STRANGE
FLESH

MICHAEL OLSON

SIMON & SCHUSTER
New York   London   Toronto   Sydney   New Delhi

Simon & Schuster
1230 Avenue of the Americas
New York, NY 10020

First Simon & Schuster hardcover edition April 2012

SIMON & SCHUSTER and colophon are registered
trademarks of Simon & Schuster, Inc.

For information about special discounts for bulk purchases,
please contact Simon & Schuster Special Sales at
1-866-506-1949 or business@simonandschuster.com.

The Simon & Schuster Speakers Bureau can bring authors
to your live event. For more information or to book an event,
contact the Simon & Schuster Speakers Bureau at 1-866-248-3049 or
visit our website at www.simonspeakers.com.

Designed by Renata Di Biase

Manufactured in the United States of America

10 9 8 7 6 5 4 3 2 1

Library of Congress Cataloging-in-Publication Data
Olson, Michael.
  Strange flesh / Michael Olson.—1st Simon & Schuster hardcover ed.
    p. cm.
  1. Computer hackers—Fiction. 2. Cyberterrorism—Fiction. 3. Sex toys—
  Fiction. I. Title.
PS3615.L75256S77   2012
813'.6 dc22   2011016615

ISBN 978-1-4516-2757-2
ISBN 978-1-4516-2759-6 (ebook)

for my parents

Even as Sodom and Gomorrah . . . giving themselves over to fornication, and going after strange flesh, are set forth for an example, suffering the vengeance of eternal fire.

—JUDE 1:7

STRANGE FLESH

PROLOGUE

The human mind is prone to infection.

I don't mean the scorching fevers of meningitis or the insidious tunneling of parasites from unclean food. These days we tend to use the language of disease to discuss ideas: viral memes, contagious media. Vectors and payloads.

We've all seen things that take root and keep us up nights. Many of us harbor thoughts that gradually poison our souls. In my case, a single vision has plagued my dreams for the past year or more, and I'm sure it will haunt me for life:

The body of a pretty, pixieish brunette with spiky hair and huge brown eyes rests on a primitive wooden seat made of a few raw boards. Behind her is bolted the upper part of a large drill press tipped on its side. Its spindle extends into the back of the chair. From there, the bit plunges through her skull.

Blood has drenched the front of her white silk robe.

The entry point is right below the hairline of her neck. Her chin is pressed all the way down on her collarbone by the restraints. The drill bit thus protrudes from her mouth: a two-inch ring of high-speed steel with a row of razor teeth around the outside.

Her bonds are subtle, appearing almost innocent. A slender white nylon line at her chin, and one low on her neck.

But they're part of the mechanism.

The cords run up through a series of pulleys set along the heavy oak ceiling supports and finally down again to a large rusty-brown rock hanging in space. Below it are the charred remains of a thick cardboard tube. A trail of burnt flooring extends back to an orange disposable lighter lying inches below her left hand.

These remnants tell a brief, violent tale. The orange Bic lit a liquid fuse of accelerant. A line of flames began licking at the cardboard support holding up the rock. When the cardboard collapsed, the rock fell, jerking her head back into the whirring drill bit.

Clearly the product of a sick imagination.

I was first exposed by watching a short video. A record of the actual event, but only a narrow view. Just a tight head shot in which all you can see is the poor girl crying while she recites a cryptic verse. There's a brief flicker of light . . .

And then carnage.

Finally, you're left with the gore-stained drill spinning relentlessly where her mouth once was. Spraying blood until the camera runs out of memory.

That picture lodged itself in some dark part of my mind and began feeding on the information I placed next to it: police photographs, the forensics report, stories I heard from those close to her. It grew into a nightmarish scene, like one of those rare cysts surgeons sometimes find filled with hair, fingernails, unseeing eyes, and, of course, teeth. The image grew until that clip stood far above all the other things I wish I'd never seen.

But you can't unsee something. There's no cure for an experience.

Learning the story behind the video would radically alter the course of my life. Like an avalanche blocking the only viable pass through a forbidding mountain range.

Looking back, I see how swiftly the illness spread. How she infected me. How her story took over mine. And the strangest thing about the fever this otherworldly woman ignited in me?

I never even met her.

I

THE JACK OF HEARTS

One Year Earlier

1

The Norn seeks you.

Eeyore, one of my friends at work, has marked the message "Urgent."
What could she want?

The project I've toiled on for the past month remains far from finished. It should be weeks before I'm due an accounting with her.

I stumble into the bathroom to get functional, trying to avoid looking in
the mirror. Not yet anyway. I take a deep breath and turn the shower on hot.

The Norn is my boss, Susan Mercer, one of the managing partners of
Red Rook, a global network security company based in DC. She's called
the Norn—after the Norse pantheon's Weavers of Fate—due to the degree of her control over the destinies of the firm's employees. The name
is made especially fitting by her habit of embroidering circuit schematics
for signals intelligence equipment from the NSA's Cold War glory days.
She is not someone you keep waiting.

The elevator opens onto Mercer's dimly lit corner suite at our New York
office. She sits at an antique desk in her Shaker rocking chair. A bright
lamp casts a circle of light on her hands, which move with preternatural
authority over an ivory hoop. Her eyes are focused on me.

"James, good of you to come," she says in a Brahmin drawl.

"No problem." I take a small glass box out of my bag and set it on her desk. It contains a rare "Bohemian Garnet" Venus flytrap for her terrarium. Mercer adores carnivorous plants, and she tolerates my gifts as sincere expressions of filial devotion. I know little about her domestic situation, but it's hard to imagine a husband, and I like the idea that at least somebody gives her something. "I hope you don't kill this one *quite* so quickly," I say.

"This plant's predecessor was a decadent vegetarian. No aptitude for hunting."

"You probably froze it."

"My office isn't a South Carolina swamp. If a thing can't adapt—"

Her look of delight fades into one of concern as she sees the scrapes on my wrist and then clocks my totally uncharacteristic turtleneck. The morning's cleanup had required some improvisation. I was robbed last night. That's how I've chosen to characterize it. Just the innocent victim of a simple theft. Happens every day.

"James . . . ?"

She lets the question hang there, but I just smile at her. Mercer is way too old-school to pry into an employee's personal life, in conversation at least. She watches me for a while but only asks, "Can I offer you some tea?"

"No thanks." I perch on one of the unstable chairs in front of her desk.

She sets down her project, the blueprint for some ancient mechanical encoding machine; pours herself a cup; and spends a moment regarding the steam as it spirals up into the shadows.

I notice her tea service rests on a set of black lace doilies that have Red Rook's logo stitched into them. A logo that says a lot about our operation. Its black circle holds a little red symbol in the center that, while decorated with simple battlements and a drawbridge, conforms to the shape of an hourglass more than the outline of our eponymous chess piece. Close observers will see the image for a rendering of the underside of a black widow spider.

Unusual that a legitimate consultancy would use the color black in its trade dress, given that the hacker term "black hat" means "outlaw." But we are by no means a normal company. Our clients are Fortune 1000 corporations and any American security-related acronym you care to name: FBI, DEA, ATF, CIA, NSA. While we ply our trade only against criminals, the means we use are often of questionable legality. In fact, we maintain a vast array of unlawful botnets, undisclosed "zero day" software exploits, salaried moles in various black hat syndicates, and even a couple agents in foreign cyber-intel organizations. So the felt of our hat is a tasteful gray.

Just as her silence begins to make me nervous, Mercer asks, "The LinkDjinn affair?"

"Looks pretty standard, and I think we already have hooks into the network the attackers used."

"One of our Ukrainian honeypots?"

"Exactly."

"I suppose we have Phissure to thank for all this mischief?" This was a group of Vietnamese net scam artists with whom we occasionally did business.

"That's what my new friends are telling me. The Brains are trying to confirm it."

Functional roles at Red Rook are classified according to retro high school social stereotypes. The Brains practice traditional hacking like network recon and searching for useful software flaws. Our Greasers run groups of informants. Jocks do "physical" penetrations.

I'm a "Soshe," a social engineer, one of the lazy reptiles who use the time-honored techniques of the confidence man to compromise our opponents. After all, why spend weeks snooping around trying to capture a password when almost anyone will just tell it to you if you ask the right way? We Socials believe that a bug in your firewall program, once discovered, can be patched in minutes, but the software running the human brain will stay broken forever.

Mercer says, "Well, that may get awkward. But I'm afraid the matter will no longer concern you."

"Okay . . ." Surely wearing a turtleneck to the office isn't grounds for a mental-health suspension.

"Tell me, James, what do you know about the Randall family?"

That gets my attention. While quieting the mental turmoil their name causes me, I stall. "The ones who own most of IMP?"

She nods slowly.

"Well, Integrated Media Properties controls enough of the mediascape to be considered, by some, a threat to American democracy. The Randalls have almost all the voting shares."

"Correct. Anything else?"

"They've got newspapers, cable, film studios . . . I understand they're picking up web start-ups like it's '99."

She arches an eyebrow. "And?"

"And I went to school with them. The twins. At Harvard. They were two years older than me. I can't say I really know them anymore, but we were in a club together."

"Phi Beta Kappa, I presume?"

"Ah, no, ma'am." Mercer is well aware of all of my affiliations, starting with the League City, Texas, Cub Scout pack number 678. The club in question was the Hasty Pudding Society, an ancient order of alcoholism.

A predatory smile. "Hmm . . . Though you claim only a passing acquaintance, apparently the Randalls remember you quite well. And have tracked you to our humble enterprise here. It's very unusual, but you've been requested for a meeting with them by name. Or by a diminutive at least. Please tell me you don't answer to 'Jimmy Jacks' anymore."

That means it must have been Blake who called her.

No one ever calls me by my real name: James John Pryce. I've been called Slim for my build, Tex for my place of origin, JJ for brevity, and Thump for reasons that were never quite clear. That's to say nothing of the brigades of online aliases marching around cyberspace on my behalf. In college what stuck were any of several variants of "Jack," which is more or less appropriate given my middle name.

J-Jacks, Jackie, Jackalope, Jackamole, Sir Jax-a-Lot. "Jimmy Jacks" was the one in general use. I received that nickname the same night I met Blake Randall.

2

For a school perceived to host a driven and introverted population, the number of social clubs one can join at Harvard is surprising. They run the gamut from coed cocktail societies like the Hasty Pudding to artistic clans such as the Signet and the Lampoon.

In the fall of 2000, I'd accepted membership to the Bat, one of the college's Final Clubs, our slightly refined version of fraternities. After the holidays, I began my pre-initiation "neophyte" period, wherein you serve as a party Sherpa to the senior members. On a bitter Tuesday evening, I was ordered to report to the club for my mandatory shift in the Texas Hold 'Em game we'd run continuously during the entire two-week reading period before exams.

Late that night, I found myself seated in our book-lined card room drinking neat bourbon and inhaling an atmosphere saturated with exotic smoke. I watched with wonder the massive pile of chips growing in front of me.

The state of my finances had been much on my mind. Like many of my classmates, my father had a blue-chip doctorate; in his case, aeronautical engineering from Stanford. I grew up within miles of the Johnson Space Center in Houston. Unfortunately, his commitment to the nation's space program was supplanted just after my mother's death, when I was too young to have formed memories of her, by a far more zealous embrace of Jim Beam. By the time I received my heavy envelope from Harvard, he was going to work in a begrimed jumpsuit, and I was left with a complex financial aid package, now proving itself hopelessly inadequate. Despite a grueling work-study job in my house's cafeteria and moonlighting at Ravelin, a nearby network security start-up, I would likely be forced to take the next semester off to work full-time in order to pay off swelling credit card balances. As I turned over a Big Slick, I contemplated the fact that while poker may contribute to my academic undoing, it would provide a respite from the debt collectors, at least until next month.

The only other player at the table with any kind of stack was a senior named William Baldwin Coles III. The son of a notorious currency trader, he was the club's vice president (in the Bat, this is the highest office) and had been playing in the game for almost four days without cease. Just as I began the theatrics to set up a devious double bluff, he looked down at his cell and grinned.

"Gentlemen, things are about to get a lot more interesting."

A couple minutes later, three new players arrived, led by the Bat's reigning carnal Achilles, Raffi Consuelo. The second was Matt Weeks, the president of the Spee Club, who spent more time at his family's Las Vegas casino than he did on campus. And finally, Blake Randall stepped inside.

Blake resembled one of the better-looking busts of a young Julius Caesar. He had the same strong nose and penetrating eyes, and his pale skin was the white of new marble. He stood a couple inches taller than my six-two and had a full head of blond hair. His chiseled physique came from hours logged on the Charles River as captain of our heavyweight crew.

Though he was a notable presence in his own right, when I looked at Blake, all I could see was his twin sister, Blythe, the legendary beauty of her class. She was also intimidatingly tall and had the same snowy complexion as her brother, which prompted her inevitable female detractors to call her "that starving vampire bitch." Of course, her rich-girl celebrity status and willowy elegance ensured all sorts of male admirers flocking to her banner.

I was utterly bewitched the first time I laid eyes on her.

The twins' glamour alone would have been enough to stimulate gossip at school, but combined with their alien mirrored beauty, we really couldn't keep ourselves from trotting out sensational fantasies, often making use of the delicious term "twincest." Further inflaming such rumors were their matching crooked ring fingers. A congenital abnormality? Had a ten-year-old Blake broken his while skiing, causing Blythe to snap her own in sympathy? Or maybe it was ritual mutilation: no wedding ring would ever pass over either finger to vitiate their perfect love.

As if to demonstrate contempt for our trifling opinions, Blythe and Blake did nothing to discourage such chatter. In a cocktail circle, her hand would seek his arm. They would clutch and whisper when they met. On formal occasions, they danced together splendidly.

Seeing these three arrive, a couple of the current players began packing up their chips. I followed suit, but Coles put his hand on my shoulder and said, "A little early for the money leader to cash in, don't you think?"

The newcomers sat down as the others hustled out like the roof was on fire. I started counting out chips.

Blake smiled benignly at me. "Evening, James. What do you say we raise the stakes?"

I found it strange that Blake would want to disrupt the game right away—and even stranger that he knew my name. I looked to Coles for guidance.

My stomach turned over when the group agreed to increase the blinds by an order of magnitude. There was simply no way I could come up with a four-figure buy-in. But the words "I can't play" wouldn't quite come out of my mouth. I stacked plastic slowly as I imagined how I might get myself out of this situation.

Coles leaned over to grab the Wild Turkey bottle and whispered, "Just deal, man. I'll cover you."

A wispy rumor tickled my bourbon-fogged brain. Coles was dating Blythe Randall. Blake supposedly didn't care for the match and did a poor job of concealing his feelings. I wanted to explain that there was no way I'd be able to pay him back. That I'd never played for that much. That it was impossible, because I'd have to drop out of school and live on the streets if I lost. But I didn't say any of that.

I dealt.

I dealt myself seven hours' worth of pocket pairs, flopped sets, and nut flush rivers. I was playing like a field mouse surrounded by hawks, and yet a mountain of valuable chips steadily accumulated under my chin.

But Blake held the chip lead all night with his unfailing instinct for the jugular. Having folded a huge pot, Raffi got up in disgust after watching him flip over a garbage hand of two-seven unsuited. Matt passed out after writing his third five-digit chit to the bank.

"And then there were three," said Coles.

My next cards were a pair of jacks, spades and clubs. I almost had to fold them in the maelstrom of pre-flop raising that went on between Blake and Coles. But with only three players, my jacks couldn't be that bad.

True to form, I flopped myself a set. The center cards were:

The pot rocketed over two grand before it got to me. It was weak, but I just called.

Coles said, "Shit!" and folded his cards. That worried me. Something about the hand scared him off. I glanced over at Blake for any sign of what Coles had seen, but he was a mannequin. He made a courteous gesture for me to deal another card.

I did, and up turned the jack of hearts. Giving me four of a kind for the first time in my life.

Silently screaming at myself to stay cool, I kept staring at the card until I had it together and then slowly raised my head to meet Blake's eye.

He betrayed nothing. "Thirty-five hundred." His bet said a full house, probably kings.

"Up five," I said, trying to lure him in.

Blake smiled cruelly. "Table," he said, indicating that he bet everything I had in front of me. At the bottom of my innocent columns of colored discs, I had three obsidian placards. These were ten-thousand-dollar markers. He raised me confidently enough that I took a second to reexamine the board and realized he could be holding cards that already beat even my fantastic hand. The ace of diamonds and queen of diamonds made a straight flush that would impoverish me utterly. I studied him, trying to evaluate whether the universe could be so unjust.

Blake had politely averted his gaze from someone wrestling with base monetary calculations. I started figuring odds but was interrupted by a voice inside me.

If you let this rich bastard muscle you off four of a kind, you might as well cash in your chips and prepare for a life of absolute mediocrity.

The black rectangles emerged. "It's thirty-seven thousand five hundred. And I call."

If Blake was surprised by the amount, he didn't show it. Maybe he became slightly more still, but my hand was the one shaking as I flipped over the last card, cultivating nightmare visions of him pulling a miracle winner.

The last card was the Queen of Hearts.

He turned over his *caballeros* and shrugged. Fortune is a cruel mistress.

I had to give him credit, though. He didn't bat an eyelash when he saw my jacks. He just took them in for a second and then murmured something I almost didn't catch.

"Knaves. How apt."

My brain was about to start leaking out my eyes as Blake casually counted off four black placards from his stack and tossed them over to me, making me wealthier than I'd ever been. Allowing me to quit my humiliating job in the cafeteria. Changing everything about my time in college. I was expecting him to insist that we keep playing for another two days, and I planned for a protracted period of trench warfare to protect my newfound riches.

But Blake said, "Well, I doubt we'll do better than that this morning. What do you say we wrap it up?"

Ten minutes later, he slipped out the door into the cold Cambridge dawn. Coles gave my shoulder a painfully hard squeeze and said, with a certain lilt of passion in his voice, "Thank you."

I lifted my glass and began an epic bender that still makes my toes curl to think of.

At the time, I was too beside myself with joy to think much about Blake's parting shot. It was only later, while researching a paper about the iconography of playing cards, that I realized what he meant. I always believed that the jack was the prince of the deck, the heir to the king and queen. But he's not. He's the servant. Another word for which is "knave." My jacks beating his kings was "apt" because the ranks of our cards matched the players. Blake the aristocrat was defeated by the scullery boy.

Once I understood this, I told myself that I'd gladly suffer far greater insult for that much money. That I would try to remember him only with gratitude.

By and large Harvard is a resolute meritocracy, free of the old overt classism. But I guess among any group of relentlessly ambitious people, weird hierarchies and castes develop. When we spoke of our aspirations, you'd occasionally hear someone disparage those choosing even such lucrative professions as the law or investment banking as "mere wage slaves," the unspoken idea being that the real elite operated on the "principal side." In business, this meant you owned the enterprise; if you didn't have one to inherit, you started one. In other fields, you'd hear similar language about acting "on your own portfolio." Being an artist, not a gallerist. Being a politician, not a consultant. Being the talent, not the handler. The subtext was that there were two classes of people: masters and servants.

Blake had called me a knave. I didn't let it bother me at the time.

But I'd be lying if I said it doesn't bother me now.

The prospect of seeing his sister is more bothersome still. I find it eerie, now that I'm once again drowning in emotional quicksand—and courting the consequent physical danger—that I'm receiving this visitation from Blythe, my original will-o'-the-wisp.

I'm supposed to go and drink their fine whiskey, pretending to be old friends, while the Randall twins interview me for a job. Though it may well demand my brand of skills, there are others they could have called.

At the end of our meeting Mercer says, "Dear boy, you *know* who these people are. I'm sure I needn't emphasize that you're to do everything in your power to accommodate their wishes."

I say, "Of course."

But I think, *Why me? Why now?*

3

Blake's assistant, a tall Caribbean beauty in a black Chanel suit, opens the door to what looks like a salon, in the eighteenth-century sense of the word. The walls are graced with finely framed paintings that I feel like I should recognize. Ritual masks from obscure religions watch from the bookshelves. She seats me in a leather armchair with brass studs along the seams.

"Mr. Randall will be with you shortly."

Once she departs, a side door opens, and out slides Blake. As he extends his hand, he flashes me a mock anxiety smile, like we're old conspirators dealing with something unpleasant, but by no means unexpected.

"Pryce, good to see you."

"You as well, Blake."

As we shake, I notice a small tattoo emerging past the cuff of his shirt, unmistakable as the head of the King of Hearts playing card.

A bit more solemnity in his eyes. "I heard about your recent, ah, troubles. But you seem to be bearing up all right. Please join us."

He ushers me into an equally opulent office. Seated at his desk, looking up at the ceiling, is Blake's twin.

"James, I'm sure you remember my sister."

Blake knows that nobody forgets Blythe Randall, least of all me.

She stands languorously. Like a cat who's had just enough time in the sun. She cocks her head and fixes me with her lambent green eyes. "James Pryce. So nice to see an old friend."

My vision twitches.

Is she toying with me? Is that an ironic twinkle in her eye?

Luckily fatigue diminishes my need to obsess over her diction. So I fall back on blank courtesy.

"It's been entirely too long . . ." I find I can't say her name yet. "I hope you're both doing well."

Blythe flicks her eyes toward Blake. She lets out a long breath, almost a sigh, and mashes a cigarette that had been burning in the ashtray next to her. Which is interesting. Blythe only ever smoked when she was drinking. Or when she was nervous.

She says, "Of course you've heard about . . . our brother."

"Well . . . I can't say I know the details," I manage, willing myself to stop gaping at her like a moonstruck toddler. "I take it he's in some kind of trouble?"

Blake frowns. "Half brother actually. Our father took it upon himself to impregnate and then marry our au pair when we were eight. Our mother never really recovered and, after we enrolled at Exeter, has been in and out—well. . ." He shrugs. "Needless to say, we were not close. He fancies himself an avant-garde artist, so some time ago he changed his name. It's now 'Coit S. D. Files.' You're meant to say it 'coitus defiles.' But nobody does."

"Everyone still calls him Billy, even when they don't know who he really is. The name followed him despite his efforts to reinvent himself," says Blythe.

Blake asks, "We assume you adhere to some principle of client confidentiality in your . . . line of work?"

"With Red Rook it's more like omertà."

Blythe nods. "So after the divorce, our father tried very hard to create a functional stepfamily. But it wasn't to be. Billy's mother Lucia was very beautiful and naturally fifteen years younger than our mother. But she was also . . . emotionally unstable. After a huge fight, they separated—this was in 2000 when we were at college."

"She was found dead at our old beach house a month later," Blake says. "Overindulgence in her twin passions for Stoli and Seconal."

Blythe pats her brother and leaves her hand on his shoulder as if trying to physically restrain him from further interruption. "Billy was the one who found her. He was only thirteen . . . Our father was devastated as well."

"And as you know, he was killed in a car accident a year later." On saying this, Blake unconsciously shoots his cuff, covering up his King of Hearts tattoo. His gesture makes me curious about its significance. That card is named the "Suicide King" for the sword he appears to be stabbing into the back of his head. The twins' father, Robert Randall, had driven his Bugatti off a cliff on Mulholland Drive. His death had been ruled an accident, but there was talk about a lack of skid marks on a dry road. I assume the tattoo is some kind of tribute. Or maybe a reminder of whatever tragic epiphany his father's death inspired.

Blythe continues. "Billy wanted nothing to do with us and went to live with his godfather, Gerhard Loring, who was our father's best friend and now chairs IMP's board. Eventually, Ger got him into the Rhode Island School of Design, and he seemed to be doing okay there. The problem with art, though, is that what it craves more than anything is attention. Despite the level of media interest our father's business has always attracted, we dislike publicity. I'm not sure what changed, but Billy began producing these . . . I don't even know what to call them. Installations? Happenings? Art games?"

Blake says, "I would call them frivolous garbage, were it not for the lawsuit."

"*Colton et al. v. Randall*. A delightful piece of civil litigation—settled out of court of course. For his thesis, Billy designed a sort of live role-playing game called *NeoRazi*. He wanted to create an oppressive celebrity culture on campus, so he set up a tabloid website that recruited participants to take photos of various attractive coeds. The more tasteless and degrading the image, the more money they got. His classmates, most of them being quick with a camera to begin with, promptly generated a litany of police complaints: invasion of privacy, stalking, assault charges against irate boyfriends. One of the girls even had some kind of breakdown." Blythe lights another cigarette. "The horrible thing was that, due to the abuse these poor women suffered, they became *actual* local celebrities, and some real paparazzi materialized to continue tormenting them after Billy's 'game' had officially ended."

"I take it his work was not well received?"

"The members of the Rhode Island State Bar were big fans. The girls suing the Razis for harassment; Razis suing them for battery; everybody suing Billy for setting the whole thing up."

"I guess one must suffer for his art."

Blake adds, "The story was nasty enough that the regional media ran with it for a cycle or two. Including some of our own stations, God damn them. And even they weren't above asking whether this was the sort of novel content we could expect as the new generation of Randalls takes the reins at IMP."

Blythe blows smoke. "But the inquiries that really worried us came from our board."

"So we made some changes in Billy's trust to take the issue off the table. He was not pleased." Blake smiles like a pride leader who has just gutted an annoying rival.

His sister examines him, something flickering in her eyes. "The *issue* could have been handled better. But there's nothing to be done about it now."

He breaks eye contact. "You could say that. But either way, we still didn't . . . solve the problem. Amazingly, our brother found a warm critical reception for this kind of stuff. Reviews complimented his refined understanding of how the internet's anonymity promotes gender oppression. So he thinks maybe there's a future in this racket, and after a couple years drifting through the far reaches of Brooklyn 'fauxhemia,' he goes to grad school to hone his 'insight.' His work gets even worse."

"Worse?"

Blake picks a glossy magazine off the coffee table and tosses it into my lap. It's a recent number of *Art Whore* with a feature set off by tape flags. Inside I find a two-page photo spread: a shot from the rear of five people standing arm in arm in front of a giant video screen. The back of each neck bears a tattoo. The title reads:

Jackanapes
Five downtown interactivists hacking your reality

The tattoos from left to right are: an Ethernet jack, a USB hub, a standard quarter-inch amplifier input jack, a drawing of an eye screw with a string running up the neck, and finally, on the only woman in the photo, a small image of the Jack of Hearts from the standard English deck of playing cards.

This last one makes me smile. I'd been spared a far less tasteful display of cards across my shoulder blades on the day after my great poker victory by Cambridge's uptight ordinance that you actually have to remain conscious in order to have ink done.

I skim quickly through the article, which describes in maddening postmodern jargon the recent work of this loose confederation of artists broadly dealing with "issues of identity malleability in digitally constructed narrative spaces." According to the caption, their brother is the one with the string running up his neck. The text covering Billy says that he's worked with LARPs (Live-Action Role Playing), BUGs (Big Urban Games), and ARGs (Alternate Reality Games). The last of these explains his tattoo.

ARGs are new-media hybrids using the whole communications spectrum—phone, email, web, forums, video—to allow a group of players to discover a hidden narrative that plays out over the course of the game. The people who organize them are called the "puppet masters." So Billy's screw-and-string tattoo favors the ARG paradigm by making him a giant living marionette. I guess *NeoRazi* could be seen as an early experiment in the genre.

I want to read the article more thoroughly, but I look up at the twins and say, "So . . . ?"

Blythe inclines her head at the magazine. "Two of the people in that picture are now dead. Second from the left, an ambiguous drug overdose a couple months ago. Then the last one, the girl, almost decapitated herself three weeks later. Billy used her as an actress in this repulsive video he made. I'm sure you can find it online somewhere."

Blake says, "Which leads us to another video . . ."

Blythe steps over to an end table on which stands a ceramic statue holding a long remote as though it's a scepter. She plucks it from his grasp, and while she thumbs a sequence of buttons, I take a moment to study the thing. It's an ugly-but-cute blue-scaled creature with spindly appendages, small pointed pig's ears, and a large head filled almost entirely with a single massive eye. I decide he must be an imp, his peculiar anatomy a mordant representation of IMP's customers: giant eyeballs dedicated to consuming company product. A private jest.

The lights dim and a white screen descends from the far wall. A projector opposite whirs quietly to life.

Blythe selects a file called Jacking-Out. "This video was sent to Blake from a dummy email account two days ago."

Darkness. Then a shot displaying a naked man of maybe twenty-seven seated in front of a bank of monitors. He presents a striking contrast to his siblings. His head is covered with a tufted anti-haircut, a few jet-black locks hanging limply over his face. His eyes are so dark that pupil and iris seem to merge into inhuman anime dots. He shares the twins' pallor, but where on them you'd describe it as luminous, on him the word that leaps to mind is "sickly." The periodic beeping of a heart monitor on one of the screens behind him enhances that impression.

Billy's sense of physical malaise is deepened by a painful-looking Prince Albert piercing through his penis. Hung from which he's got a large golden crocodile pendant that closely replicates the world-famous logo for Lacoste sportswear, the touchstone of preppy culture until Ralph Lauren's polo ponies nearly trampled it to death in the eighties.

The chair he's sitting on is made of rough planks. Affixed to its back is a rusty metal band that's fastened around his forehead. Thick wires descend from the band and attach to a bank of car batteries at his feet. While it's impossible to follow exactly, a large throw-switch next to his right hand appears to control the circuit.

An improvised electric chair. I tense in anticipation.

Billy declaims in a slow rasp:

As a final farewell, Blake, I thought to indulge your greatest fantasy. I know you've often wished that I'd just jack out like she did. But be careful what you wish for. My ghost may come back to haunt you. And lead you down your own path of torment. For I will rain down brimstone and fire upon your festering Sodom. And when you look, lo, the smoke from your life will rise up like the smoke from a furnace.

He then throws the switch, sending his body into violent convulsions. His eyes bulge, and his hands form unnatural claws. Blood trickles down his chin after he bites his tongue. It goes on for an excruciating ten seconds or so, his skin blackening around the metal head restraint. The heart monitor becomes a frenetic screech of trauma. Then the beeping abruptly stops. At this point, the juice must have cut off, since Billy's body relaxes. Foamy mucus drips from his nose and mixes with the blood now freely coursing from his mouth.

The camera lingers on his still form and then cuts to black.

Blake brings up the lights, and the three of us sit looking at one another. I'm not altogether sure what I've been shown, so I just say, "I'm sorry."

He sniffs. "Don't be. It's a fake. Our brother is extremely disturbed, and—"

"He needs help." Blythe's words are soft and almost without affect. I can see Blake framing a sarcastic reply, but some subtle detail of her posture must alert him to the fact that she's holding back a reservoir of pain. His initially dismissive gesture blends into one of apology. He stares at her expectantly. I'm no longer in the room.

I clear my throat and ask, "Why do you say it's fake?"

Blake looks away from his sister. He pulls up the video again. "It's just his typical plug-head drivel." He stands up and points to one of the monitors behind Billy.

It shows a 3D scene set in the courtyard of a ruined castle.

Blake says, "Watch this space when the heart monitor stops." He plays the video, and sure enough, as Billy's body slumps, an avatar modeled to resemble him slowly fades into the game world with a ghostly particle effect.

"He's not dying. He's just virtualizing himself. Which, at least for the moment, is science fiction. Ergo, this video is bullshit."

"It certainly looks convincing."

"He may have used real electricity. Maybe even harmed himself for the sake of realism. But we don't believe Billy has the good grace to actually . . . Well, anyway, this is just another stupid shock-art project." Blake grimaces at the rogue pun. "So to speak."

"You know it's more than that, Blake," says Blythe.

"What do you mean?" I ask her.

"We can't find him. It's like he really has dematerialized."

Blake adds, "His apartment is cleared out. None of his . . . associates have seen him in weeks. He hasn't been at work. No financial transactions, cell phone calls. Nothing."

"But you think he's alive. He's just"—I'm reaching here—"faked his own death? Why?"

"Why does someone like him do anything? He's totally bug-fuck. I'm sorry, Blythe, but it's true."

"I understand that his work is, ah, on the dark side, but what makes you believe he's actually crazy?"

"Oh, I don't know." Blake starts ticking things off his fingers. "In the years since our differences over that first lawsuit, he's sent me a ream of threatening emails. His work has become even more depraved. Recently he's taken to getting himself arrested for petty outbursts."

"But this feels like . . . a more significant departure. Like he's planning to target Blake in some way," Blythe continues. "That online world you see Billy enter is the ever-popular NOD. The only clue we have to his whereabouts is this place that doesn't really exist."

"I see."

Blake says, "Ms. Mercer assures us your technical skills are top-notch. She also says you've had a number of assignments involving . . . undercover work."

Blythe says, "We want you to find our brother. Before he really does harm himself. Or someone else."

4

Standing under the imploring gaze of the woman who, it could be argued, ruined my life, you'd think I might exercise some caution. Obviously this assignment will place me in a mental landscape so perilous that I should refuse it point-blank. All I'd ever wanted was to be there for Blythe when she needed me. In the end, she declined. Back then, I was devastated, and turned my sorrow inward. I told myself that I'd manufactured an epochal love story purely in my imagination. Blythe never made me any promises.

Why then, after all these years, do you feel the need to make promises to her?

The answer of course comes from my abraded wrists and the scabby bruise around my neck. Wherever this work takes me can't possibly be worse than where I am now.

Those were my thoughts after the meeting. In that moment, though, accepting Blythe's charge had the feel of a spinal reflex.

"I'll find your brother," I said.

Blythe smiled at me, and that was all it took.

Pathetic, sure. But my pride has deserted me these days.

To say that I have a weakness for women is like saying Ernest Hemingway enjoyed the occasional cocktail.

After my mother's death, my father made the disastrous decision to enroll me at an all-boys former military academy in an effort to curtail some of the tantrums brought on by her absence. The education, dispensed by a staff of retired air force officers, was exceptional, but by age eight, I was spying on my friends' mothers. One of them caught me observing her step out of the shower. She was really kind and understanding about it, and even hugged me once she got her clothes on. But I was never invited back.

The advent of my interest in computers can be precisely fixed at the instant a low-res image of a nude Victoria Principal rolled off Rory Cullenden's dot matrix printer when we were in the fourth grade. My hacking skills went critical after I discovered those underground bulletin boards for swapping naughty files. I spent high school knowing that I'd do the computer science course at Stanford.

So, how did I end up at Harvard? Sonali Mehta. I followed my rival high school's gorgeous Intel Talent Search winner there. Though she declined all my advances, my grief didn't last long, since there were any number of distinguished young ladies for me to spend my freshman year mooning over.

Then I met Blythe Randall.

I've always known that the idea of perfect, all-consuming love is a myth invented by ancient writers in order to move units. And yet acknowledging that left me without an explanation for the unprecedented feelings she aroused in me. After Coles introduced us at the Pudding one night, I felt like I'd discovered an alien species, awe and fear wrangling for control of my brain.

What was it about her?

Blythe's beauty was somehow original. She had a refinement of face and figure that you hadn't seen a million times on magazine covers. And she used that peerless vessel to radiate goodwill. Not a common sort of gushy niceness, nor the protective shell of polite reserve often found in the insanely rich. She seemed to instantly hold the conviction that you were an interesting person, and even if that wasn't true, she had the confidence and alchemical grace to make you so. In her presence, people, at least those not prone to jealousy, would just beam with pleasure.

A month after that monumental poker game, her relationship with Coles ended in a pyrotechnic argument in front of the Bat. I'd heard that the subject was her brother.

For a dismal couple of weeks I didn't see her at all. Then one night just after winter break, Rex Ainsley and Raffi Consuelo burst into the card room to demand that at least three of us make ourselves presentable for some ladies coming over from Pine Manor, a local women's college, for a round of Circle of Death. This was a drinking game expected to segue into strip poker and hopefully some kind of orgy-type activity. We were skeptical since these often-promised orgies never really seemed to materialize.

Ainsley said, "And Coles is coming by for this, so whichever one of you cum dumpsters let in Blythe Randall, you need to get her out of here. Now."

"She's here? Where?" asked Tim Fielding, the dealer.

"Upstairs, bombed out of her skull, and looking to make trouble. We are her friends, so clearly we're not going to deal with her. It has to be one of you lot."

"You want us to throw her out?" This from a fellow sophomore.

Ainsley snorted. "I'd like to see you try. That woman could crush your testicles with her *mind*. No, one of you must use his feminine wiles to lure her nicely out of here, so she doesn't suspect that her ex-boyfriend is coming over to molest wet-brained goo poodles before a decent mourning period elapses. We Batsmen are classier than that."

There were blank looks all around.

"Jesus, what a bunch of worthless—"

I was astonished to hear myself say, "I'll do it." I flipped over the pair of queens I was betting, drawing a sigh from the nut flush.

Blythe was sprawled in a wingback chair in the upstairs members-only lounge. Eyes closed, ashing into a full tumbler of scotch. Around her neck hung her trademark pearls, a stunning string that glowed with an extraordinary scarlet luster.

To me such unique jewelry spoke to the ethereal nature of its owner, but I'd heard a sour-pussed Grotonian complain that they were just "tacky dye-cultured fakes." Spiteful, yes, but I later found out she was right in a sense. They *were* a replica of a strand that had been assembled over centuries, but only because to wear the originals demanded a massive security detail. Anyway, those were on loan to a museum in Kyoto because a small war had been fought over them during the Tokugawa shogunate.

According to legend, the pearls were collected by a bloodthirsty witch-queen who had a special hidden grotto over which she liked to hang her victims after they'd submitted to her twisted pleasures. Eventually their bodies would fall and be consumed by the local sharks, their blood seeping into the oyster beds below. After each victim, the queen then sent a virgin village girl to harvest a single pearl. Blythe's strand grew to over a hundred stones before the peasants revolted, and a minor warlord, sensing opportunity, invaded the prefecture. Though the evil queen was eventually fed to her rather ungrateful familiars, members of her cult retrieved the pearls, and the strand continued to grow. How Blythe ended up with them is a saga unto itself.

I stood there for a minute thinking desperately of what to say. An attitude of servility seemed best.

"Would the lady care for a fresh adult beverage?"

She smiled but didn't open her eyes. "They've made poor little Jimmy the hatchet man, huh?"

"Not at all. *Nous casa, vous casa.* I think you'd make a fine member here."

One eye opened. "What a revolting idea."

"That's not likely to be the most revolting idea you hear tonight if you stay with us."

"Pryce, go away. I'm looking for someone to fight with."

"Try me. I can be very irritating when called upon."

"I don't know who put you up to this, but I'm not leaving."

"'Course not. Why would you? You'll be thrilled to know we have a lively round of COD on tap, followed by strip poker. We may even have an orgy, at which you'd be more than welcome."

"Oh, barf. Wellesley?"

"No, I believe our guests tonight hail from Brookline High School."

"Liar. You're not going to have any orgy."

I cut my eyes over to the giant stuffed fruit bat perched over the bar and winced. "I think Fulgencio may beg to differ." The club mascot's head came off to reveal a secret compartment intended for Cuban cigars but in practice used as our ceremonial stash locker. It was generally filled with at least ten hits of Ecstasy.

"You are all vermin . . . Fine, you can walk me home."

"And miss my first orgy?"

"If you think *you're* in line for an orgy, you're probably too stupid to help me find my way. Enjoy yourself with your boyfriends." She got up, a trace of sway in her step. I offered her my arm.

Despite having devoted long hours to speculating about what I might do to please Blythe Randall, all I could come up with was a plan so ridiculous, I suppose it had a certain childish charm. "Why don't we go to the vault at Herrell's and tell each other secrets? They have milk shakes there." Herrell's was an ice cream parlor housed in an old bank.

She gave me a long appraising look and finally pointed to our bar. "Might I suggest you liberate that scotch?"

Out on the street, Blythe was less stable. She whispered into my neck, "You know, you're very sweet, but all this really isn't necessary."

"Well, I'm getting a milk shake, and it's going to seem a little strange if I'm sitting there by myself mumbling about how I used to jerk off to *Murder, She Wrote* in junior high."

Blythe allowed a ripple of laughter and slapped me on the chest. She turned to face me and said, "Milk shakes, then. But I must warn you, I have a lot of secrets." She wobbled, and I caught her in a half embrace.

Behind me I heard a soft male voice say, "Blythe."

At first I thought it was Coles, in which case I'd have retreated and let her have the fight she was looking for. On turning, however, I saw that it was Blake, headed toward the Bat. Blythe stiffened, her buzz draining right out of her.

I said, "Hey, Blake."

"How are you doing tonight, Blythe?"

"I guess I'm getting by. James was just taking me for a milk shake to cheer me up."

"Well . . . What a gentleman you are, James. Listen, I need to have a word with my sister. Would you mind having your milk shake another time?"

I shrugged and gestured to her.

Blythe closed her eyes briefly and said, "Fine. What do you want?"

He put his arm around her, saying, "Let's talk on the way back to your room."

I watched them cross Mt. Auburn Street, Blake speaking into his sister's ear. She began rubbing a temple. After another moment of his rebuke, Blythe stopped in the middle of the still, snow-covered street and said, "Blake, I can do whatever *the fuck* I want."

Blake raised his voice too, but he was turned away from me, so I couldn't hear him.

Whatever he said, the last bit of his speech caused Blythe's face to freeze. She slowly straightened, and then unleashed a wicked backhand that connected with Blake's cheek so hard he stumbled sideways. He grabbed her and shook as if building up to further violence.

I had enough Texan chivalry in me that I wasn't going to stand by while a woman was assaulted in the street. I started walking over to where the Randall twins were locked in their vehement pas de deux.

Blythe saw me move, and she went rigid. Blake, always attuned to her, let go instantly and turned. Doing so snapped him out of his rage, and his face displayed plummeting grief as it dawned on him what had almost happened. A desperate urge to make amends flowed into his eyes, and he reached out to his sister.

But Blythe was having none of it. Looking back to ensure he was still watching, she marched up to me, took a deep breath, and then, incredibly, kissed me gently on the mouth.

Even at the time, I was well aware of my role as a mere prop in their family drama, but nonetheless, the touch of her lips was clearly the greatest thing that had ever happened to me. All my thousand versions of this dream uniting in one surpassing moment of consummation.

I might have felt differently had I known that when she kissed me, that surge of divine electricity she sent through my mind would prove overpowering. So strong that it melted the delicate reset circuitry that would allow me to ever really love anyone else.

5

After Blythe, I, like my father, transferred my passion for women to one for men: Jim Beam, Jack Daniel, and Basil Hayden.

Memories of my sophomore summer are pretty blurred around the edges. By the end of it, a vast misunderstanding with the Cambridge police had landed me in a tense meeting with my house master, an old Bat alum. He suggested that I could avoid a dire encounter with the Administrative Board—famously eager to make disciplinary examples at the beginning of a term—by voluntarily taking a year off in order to "better reach my full maturity." The date was September 8, 2001.

A week later, I got a message that a grad was looking for me at the Bat. He was a fairly young but professorial guy, and without so much as an introduction, he asked me, "So how'd you like to help us rat-fuck Osama?"

Seeking vengeance quickly cured my depression, and I developed a reputation as a technical asset who also enjoyed the "operational" side of our work. This led to training across a wide spectrum of the clandestine arts, and I discovered a certain bloodlust and an aptitude for duplicity, both of which served me well during several pretty hairy undercover assignments.

All told, I guess we know that bin Laden's life wasn't much affected by my efforts in the Global War on Terror. But there are several Saudi financiers who are right now wondering how the hand of Allah guided them to Kazakhstani prison camps.

I never went back to school, and five years of such quiet victories garnered me Susan Mercer's contact information. Which proved to be worth a quadrupling of my salary upon joining Red Rook Security.

I found myself well suited to my new job and advanced rapidly. But my pleasant routine was again swamped by romance. I managed to meet and hang on to a lovely girl named Erica, a whip-smart redhead brimming with levity. Though a member of the class two years below mine at school, she'd already made vice president at a stylish record label. We spent long nights at outer-borough rock clubs and abused the flexibility of our work schedules with endless mornings of canoodling sloth. Last winter I tendered a big diamond on a Balinese beach under an almost unrealistic canopy of stars. We'd been very happy.

Six weeks before our wedding, I walked into my study to find Erica leaning over a series of pictures spread out on my desk. I prepared a guilty cringe, thinking of the palliative measures my friends had recommended for when the fiancée discovers your porn stash. But as she turned, I noticed that the photos had been scattered with wet blotches.

She regarded me red-eyed, evaluating. And I realized how bad this was. Which pictures she'd found. I stayed silent for a moment, thinking, *I'm not that awful. It's not as terrible as it seems.*

"You know there's really nothing you can say."

She was right.

I'd often marveled at the way my peers tended to date bad women. Bossy drunks and fashion monsters. But the peril of living with a brilliant and marvelous lady is that she's hard to fool, and the guilt is crushing when you disappoint her.

The images would look almost innocuous to most people. The surprisingly tasteful artifacts of an intimate photo session between two young lovers. But the model was a slender collegiate woman with long blond hair. You'd have to call her willowy. Her only adornment in the last of them: a string of pale scarlet pearls. I was always amazed that Blythe had let me photograph her, and I savored those demonstrations of her trust.

"James, I just can't ever be her. I'm sorry."

I wanted to explain. Not to defend myself; I'd have gladly swallowed a puffer fish if I thought it could magically draw away her pain. I wanted her to know that I'd kept those pictures not as fetishes to creep in and venerate late at night, but rather as proof that I could bear thinking about Blythe. That it was safe to revisit those moments. In the same sense that former smokers always say, "You haven't really quit until you can walk around for a month with a pack in your pocket." The fact that I hadn't pulled them out in years proved that I was cured.

But the last stage of beating cigarettes is when you tire of carrying around that stupid box and finally discard it. Erica had said to me at the beginning, "Creature, I know what she meant to you back then. I know how intense young love can be. So I *need* to know, once and for all: you're not still holding on to any of that, are you?"

And now she'd run the numbers and come up with the only logical answer. Weaselly quant that I am, I fought to suppress the protest that numbers are just symbols and thus are infinitely malleable. Two and two *doesn't always* equal four. But normal people view those who make such arguments with even greater contempt than the ones who can't do the arithmetic to begin with.

The undeniable fact of the matter remained: when I bought the ring, those pictures had to go into the fire.

Classy to the end, Erica departed without hysteria. She left me alone with the images I had kept to help master the moment when the fissure in my heart had first formed. But the spell had backfired, and now my protective wards were streaked with tears from the wonderful woman whose heart they broke in turn.

Harvard's tragedy telegraph operates with shameful efficiency. Though six months have passed since our broken engagement, I'm sure I have that episode to thank for Blythe's reappearance in my life. Blake hears of my "troubles" and then thinks of me when he has some trouble of his own.

Of course, mine have gotten even worse in the interim. Women, naturally, remain the problem.

Men invariably prescribe a single remedy for a serious breakup: get as many bodies as possible between you and her. The underlying theory being that your anatomy will convince your pining mind that there isn't really any "one" woman. There is only all women. And that by screwing a diverse cast of these lovelies, you're reminded of all the scintillating possibilities life has to offer.

Though I've fully adopted that course of treatment in recent months, the difficulty has been recruiting willing therapists. I don't know what does it; maybe my eyes skitter away from theirs, maybe my manufactured smile betrays the flux of pain within. But most women can sense that there's something a little broken with me. And the ones who can't, well, there's usually something very broken with them.

This state of affairs leaves me, like the majority of my demographic, to content myself with the fire hydrant of pornography that is my cable modem. I can't imagine what people did before the internet arrived with its grand smorgasbord of pictures, video, chat, and webcam girls. But too much netporn turns one's mind into a Superfund site of frustrated lust. I find myself wearing out into the world the subtle but alienating caul of shame one gets from constantly wallowing in commodified filth. Another thing women can sense. Which makes me a more and more permanent citizen of this virtual Gomorrah we've built, the gateway to which sits innocently on our desks, pretending it's for work.

But on occasion, the ache of solitude simply demands real human warmth. So I've recently been driven to the teeming swamp of no-strings dating sites, erotic social networks, and "casual encounters" ads on Craigslist. In that arena, "real" becomes a somewhat loaded term.

One thing the internet reveals is that the world contains multitudes of people *just like you*. We've always known that there's this vast nation of lonely, isolated people out there, but now we're not just watching TV anymore. We've started coming up with ways to reach out. Some people are looking to share their thoughts, others are looking to share . . . other things.

Usually one finds a fellow forsaken soul who just wants a dose of companionship or a specific act performed and isn't very particular about the details. But often enough, you'll open the door on a lunatic or a criminal. The varieties of each are astounding.

On the crazy side, I've found everything from garden-variety weepies to scary "Miss Andreas"—women trying to work out profound man-hatred through anonymous sexual episodes. They want to hurt you, or at least scare you.

For example, Penny_S_Evers delivers a very hot oral experience with perhaps a little too much biting. In the morning, you wake to find "AIDS" scrawled on your mirror in lipstick. Of course, we've all already heard that story, but it's still enough to make you upchuck your Cheerios. I took the time to scope her medical records. She doesn't have AIDS, just a whopper of a borderline personality disorder. There are freelance voodoo surgeons and ladies possessed by dead celebrities. I'm still not able to parse the treatment I suffered at the hands, or rather other body parts, of Ms_Ophelia.

It all makes me curious what kind of ghastly characters the W4M dredge up.

The criminal side is occupied mostly by those aspiring to blackmail straying husbands. Rumors of organ harvesters abound, but I've never uncovered a credible case. Though as illustrated by my most recent debacle, I have run across plenty of more traditional thieves.

Last night, I'd found someone calling herself 1Ton_1—which I read as "wanton one" rather than "one-ton Juan"—posting about her desire to "party with an open-minded stud." A possible sneeze hooker, but since she didn't actually demand "skiing" (cocaine), I thought I'd take a chance with the pic4pic exchange. She emailed me an authentic-looking shot from her phone that showed a slender Mediterranean girl who could well have been the nursing student she claimed to be. I traced her IP and ran the name and address on her account through the NICS and KnowX crime databases just to make sure. She came up clean, so I invited her over.

In my foyer, she seemed a little nervous, but that's not unusual. Some guys like to play up the erotic tension of walking into a complete stranger's home for sex with dangerous looks and chilly silence, but I try to put people at ease with church-social friendliness.

I made drinks while she took off her shoes and got cozy on the couch. She savored the first sip of her rum and Coke and then asked slyly if perhaps I might have a lime. Something breathy in her voice implied she had perverse intentions toward the fruit, so I eagerly brought her drink back to the kitchen and sliced up a garnish.

A rookie mistake.

When I got back, she'd shed a layer of clothing and had draped herself with a blanket, which helped prevent me from thinking clearly. We clinked glasses, and she downed her entire cocktail, a gesture meant to impatiently dispense with the preliminaries. I slammed mine too, liking this girl more by the moment.

I registered the faintest hint of an acrid taste to my bourbon, like an evil spirit had crawled into the barrel while it aged. But she started kissing me with an ardor that emptied my head of petty cares. My last impressions were that her mouth didn't feel quite right, and for that matter, neither did mine. And why was I drooling down my chin?

I woke up bound, choking on an inexpertly applied gag. 1Ton_1 was a honey trap after all. I assume her boyfriend had been waiting in a car downstairs.

The appalling thing is that this has happened before. I've been prowling the no-strings world relentlessly in the past months. The incessant probing of my day job now leeching into my nightlife. Always searching, always trying to connect. In the past six months, I've been left tied up three times, robbed four times, and assaulted twice. Yet none of it has been enough to make me stop. The compulsion is strong, the risk outweighed by what I'm seeking.

But what exactly am I looking for? Solace? Pleasure? Action?

This last incident makes me fear the real answer is a darker word.

In penance for my behavior, I make it a point to flag or otherwise warn the community about the more egregious scams, blackmailers, and crooks I happen upon, alerting the police when it feels warranted. As though I fancy myself some kind of prurient superhero. Of course, the lonely and lustful are ever willing to make themselves victims. The police are correspondingly unsympathetic.

Despite this, my nighttime search goes on. And it had appeared I'd keep collecting rope burns until one day, not unlike this morning, the devil would take his due, and I'd miss my next meeting with Mercer.

But now I've felt the earth shift, and a new passageway has opened. This morning, Blythe's delicate smile made me remember a time when I felt almost normal. And she's asking me to take on an undercover assignment that offers a brand-new artificial world to inhabit. Just the thing for someone who insists on making a shambles of his real one.

6

Even if I wanted to ponder the merits of their cause, the Randall twins don't allow me the leisure. Judging from the welcome message I get from the director of Billy's most recent "place of business," my assignment has already begun.

They want me to infiltrate GAME, the Gnostic Atelier for Machined Experience. Founded as a colony for artists working in tech-heavy media, it's become the forward operating base for the Jackanapes movement.

The abuse of the term "Gnostic" by so many New Age sects has drained it of precise meaning. I gather from reading their online manifesto that GAME uses its original definition: that certain esoteric knowledge allows one to transcend the corrupt material universe into the realm of mystical Truth. This idea has been repurposed by hard-core transhumanists who believe that as mankind merges with machines, we'll be able to remake reality into a Platonic wonder of pure data. Thus liberating ourselves from the scarcity, ugliness, and strife of physical existence. Unsurprisingly, obsessive gamers make up the bulk of adherents to that theory.

The twins have secured a position for me at GAME based on a large donation that eliminated whatever red tape might otherwise complicate the process of adding a new fellow. My cover is that I'm a "conceptual video artist" with a manufactured portfolio who wants to make a documentary about Coit S. D. Files and his cohort of avant-gamers.

My real objective is to integrate myself into the community by joining whatever backgammon tournaments or tantra workshops they might hold to keep themselves occupied while awaiting the digital rapture, with an eye toward finding out whether anyone might know where Billy is. There's likely to be only some trivial hacking and casual surveillance. Best of all, GAME is reputed to throw fantastic parties. If you're into strip Twister and prescription bingo.

Since I'm officially undercover as of now, I'm banned from the Red Rook offices. So I go home to my apartment, a spacious loft at Lafayette and Bond near NYU, to change out of my suit, pour myself a Kentucky coffee, and get up to speed on this online world called NOD. The Randalls hadn't really touched on why their brother might want to symbolically electrocute himself into it, but I suppose that's a question I'll ask when I speak with IMP's security chief about Billy's recent corporeal whereabouts.

One of the biggest cultural trends of this century's first decade was the rise of the Massively Multiplayer Online (MMO) world as a truly widespread phenomenon, consuming an ever-growing share of the public's spare time. NOD is one of these digital environments that range from Tolkienian role playing like World of Warcraft to kiddie-crack mini-gaming like Club Penguin.

Akin to Second Life and IMVU, NOD appears on-screen as a 3D game, though there's no actual objective other than to amuse yourself if you can. This pursuit of virtual happiness can inspire people to do curious things. They quit their real-life jobs to become pretend haberdashers and legally marry people whom they first met as lime-green panda bears. Once in NOD, you quickly find yourself reducing the whole concept of "real life" to mere initials: RL. And untold millions of people worldwide have taken on new identities in one of these microtopias.

To start, you sign up and create a character called an avatar, which could be anything from a busty milkmaid to a ham sandwich. I already have one: Jacques_Ynne (pronounced "Jack In"). NODlings harbor a passion for double entendres equaled only by professionals in the adult film industry. Sadly, I never really bonded with my av. Poor Jacques has been even more lonely than I have in the past weeks.

After I log in to my account, the default location resolves from wireframe to lushly shaded volumes like a skeletal mummy coming back to life.

NOD Zero (NOD0), the center of the world, is a cross between an interplanetary Epcot Center and Bangkok's Patpong red-light district. Giant garishly colored buildings loom around the Tiananmen-sized central square. Like a NASCAR driver's uniform, every square inch of real estate is drafted to serve commerce, which is denominated in "Noodles" (NOD dollars). Blinking animated advertisements offer to satisfy unbelievably specialized fetishes:

```
Victorian Firefighters for your discreet pleasure.


Fraggle Bed-wetter?


Cum 2 Hershel's Hate Hotel. U WILL Regret It.
```

Throngs of ersatz Wookies, zombies, and anatomically enhanced Pokémon stand around chatting.

Immediately I'm besieged by avs teleporting to my location to make lewd pitches in Viagra-spam patois. The first in line are a woolly mammoth, a female Napoleon, and a little Oliver Twist clone.

```
DeeDee_Pea:                Caveman Enema??? Don't wait!

Jessica_A_Belle:           Hottt Machinima Man-Sluts ONLY
                           N$399.99 / min. Yes!!! HAVE
                           SOME!

Raymond_Richard_Euliss:    Hello, fine sir! Might I be of
                           some assistance?
```

Their appeals are unsurprising. I'd first rezzed into NOD a couple months ago, in an attempt to add some variety to my diet of online smut. "Cybering," slang for in-game sexual activity, is a favorite MMO pastime, and NOD is notorious among the major social worlds for having the best cybering tools by a long shot. NODlings like to flaunt this fact by making huge libraries of 3D animation, called machinima, that document their skills in the v-rotic arts. Recently, an anonymous developer produced LibIA (Library of Intercourse Applications), an extremely swanky tool set for neterosexuals that has the population of NOD acting like bonobos on crystal meth.

I dispel the first two avs as obvious NoBots (NOD robots are avatars controlled by programs rather than people). Raymond might be worth talking to. Right-clicking him shows me his profile data:

```
Name:              Jonathan Gurwicsz
RL Location:       Boca Raton, FL, USA
Rez Date:          03/16/2008
Interests:           . . .
```

Only the elderly and fraudulent chat-bot operators trying to make their automata more convincing use actual information in their profiles. I decide to give little Raymond a Turing test—queries meant to determine whether a fellow av is an actual person.

```
Jacques_Ynne:              What does NOD stand for?
```

A trick question. The world's denizens love debating what its name signifies. The obvious answer comes from the Bible. The Land of Nod is the place to which Cain fled after killing Abel. Scholars observed that the Hebrew root of the word means "wandering," so the verse could refer less to an actual place than to the act of fleeing. Nod later came to be known as the "land of dreams," primarily through the popular children's poem by Robert Louis Stevenson. So most people see the name as derived from the idea of "wandering through a dreamscape."

```
Raymond_Richard_Euliss:    Nerds Only Dungeon
                           Network Often Down
                           No Obscenity Denied
                           Take your pick. I've got
                           others.


Jacques_Ynne:              Thanks.
```

Raymond_Richard_Euliss: You're welcome . . .

                               So does the noob want to spank

                               me, or what?

Before I can evaluate his proposal, my screen goes black. Eventually I determine that some asshole griefer has affixed a giant black starfish to my face, and I can't see any obvious way to remove it.

Such is life in NOD.

Which raises the question of why Billy would choose this world as the place to receive his final reward. It's only to be expected that a game-focused artist would take an interest in MMOs. Though taking an interest in one and faking your death to send some kind of message to your brother are very different things. Not to mention the meaning conveyed by flipping the switch wearing nothing but a gilded lizard dangling from your urethra.

And if Billy's motivations are opaque, I'm also uneasy about the twins'. Why are they so concerned about his virtualization video? If there's so little love lost with their obnoxious sibling, why do they want to find him so badly?

What is it they're afraid of?

7

That evening I start getting some answers.

I'm at my desk, still starfish encumbered, when I feel a sudden twinge of apprehension. I turn off my music and listen. A soft ticking sound comes from my entryway. It stops for a second, and I'm halfway to convincing myself I'm imagining things, but then I hear my door's dead bolt slide against its strike plate. Someone is breaking into my apartment.

Given my professional propensity for making enemies within the criminal element, I try to keep two pistols around for ready access. From my file cabinet I grab the one that wasn't stolen by my recent house-guests. I flick the gun's custom-installed external safety and ease past the corner to take a bead on the intruder.

There's a man in my entryway with his back to me quietly shutting the door. He wears a plain gray suit and stands about five foot ten with a triathlete's build. He hears me come around the corner and turns fluidly.

The man actually smiles and says, "Nice Glock, bud."

Embarrassingly, I yell, "Freeze!"

He takes no notice of the "nice Glock" aimed at him and starts pulling open his jacket with his left hand. I can't believe he's doing this and can only come up with, "Hands up, motherfucker. I will fucking—"

"Let's just take it easy, killer."

Before I can track what's happening, he's retrieved a black object from his coat pocket, like he's performing a magic trick. I almost fire but am just able to restrain myself. He simply doesn't seem overtly threatening.

The object in his hand is a leather tri-fold he flips open and holds out for my inspection. He says, "John McClaren. IMP security. I thought you'd be expecting me."

I let out the breath I've been holding. "I wasn't expecting you to break into my apartment."

"Oh, I didn't break anything. But if you want to work with the Imp, we got to talk about hardening your perimeter."

He snickers, reviving my urge to pull the trigger. I just shake my head and lower the pistol.

He looks around brightly and says, "Got any scotch?"

I decide to just relax and go to the kitchen for some ice. He makes himself comfortable on my couch while I pour us each a slug.

Still a little suspicious, I use my phone to pull up his online bio. West Point class of '89. Fought with Special Forces in the first Gulf War. He spent the next decade with KBR and DynCorp. Then there's a dead space in his CV starting right around our invasion of Afghanistan. In '04 he set up his own modest security firm, McClaren Partners, which an IMP acquisition vehicle purchased four years ago. His picture matches the guy lounging in my living room.

I hand him his lowball and say, "Now that we've got whiskey, I guess the laws of hospitality say I can't shoot you."

"Well, I'm glad that's settled." McClaren speaks with a sunny Georgia twang. He doesn't use it to apologize. "I been looking forward to meeting you. Did some recon, and I must say I'm impressed." He rattles the ice in his glass. "I've got some former spooks sitting on Billy's last knowns. A couple ex-Bureau agents doing the normal shoe-leather inquiries. We've got plenty of tech people, but none with your shop's particular, ah, o-ffensive posture. And you, an honest-to-God covert operative too. Just the guy to help us find our Billy." He shakes his head in disbelief. "Boy's been nothing but trouble since I joined the enterprise. Nothing too serious. Has a fiery temperament, you know? But now he's got his loving family real worried. Haven't seen head nor tail of him in over a month."

"So I hear."

"But you're on the case now, so I'm sure we'll find him in no time. 'Course his safety is our top priority. We just want to take care of him. And plus, he's one of the Imp's biggest shareholders." He nods thoughtfully at his drink.

"What makes you think his safety's at risk?"

"Ah, well, I'd say he's exhibiting what his brother calls 'a crescendo of aberrant behavior.' Let me run you through the timeline." McClaren settles deeper into my sofa. "So after his dust-up with Blake over his trust, Billy moves to New York and a few years later enrolls himself in this techy art program called PiMP. NYU's Pervasive Media Program. He gets sued again over some project he did there, but with his new name, none of it bothers the twins all that much. After that stuff in college, he doesn't want to advertise who he is. Distracts from the work, I guess. Anyway, he graduates last spring and gets himself a fellowship at this GAME place, where you're going to be. Right?"

McClaren pulls from his jacket a folded set of eight-by-ten photos. He places one on the table between us. It shows Billy walking into an indistinct building.

"Wait a minute, you had Billy under surveillance?"

"Yeah, the twins just wanted to check up on him when that first Jackanapes guy kicked off—they showed you that article?"

I nod.

"Right, so Trevor Rothstein injects an unhealthy amount of herowine. There's this video of him shooting up and going on about how much everything sucks. Which the cops take as a suicide note."

"Was Billy close with him?"

"We don't think so. If anything, they didn't care for each other. But the next one to go *was* a big deal. Gina Delaney. A good friend of Billy's from grad school. She offed herself two months ago. Videotaped it, too. And what a mess that was."

"Blythe said she almost decapitated herself?"

McClaren winces. "Yeah, best you hear about that from the horse's mouth. I'll hook you up with the detective who investigated, and he'll give you all the gory details. We don't think they had an actual romantic relationship, but suffice it to say, Billy's a little more broken up about this one. After the funeral, he gets arrested for disorderly conduct outside some bar in Boston."

"What did he do?"

"From what the officers say, he got in a fight. By the time they arrived, the other party had taken off, and they ended up letting him go. Said he looked like he got the worst of it. A couple weeks later, he gets arrested again. Another disorderly-conduct citation from the NYPD. Late night, up around Forty-sixth and the West Side Highway."

"What was that about?"

"We don't really know. We got hold of the ticket, but it doesn't say much beyond the charge. Talked to the guy who busted him, but he was uncooperative."

"So all this is acting out because his friend killed herself. And you're worried that the end point is him following her? That these suicides are contagious?"

"You don't watch out, you wind up with an epidemic. Recent rash in Wales finally petered out at twenty-five corpses. So yeah, that kind of stuff worries us. Just on its face. But with Billy it gets worse."

"Worse than him dying?"

He smiles. "No, our worry gets worse. When he disappeared, some of these extreme-gaming blogs wondered if he'd gone the way of his friends. The curse of the Jackanapes, they called it. So we took the liberty of checking his apartment and found this." He hands me a series of photos taken in a sparsely furnished luxury apartment. The element that jumps out is that all the appliances have been disassembled. "So that just don't seem right. Like maybe he's gone paranoid. Hearing voices from the TV and all that. We get ahold of his bank and credit card statements."

McClaren places some papers in front of me. The statement for Billy's private bank, which begins with a seven-figure cash balance, shows normal activity and then a large wire transfer to another bank in Lichtenstein.

"So from this we concluded Billy was planning to go incognito. Probably had lawyers set up an offshore corporation to get new accounts and credit cards through. We're afraid he's trying to put himself beyond help. Then the twins get that electrocution video. All in all, not the behavior of a sane person, is it?"

"I don't know. Maybe he spotted your surveillance. That could explain the disassembled electronics. Could be the main thing he's doing is hiding from his siblings. The video is just an artistic 'fuck you.'" I shrug. "Maybe he's protecting himself."

"Protecting himself?"

"Yeah. I know I'm the new guy here. But I wouldn't call him crazy for believing his big brother is trying to put him in a place where the people with electrodes strapped to their heads aren't performance artists."

McClaren takes a moment to ponder this. A little of the cornball friendliness departs from his voice. "It's always good to try to think like your quarry, bud. I just hope you remember that your job is to help find him. What happens after that ain't your concern."

He knocks back his drink and stands, glancing at his watch. "Well, no rest for the wicked, right?"

On his way out, he's kind enough to lock the door behind him.

Curious now about the gears grinding in Billy's head, I find online a copy of the video he created with his friend Gina Delaney. Blythe had mentioned it with sincere distaste, and its title indicates why: the clip opens with the words "Getting Wet."

A profile shot of a delicate girl seated in a high-backed wooden chair. Attached to its central post is a wide band of rusted iron that encircles the girl's neck. She struggles against the leather restraining straps and whimpers. I recognize the contraption from a James Bond film. It's a vile garrote, beloved as an execution device by the Spanish up to the end of General Franco's reign. These machines employed a dowel, or if the executioner was merciful, a spike that was screwed into the back of one's neck, creating the pressure necessary for strangulation. In this case, Billy has replaced the spike with an oversized male Ethernet plug pressing insistently against the nape of her neck. Her breathing is labored, and as the thing presses harder, she starts to moan with progressively more erotic energy. Her body arches forward against the metal collar, throwing her small breasts into relief against the white silk of her robe. This goes on for a few beats until the network cable rears back like a snake and drives itself into her spine with a small spurt of blood. A close-up of her face as she inhales sharply in a sudden apex of ecstasy. The camera zooms in on her left eye, where, via some nifty special effects work, the spiderweb of broken veins slowly morphs into hexadecimal code.

The screen cuts to black.

Getting Wet isn't the first video I've seen that sexualizes the now classic sci-fi concept of the "wet interface." To create a direct connection between one's nervous system and a computer, you must penetrate the skin. So the idea really doesn't need a lot more sexualizing. Billy's video takes a dim view of the prospect in suggesting that Gina is actually being strangled in her moment of networked transcendence. Making such a video might well get a woman interested in sexual asphyxia. And certainly there are a lot of both suicides and accidental deaths that stem from this sort of fantasy.

But I'd like to know how this girl went from risqué playacting to almost decapitating herself.

8

Suffocating images from Gina's video invade my dreams, and I wake the next morning with a drained and uneasy feeling, like a family of affectionate pythons has shared my bed. But better rest will have to wait. I have an early orientation meeting with a woman named Alexandra Xiao.

The GAME facility stands just on the edge of New York's Lower East Side nightlife mecca. The building is a seven-story neo-Gothic that takes up half the block. Ringed by intricate iron railings, fronted with mullioned windows, and embellished with irate gargoyles, it looks more like a place to house impenitent nuns than a modern interactive arts facility.

I find Ms. Xiao in the large front hall that serves as one of their public event spaces. Her online bio says that she's an '11 alumna of PiMP and already an adjunct professor there as well as a senior GAME fellow. An accomplished 3D artist, she's best known for a series of female characters from a hit martial arts title whose images now decorate the walls of fanboys the world over.

She's supervising the installation of a large aquarium, pointing with one hand and holding an iPhone in the other. "And you're absolutely sure we don't need any kind of permits for transgenic piranhas?" She sees me and says, "Look, I have to call you back."

While the exquisite planes of her face speak of northern China, her musical English accent indicates a Hong Kong childhood. She's wearing a navy pinstripe pantsuit over an *Urotsukidoji* T-shirt. The film is an

X-rated anime about a shy young student who grows a three-headed prehensile penis that ends up destroying Tokyo. My kind of woman.

"You must be our new resident. I'm Xan, your welcome committee as it were. Come to my office, and let's chat."

She leads me down a long hallway into a room whose every available surface is occupied by screens. There are banks of monitors connected to expensive workstations, multiple game consoles, and a group of wifi picture frames cycling through landscapes from popular shooters. I sit across from her desk, and she surveys me intently.

"Are you a gamer, Mr. Pryce?"

"James, please. And no, I'm more of a spectator by nature."

Her mouth forms an evil smile. "I'm not sure your fellow residents will allow that. Passive engagement is considered *quite* last-century here. Abstinence is not an option. In this place if you're not playing the game, the game plays you."

"You're obviously quite the ambassador."

"Well, we have you in our clutches now, so better you understand right away that GAME is no fun if you don't know the rules. Fancy a bit of background on the place?"

I nod.

"We humans have played games since the very dawn of time. But as we digitize them, it's got to where, for some of us, that's *all* we do. Our generation grew up playing video games, but those were just dollhouses: tidy wee worlds that live in your monitor. Today we're capable of far more immersion. Not just modeling reality anymore. Now we want to manipulate it. To 'machine' it, if you will. Maybe even *replace* it."

"I can think of a few improvements."

Xan smiles. "Quite so. But a bit of caution's in order. Something about treading the line between the virtual and real makes GAME's little monsters hopelessly transgressive. If there's an observable border of decency or prudence, the hateful players we breed here want to cross it like fighting cocks."

She adopts a long-suffering expression. "Just this year we've seen the premiere of *Kewpie*, a game intended as a profound comment on the casual misogyny you find with internet culture. But in playing it, you'd be forgiven for mistaking it for the real thing. Then there was the staging of a piece called *Flash Mob*, which resulted in several residents getting nicked for indecent exposure. If we GAMErs hold the keys to the future, I'm not sure I want to live there."

"What about Coit Files?"

"Coit? Ah, you mean *Billy*." Apparently Xan disapproves of people inventing absurd handles for themselves in RL.

"How would you characterize his art?"

Xan weighs my question. "I can say this: it ain't pretty."

I raise my eyebrows, looking for more. But she stands and takes my arm. "Why don't I show you?"

As we walk back to GAME's main entrance hall, Xan says, "Your Billy's idée fixe is something he calls 'The Bleed.'"

She treats me to a disquisition about how throughout history we've tended to surround ourselves with ever more sophisticated imaginary environments. It used to be books and plays, then film, but now we have these giant online spaces. Part of their allure is how they grant us the ability to act as someone else, through the use of these ornate masks we call avatars.

Xan tells me that Billy liked to explore how our enthrallment to lavish fantasy worlds can have a pronounced impact on the real one. He sought to inspire moments when your biological self *bleeds* into your avatar, and vice versa.

She leads me to a small alcove set up as a public gallery space. While most of the "work" produced at GAME is intangible, they've filled the room with posters and exhibits illustrating demos, play-tests, and events. A corner of the space is dedicated to one of Billy's previous offerings.

On a glass pedestal poses a hideous sculpture of Satan. Spiraling ram horns, cloven feet, barbed tail. Oddly, he appears as though he's been burned by his own hellfire. His crimson skin shows large black and brown spots. The latex has bubbled in some places, melted all the way through in others. I look closer and find not a statue, but rather a devil costume arrayed on a neutral mannequin. He's reaching forward with one of his clawed hands holding a charred wooden frame that houses a fifteen-inch video screen. A small brass nameplate reads HELL IS OTHER PEOPLE. The screen cycles shots of human faces contorted in horror.

Xan explains, "So one advantage of having this scary old building is that it makes a jolly good venue for our annual haunted house fund-raiser. We often invite visiting artists to do special 'installations' exploring fear."

"That sounds scary."

"No, they're generally quite good. We only select those who don't place themselves above delivering cheap thrills. Many of our residents hail from PiMP, and so in 2012 a couple of the new ones had met Billy. Just starting the program, wasn't he? They knew he had a yen for high-concept nastiness, so why not see what he could do with a room?"

"I suppose you're about to tell me."

"On the contrary, many thought it a smashing success. At the debut, we were disappointed to find a cheesy mockery of those evangelist hell houses that dress some oaf in a Satan costume"—she gestures to the thing in front of us—"to frighten teens into preserving their virtue. We asked, 'Is this really the best he can do?' But just watch."

She touches the screen a few times, and a video starts rolling.

In a dark room packed with people, the actor dressed as Satan stands on a slightly elevated stage. He makes a showy gesture to summon his dark powers. Behind him erupts a shower of sparks. Flames jet toward the ceiling. The devil turns and throws up his hands with malign ecstasy. But in doing so, his tail drags through one of the gas jets. His costume catches fire like rayon pajamas. Spasming with terror, he trips into the room's painted backdrop, which ignites in a blazing sheet. The devil starts screaming. After an agonizing moment of indecision, so does the crowd. Two GAME staffers run from offstage to extinguish the actor, but by now the flames have ascended to the heavy curtains draped around the room, and the fire is clearly out of control.

The crowd surges to flee, and you can make out the accordion impact as they hit the exits. Then the cascading frenzy of panic when they realize: *the doors are locked.*

But those nearer the fire keep pressing forward. A petite woman goes down calling for help. This is obviously the moment at which Billy's portraits of horror were taken. Someone being pulverized against the doors screams, "I can't breathe!"

The video cuts to black.

— — —

"Ouch," I say.

"Yeah. Anyone who's been near the stage at a big music festival can tell you it's not a pleasant feeling. But with an inferno at your back . . ."

Xan pauses, remembering the experience. "Billy had rigged that wall with sensors that tripped when a certain 'safe' amount of pressure was applied. At the critical moment, it just fell down like a drawbridge, and people got out without any serious injuries. The fire was all just special effects. He'd hired some guys from the Madagascar Institute to teach him how to rig them." Madagascar is a Brooklyn-based collective known for staging wild bashes involving flamethrowers, pyrotechnics, and rocket-powered carnival rides. "But needless to say, that was the one and only performance of Billy's hell house."

"Not afraid to set fire to a crowded theater."

"Yeah, he has a pretty aggressive attitude toward your First Amendment. Toward his audiences too. The guy goes around saying, 'Art, like games, must have something at stake.' You can see why, even here, people find him hard to take. But I have to credit the little blighter. He set himself the task of creating real fear in the most contrived setting. People come to a haunted house *knowing* that you're going to try to scare them. It's easy to get a yelp when you have someone in a funny wig jump out at them. But then they're laughing about it the next second."

"But no one was laughing after this."

"More like hyperventilating. Billy was really able to jar us out of our role as 'fake' victims. The way he'd built the context helped. Prominent fire code warnings posted at the building's entrance. He search-optimized a news story to appear just under the links to our ticketing website so almost everyone would read the headline 'Ninety-six die in Rhode Island concert blaze,' before they came to the show." She shakes her head in admiration.

"With all that in our subconscious, his artificial fire shattered our superficial suspension of *disbelief* and made us actually *believe* we were about to die. That, for him, is the Bleed, the moment when the imaginary becomes shockingly real. When you and your persona fuse."

"People must have gone crazy."

"Across the board. One critic wrote that it was the most transformative artistic experience he's had in years. Another coined the term 'terrartist.'

An audience member filed a suit asking ten million in damages for giving her PTSD."

"Do all of his projects end in lawsuits?"

"I think he'd be disappointed otherwise. He believes litigation is America's only authentic form of public discourse. If no one is suing you, you're obviously not very interesting. He indemnified GAME against that little stunt, and we actually saw a marked increase in donations when news broke about the legal action. Seems supporting the arts is tedious, but defending them stirs the blood."

Xan smiles at me and then steps back toward the hall. "Come along then. I'll show you around."

I'm impressed by the building's size and scope. Along with the main gallery on the first floor is a performance space fit for an audience of over two hundred. The next three levels house studios, increasingly industrial in nature. There's a state-of-the-art computer lab and a full-service metal shop bedecked with warning signs emphasizing the dangers of welding while under the influence of controlled substances. The fifth floor is divided into "collaborative spaces" that all seem to be padlocked, and the last two floors, Xan informs me, consist of garrets for those residents who need "accommodations suitable for alternative lifestyles."

She adds, "But I'll spare you the zoo tour. I'm sure the beasts are still asleep."

Xan then takes me to find an office. Given the sort of work I need to do, I ask for one that's fairly out of the way.

She says, "A cave dweller, are you? Well, we can give you one of the PODs, but—"

"PODs?"

"The work spaces in the Pit of Despair. Here, follow me." We walk toward a small antique elevator. It descends creakily after Xan hits the button for the basement.

"I have to warn you," she says, "your associates down here are a different breed. POD people, we call them. Not the most gregarious."

We step out into an area that looks like the set of a grindhouse feature. It's a rat's nest of narrow brick corridors with rusty pipes overhead and industrial doors spaced at irregular intervals. To enhance the atmosphere, residents have covered the walls with prison graffiti, and at one intersection, a realistic skeleton hangs from shackles.

Xan stops at an office and appears surprised at the oversized Master Lock hanging from its latch. She consults a sheet in her portfolio and mumbles, "Bollocks. This is supposed to be open."

I drift halfway down the hall to where a rickety door stands ajar. A naked overhead bulb reveals the room to be a tiny dank cell with a slouching brick wall running along one side and a set of water-stained drywall planes composing the other three. In the back, an ancient desk stands devoid of contents.

"This looks okay," I call out.

Xan seems hesitant to abandon the room listed on her clipboard, but she walks slowly over and checks out the one I've selected. She darts a glance across the hall at a sturdy steel door.

Finally, she says, "Right. Well, I hope you're very happy here. I should say that we're having a bit of a fete tonight. If you meet me outside at eleven, I'll hand you around to your new colleagues."

"Sounds great."

"Welcome to the GAME, James. You know where I am. If you need anything, don't hesitate to ask."

"Well, there is one thing. I understand Billy has disappeared. You haven't seen him recently, have you?"

Xan chuckles softly. "Billy? I don't believe I've laid eyes on him for quite a while. But that's not so unusual."

"Seems like there's some reason to worry. What with the Jackanapes suicide epidemic."

"Now James, I like lurid drama as much as the next girl, but two separate tragedies hardly make an epidemic."

I nod amenably but silently reply, *Yeah, but who says it's over?*

9

Approaching the GAME building that night, I'm surprised to see a scene resembling the sidewalk of a hot nightclub. There's a brace of enormous black bouncers accompanied by a transvestite in an astro-Krishna getup holding a clipboard. Beyond the perimeter, a group of the unnamed angrily thumb their phones. Xan, ravishing in leather pants and black cashmere, leads me smoothly past the doorgoyles.

Inside is a labyrinth of giant screens, each providing a window into some strange universe of grave jeopardy and eternal resurrection. Projectors mounted in any available corner make surfaces crawl with a chaos of ill-defined images. Smoke from DIY holographic displays pervades the place with a sense of spectral menace. Condensing mist drips onto the cables crisscrossing the floor. Having considered the topic recently, I assess the possibility of electrocution.

The crowd is a pan-tribal confab representing suits, geeks, and the new-media media. Omnipresent black lights impart a *Tron*-ish computer glow even to those guests not dressed like gaudy NOD avatars. A series of statuesque women, faces hidden by Boschian beaked-creature masks, are dancing up on platforms.

A DJ I dimly recognize is working through a dissonant eight-bit set, occasionally manipulating a panel of raw circuitry.

Though it seems like typical art-rave eclecticism, eventually I notice that the unifying undercurrent here is *play*. Scanning the room I see a group of what I'm forced to characterize as upscale punk intelligentsia running around trying to assassinate each other with their cell phones. There are several home-brewed *Magic: The Gathering*–style card games going, hardcore LARPers fencing with prop-quality light sabers, and a techno-hippie drum circle gathered around an iPhone collaborative music app. They're wearing headphones, so the group's synchronized nodding comes off eerie in its silence. The aquarium I saw Xan working on earlier now allows players to fight phosphorescent piranhas with a remote-control submarine.

My host sees a passing waiter, all of whom are dressed as snow ninjas, and liberates two magenta drinks. She hands one to me.

"*Gan bei,* James." We clink glasses. "So here you have GAME in all its degenerate glory."

She gestures to a group way out on the thrash end of the spectrum who have imported a bottle of Everclear and some powdery substance and are lighting their sneezes on fire.

Xan downs the better part of her drink and then grabs the elbow of someone behind her. "Looks like I'll need another cocktail. Be right back, but in the meantime, meet Andrew Garriott."

Garriott is a diminutive Brit with short hair and dancing eyes that give him a sprightly quality. He shows the well-wrought smile of someone groomed to be a child star. After a warm handshake and some preliminaries, he asks me what I do.

"Video, mostly. What's your game of choice?"

"Game? Oh, I'm complete crap at games. More of a gearhead, really. I was making robots at Cambridge . . . I suffer to think how I ended up here. Good parties though. I guess you could say I—"

Garriott is nearly carried off his feet by the ardent embrace of a strikingly tall blonde. Her back to me, she puts him into a precarious dip while whispering into his ear. Garriott's initial frown at being mauled smooths into an expression approaching bliss. She sets him back on balance, grabs his hair, and gives him a violent kiss on the forehead. I begin to turn away, as it seems clear they have something important to discuss, but Xan reappears by my side and taps her shoulder, saying, "Olya, how beastly! You're alienating our new man here."

She turns, and I have to strain to keep my mouth closed and my eyes from wandering along uncivil trajectories. Olya puts one in mind of mythology. With cascades of nearly white hair, eyes a color of blue Icelandic geneticists are no doubt struggling to patent, and a radiant complexion, she has all the unnatural perfection of the Valkyrie one might find painted on the side of a van at Comic-Con. This impression is not hindered by her wearing a metallic corset that, while possibly providing some protection in battle, seems more contrived to bring confusion to her enemies by what it does for her tremendous décolletage. Her voice is the low Slavic purr of a Bond villain:

"Ah. Hello. I am Olya Zhavinskaya."

I start to offer my hand, but she envelops me in a Russian triple kiss. The last one lingering enough to make me fumble my own name. Olya seems to ignore it anyway and says, "Now, *zaichik,* we welcome you here, and I'm sure we'll be great friends. It is very rude of me, but I must take away the little ones. We have business."

She puts her arms around the shoulders of Garriott and Xan and marches them off toward a dimly lit corner by the DJ booth. Xan puts up a mollifying finger for me, but something Olya says makes her head snap around as they disappear into the crowd.

After some time spent making small talk with other GAMErs, I notice, across the crowded main gallery, Olya stepping up onto the DJ's stage.

"Shitfire," observes a guy standing nearby.

The DJ shakes his head at whatever she's asking. But with her lips at his ear, he finally nods reluctantly, earning a brisk pat on the ass. The DJ abandons his abstract composition of low-fi bleeps and segues into an up-tempo version of the Smiths' "Girlfriend in a Coma," but with Morrissey's bleak baritone artfully mixed with a James Brown classic:

Girlfriend in a coma I know I know it's serious—Get up! Get on up!

Olya then steps back to Xan and Garriott, who are wrestling with a bottle of champagne. There's a barely audible squeal of delight as the cork goes and foam explodes all over them.

I feel a strong impulse to slip over and play cabana boy with my cocktail napkin. But I make it only a few steps in their direction when I'm thwarted by a girl turning away in disgust from losing at some handheld game. This hefty cyber-goth with Muppet hair and a pincushion face slams into me, and my drink spills all over the most incongruous part of her outfit: a pastel pink polo shirt she's wearing along with plaid vinyl pants. I apologize and offer her the napkin meant for Olya.

She says, "Ha. Forget it, dude. That won't be the worst thing I'll have—well, anyway, don't worry about it."

Then she's distracted by one of her friends hollering at her. I check out the mess I've made. Curiously, her soiled shirt bears a crocodile logo over her left breast. But this one isn't the usual preppy embroidery. It looks more like it's been embossed into the fabric. I guess she notices me staring at her chest. When I glance up, she smiles and flicks the crocodile with a black fingernail, making a soft click.

"See anything you like?" she asks.

I realize that the logo is actually a metal pendant affixed to her nipple. Having recently seen its twin dangling from Billy's pecker, I know I have to overcome my mortification to ask her about it. But she's already wheeled away from me back into the crowd.

I push forward to follow her but can't see where she's gone. As I scope the nearby guests, however, I discover that several of them are also wearing gold croc insignia through a wide variety of piercings.

In the bar line I find a bored-looking man with the pendant hanging from a bull ring through his nose. "I've seen a bunch of people wearing that crocodile tonight. What does it mean?"

"Just swag, man. This stupid guerilla marketing thing. We thought we might win something."

"Can I see it?"

He takes it out, and I examine it, feeling like he's handed me the key to a treasure vault.

"Where'd you get it?"

"It came in the mail a couple days ago. I've been wearing it this whole time, but nothing's happened. Which is bullshit if you ask me."

"Did it say who sent it?"

"No. No return address or anything. It was clipped to a card with this fucking poem. I brought it in case we needed it to get our prize."

He pulls out a small ivory square of heavy-gauge card stock. Printed in a medieval script are the words:

For reward look to me,
Your divine Louis Markey,
And so yoke your breath
To the Narration Of Death.
Let my word be your bond,
Et voilà: my beau monde.

Underneath the last line are the two holes from the pendant's pin.

The guy sees my quizzical expression and says, "People here think it's from a new game someone's starting. But I bet it's just some corporate hipster anti-fashion irony thing."

New York is rife with dernier cri marketing agencies that promote brands through in-crowd secrets rather than the traditional media blare. Some of these PR judo techniques were actually developed as launch strategies for various bleeding-edge games like *The Beast* and *I Love Bees*. The "inscrutable mailed item" being a favorite device.

The guy refuses my offer to buy the pendant, saying I can just keep it.

I go outside for a cigarette and contemplate my good fortune.

My fortune gets even better a few minutes later when Olya emerges from GAME heading toward me. She glides smoothly down the steps despite her rapier heels. The giant martini glass she's carrying contains enough alcohol to sicken a hippo.

"Ah, my new friend. Maybe you have a cigarette for a poor babushka?"

I offer her one, and she demonstrates her contempt for my choice of Camel Lights by removing the filter with a flick of her thumbnail. She deftly tends the ragged end with her tongue and leans into me for a light. Then a long French inhale.

"Xan tells me you are making a film about Billy. I very much wonder why you want to glorify this person with documentary."

"I take it you're not a fan? Do you mind telling me why?"

Olya makes a staccato teeth-sucking sound. "I don't think so. I know him for long while now. From graduate school. And he is not a good topic for conversation, I think." She finishes her drink and tosses the glass into a nearby tree planter. With a sleepy smile, she slaps me lightly on the cheek, saying, "Maybe I see you tomorrow."

This woman's every departure must be closely observed by frustrated men. My lizard brain is certainly screaming furiously as she recedes down the block. She turns right at the corner, and I notice that a fellow admirer, smoking on the opposite side of the street, is taking in her progress as well. As he steps off the curb in her direction, I think, *moths to the flame,* and wish that the cloak of anonymity permitted me a few more minutes witnessing the glorious pendulum of her hips.

But what sets me in motion isn't the natural jealousy of a rival. It's when our casual peeper affects tossing away a half-smoked butt and glances up the street. The hours of surveillance I've clocked at Red Rook have imparted a keen appreciation of body language, and this subtle action was clearly taken *to check if anyone is watching.* Suddenly the guy flashes from just another devotee of the female form to a potentially dangerous creep. And now I've found a reason to follow Olya after all.

I hustle after them down Delancey and check myself as I turn left onto Allen. The street is crowded with late-night revelers. Olya crosses an intersection about a block ahead of me. She ignores some appreciative whoops from a pack of men coming the other way. I start thinking that maybe my mind's reptile regions are making me overreact. Then I see the guy speed up to make the light and slide in behind a group heading in the same direction. He's definitely following her, and trying not to be seen.

A lucky gap in traffic allows me to keep her in sight. She turns right at Grand, and the guy stops to light another cigarette before pacing her down the block. I merge into a line formed at the ropes in front of an unmarked bar. From here I can see that he's a short but thick man, with stringy hair and a mean, acne-scarred face. He's wearing a bulky black jacket and baggy jeans. Thick glasses disrupt his otherwise thuggish look.

He waits a beat and then proceeds after her, and I hurry to the corner. I start to cross the street, thinking I'll watch from the opposite side, but Olya extracts her keys at the door of an old tenement building, no doubt converted into resplendent lofts. The guy has picked up speed. He's turning into the doorway. I go into a dead run.

Fifty yards ahead of me, Olya startles as she notices someone behind her. Too late. He's already on her. He grabs her shoulder with one hand, his other reaching toward her chest. His face is close to her ear, and he seems to be giving her some kind of order. Her gaze drops down to his hand for a split second.

Then Olya fights. She twists in his grasp and aims her keys at his eyes. He takes the blow on the side of his head, but it knocks off his glasses. When he grabs her hair, something small and shiny drops to the ground.

That's when I hit him full tilt. My shoulder nails him at the base of his neck, rocketing his face into the glass door and leaving an impressive splatter of blood from a long gash that opens over his eye. He slumps, dragging Olya down. I take his wrist, twisting it backward to break his grip. Olya jerks upright, strands of her hair tearing free. I grab the guy under his jaw and hurl him out of the entryway. He collapses on the sidewalk stunned, blood running down his face.

I start dialing 911, but Olya puts her hand over my cell.

"No! . . . James. I—I'm sorry. Thank you, but—"

"Are you out of your mind? This guy just attacked you. We need to call the police."

Olya takes a long trembling breath. "No, please. Do not call police." She looks away, and I see a sad expression steal across her face. She lowers her voice. "James, I don't want to say this . . . But my papers. My, ah, immigration status. Maybe it is not quite current. I'm fixing, but you see . . ."

So that's it. She's overstaying a student visa. And GAME is probably quite lax about its payroll. I let the phone fall to my side. "Olya—"

But she can tell she's prevailed and follows up with a deep embrace. She kisses my neck and ear, whispering, "Thank you so much. My guarding angel."

"Well, are you okay?" I can't help adding, "Do you need some company?"

Her eyes slide away from mine. "Oh . . . James, I appreciate—"

"I didn't mean it like that."

Olya's smile blooms at my discomfort. "Of course not, you silly man. But no, I am fine. I have a hot bath and some tea. Everything's okay." She brushes my cheek with her hand. "Again, thank you." She reaches down for her keys.

Not quite ready to let it go, I ask, "What about him?"

Offhandedly, she grabs the neck of a wine bottle poking out of the adjacent recycling bin and hurls it at him, shouting, *"Poshol ty na khuy!"*

It shatters next to his head, which seems to revive him somewhat, and he slowly crawls to his knees. When he sees me advance, it prompts him to lurch to his feet and hasten away, cradling his injured wrist. Olya and I watch him limp down the street, but he turns and, pointing at her with his good hand, yells something that sounds like "Don't pretend you didn't want it, you fucking bitch."

I glance back at Olya, but she's sliding through her door. She turns at the stairs and blows me a kiss.

As I stand there in the entryway trying to understand what just happened, a sparkle catches my eye. In a clump of dirty snow next to the trash cans, there's a necklace. I pick it up.

A simple platinum chain suspends a large deep-purple stone carved into an icosahedron. Tiny integers are engraved into each of its faces. The necklace isn't Olya's. I would have noticed her wearing it, and I have trouble believing that she'd adorn herself with a universal emblem of the über game-geek: the twenty-sided die from Dungeons and Dragons.

But if it's not Olya's, where did it come from?

I know I saw it hit the ground earlier, which brings me to a strange conclusion. Rather than trying to steal from her (or worse), could the guy have been attempting to give her a present? If so, he received poor thanks for it.

But that doesn't feel right. There was something off about that encounter and Olya's reaction to it. Something else is going on.

That brilliant insight's confirmed when I suddenly realize that I'm not alone on the street. Almost obscured between two parked SUVs, there's a short guy with a shaggy beard pointing a small black object at me. I flinch, thinking, *Gun.* He sees this and smirks before he backs into the shadows. I hear him jogging up the street.

What was that? Not a gun. He was looking at it, not me. So . . . a camera, I guess.

I start running, but he's got too much of a lead for me to catch him. I pull up at the corner and check in every direction. Nothing.

My familiar cityscape now vibes weird and hostile. A cold fog is sweeping in, giving the street a disquieting, dreamlike feel.

Who were those guys? Why would they record themselves giving Olya a neck-lace?

It can't be a coincidence that in one night I've come across two myste-rious pieces of jewelry that seem like cryptic symbols. Separately they'd rate as minor oddities. But together they feel like, what?

Game pieces.

I think about Billy and his "Bleed" and suspect that maybe I've been cut.

10

At breakfast I reexamine the ornaments I acquired last night, puzzling over their significance. I figure I'll just ask Olya about the die. But the crocodile pendants trouble me since their prevalence means others far more familiar with Billy's games must be working on the riddle. I can't see McClaren's team of spooks being much help, so I settle in and resolve to crack it myself.

> For reward look to me,
> Your divine Louis Markey,
> And so yoke your breath
> To the Narration Of Death.
> Let my word be your bond,
> Et voilà: my beau monde.

At first, the verse reads like nonsensical doggerel, though I catch another reference to NOD in the capitalization of "Narration Of Death."

What is this project Billy's asking people to undertake for some reward? Who is Louis Markey? Where is this beau monde *he wants us to find?*

I suspect the GAMErs will have a much easier time with these questions. I hold one advantage over them, however: I've seen the video he sent his siblings, which gives me a set of clues no one else has. So maybe I should begin with that speech.

He starts with:

*As a final farewell, Blake, I thought to indulge your greatest fantasy. I know
you've often wished that I'd just jack out like she did.*

I assume "she" is his mother. Billy's implying here that Blake celebrated
the loss of the au pair home wrecker and hoped her unloved spawn
would follow her example, thus cleansing the Randall family history of
that unfortunate chapter.

Then Billy threatens this occult revenge:

*But be careful what you wish for. My ghost may come
back to haunt you. And lead you down your own path of torment.*

After which he invokes the Old Testament story of Sodom and Gomorrah, promising some end-times punishment for Blake's sins against
him.

*For I will rain down brimstone and fire upon your festering Sodom. And
when you look, lo, the smoke from your life will rise up like the smoke from
a furnace.*

My biblical knowledge is weak, so I have to review an online summary of
the story from Genesis.

God sends two angels to ascertain the level of evil shit going on in
Sodom. They meet Abraham's nephew Lot at the city gate, and he offers
them hospitality for the night. Lamentably, the other Sodomites notice
the strangers and gather outside Lot's house, demanding access to his
guests. My summary quotes the King James version:

```
And they called unto Lot, and said unto him, Where are the
men which came in to thee this night? Bring them out unto
us, that we may know them.
```

Does that "know" refer to knowledge in the *biblical* sense? Are the people
saying, "Lot has two houseguests. Let's go over there and anally rape

them," or are they just looking for an introduction, and who knows what might happen after a couple glasses of date palm brandy?

In light of his obligations to his visitors, and knowing the propensities of his neighbors, Lot feels that he can't allow this. So the gracious host offers the mob his two virgin daughters instead. Which doesn't speak well of the family feeling in the Lot household. I'm not sure that angels possess the anatomical equipment in which the Sodomites were interested, but regardless, they obviate Lot's proposition by striking the villagers with a spell. The summary is vague on the details.

Was it blindness? Impotence?

I can't remember. At any rate, because of their churlishness, the fate of the Sodomites is sealed. For reasons that aren't made clear, the Gomorreans are lumped in with them to share their punishment.

The angels offer Lot the chance to escape with his family, provided they don't look back once the show starts. They make it out just as the fire and brimstone start to fall. Of course, Lot's wife looks back, and, in a rather arbitrary twist, she becomes a pillar of salt. But Lot escapes with the rest of his family. This is where the summary ends, but if I recall correctly, their descendants become some important tribe until the Assyrians come in and kill everyone.

What I can't figure out from Billy's speech is how NOD plays into all this. His electrocution video implies that this online world is somehow going to be the medium of his revenge. Maybe the location his ghost rezzed into would tell me more. The riddle he sent to his fellow GAMErs solicits them to find or do something in NOD as well, a mystery to which the croc pendant seems the most important clue.

I fire up NOD and send Jacques_Ynne searching for crocodile-related content. I visit a simulated crocodile farm. Then an overwrought Steve Irwin memorial. I try an actual Lacoste sportswear store for virtual clothes. Finally, I exhaust Jacques searching locations tangentially related to the company's namesake, tennis great René Lacoste.

At none of these builds do I find anything resembling Billy's fingerprints. No answers. No further puzzles. And no suspicious characters lurking around to interrogate. Though in a place where representing as a psychedelic amoeba is considered de rigueur, "suspicious" can be a hard quality to pin down.

Despite all of NOD's vastness, I end up nowhere.

At a loss, I try placing the pendant in its original context by reattaching it to the card. Now I notice the last line above it, "*Et voilà:* my *beau monde.*"

The French word "voilà" means "there" or "there it is." "Beau monde" is a term for "fashionable society," but taken more literally from the French it means "beautiful world." So the line would read, "There it is: my beautiful world." And then we have this crocodile pendant. Maybe it refers to a place rather than a person or company.

I search for Lacoste on Wikipedia. I'm confronted with a disambiguation page that mentions several other prominent people, including Carlos Lacoste, the former president of Argentina; and Jean-Yves Lacoste, a "postmodern theologian," whatever that might be. But also listed are a few specific places. The Bordeaux winery Grand-Puy-Lacoste and also Lacoste, Vaucluse, an ancient town in Provence.

Something about this last one resonates ever so slightly.

There's nothing like the endorphin bath you get in reward for making a successful guess. My mind wallows in pleasure upon reading the first sentence of the history section that appears when I click through:

```
Lacoste is best known for its most notorious resident,
Donatien Alphonse Francois comte de Sade, the Marquis
de Sade, who in the 18th century lived in the castle
overlooking the village.
```

The identity of the town's favorite son fits with enough contrived perfection that I know I've solved my riddle. The Louis Markey of Billy's verse isn't a real person, it's his NODName. Via "Lou Markey," you arrive at "Le Marquis." Sade enthusiasts often style him the Divine Marquis. A curious title for one of history's most infamous villains.

To find out where Billy's going with all this, I guess I need to take a trip.

NOD's geography is based on our real-life Global Positioning System, so I just type the coordinates of Lacoste into the teleport box. Before hitting return, I make sure to mask my IP address so it looks like any session I start with Jacques comes from GAME's open wifi network.

Jacques materializes on top of one of the few remaining walls ringing the ruins of the Château de Sade. The little town of Lacoste, with its cobbled streets and ancient buildings sagging under red tile roofs, nestles into the forested Provençal hill below. A roman bridge spans a small stream as it meanders through the village.

Billy's castle, which I see matches his virtual destination at the end of *Jacking Out,* is a limestone husk with a crumbling curtain wall rising to the east. A maze of walled ditches and open cellars surrounds the empty courtyard, and only a two-story side building attached to a stubby tower remains intact. I walk in there and see that Billy has created a modest presentation of biographical artifacts commemorating Sade's exploits.

His biography disappoints at first blush. Sade was really more of a persecuted writer than anything else and spent much of his life in prison at the behest of his formidable mother-in-law. The crimes for which he was actually convicted consisted primarily of some minor assaults on prostitutes. Poor behavior, of course, but hardly the stuff of enduring infamy.

The tour begins with a display of the bloody shirt taken off the Prince of Conde after the ferocious beating Sade gave him when they were childhood playmates, an incident that would prefigure a lifetime of conflict with authority. We then move to the box of anisette candies he used to allegedly poison three prostitutes with Spanish Fly in the Marseilles affair, which resulted in one of his many stays in prison. The associated info card points out that Sade most likely had them eat the candy solely intending to make them copiously flatulent. Which was apparently how he liked his courtesans.

There's a collection of props from the plays he staged at Lacoste once he escaped prison for the first time. Then the dreaded *lettres du cachet* his mother-in-law obtained that condemned him to the Bastille.

Next up are the giant glass dildos he had his poor wife Renée procure for him while he was imprisoned. These "engines," or "prestiges," as he called them, used in his superhuman jailhouse masturbatory regime, were the source of considerable marital strife.

The last exhibit is a straitjacket of massive proportions that conveys how grossly fat he had become after the revolution, when he was jailed again for obscenity and confined to the lunatic asylum at Charenton. Thus did Donatien Alphonse François, *comte* de Sade, die: fat, impoverished, and officially insane.

But he left an immortal legacy due to the body of written work he created in life. The château's exhibits end in a library up a narrow spiral staircase into the castle's lone remaining tower. There I find volumes that, when selected, offer to download PDFs of all Sade's major works: his plays, essays, and novels. These writings explore the pleasures to be found in cruelty at such length that the word "sadism" was coined in his honor. Furthermore, his books serve as the foundational documents for the genre of sex practices known as "bondage." The line in Billy's rhyme "Let my word be your bond" could refer to no one else. Indeed, all the submissives right now tied up in dungeons across the city surely have him to thank for their restraints.

I download all of them and point my av out of the room. But right at the exit there's a tasteful placard written with a calligraphic font that says:

I hope you enjoyed my small exhibition,
And that you're inflamed past all thoughts of contrition.
If now there is more that you desire to know,
Then find and explore my eternal château.

—Louis_Markey

If the Château de Sade isn't his eternal château, then what is?

For that matter, why would Billy want to send his players to this place? Judging by some of his work, I can see that he might harbor an affinity for Sade, but the renowned rake doesn't seem to have much to do with either GAME or the Randall family. Still, the card suggests an obvious next move, alleviating any doubt that I've discovered a space on Billy's game board.

I feel a rare tingle of excitement as I start sorting possibilities. Though I haven't so much as stood up in hours, finding this place in virtual France makes me feel like I'm getting somewhere.

Minutes later, an even more exciting aspect of my investigation demands cycles. I get an email from Olya expressing with the charming formality of a non-native writer her gratitude for my help last night. A quick look at the header tells me she sent it from GAME's internal network.

Rather than reply, I jog downtown in the hopes of catching her. Of course I'd like to question her about the incident and her relationship with Billy, but my overriding motivation is that I want to accept her thanks in person.

And to see what more I can do for her.

1 1

But she's not there. I must have just missed her.

Irritated, I start scouting locations for the hidden cameras I'll install to better monitor the GAMErs' movements, on the off chance that Billy decides to drop in on his old friends.

As my eyes trace the moldings above the main elevator, I'm surprised to find a small video camera on a gimbal mount already focused straight at me. This must be the detritus of a surveillance game called *Gotcha* someone last night told me took over the building during the previous spring like some form of voyeuristic kudzu. I'm amazed the other residents tolerated it, but for me the remaining network is a blessing from above.

It's only a few minutes' work to track a couple cables to a file server dumped in an otherwise abandoned rack room. I glom its address and network ID and head back to my office to probe the box.

Whoever set up the project lacked any notion of network security. I find their server riddled with yawning orifices, and I have root-level control over it within the hour. The box contains about a terabyte of compressed video streams captured at irregular intervals over the past several months.

The last image recorded in many of these is Olya's stunning countenance, squinting angrily. Then static. She represents a *Ringu*-like supernatural force for them: the last thing the cameras see before they die. Why would such a broadcast-quality woman be so protective of her privacy?

I don't have time to wade through all this video. Luckily Red Rook has availed itself of a Defense Department development grant to explore robust facial recognition. The software is called ProSoap, from a combination of "*prosopon,*" Greek for "face," and its ability to "scrub" non-useful frames from a video file. I train the engine with photos from the GAME website's profile pages. The goal here is to see if the cameras can tell me the last time Billy was at GAME, and with whom he spent time before he disappeared.

While I'm waiting for results, I get up in search of a bathroom. As I'm passing by the steel door across the hall from me, Andrew Garriott peeks his head out. He offers a disappointed, "Hey, mate," before ducking back in.

It takes quite a while, but ProSoap picks out some interesting action.

As I click through videos starring Billy, they paint a pretty clear portrait of a guy not well liked. He sets down a plate of takeout in the upstairs dining area, and his neighbors promptly get up. He joins a conversation at a bank of vending machines, and the group disperses until he's left staring at a girl who's too stoned to acknowledge his presence. He leans over the shoulder of a fellow resident working at a computer, making what seems like a well-intentioned comment. But the guy gives him the bird without even looking at him.

This ostracism feels strange to me. Normally any number of people would be willing to make nice with someone like Billy simply due to the gravitational pull of his bank account. Although his name-change indicates that he was tired of that sort of attention and wanted to be taken on his (apparently dubious) merits. After about a month, almost all of Billy's appearances consist of his entering at the front, going down to his workspace in the POD for a few hours, and leaving without speaking to a soul.

One of the most recent feeds shows him carrying a stepladder down the hallway outside my office. He stops right in front of my door. His other hand holds a tiny piece of electronics, which he carefully places on top of the doorjamb. Then he checks his iPhone's screen and makes a twisting motion with his finger on the gear he's setting up. Finally satisfied, he departs.

Looks like the surveillance gamers aren't the only ones installing hardware around the building. And if a wireless camera was sitting on my doorjamb, then it must have been pointed at the door behind which Garriott is currently working. The one Xan seemed slightly nervous about when I chose my office.

So Billy was eavesdropping on Garriott? Now, why would that be?

I gathered from their group champagne bath at the party that Olya, Garriott, and Xan are working on some joint endeavor. And if Billy's paying them special attention, so should I.

Hours pass as I sift through more results. I linger on a selection that shows a cocktail party for the summer's new residents, at which there is a lot of handshaking and convivial chatter. I see Olya has already made friends with Xan and Garriott, and the three stand in a circle conversing. Billy steps into the frame, causing them to stop talking. Olya glares at him like an angry wildebeest, while the other two look away in discomfort.

As Billy shuffles off, shoulders slumped, a small brunette puts her hand on his arm. She says something in his ear and then kisses him on the cheek before skipping away. Billy's gaze follows her, abject devotion in his eyes, his face growing a fragile smile.

I rewind and zoom in on the girl: Gina Delaney.

So Billy had at least one friend, though evidently there's some bad blood pulsing in from PiMP between Billy and Olya. Yet in the clip it seemed like he was trying to edge closer to his former classmate. That's not surprising given her gale-force sexuality. But she despises him. So maybe it's something else between them.

Which brings me back to that guy who accosted her. He said, "Don't pretend you didn't want it." And tried to give her that necklace. The street asylum of New York is replete with Delphic utterances and aberrant behavior, but the guy following her just as Billy starts his new game? And sidewalk crazies don't normally employ cameramen. Is it possible that Billy would have recruited someone to attack one of his colleagues as an opening move? For a guy willing to create a dangerous stampede in a haunted house, I'd have to say, "Sure." But if so, why?

Then I realize I'm looking right at the answer. I zoom in again on the shot of Gina kissing Billy and sharpen the area around her neck. Hanging there is a purple twenty-sided die. So the necklace I found was either Gina's or a replica of one she used to wear.

What's the implication? That the necklace was some kind of trophy? Maybe "Don't pretend you didn't want it" was an accusation. But of what?

It's clear I'm going to have to crawl inside Billy Randall's head to get through his game. Digging into what goes on in this building will help. But where he made mostly enemies, I want to make friends.

I get my first opportunity half an hour later when I hear an outburst of plummy cursing through the door of Garriott's work space. After a brief interval of quiet, there's some keyboard banging accompanied by "Bloody arseing swine-fucker!" The bump of his chair being kicked against the wall. I go to his door, which opens slightly at my knock.

"Everything okay?"

As I step into the room, I see it's a raw but spacious studio dominated by five large worktables arranged in a U shape. Garriott is bent over in front of his computer clawing his head. Hearing me, he jerks upright. "Oh, yeah. You know these damn retromingent machines."

I have no idea what that means, but I ask, "Anything I can help with?"

Garriott resumes his seat, and I notice one of his windows minimizing without him touching the keyboard. He's got a series of foot pedals below his desk. These are used by very serious programmers to replicate the CTRL, ALT, SHIFT, and TAB keys.

"Oh, I'm okay, it's just—" He examines me with a sense of desperation. I can see him mentally dismiss my offer as coming from an ineffectual "video artist."

He says, "That's all right, mate. I think only God can help me at this point."

I nod slowly, reading the code remaining on his screen. On a hunch, I say, "Okay. But you know our God is a jealous God and responds to the recursion of fathers by dealing buffer overflows unto the third and fourth generations."

He looks from me to his monitor. "Wait, what? How do you know that?"

"I don't. But it's often a problem when you're starting from scratch."

"I'm a bot jock. This networking shit . . . How is it you know so much about—"

"I wasn't always a video drone. Mind if I sit?"

Garriott pulls over another chair, and I start scrolling through his code. For someone who's spent the better part of thirty years getting reluctant or even hostile systems to follow orders from a distance, it's pretty elementary. I haven't done much real programming in a while, but I'm sure I can assist him.

"What's all this for, anyway?"

"Sorry, mate. Can't really say. I mean, *I'd* tell you, but my team is sensitive to—"

"You're working on this with Xan and Olya?"

"Yeah," he says with a slight wince at the disclosure.

"Right on. Well, I respect that. Sometimes things need to gestate until they can spring upon the world fully formed."

"This brat is like to kill her mother in the process."

"Anyway, all this stuff is pretty abstracted. I'd be happy to help you with it."

He's clearly torn, but I guess the late hour and his frustrating lack of progress combine to force his assent.

A little after two AM, Garriott hits the compile button and says, "It better work this time."

We've scrapped most of his original code, and I put him onto an open-source library that rigorously implements the bulk of what he's trying to do.

We see our test data start whizzing through various monitoring programs. After about a minute, we cut it off and get a readout of "exceptions: 0." This elicits more keyboard banging, but now in unrestrained joy. These are the occasions engineers live for: when hours of tedious effort result in a lone number that means success. Seeing that simple flag come up is better than all the slot machine cherries in Vegas. Because you know your baby has taken its first step. Garriott slaps my back.

"Thanks, mate. That could have taken me weeks."

"No problem. It's nice to stay sharp on this stuff."

He checks his watch. "Well, I'm not going right to sleep after this; why don't you let me stand you a—I mean several—pints?"

So here's the perfect chance to establish trust with someone using the most time-honored of methods: get drunk with him.

"Done."

We walk over to Foo Bar, an underground cocktail fetishist's joint south of Delancey. Garriott texts for part of the walk, perhaps extolling his recent triumph. As we enter, it's clear that he spends enough time in this place to have achieved a Vulcan mind-meld with the staff. A waitress delivers three Guinnesses just after we sit down.

A minute later, Xan slips into our booth. She says, "My fierce warriors retire to the mead hall to sing of their great victory."

Garriott raises his glass. "I propose a bumper to it!"

Guinness isn't my normal choice for high-volume drinking, but I follow the other two in draining my glass. These children of the Commonwealth were probably fed stout in their baby bottles. I prepare myself for a long evening.

Shots of Jameson and more beer appear unordered. Garriott and Xan grin at each other and then make a series of hand gestures: first a V-sign, then they point at themselves, and finally, a pinkies-extended pantomime of sipping from a cup. Then they drop their shots into the beers and chug them. They look at me, and I do the same, finishing with a contented gasp as the ethanol and oxygen deprivation set about working their sweet magic.

"I take it y'all served in some kind of alcoholic militia together."

Xan says to Garriott, "I'm sure we're not supposed to tell him."

"Luv, tonight he earned the juice, and it has to be consecrated. So, he might as well do it properly."

"What does it mean?" I ask.

Xan repeats the gestures, saying, "Two, I, tea. That's the toast."

"I like Information Technology as much as anyone—"

"No, no. Not the acronym. The neuter pronoun: 'it.'"

"I've never lifted my glass to grammar. Why do we do that?"

Xan says, "We mean 'it' in the sense of 'the thing of the moment,' like an it-girl. Or the sui generis, if you will. As in, 'That is *it*!'"

I shake my head. Their toast lacks the gravity of "God save the king" or "*Viva la revolución.*"

Garriott explains, "Mate, you know Dean Kamen, right?"

"Yeah, the famous inventor; he made one of the first insulin pumps."

"So remember back in 2002, there was all this buzz coming out of his shop in New Hampshire that they were about to unleash a new device— something that would totally change the world. Which they code-named 'IT.' And the net went nuts theorizing about what 'IT' was."

"Yeah. IT was the Segway. Big deal."

"Exactly. A *scooter.* I mean, where's my fucking *jet pack?*"

Xan adds, "Now, granted, it was the greatest scooter ever made, and they had all these bollocks theories about how such a thing might change urban transportation, yea, even the very fabric of our cities—"

"But it was all just hype," I say.

"An *Attack of the Clones*–level disappointment." Garriott winks at the waitress, calling for more whiskey.

Xan continues. "So GAME is this rare place where you get paid to do whatever you want. And yet somehow we end up with all this derivative metagame crap. So we'd sit around bitching and ask ourselves why we weren't working on something really amazing. *Game changing,* if you will. Something that would be worthy of the name 'IT.'"

Garriott says, "Xan and I spend my first months there arguing about what might fit the bill. Eventually Olya comes to us with this idea—"

"Cold fusion?" I ask.

Xan giggles. "No."

"A laser death ray?"

"Nope."

"Total enlightenment delivered in a convenient suppository?"

She and Garriott stare at each other, obviously contemplating whether or not to tell me.

Suddenly there's a bang on the table that makes our glasses jump. We look up to behold Olya wrapped in the type of leather trench coat favored by Hollywood SS officers. Her eyes blaze with fury.

"So, I must find you drunk and gossiping like peasants? What is this?"

Garriott closes his eyes in sorrow. Xan hits a button on her phone and groans, saying, "My Foursquare. I left it on auto check in. Sorry."

"Oh, so you think you must hide from me? Why is this, little ones? What is it that you are doing?"

Garriott musters himself. "We are celebrating the birth of our primary network interface."

"And this tiny bit of code is such heroic feat that you need a videographer?" she asks, eyeballing me.

Garriott breaks the tense silence. "Our man James here is the finest net-coding documentarian GAME has ever seen. We're buying him a couple rounds in thanks. So stop glowering and join us."

I try to soothe things. "Hey, guys, I'm going to go ahead and take off. Let y'all have a meeting or whatever."

Olya puts a firm hand on my shoulder. She gives me an almost warm smile. "No, no. Please stay. We are very grateful for . . . all of your assistance." She motions to the waitress, who's already on the way over with a round. A glass of neat vodka for Olya. She makes an impatient sketch of their toast, murmurs, *"Na zdorovye,"* and downs it at a smooth draw. The other two look askance at their fourth round but bear up and get it down. I just sip mine.

Olya raises her empty glass. "Mr. Pryce, thank you . . . But I think now you must not do the work of the little ones. In English you say something about lazy people and Satan?"

"Idle hands make the devil's work."

"Just so." She slaps a crisp C-note on the table and glares at her teammates. "So now we have nice party. Tomorrow, I think we meet at seven in the morning, yes?"

With that, Olya marches off. Xan and Garriott make comic faces at each other.

I ask, "Why do you put up with that? Not like you're Spetsnaz troops trying to kill Chechens."

Garriott laughs. "Olya's like a Soviet supercollider. You're not sure the wiring's all straight, but she does generate strong impulses in a man."

Xan adds in a low voice, "Women too." Garriott glances at her inquiringly but then looks down and sighs.

Xan grabs his arm. "Come on, let's share a cab. You okay, James?"

Without waiting for my reply she takes my cheek and lightly kisses me good night. The tingle left from her lips takes me well past okay.

Since losing Erica, I would normally let myself obsess over even a casual kiss from a woman like Xan. Which might lead to a risky online search for a surrogate. But tonight, my mind wants only to hammer away at this vein of secrets I've discovered at GAME. I hurry home so I can start delving into today's most pressing lead:

Billy was in love with a dead girl. And he doesn't seem inclined to let her rest in peace.

12

People with elite tech degrees usually maintain pretty extensive online identities. But Gina has left only a void. Old links to her pages on various social networking sites now come up empty. Her blog returns "404—page not found." While she appears in the alumni list at the PiMP website, her profile has been removed. After dredging up the name of her main NODSkin, Joanne_Dark, I see that she's been "transcended," NOD's euphemism for having terminated the underlying account. She seems to have taken pains before her death to wipe out any online evidence of her life.

A lot of recent websites are totally dynamic and therefore hard to record. But leave it to the creaking IT systems of a university to save the day. The Wayback Machine crawls of the PiMP site from September of '12 give me a hit on Gina that includes a fairly recent résumé.

She describes her academic specialties as "Interface Design and Social Computing." Her picture shows an old City of Heroes avatar in place of herself. She did her undergrad at MIT: a Course Six (electrical engineering) degree awarded in 2003 with a minor in mech-E. Right out of college she racked up some pretty impressive publication credits for work she did at Monotreme Research on novel collaboration environments. Then a stint at her lab's spin-off, Ichidna Interface, which made prototypes of new training gear for the military market. In 2012, she headed to PiMP for another degree. Her skills section is a dense block of trendy acronyms. For personal interests, she simply lists "pwning." Gamer slang for "owning" or dominating other players.

Her death on October 29 of last year didn't elicit a whole lot of media interest. Mentions in the major papers rate only a brief unembellished blurb, as if the reporters were quickly frustrated by a lack of forthcoming information. A weepy *Washington Square News* article quotes friends evincing shock, one going so far as to say, "She's the nicest, most talented person I know." Her parents didn't have any comment for the student reporter.

In contrast, the write-up on the other recent GAME suicide, Trevor Rothstein, diplomatically refers to his "struggles with substance abuse," and his mother's requiem strikes a weirdly positive tone: "We're just happy he's finally at peace."

Gina's death leaves one with nothing but questions.

Why does an attractive, brilliant, successful young woman commit suicide? And why do people grimace whenever they mention her death?

I send an email to McClaren reminding him of his offer to hook me up with the officer who handled Gina's case.

With disturbing promptness he replies:

```
Go see Detective Paul Nash tomorrow at the Union St.
Station House. He'll be expecting you. Nash is a friend,
but for op-sec keep your current cover. He's been told
the twins are "privately supporting" your work.
```

13

The staff sergeant at the precinct office sends me to a small conference room on the second floor. Standing up to shake my hand is Detective Paul Nash, a tall man in his early forties. I expected an overweight mustached guy, so it's interesting to find this clean-cut, soft-spoken person who looks like a business retreat leader and whose tan indicates a lot of time spent on the links. As we sit, he asks what he can do for me.

"Well, I'm mostly here to talk about Gina Delaney, but before we get to that, can you tell me anything about Trevor Rothstein?"

He cocks his head. "Not my body. But since he was sort of connected to Gina, I heard about it. What do you want to know?"

"Was there anything unusual about the case?"

Nash shrugs. "Nothing unusual about a dead junkie. These are people who poison themselves daily."

"His was like any other overdose? Nothing noteworthy?"

"Just that he wasn't already dead, the amount of smack that guy was doing."

Trevor seems like a blind alley, so I switch gears. "Okay. So you caught the call for Gina Delaney."

He slides me a file containing her casework.

"Of course that can't leave the room," he says.

"I see. I'm just trying to understand what happened."

"The pictures make that pretty clear."

I open the envelope and pull out a report that is several pages of forms stapled together and a set of glossy eight-by-ten photographs of the scene. The first is the worst: a wide shot of Gina slumped against a horrible contraption, impaled through the mouth by a large circular cutting bit. Called a hole saw, I think.

The close-ups of her corpse are bad enough, but the Byzantine sickness of her machine makes my fingers shrink from touching the photos that follow. Restraining cords, pulleys, burnt cardboard tube, blood puddle on the floor. I'm struck by the lethal similarities to Billy's *Getting Wet* video, which now seems tame in comparison.

When planning their end, most people don't look to Rube Goldberg for inspiration. Or maybe it's surprising that the many artist suicides over the years are so unbelievably pedestrian.

I say, "Bizarre way to go."

Nash nods grimly. "I think all suicides are bizarre. But this . . ." He whistles.

"You get any idea what led her to this particular method?"

"I suppose you've seen that *Getting Wet* video she made? Normally I'd say it's this gasper obsession people have, but the drill makes that seem wrong. 'Course, she *was* an engineer. She had all the tools at hand. But to be honest, we don't really know."

"It didn't seem like there was much press interest in the story."

"True. We suppressed the details, for the family's sake."

I flip through a series of pictures, presumably taken by the medical examiner, depicting the extent of her injuries. The coverage of her back shows that the drill bit went in smoothly, creating a surgically precise two-inch hole. The facial photos reveal the horrendous mess of her mouth. A full-length shot shows some scratches on her torso, as well as jagged stripes of scar tissue on either wrist.

Nash sees my finger hover over this detail. He says, "This wasn't the first attempt. Maybe the machine was meant to take it out of her hands."

"They do follow orders," I mumble. Paging through the paperwork, I pause at the ME's death certificate. "No autopsy? I thought they're required for suicides."

"Generally, yes. But in this case the family requested a religious exemption. They're an offshoot of some Pentecostal denomination. Can't have organs missing come Judgment Day." Nash frowns. "There might have been a hearing, but at the time, the ME was dealing with a bad meth package hitting East New York and a shipment of contaminated beef getting served through a food bank for the elderly. There wasn't any doubt about the cause of death, so I guess they just let it go."

"What did her family have to say about all this?"

Nash pinches his temples and lets out a long breath. "Not a whole lot. Dad was ready to explode. Barely keeping it together. Her mother looked like she was planning to join her daughter any minute. I got the impression that the Delaney home was not a happy one."

I lift an eyebrow. But he just shrugs.

I return to the shot of her back. Another image I've seen of Gina flickers through my mind.

"Huh. The entry wound here. It's right over her tattoo."

"Tattoo?"

"She had a little Jack of Hearts playing card inked there on the back of her neck. The wound obliterates it."

"There are easier ways to remove a tattoo."

"Yeah. But she was part of this group of artists into virtual reality, so it's interesting she'd want to destroy that symbol. Her brand of membership. If that was a big part of her identity, maybe this reads as a repudiation. Like she's saying she wanted out of the Jack—"

Those words suddenly click for me. "Jacking out" was exactly what Gina was doing. Taking out her jack. Decoupling from life. The same act Billy was simulating with his video to Blake. But he also used the term explicitly. What was the line? *I know you've often wished that I'd just jack out like she did.* I'd thought he meant his mother, but having seen Gina's fatal wound, I'm now certain he was talking about her.

But why refer to her death in his message to Blake?

Nash seems disinterested in my theories but politely prompts me: "What's that?"

"Ah, never mind . . . She leave a note?"

"No. This one was all electronic. Almost no paper in the entire apartment. Except these framed pictures. Like most people have shots of their friends at parties? She's got a bunch too, but they're all video game characters. No books, just one of those tablet things. We fired up her computer to see if she might have left a statement, but she'd wiped it."

He sees me starting to interrupt and puts up his hand. "We checked the hard disk: it was overwritten up and down. Completely destroyed her phone too. Really just erasing everything about herself that she could."

"So you have a dead girl, this ugly mechanism, some previous attempts, but if you don't mind my asking, how did you establish for sure that this was a suicide? I don't mean to be ridiculous, but couldn't—"

"Yeah, I thought the same thing at first. But she taped it."

"She taped it?"

He nods.

"Can I see it?"

Nash twists his face into a portrait of unease. Thinks for a moment, but then says, "The thing's in total lockdown. We had problems a while back with people leaking shit to snuff sites, creeps, even the straight press. This, well, this is bad enough that if her mother ever saw it, I don't think she'd last the day. Other kids see it, maybe it sparks their imaginations. I can't have anything like that on my conscience. I'm sorry."

"Okay. Maybe I don't need a copy. Can you just show it to me?"

"Look, I've been real cooperative here, per my understanding with your friend. But I'm afraid I just can't do that. Why do you need to see it anyway?"

I sense he's not going to budge. Because we may need him later, I decide not to push it. "I guess I don't. I understand your position. Can you tell me, though, did she make any kind of statement? Say anything to the camera?"

"Yeah. She said, 'You must have thought / I'd play the daughter of Lot / but I will not.'"

"The daughter of Lot?"

Maybe that explains the Genesis reference in the video Billy sent to his brother. How does Billy know Gina's last words? Has he seen the video?

"That's what she said."

"What did you make of that?"

"A lot of people cite the Bible in their final words."

"Yeah, right . . . But that's not quoted in this report here. Did you tell anyone else about it?"

"No." A waver in his intonation makes me think there's more to it.

"But maybe someone else did?" I ask.

Nash frowns. "We had an incident a couple days after we found her. One of the crime scene techs was trying to access the video in our evidence repository. Something he wasn't authorized to do since the case had been closed. I asked him about it, and he said he was 'doing follow-up.'"

"And you think he was going to leak it to someone interested in the case?"

"Seemed that way. But people do things for all kinds of crazy reasons."

Maybe this tech's reason came from Billy seeking answers about his friend's death.

"So this tech didn't have access to the video. What information might he have turned over?"

"He'd have his own crime scene photos, and he was the guy who found the video, so he'd be able to tell someone what was on it."

"Can I talk to him?"

"I'd rather you didn't. Guy's mad enough at me already. They put him on leave pending an inquiry."

"Really? That seems pretty severe."

"Yeah. Well, when pressed on his 'follow-up,' rather than come up with some exculpatory bullshit, he calls a fancy lawyer. Which is an extreme reaction to a minor disciplinary matter."

"Strange."

Though not so strange if money had already changed hands.

"Yeah. Strange that you'd be asking that. You know something about this that I don't?"

"I seriously doubt it."

"You want to tell me exactly why you're interested in this girl?"

"She was a friend of my subject. They were part of the same art group as Trevor Rothstein too."

"Well I'd keep an eye on him then."

"I'm trying to."

14

zip over to GAME on my way back from the police station, trying again to catch up with Olya.

I can hear her as soon as the elevator door opens. There's a high-volume stream of Russian cursing coming from outside the room belonging to her group. Which I've mentally named the "iTeam."

As I turn the corner, I see Olya snatch a disposable video camera from one of a pair of GAMErs and smash it on the floor.

The guy steps back from her and says, "Take it easy, bitch. It's just a game."

"Gina is dead," she says, her voice climbing registers of distress, "and you want to make a game of this? What kind of sick fucking perverts are you?"

The other guy puts his hands up. "Look, we're sorry, Olya. We thought that you were part of it."

Olya takes a deep breath and says with a thick voice, "Dixon, you have seen what I think about this *dolboeb* Billy and his games. Maybe you tell your little friends what happen to them if I hear any more of this."

She pushes past them and stomps the opposite way down the hall without seeing me. I decide it's not the right time to interrogate her. Dixon and his buddy follow her at a respectful distance.

That scene certainly confirms that Billy's recruiting GAMErs to harass Olya. At first I'd thought Blake would be his primary target, but maybe he harbors a whole list of enemies he plans to sic his players on. Given

what the twins told me about *NeoRazi*, I'm not surprised. Game design-
ers will often co-opt early participants into an elite cadre they use to help
advance the narrative.

Olya however clearly has no intention of cooperating, though Billy
seems bent on forcing her to play along. Maybe he sees her as the white
queen he's beset with pawns from GAME.

I spot Garriott standing just inside their workroom.

"Trouble in paradise?" I ask.

He peeks out to make sure she's departed. "What, that? That's nothing.
You should see what happens when she gets stroppy. I think your man
Billy disappeared to prevent her from killing him."

"They fought a lot?"

"Hammer and tongs, mate. You didn't hear about the funeral?"

"You mean Gina Delaney's?" McClaren had mentioned that Billy's
first arrest happened at her funeral.

Garriott tilts his head with an anxious grin, like he's considering something that he's supposed to abhor but secretly loves. "You *must* see this."

He brings his laptop over to my office and pulls up a video.

Someone's cell captures a group somberly toasting the departed. The person leading the toast addresses the camera. Maybe they're streaming the
recording to friends who couldn't make it to Boston.

In the far left of the shot, there's a violent motion. Garriott stops it,
expands that part of the clip, and starts a frame-by-frame. He's got it
focused on the back of a tall blonde in a black dress, clearly Olya. Then
Billy enters the frame and leans over to say something to her. Olya
doesn't look at him, but almost lazily, she pulls her right hand across
her body and then rams her elbow hard into Billy's face. He goes down,
lights out, and the camera now pans over to the commotion.

Olya steps forward to continue her assault, but someone grabs her and
wrestles her away. The camera stays on Billy, but you can see her in the
background breaking free and striding coolly out of the frame. We do not
see Billy get up.

The feed ends.

— — —

I blink at Garriott. "I guess y'all won't be putting that in your team re-cruiting videos."

Garriott grins. "Isn't that just *fucked* though?"

"What happened to him?"

"Oh, nothing life-threatening. Badly split lip, a bit of a bump on his head. I don't think his nose was broken. But all in all, a rather poor show-ing. Especially given all his aggro theatrics from earlier."

"What was he doing?"

"So the service was closed casket, and when Billy walks by, he tries to lift the bloody lid. He wants to place something in the coffin with her. Her dad sees this and is having none of it, and he confiscates whatever it was. Makes it known that poor Billy isn't welcome. Fine. But then the barmy bastard comes back for the actual burial, and he's taking photos. And again, her dad, who is a bit off it himself, goes over, grabs his camera, and tosses the kid out on his ear. Sasha, one of their PiMP friends, goes off to try to console him, and that's the last we expect to hear of him."

"But he came back again."

"There wasn't a reception, so her friends gathered at that bar for a post-funeral piss-up. Imagine our consternation when he shows up there. The family wasn't around, and we knew he was close to Genes, so we don't say anything, just avoid him like the plague, right? And everything's aces for a bit while he's downing Bombay and sort of talking to himself. Then he fancies having a chat with our savage Siberian, and . . . well, you saw how that interaction turned out."

"Scary."

"After all that shite, I suppose he deserved it."

"What did he say to her?"

"I didn't hear it, but our mate Dix was standing right there. Told me he said, 'Are you happy now?'"

15

Later that night, as I return from GAME, I see three orange-vested municipal workers standing around a steaming manhole. They peer into it as if one of their number just disappeared down there and they're about to draw straws to see who has to go after him and wrestle the albino alligators. The scene reminds me that I've yet to discover an entry point to Billy's latest rabbit hole from the clues he's offered. So by the time I flop down on my bed, my mind is spinning up on the problem, and I know I won't be able to sleep.

I send Jacques back to Sade's castle to stare at its crumbled crenellations. This can't possibly be a dead end. The placard inside speaks of an "eternal château," so must I now canvass all the period theme communities in NOD for another stupid castle? In the Nerds Only Dungeon every other build is a fortress, and the place's swarming immensity would swallow any direct search. So where in the world should I start looking?

Well, how did I find my way here?

I followed a reference from the poem that came with the croc pendants. Maybe it has yet to yield all its instructions.

The verse invokes NOD with the phrase "Narration Of Death." Focusing on those words again, I decide that an "eternal" castle wouldn't be one subject to the entropy of the real world. But such a building could be preserved forever through art, like the castle in a painting. Or a book.

All of Sade's work deals liberally with death and the suffering that precedes it, but "Narration Of Death" would apply to one title above all the others. One that also happens to feature a castle infamous in the history of literature.

I scan through the first several pages of the book, and then start typing coordinates into Jacques's teleport box.

My av winds up staring into a thousand-foot ravine. I take a second to pull up the sim's property page and confirm that it's owned by an av named Louis_Markey. The ruined castle at Lacoste was just a set of virtual objects on one of NOD's public servers—the equivalent of an inert brochure. But now I've discovered a complete, privately hosted NOD build, which is more like someone's personal website.

Panning my view, I see a mountain landscape with jagged peaks looming all around me. Just to the side is a stout wooden bridge that leads across the chasm toward an ominous gothic castle. The kind of place a monster would take his kidnapped princess in one of the darker fairy tales. One that revolves around revenge rather than escape.

Chiseled below the ramparts of the gatehouse I see the name of the fortress: the Château de Silling.

This castle is the setting of Sade's epic of filth *Les cent vingt journées de Sodome, ou l'Ecole du libertinage,* known in English as *The 120 Days of Sodom.* I'd first flipped through it in college, where it was somebody's bright idea that the Bat call our big winter party "120 Minutes of Sodom."

Unfortunately the book is more of a catalog of heinous atrocities than a novel. The entries run along the lines of:

```
31. He fucks a goat from behind while being flogged; the
goat conceives and gives birth to a monster. Monster
though it be, he embuggers it.
```

While such a spectacle would certainly be entertaining, we didn't have the special effects budget to bring it about. Given that even the very first, ostensibly mild, crimes mentioned involve priests, children, and urophilia, we quickly realized that this wasn't going to work as a party template.

The self-described "most impure tale ever told" concerns four wealthy libertines: a bishop, the banker Durcet, a judge named Curval, and their leader, the Duc de Blangis, who serves as a sort of Sadean superhero.

He's an aristocrat blessed with the ability to ejaculate at will, an attribute as important as any to the basic plotline.

These four hit on the idea of sequestering themselves for the winter in an impregnable fortress where they'll aspire toward an eternal pinnacle of debauchery. Perhaps an honorable goal, except that these characters' tastes run to pedophilia, coprophilia, torture (not the slap-and-tickle variety), and murder. To aid them in their endeavors, they kidnap sixteen of the most noble and beautiful children from across the country. Four wizened whores (Madames Duclos, Champville, Martaine, and Desgranges) come along to stimulate the goings-on by telling stories from their lifetimes spent in carnal riot.

The book consists of descriptions of the six hundred tortures inflicted upon the castle's inmates over the course of the winter. Sade wrote this monstrosity in thirty-seven days while in prison. Due to his incarceration, he had to write the book on a twelve-meter toilet paper–like scroll that he could easily hide from his jailers. He claimed to have "wept tears of blood" when his manuscript was lost during the storming of the Bastille.

But after the rioters looted his former cell, someone found the scroll and kept it in his family for over a hundred years before a German psychologist discovered it and had the nerve to publish it in 1905. Of course, it was immediately banned, but by the midfifties Sade was receiving a radical rethink among certain intellectuals, and they started printing it again.

One can now easily find Sadean ideas and aesthetics throughout popular culture. Indeed, NOD already has several builds that pay homage to his work. It seems Billy's decided we need another one, which means I have to search the place until I find out why.

Just to the side of the portcullis is a small iron door over which is engraved a double-headed eagle, the Sade family crest. Beside this entrance I find the Château de Silling's guest registry. I have to fill in a bunch of personal information, including email address and phone number, in order to unlock the postern gate. For these I use new Gmail and Google Voice accounts forwarded to a brand-new work cell. Upon doing so, I get a message telling me that I have to install this NOD build's special plug-ins for "enhanced features." I shudder to think what those might be, but I agree.

Through the courtyard is a spooky gallery lit with torches standing in bronze sconces. The seeping stone walls are hung with obscene tapestries. After wandering through several hallways admiring the period detail, I enter a room I remember well from the text: the amphitheater.

This is the chamber in which much of the book is set, the place where the Libertines gather every evening to hear the whores' stories. There's a small stage in front that supports an extravagant gilded throne. Madame Duclos, the first of Sade's courtesan raconteurs, sits there. Cut into the curved back wall of the room is a series of five alcoves, each containing a comfortable couch. Four of them seat avatars representing each of the Libertines.

The fifth one, in the center, is empty. I presume it is meant for me.

I trip a hidden switch somewhere that causes the Duke to rise and say, "Welcome to Château de Silling. Our redoubt was built for those who wish to walk in the shadow of the Divine Marquis. Enjoy yourself. We'll be watching."

I walk over to the center niche and sit on the chaise. As my av relaxes into it, Madame Duclos begins her narration in a deep French-inflected voice:

```
Although I had not yet attained my fifth year, one day,
returning from my holy occupations in the monastery, my
sister asked me whether I had yet encountered Father
Laurent.
```

I get impatient quickly. I've always thought audiobooks proceed at an insufferably slow pace, and with Sade you know generally what's about to happen anyway (here, a golden shower). So I drop a "listener" object to keep streaming her stories aloud and then begin a tour of the rest of the castle.

The door on the other side of the great hall leads to the chapel. Sade was rabidly anticlerical throughout his life, so this room is tricked out as a voyeur's privy with an abundance of peculiar glass furniture, containers, and tools. I carefully search the chamber and finally settle on the stone step in front of the altar. It opens to reveal a staircase spiraling into the floor.

The entrance to the dungeon.

Silling's dungeon is the site of the worst crimes that take place at the climax of the book. It's supposed to contain all the specialized torture mechanisms needed to mount a successful Inquisition. However, Billy's rendition has only a dark stone hallway that passes a long row of wooden doors. I randomly try the fourth one, which opens onto the av of a frail girl around seven years old. Next to her is a small table with some cups and a glass tube with a rubber bulb at its end.

The waif sniffles. Then she turns to me, and a text bubble says:

Zelmire: You wanted to see me?

I stare at the odd configuration of objects and the little girl, and it dawns on me that this is an exact staging of the story Duclos is telling now: a bracing episode involving the ingestion of a child's snot. I hit F6 to bring up NOD's machinima interface. Sure enough, Billy has help-fully placed a series of pose balls, sound effect notes, and camera tracks around the room. Handy props for making some virtual kiddie porn. That is, if the act in question can be considered pornographic. By any reckoning, it isn't *Sesame Street*.

I shut the door.

What is this place?

I doubt it's just a celebration of one of literature's more demented imaginations. Billy's recent behavior points to a larger agenda. Also, his Château de Silling appears to make demands on its guests. He's con-structed a factory for twisted animation that will probably make the stuff currently coming out of NOD look downright quaint.

But why?

In the threatening video he sent Blake, Billy alludes to his friend Gina's death. Here I find the word "Sodom" connecting the most loath-some book ever written to Lot's story in the Bible, which Gina men-tioned in her last words.

This elaborate NOD build suggests a major investment of time and resources, so Billy must have been planning it for quite a while. And yet, Gina died only two months ago. So maybe he decided to transform a project already in progress into a kind of eulogy. But though Gina may have loved NOD, this virtual porn studio is a strange form of tribute.

Billy's creation will demand a detailed exploration, but I have a feeling it's not going anywhere, and I'm well overdue a trip to the real Land of Nod. Before signing off, I fire up a sniffer program to trace the details of my connection. I'm talking to a box hosted at a server farm here in New York owned by a company called Scream Communications.

So now I've got a fixed internet address Billy must use to run his game. I briefly indulge myself by picturing Blythe's smile when I bring this to her. Our first real line on her brother. One I'm sure we can use to start reeling him in.

16

Early the next morning I shift my attention from Billy's virtual fortress to the iTeam's dungeon laboratory. Learning more about their endeavor might help me worm my way into their confidence. I hope someone in the group will then illuminate why Billy's so fixated on Olya.

As befits a secret project, the iTeam likes to be alone during the wee hours. Excepting Olya's occasional morning punishment meetings, they have yet to arrive in time for breakfast, so now is a good time for some light recon.

Unlike most of the workrooms, the iTeam's studio outside my office has a new Yale dead bolt securing its door to a steel frame. I have some primitive lock-picking skills, but this imposing matron would take a far surer hand than mine. I'll need to find an alternative.

The basement's center hallway runs from the elevator to the back bulkhead doors that lead to a thin, grimy alleyway at the south side of the building. The iTeam workroom's door opens off this hall, so I'll see if there's another way in from the back.

A simple lock bump gets me into the office of David Cross, GAME's resident puppeteer, who has permanent tenure as the person most essential to mounting the haunted house. The back wall of his office is penetrated by a huge air-handler duct running along the low ceiling. Cross has rigged a decorative curtain that pulls back to expose a large piece of plywood roughly cut to cover the much larger hole in the wall created during the duct's installation. Only a couple screws connect it to the surrounding drywall, and removing it opens a space I can just wriggle through.

The beam from my Maglite cuts through the dark, illuminating a three-sided storage niche adjoining the main work area. Some strenuous contortions get me through the gap, and I roll onto the floor below.

In the center of the room I now find two odd pieces of equipment that look like lawn chairs from the future. They're made of nested aluminum tubes, and each has three mesh surfaces that permit a wide range of orientations. One is set up as a straight-backed chair, the other is configured to resemble a camp bed. Draped over these things is an array of exotic devices including a pair of late-model eMagin head-mounted displays (HMDs) and matching CyberGloves that allow one to control a computer with finger gestures. There's a pile of black fabric decorated with shiny polka dots. Off to the side of the chairs are six high-resolution video cameras with tiny infrared lights clustered around their lenses. While not really my technical bailiwick, I can identify this stuff as mocap—motion capture—gear used to track the movement of one's body. Toward the front of the room, a bank of new PCs rounds out the setup.

So the iTeam is working on a virtual reality project.

Not at all what I would have predicted. While online worlds have seen amazing growth recently, we still interact with them using mostly the same interface technology as we did in 1983. The hardware side of VR has long been a graveyard of broken dreams for its visionaries.

I'm disappointed. The idea that some gamer-artists are going to revolutionize anything with the outdated technical notions of the late eighties strains credulity. And yet the iTeam members are far from stupid, and they seem genuinely consumed with their secret project.

What could it be?

Next to the bank of computers are two large metal cabinets, each fastened with a rugged padlock. Maybe this is where the real treasure is stored. I unroll my picks and am just starting to fiddle with the first when I hear steps coming down the hall.

Could be nothing, but it wouldn't do to get caught in here, so I grab my tools and retreat to the storage nook. A wedge of light breaks the darkness, and I hear something dropping onto one of the tables. The room's fluorescent lights flicker to life.

Damn.

Xan and Garriott enter. They're in the midst of a dispute about the quality of data passing between two elements of their project. There are some brief clicking sounds, and then I hear the squeak of one of the cabinets' doors swinging open. I'm dying to take a look but decide I can't risk it.

They argue for another minute until I hear the sound of someone relocking the cabinet. The lights go out, and the second they throw the dead bolt, I scamper back through the hole in the wall and drop into Cross's office. I run out the door and around to the main hallway.

Xan is saying, "—never going to work unless you can clean the stream—"

I almost slam into Garriott as I turn the corner.

Xan yelps. Her hand snaps to her mouth. Andrew jumps back, bumping into her. He drops the handle of the large aluminum case he's rolling behind him. It hits the ground with a loud crack.

I try to mollify them, saying, "I didn't mean to—"

"Christ's tits, mate, I think my testicles have undescended," he says.

Xan is cross. "James, what are you doing racing about in the dark?"

I can see hackles rising, so I temporize. "I, ah, was getting a drink, and I heard y'all come in. So I just wanted to catch you before you left again."

They both squint at me.

"I'm crawling the walls with boredom. Capturing hours of video. I thought maybe I could help y'all if you want."

Xan starts to say, "Thank you, but no, we'll—"

Garriott interrupts her. "Xan . . . Let him have at it. You know we don't have time for arsing around. Give him the simulated stuff and see what's what. He sorted me the other night." Garriott suppresses a yawn and consults his watch. With a shriek, he grabs his case and scurries toward his office.

Xan gives me a long appraising look and says, "Really, I can handle it myself. I've no need to impose on your rather suspicious generosity."

"It's not suspicious at all. Maybe I need a favor from you."

"All right, what?"

"I'd like to interview you. But we'll get to that later. For now, show me this dastardly data."

Nine hours pass. Xan and I are cloistered in her office, sitting close, staring at her monitors. I stretch my wrist and solemnly tap F7 to test the latest version of her program. "This is it. We got it this time."

Xan drops her head, her fingers digging at pressure points around her face.

The problem we've been working on is a thorny one. Xan is trying to use a stream of sensor values to determine the position of a number of points linked together like the joints of a robot arm. That would be straightforward, but the underlying points' ability to shift of their own accord makes them jump around crazily. We need them to move smoothly, but it's like we're trying to deduce the exact postures of two fencers only knowing the forces on their foils.

I run the program. The graphed output of the data looks different than it has all night.

I say cautiously, "I think we may have a win—"

"Wait."

None of our debug breakpoints trip, and the program runs to completion for the first time. This triggers a burst of graphic fireworks we rigged on the end line.

Xan wraps me in such an exuberant hug that the ball chair I'm sitting on tips over backward, and we thump onto the floor. She screams comically, levers herself off my chest, and then gives me a hand up. She's concerned that I hit my head and starts inspecting it for a bump. I should say that I'm fine, but the feel of her fingers running through my hair has dissolved my capacity for speech. I want to turn to face her, but my spine has locked itself in place.

Perhaps she picks up on this, because seconds later my head is pronounced "quite sound," and I'm dismissed with effusive thanks and a sisterly peck on the cheek.

Sisterly, but this is the second time she's kissed me.

17

Billy's virtual Silling remains the province of a select few until someone posts this thread to the NOD forums on Saturday night:

Thread: New Game Trailhead?

Cal_Iglooa	So here's something:
Joined:9/17/11 Posts: 357 Location: your business	Check out this NOD shard we found at: http://nod.com/ule_find/grid:334.118.797 Screen Grabs: [http://www.flickr.com/photos/Cal_ Iglooa/737027084/] Those among us who actually still read might recognize that castle. We've now got a sim based on *120 Days of Sodom*. The stakes? Foul lucre it seems. And any of you who have read *120* will know that I mean *foul*. For those that haven't, *educate* yourselves: A summary The full text

We've only explored a little, but here's how it works:

Every day one of the whores tells a story involving 5 "passions."

Once she starts telling each, you can go into the dungeon and there are rooms set up corresponding to each situation. You reenact the stories with the provided NoBots, sounds, and cameras. Then post your videos back in the amphitheater.

Good ones play up on the wall above the whore's head. After a submission, the Duke puts out his hand with a Louis d'Or. When you take this, your NOD account is credited with 7,500 Noodles [about $5 per video].

Not even minimum wage, you complain? Wait, it gets better. After we tipped him off, Hal_LaCoste took his time and made a couple quality nut nuggets, like the ones already playing in the rotation. We rezzed in today, and when we entered the theater, the Duke got up and said to him, "Your work has pleased us. It is now part of the Telling." He holds out his hand, and in it there's a purse: 75,000 Noodles! That's $50 per video. For all 600 tortures, that == serious spaghetti.

So much pasta raises questions:

1) I can haz?

2) If not, why would someone want to spend so much to crowdsource a machinima version of *120 Days*?

> 3) Is this new game related to the recent
> bubble in NOD cybering tools like our
> much-loved LibIA?
>
> Those of you up for finding out the
> answers, hit us up at our new forum:
>
> Savant

I gather from browsing around in the forum that "Savant" is the nickname for this new place that emerged during chats between early explorers. It's a corruption of "*cent vingt,*" the French word for 120. There are already a number of replies to the post, most expressing "OMF-GROFJUADBBQ" enthusiasm.

But there are also some comments like this one from Anne_Sasha_Ball:

> Is it just me, or does ANYONE maybe have a problem with
> this? I cyber every day, but I have to draw the line at
> making virtual kiddie porn. I mean is this even legal?

Her question ignites a firestorm of responses, and the discussion degenerates into First Amendment bickering that then wades off into tendrils about whether George W. Bush was a "genocibal rapist" and the extent to which communist Jews control the media.

I check Cal_Iglooa's initial *Savant* forum posts in which he outlines essentially the same path I took to find Château de Silling. I'll bet the guy is one of the original GAMErs who received a pendant. What bothers me is that the number of active participants has reached three hundred in the few hours since he posted to the NOD forums. So Billy's game has now infected a broad population of bored net people looking for something to do.

Savant is spreading.

18

The New York Harvard Club's two buildings neatly embody the dual nature of the university itself. The original neo-Georgian edifice features an old-boy décor of polished wood and animal heads, reputed to be the spoils of Teddy Roosevelt's shooting expeditions. The resolutely modern addition next door resembles the headquarters of an EU agency, more in the spirit of the school's current inclination toward international technocracy.

Blythe had texted me asking if I'd meet her for a drink after she finished with a speaking engagement here.

I can't think why she would have agreed to debate Mark Cooper '96, a communications professor at Hunter College, on the subject of media consolidation. Perhaps she considered it a practice bout to hone her message in advance of her imminent congressional hearings.

The big news at IMP is that they've agreed to buy TelAmerica, one of their East Coast rivals, in a twenty-six-billion-dollar combination that will make them the largest cable provider in the country. As VP for cable operations, the deal is very much Blythe's baby. Congress loves to make a circus out of major media mergers, so she's been called to Washington early this spring.

The press quickly jumped on the atavistic nature of the deal. Blythe's father first put himself on the map with a daring bid for CalCast, a much larger rival, in 1974, well before the leveraged buyout boom really caught fire. While analysts complained that Randall's balance sheet couldn't justify the debt required, interest soon shifted to larger deals elsewhere. Randall digested his prey and proceeded to ever-greater conquests. In taking a swing at TelAmerica, Blythe is paying tribute to her father's legacy.

I step in just as Blythe is winding up her closing argument. Judging by the way the crowd is nodding at her every sally, poor Dr. Cooper was badly overmatched.

She spends a long time chatting with the attendees afterward. Her performance has compelled even some of the audience's avowed socialists to try slipping her their résumés. Eventually she catches my eye and, covertly rattling a notional lowball, sends me to the bar to secure refreshment.

The words "double Laphroaig neat" come out a little husky and get me a double take from the bartender. I'm repulsed by my sentimentality, but the drink is ingrained in my mind as the enchanted love potion in my secret history with Blythe.

After the night she kissed me by the snowdrifts of Mt. Auburn Street, I took on the lone goal of wooing her. The project seemed futile to the heartsick adolescent in me, which left my autistic engineer side to take control by asking, "Isn't courting someone really just the oldest and most fundamental form of social engineering? Well, isn't it?"

A woman like Blythe, with legions of men falling all over her, looked like an exceedingly hard target. But I had a few advantages. I was already a more-or-less trusted party, I had ample resources harvested from her twin brother, and I had the determination fostered by my sincere belief in the hacker's creed:

There's always a way in.

One begins such an operation with detailed reconnaissance. I admit some pretty stalkerish gambits leapt to mind, but I decided that reading her email would be dishonorable. However, I did hack the registrar's systems to get her class schedule.

That prompted my rising early twice a week to stake out a cozy table at the always packed café at the Science Center so I could turn it over to her and her friends when they came out of Stats 139. After a couple weeks of this, she finally showed up alone, and I blew off my imaginary class to keep her company.

I was "delighted" by the coincidence of finding her in charge of the math/science tutoring program for Roxbury kids that I'd just joined to indulge my previously unexpressed need to serve the community.

I wandered Cambridge scanning for the minutest signal of her presence. Like a drug-sniffing dog let off his leash and free to pursue his fixations.

Finally, a breakthrough: I saw her coming out of the Harvard Provision Company carrying a box of liquor. In my first experience with dumpster diving, I fished her receipt out of the trash bin and found that she'd just purchased half a case of Laphroaig twenty-year. This fact evoked a memory of the slight tug of displeasure at her lips when the Hasty Pudding staff informed her that they only served Johnnie Walker.

The next Thursday, I stood in the Pudding rehearsing the details of my admittedly thin plan to start a conversation about scotch. Isn't it funny we're both Laphroaig fanciers? Perhaps she'd like to sample some rare Quarter Cask I have stashed back at my room?

As it happened, my contrived place at the bar simply allowed me an ideal vantage from which to observe our leading hockey stud, Pete Novak, asking Blythe to the next evening's Mather House formal.

Novak was one of those rare athletes who wanted at least part of a fancy degree before exploring his prospects in the NHL. He had a testosterone-soaked pulchritude, and I guess he represented a passable antithesis of William Coles. But I was still mortified when I heard her say yes.

Seething with jealousy the next morning, I couldn't help torturing myself with online pictures of him celebrating the winning goal in the Junior National Championship. But Novak was an academic all-star as well, so my rival had more substance than a mere well-marbled boy toy. He grew up in a tony suburb near Princeton, mother a professor, father a prominent local sportscaster. *Probably worked for her dad,* I thought bitterly.

Digging deeper, I learned that Robert Randall *had* in fact acquired Joe Novak's station ten years ago, but had fired him in the first round of automatic layoffs. Novak's parents divorced early the next year. Shortly after, Joe Novak killed two people in a DWI accident and was still in jail. So any relationship between Pete and Blythe would have heavier baggage than the First Armored Division.

Though I'd hesitated to invade Blythe's privacy, I had no compunctions about Novak's. He wasn't a heavy emailer, but his browsing history yielded an undue amount of research on powerful sedatives and queries about local doctors with liberal views on their use.

That seemed pretty dark, so I Photoshopped myself an invite to the Mather formal and started trying to figure out how I was going to warn Blythe.

But she didn't even show. I stood there nervously sipping club soda for two hours until I heard a couple of her friends talking about how after pre-gaming with them, she'd "stumbled off" for some "steak and cheese."

Where?

To get to Novak's dorm they'd have to walk right by the party. Not another bar. The Pudding was closed. If Blythe was still conscious, she'd probably balk at a hotel room. So a plausibly innocent place he could take her that would nonetheless offer plenty of opportunity to get her alone?

I called Blake and then ran all the way to the Zeta house.

The front door of the frat's dingy clapboard lair was propped open, and I could hear members bellowing out back. I sprinted up the stairs and wound through the dim hallway leading toward their den. Adjoining which I knew they had two former bedrooms pressed into duty as the "bong room" and the dismal "mattress room," where I thought I might find Blythe.

But the mattress room's door hung ajar, revealing only darkness. I turned back, trying to think where else she could be. Then, a bright light flashed from the alcove next to their most remote bathroom. Deep voices accompanied another flash.

"—society whore's not so pretty now, are you?"

"Daddy Randall's going to *love* this."

I crept around the corner and saw Novak standing in the doorway taking pictures with a digital camera. He was flanked by two of his team-mates, one of whom was struggling with his fly. I had to sneak right up behind them before I finally saw her.

Blythe hunched over the toilet, her lips resting on its soiled rim. Vomit covered the floor. Her backless dress had fallen to expose her breasts. I supposed she'd felt something wrong and tried to make herself sick but was too late. As the flash went off again, she looked up in mute appeal and reached for the plunger in the corner. To use as a weapon? The effort destroyed the remnants of her balance, and her face made a splashy thump as it hit the floor.

I shouldered my way in and reached for her. "Jesus Christ, guys, what kind of shit—"

Novak checked me with his forearm so hard that the back of my head bounced off the wall, and if he hadn't been holding me in place, I'd have joined Blythe on the floor.

"Who the fuck are you?"

As I closed my eyes against the next blow, I saw a pair of pale hands reach from the dark, fasten onto Novak's neck, and rip him back out of the doorway. His minions turned to confront the better part of our heavyweight crew's first boat. Several more hockey players followed just behind them. Seeing Blake and Novak wrestling viciously on the floor, they threw themselves at the rowers. Though the hockey team were surely the better fighters, the rowers had an average of twenty pounds on them, so the brawl escalated fast as more people kept coming up the stairs.

After wiping Blythe's face, I hauled her out of the bathroom and pushed my way along the left-hand wall to a short, dark hallway that led to the back stairwell.

I set her down on the sidewalk outside and tried to revive her. Seconds later Blake loomed behind me, bloody and breathing hard. Without a word, he tenderly picked up his sister and stalked out into the night.

The wee hours passed while I hacked the Mather House key card security system to give myself access to Novak's suite. At six in the morning, he and his roommates were passed out, presumably from celebrating their coup against the "society whore." I found Novak in an almost adorable state of helplessness: snoring loudly on his futon mattress, still in his shirt and tie, but sans pants. One hand remained inside his dingy white briefs, the other cradled his camera.

I grabbed the camera, my primary objective, but couldn't resist a little more payback. A quick sweep of their common room delivered the obligatory gay porn mag, always useful for infantile japery, which I opened on his chest. Then I tightened his tie and placed the tensioning end in his free hand. The dawn lent enough light for several pictures without the flash.

But it still wasn't enough. He'd gone after *Blythe*.

Inspiration struck, and I used Novak's phone to send a quick message.

The Bat's preferred Fulgencio-filler was eager to make a house call and supply me with the powdered methamphetamine that I slipped into the giant Gatorade bottle next to Novak's bed. Not so much that he'd go to the infirmary, but enough that he'd have an invigorating morning. And difficulty passing a drug test. And a sharp end to his hockey season. And a big problem with his scholarship.

At midnight the next evening Blythe knocked on my door. She looked the opposite of how she did the last time I'd seen her, crisp jeans and an immaculate white blouse covering her pearls. Heavier makeup than she usually wore.

Rooted in place on my doormat, she started a stilted speech. "James, I thought I should stop by to express to you my deepest gratitude . . ."

This was not at all what I wanted. She obviously loathed that I'd seen her in such a state.

I interrupted. "Hey, come on in. I have something for you."

She hesitated but stepped inside. As I closed the door behind her, I handed over Novak's camera, cued to my early-morning photo shoot.

She flipped back to the pictures of her and asked the question with her eyes.

"I checked the log. He hadn't downloaded them yet. I think everything will turn out fine. But you should be more careful."

Her silence stretched on, so I asked, "Are you going to be okay?"

She stared at me for another moment, visibly reassessing. Finally she said, "Yeah . . . I'll just need . . ." She glanced around abstractly, as though searching some alternate dimension for what could possibly redeem that awful experience. But then her gaze settled on my mantelpiece bar prominently stocked with exotic bottlings of her favorite alcoholic balm.

I guess its presence served as a celestial confirmation of my virtue, because her voice relaxed when she said, "I'll just need a drink."

She then drifted to my window and stared into the night. I couldn't believe she'd turn her back to me as I poured.

Blythe arrives down at the club bar minutes later and inhales deeply from the lowball I ordered for her.

I raise my drink and say, "To victory."

We tap glasses. "Kind of you. But one can't really declare victory in a training exercise."

"You can if you learn something. And you learned that you need a better class of opponent."

"I think my opponents are talented enough these days. If I—" She stops herself and takes a sip of her drink.

I wait for her to resume, but when she doesn't, I ask, "To what do I owe the honor?"

"Business, sadly. Though I hope that soon we can drink for pleasure."

Lightning surges down my spine. But it dissipates as I realize she probably means that I need to move my ass on locating Billy. She's also not necessarily implying that we'll be drinking *together* at the end of it.

She continues. "How are you finding the new you?"

"Liberating. I'm thinking of installing some new holes in myself. Turns out your brother isn't the only GAMEr with a soft spot for retro prep."

I show her the croc pendant I got at the party. Blythe stares at it. "I won't ask how you came by this."

I laugh. "Nothing like that. He mailed them out to some of his colleagues. An advertisement for this place he's set up in NOD."

She says, "So another game . . . Just a little harmless fun?"

"Well, I wouldn't—"

"Pardon my sarcasm. I know he's always taken them quite seriously." She thinks for a moment. Then changes the subject. "James, I also need to clarify a few things from our last meeting."

"Okay."

"Because of our past, ah, relationship, Blake thought it would be best if you worked mostly with him on this to prevent any . . . awkwardness."

"I see."

"I told him that was ludicrous, but he's obsessively protective of me, and once he gets an idea in his head—"

"I understand."

"But I just wanted to make sure you don't have any difficulty—"

"Blythe, I'm here to help you. Not create new problems."

She smiles. "Ah, good. The one we have is bad enough."

"I get the impression this isn't just an everyday sibling rivalry."

"It's beginning to display the hallmarks of a war of succession."

I nod as she takes a long sip.

"My father badly wanted the enterprise he built to last for generations. He set up the estate so we'd retain voting shares and, therefore, control of the company. Dad was acutely aware that family disputes can lead to dreadful headlines, lawsuits, and sometimes fire sales."

"And you see yourselves heading in that direction?"

"We'd have been there long ago, but my father took steps to prevent that. In his will, he divided financial ownership of IMP equally among the three of us, but not the supervotes. Coherence of control came before equal treatment."

Though it's forbidden throughout the club, she lights a cigarette. "So Dad gave each of us enough voting shares to guarantee a seat, but the full board decides which child will be placed in charge. A sort of meritocratic primogeniture. There wasn't a set deadline, but Ger Loring has started flouncing around in Hawaiian shirts, so everyone thinks the decision will be made soon."

"Sounds like a recipe for a strong company, but a broken family."

A sad smile emerges from the lip of her glass. "Of course Blake and I have stayed quite close. We are twins after all."

She tells me how they carved out separate spheres of influence in the company. Blake on the business development side, and Blythe in cable ops.

She continues. "Billy, on the other hand—"

"Is he even interested in IMP? I thought he dreamed of being a sort of Caravaggio two-point-oh."

"Maybe so. But he never got to make a choice. Blake was so enraged at the publicity from Billy's early legal troubles that he seized on a minor provision in the trust that allowed the board to delay giving Billy his seat when he turned twenty-one. He got the money from his regular equity but no real voice in the company."

"Your father gave the board the power to disenfranchise one of his children?"

"My father trusted Ger more than us, I suppose. He was sensitive to the fact that later generations often take an axe to the family tree. So he put in this 'against the interests' clause. I'm sure it was aimed at situations where the black sheep turns pinko, but Blake deployed it against Billy's freedom of expression. My family has an unfortunate belief that scorched earth is good ground for negotiation."

"I don't suppose he took it well."

"No. We had dinner to try to reach an understanding. To keep our dissension out of the press and maybe make peace." She closes her eyes. "Billy accused Blake of hypocrisy, idiocy, philistinism. Blake . . . There was an altercation. Quite undignified."

She sighs. "Blake thought he was doing it for the good of IMP, but sometimes I think the imp to which my brother seems most attuned is Poe's, not our father's."

She's referring to Edgar Allan Poe's short story in which he lays out a theory about the irresistible allure of self-destructive actions. The Imp of the Perverse, a creature with whom I'm all too familiar.

"Blake thinks I'm too soft on Billy. And maybe he's right. I won't pretend we ever had a warm relationship. But my father loved him, and I try to honor that. I constantly come back to this image I have of him when we picked him up at the airport after his mother died. The way he stood there with his little backpack and seemed so grief-stricken. So vulnerable. Even Blake felt sorry for him. And the look on my father's face was almost worse. I had this idea then that I could try to help them both with that pain . . . As it turned out, there wasn't much I could do. But now, I—I just know my father would want me to help Billy if I can. Blake too. Try to end all this senseless conflict."

"And your concern is—"

"I'm concerned that my two brothers are intent on harming each other. And that they're getting to the point where they don't care about the consequences. That's the message I see in Billy's video. So . . . though you'll be working mostly with Blake, please keep me informed. There may come a point where I'll have to ask you to help protect my brothers from themselves."

Saying this seems to cost Blythe something. She turns away from me. I lift my hand behind her, thinking to comfort her with a gentle pat. But it just hangs there, and I can't bring myself to touch her. I withdraw it and clear my throat.

"Don't worry. Everything will turn out fine."

Her eyes search for something in mine. "I'm sure we both remember what happened the last time you said that to me."

Then, with a subtle arch of her eyebrow, she knocks back her drink.

19

That arched eyebrow ignited a mental wildfire that consumed any thought I might've had beyond ransacking cyberspace for traces of her brother.

At midnight, several hours into my minute forensic probe of Billy's Château de Silling build, I receive the kind of jackpot break you forbid yourself from hoping for. A ProSoap alert from the elevator camera at GAME with recognition results on Olya, Xan, and Garriott.

After rewinding the stream to ten seconds ago, I see the trio troop into the frame, Olya and Garriott dragging large aluminum cases behind them.

I run the eleven blocks over to GAME, sure that seeing the contents of those cases will tell me what their techno-coven is all about. Since coming down the main elevator would probably alert them, I sneak around back to the metal cellar doors that lead to the basement. The doors are secured with a key card system, which only makes a slight click when the lock disengages. I haul one open as quietly as I can.

I tiptoe back to my office and see that the door to their workroom across the hall is closed tight with only a thin ribbon of light running underneath. Olya's sharp tones ring out behind it.

"No. We said we run trial tonight, so we must do this. We don't just slip and slip and slip every time."

"It's *supposed* to slip." This is Garriott's voice. "If it doesn't, it's going to break, and then where will we be? If we just take—"

"If it breaks, it breaks. Then maybe we build it better. They cannot be so fragile."

"But—"

"And we need to know *how* it breaks, yes?"

"Olya, we're not even done with all the component tests. Xan just got her last one fixed today."

Olya's heels click briskly as she walks across the room. She adopts a sugary, mollifying tone. "Little one. Don't you want to know how it feels? Not just the surface, but the connection?"

Andrew sighs. "I just—"

There's a smacking sound. "For luck. Now, let's go. You know it must be tonight."

A moment of silence. Then Olya again: "What is wrong? We work on this all these months, don't tell me now you are timid?"

"Olya, I just don't—"

"I won't laugh, I promise."

Xan intervenes. "Olya, take it easy."

"Andrew! It must be you. Why must I explain this?"

Garriott takes a deep breath and says, "Olya, I don't know what's gotten into you tonight, but I'm going to get some coffee, and we can discuss it after."

Their door cracks open a few inches.

Olya yells, "Get back here, you little—"

I figure this will be my best shot, so I push the door open hard and barge into the room with my BlackBerry in front of me like I'm finishing a text. I say, "Hey, Garriott, I had a new idea on that network problem we were working on that I want to run by—"

I stop about eight feet into the now completely silent room. I look up as though just realizing where I am.

"Oh . . . shit. Sorry, guys. I didn't mean to interrupt."

Eyes closed, Garriott massages his temples like he's trying to keep his skull from fragmenting. Olya has gone apoplectic and alternately stares at him and me as if trying to decide on whom to release the brewing tempest of her rage.

I take the opportunity to glance at the middle of the room, where I am finally confronted by IT.

Or make that THEM, since the top-secret project is composed of a pair of robots linked through a tangle of cables to matched high-end PCs. They resemble oversized swans in form, albeit with ungracefully large heads. Each has a rounded bulk of motors, electronics, and a small air compressor mounted on a wide stationary platform. From there a thinner neck of four motorized segments rises about three feet to culminate in an oblong cylindrical head of maybe nine inches in length and four in diameter. Two arms rise from points corresponding to where the wings would attach. They end in round pads supported by an array of small pistons set up so that the surfaces can quickly change shape. A vasculature of narrow tubes snakes up the neck into the head. At the head's other end, a circular opening is padded with bright red silicone rubber. The heads point downward, as if the machines are bowing in prayer, so I can't tell what's inside the holes. But having seen the rest of the devices, I can guess.

"So this is IT," I say.

My words snap Olya out of her shock. She walks toward me, her arm extended to the exit. "Out, goddamn you!"

She reaches as though intending to bodily throw me through the steel door. But I pivot around her and put up my hands soothingly. "Come on. I've already seen them. At least show me what they do. I'll be your lab rat, and you can kill me afterward if you have to."

Olya looks around for a weapon. "I think we kill you now."

Garriott lifts his head and says with resignation, or maybe relief, "Just let him do it, Olya. We're going to have to test it on other people soon anyway."

Xan is staring at me with a blank expression. Not hostile, more like evaluating. She doesn't speak for a second but then whispers something into Olya's ear.

Olya gives me a gimlet-eyed once-over. Her eyes flick disdainfully at Garriott, and then she says softly, "Well, Mr. Pryce, you want to be the first victim? Come and try our little project."

She edges past me to sit on one of the configurable chairs, where she reaches down and hikes up her skirt. She then leans back and whips off her panties with a lissome flourish of her legs.

This prods everyone into motion. Xan starts plugging more cables from the robots into the workstations, while Garriott tosses a motion-capture rig to Olya.

Olya places her hands on the nearest robot, and I hear a series of mechanical clicks and whirrs and what might be the sound of a fan coming up to speed.

Garriott then steps over to me and points at my belt buckle. A smile forms as he sees me hesitate. The implications of what is required here hit me suddenly, and I feel my whole body start to blush. I have disrobed in the presence of relative strangers before, but this situation represents a new level of weird. But if my duty to Blythe demands that I sacrifice my sense of propriety, so be it.

Besides, how bad can it be?

I drop my pants.

"So put these on. But first, I'm going to need the boxers as well, mate."

I expected this but am paralyzed by the sight of Olya shrugging out of her shirt, revealing a lace-encased bosom that could make Shakespeare's desiccated skeleton compose a 155th sonnet. She quickly pulls over her mocap rig. But for a net nerd like myself, that only makes my erection totally unavoidable.

Andrew glances down and smirks. "I see stage fright won't be a problem."

I snatch the mocap tights he's proffering and wriggle into them as quickly as I can. Naturally, I find they're crotchless and only serve to emphasize my rapid swelling. Along with the standard IR patches at the joints, there are reflective bits lining the seams along the tights' inner thighs, like rhinestones for a glammy fetish act. Xan tugs my shirt over my head and then drapes me with the mocap tunic as though I'm a futuristic knight about to sally forth. She does not resist lightly goosing me for good measure, which marks the end of my battle with modesty. I'm forced to brazen it out with my engorged tool waving in the chilly air.

The next article is my head-mounted display, so at least I don't have to look anyone in the eye. Garriott takes my hand, and with Xan guiding my hips, they recline me on the other chair and position one of the robots between my legs with its head in very intimate proximity.

As I settle in, I ask, "What do I do now?"

Xan, her lips alluringly close to my ear, says, "Now we let nature take its course."

The screens in my visor fade into a 3D rendering of a dungeon scene. I swivel my head and decide that it must be Hell due to the river of molten lava at my left. I'm sitting on a pagan altar in the center of a rock outcropping. A cavern opens to my right, out of which smoke billows lazily.

From the haze emerges a raven-haired succubus character, naked but for some beguiling cuneiform tattoos. Her barbed tail sways seductively as she walks toward me. She grins, and I hear a deepened version of Olya's voice intone, "So, Zhimbo, are you ready to play with me?"

"Mmm-hmm," is all I can manage.

"Well, I am yours to command. What do you want to do?" She's slowly moving closer.

"Uh . . . What *can* we do?"

"Why don't I show you?" she says as she's almost within range of an embrace. But instead she drops to her knees and motions with her hands for me to spread my knees apart. She moves in between, teasingly making sure not to touch me yet. Though I know this gorgeous demon is only a binary figment, my cock jumps at the proximity of her crimson lips. SuccubOlya's right hand darts out and she catches it with two fingers right at the base. The miraculous thing is that I actually feel this. I know it's just the robot. Just a lifeless mechanism. But it doesn't hurt to have Olya's sultry whisper in my ear, and the visuals are marvelous. Indeed, my game-cock, with its full Brazilian wax, lack of unsightly veins, and extra virtual inch or so, looks much better than in real life. But I'm not allowed much time to admire it.

What follows, as SuccubOlya's mouth descends, is without a doubt the most amazing thing I've ever experienced.

A feeling like warm wet flesh pours all the way down my length, but it's unusually hot and soft. I gasp as a glissando of small squeezes runs from stem to stern, and I almost lift my visor to see who's gotten hold of me, so convinced am I that the iTeam is pulling a bait and switch. But as the velvet wave pulls back by slow, agonizing increments, I observe that really it doesn't feel anything like an actual woman.

It feels *better*.

Olya's sex devil seems sprung from a lubricious reverie, but it's the thought of the real person behind her av that lends the scenario its blistering power. Far from the sterile repetition of porn, and yet still maintaining a pleasant buffer of fantasy, she's an ideal balance between the virtual and the real. While my brain indulges itself, my skin just believes.

But I quickly lose this train of thought as she plunges into a rapid full-stroke deep throat. No frightening snags on her hard palate. Super-human muscle control, like she's somehow able to use her very vocal cords to pleasure me. As she comes back up, I wiggle and notice the lack of teeth. She squeezes hard at the base, bares her fangs, and murmurs, "Hold still, *dorogoi.*"

She speeds up the rhythm, and my jaw drops. I suppress the urge to place my hands on her head.

Well, what would happen if I did?

I send out an exploratory finger. Incredibly, something's there. Not exactly the silky black tresses I'm seeing, but there's a soft surface exactly where her cranium should be.

As sometimes happens in real life, SuccubOlya stops, but she leers at me, saying, "You like that?"

"Yeah."

"Why don't you stand up and really fuck my mouth?"

That's sufficient invitation for me. It's not like I'm going to stimulate any unfortunate reflexes in a robot. Being able to put my hips into it re-ally adds a dimension to the feeling. SuccubOlya even offers a few dirty words of encouragement that she couldn't possibly say under the circum-stances. Her av throws in some pornographic visual grace notes, but it feels so good that I actually close my eyes.

She allows me a few joyous moments of that before pressing me lightly back against the altar and then straddling me in a reverse cowgirl. The sensation is totally different, but I don't have time to analyze the variation, since seconds later, I realize this episode is about to come to its unnatural conclusion. Olya must sense this, because right then she dials up the heat and pressure. I don't want it to end, and I wonder if I can prolong things, or if I should just surrender to the inevitable. As usual, my genitals reach their own decision, and I'm helpless in the face of an all-consuming orgasm that feels like it's never going to stop.

Then suddenly—pain. It shoots into me like a bear trap just snapped shut on my package. The vids go out, so I'm drowned in blackness. Total agony throbs up into my groin, and I try to slap this horrible thing off my cock. It seems dead now, but there's still suction remaining. And *fuck!* It's completely unbearable!

Finally I wrench it off, and the pain starts to abate. A burnt, ozone-ish smell fills the air. I tear away my HMD to see what happened to James Jr.

This British twit is yelling, "Oh my God, what's he done?"

I still can't see my injury because the lights are inexplicably out, and Garriott is in my face with a flashlight.

I shout at him, "You people fried my dick!"

"You were supposed pull out!"

"You didn't tell me that!"

"It's a prototype. What did you think was going to happen?"

Xan comes over giggling. She grabs Garriott's light, places a steadying hand on my shoulder, and bends low to inspect me.

"Your penis is intact, Mr. Pryce, I assure you. There may be a small blister here at the end, but a little unguent will have you back at it in no time."

I take stock. The pain has lessened, and the stress hormones are slowly falling off. I get embarrassed about the spooge dripping down my tights. Garriott examines his gently smoking apparatus.

The overhead lights twinkle to life, and we see Olya over by the fuse box. She's out of her mocap gear, in a demure bathrobe, but I can see a rosy flush creeping up around the hollow of her throat.

"So, Zhimbo, how was I?"

I pause for a second, assessing what I've just experienced. The word forces itself out of my mouth:

"Electrifying."

20

___

We're gathered around their usual table at Foo Bar. Xan twists the key to a magnum of Veuve Clicquot and says, "James will not be the only one popping a cork tonight." She thumbs off the foil while caressing the bottle's neck suggestively. Garriott begins moaning in falsetto. Xan is not afraid to hose down the table, and I become damp for the second time that evening.

When what's left is poured, Olya raises her glass and says solemnly, "Team . . . To a great fucking day at the office."

We all make the "2-I-T" sign, but Xan puts up a hand to stop the toast. "I guess we can tell James what 'IT' really stands for."

"What?"

"Imminent Teledildonics, mate," says Garriott.

"Teledildonics" is the fancy word for virtual sex coined by Theodor Nelson of "hypertext" fame. The term gained currency due to its fine blend of nerdy and naughty, though I think we'll need a new one to describe what I just went through.

After a boisterous clink that leaves much of the remaining champagne on the table, a waitress appears with an armful of Guinness and Jameson.

Garriott takes his shot glass and says, "To Fred!"

Xan follows, holding up her stout: "To Ginger. May she rest in peace." We drop our whiskey into the beer. Garriott is steeling himself for the race and says to me, "I can't believe you killed my girlfriend."

This causes a choking fit on Xan's part. Olya finishes smoothly and slams down her pint. She immediately waves to the waitress. I'm just behind her, and after a deep breath, I ask, "Why do y'all call the bots Fred and Ginger?"

Olya says, "This stupid obsession with scooters."

Garriott finishes quickly to defend himself. "Right. Remember how we were talking about that infuriating Segway hype? So the first prototypes were named Fred and Ginger, because they glided around so gracefully. And yet . . . there's something asexual about a scooter. So we took the names for our little darlings. Who *really* aspire to glide gracefully. They seem to move together well enough for you?"

"I guess the proof was in the pudding."

Olya, ever the heavy, says, "Of course, like any good demo, maybe eighty percent of it was faked."

"I'd say that's about par for the course."

Olya frowns. Xan clarifies. "He's talking about real women, and has betrayed the fact that he's never met one."

Olya rolls her eyes, as if the idea of women faking orgasms were a childish fairy tale. "Maybe now you can fuck penguins if you don't like women."

I want to change the subject from my bedtime preferences, so I try, "What do you mean it was faked? If it's virtual—"

Xan says, "No, she means the machines' capabilities. They can't really do everything you might think from your experience tonight. We preloaded most of that. It wasn't all real-time."

"You could have fooled me."

"Yeah, we're counting on the natural phenomenon that men don't tend to ask a lot of questions when they're getting blown," Garriott says. "Which is why certain transsexual prostitutes—"

"The point is we have very much work still to do," says Olya.

Xan and Garriott put on pouty faces. Olya throws her hands up. "But not tonight, not tonight. Now we celebrate the coming of Zhimbo."

"Well then," says Xan, "with apologies to Richard Powers and his beautiful, if rather chaste, book about our vocation, let me propose: to plowing the dark."

Our glasses clink again. Xan winks at me over the rim of her whiskey, and I feel like I'm finally inside.

— — —

Hours later, we're at an unlicensed club in a big loft in Greenpoint. Olya insisted we go due to the presence of some Polish DJ she knows, and she and Xan are out on the dance floor causing tension to flare between the male patrons and their dates. Garriott tries to train me in some of the simpler rituals of the iTeam, such as learning all the words (and grunts) to James Brown's "Get Up (I Feel Like Being a) Sex Machine."

After quite a while of failing to meet his rigorous but rapidly deteriorating standards, Xan comes over to take her leave. Olya leans over to finish Garriott's drink and bite him on the ear, which I suppose is what passes for affection with her.

She pours me a shot and says, "The little one always leaves early. She is delicate. Not like Andy here. But he is small too. He stays, but he can barely talk."

Garriott primly downs a shot in silence. Olya continues. "Speaking of talking. James, you are a smart man. And not afraid of sex. We have to complete this very fast. Maybe you want to help us. It's good work I think."

"I think I'd like that."

"Da. Good. Well, before you are officially on the team, you and I, we sit down. Have what they call the 'Come into Jesus' talk. Maybe eight AM?"

Only three hours from now. But I can't keep myself from saying yes.

21

All the champagne and stardust has fled from Olya's demeanor when I roll into GAME very near the appointed hour. I meet Garriott in the hall, and he mumbles that he's going to Bellevue to see about getting his stomach pumped, if not replaced. Olya seems completely fine. She's wearing a conservative charcoal pantsuit, albeit with a see-through blouse and patent leather demi bra. Her head starts shaking before I can even sit down.

"Zhimbo, this is no condition for serious talk—"

"Olya, trust me. You have my undivided attention."

A frustrated exhalation and pursed lips. Not much of a welcome, but what would someone raised under communism know about how to conduct a "Come to Jesus" meeting?

"So for background, you know I was at this Pervasive Media Program—where Xan teaches. A place for people who *love* computers. Webcams, online dating, social networking, all these things. So of course we *talk* of having sex with them all the time. But no one ever *thinks* about it. I have degree in materials engineering, so my knowledge of *surfaces* is very deep. But I spend my summers at boring design firm. Eventually I think, *Enough of this!*" A bona fide fist-thump on the desk. "Why not try to do this thing we all want? So at GAME I find the little ones—they are very bright, you know—and we start work. Now maybe we have you too."

"You had *me* at 'fuck my mouth.'" Olya squints quizzically. I realize that paraphrasing *Jerry Maguire* to a recent Russian immigrant is silly. "But do you really think normal people are going to want this?"

"Who is normal? No, it's not whether people want to do virtual sex. The question is, once you give it to them, will they want to do anything else?"

I chuckle and concede the point.

She continues. "Everybody in the world wants real VR. We know what it looks like, but we don't know how to get there. In the science fiction it is always these jacks you plug into network with. Jacks in the neck, chips in the head. Like Billy, this foolish *artiste* you are so interested in." She waves dismissively. "I think nature already has given us the right sort of jack." She places a hand over the juncture of her legs. "And this is the channel that will give birth to the technology. VR will arrive when it *comes.*"

Her head tilts thoughtfully for a moment. "Now, are we the first ones to think of this? Of course not. People have always made love to objects. Sailors used dolls made of wood, burlap, and hair of horse. They called them 'sea wives.' Now we can do a little better."

She goes on to detail the more recent history of teledildonics. The subtleties of Allen Stein's "Thrillhammer," an internet-enabled dildo chair that, while something to behold, provides only a visual experience for hetero males. Many device enthusiasts swear by their Venus 2000 / Sybian setups; these are a powerful pair of his-and-hers sex machines, but they're operated only by simple remotes and cannot actually communicate. At the other end of the technological continuum, one finds the purely mechanical charms of a contraption called the Monkey Rocker.

If one artificial coupling strategy has been to sexually enable furniture, another is to simulate actual humans. In response to a crackdown on prostitutes, the Koreans created Robot Hotels, populated with anatomically equipped mannequins. The U.S. has seen the debut of the gorgeous but inert Real Dolls and their more cerebral cousin Roxxxy, who actually runs some pretty respectable AI.

But Olya scorns such literal substitutes. "All these robo-whores give new meaning to the term 'uncanny valley.'" She means the hypothesis that *almost*-lifelike human facsimiles produce feelings of revulsion in their living counterparts.

"Maybe one day, perhaps they will be very sexy, but now I think our way is better. We want the machine, the interface, to disappear, and leave you with two *real people* making love."

Other companies have taken the iTeam's approach as well. Currently on the market is the RealTouch, which is a belt-driven device for men that produces friction in concert with specially produced porn loops. For the ladies, there's the Sinulator, a vibrator control module that they've hooked up to Second Life. Olya sniffs, "A broken metaphor. I do not need someone else to run my Rabbit. If you're fucking, there must be thrust. We are trying to simulate, not just interact. The problem, it is much harder."

I'd like to explore Olya's ideas at length, but she abruptly stands up and moves over to the room's giant whiteboard. She wipes out a small colony of Garriott's intricate drawings and with precise strokes sketches a block diagram of the system. As she's doing this, she describes the team members' respective roles.

She handles what they call the "skinterface," literally where the machines touch the users. This includes much of the sensing package, which is currently being upgraded. The anatomical rendering is a series of air muscles operated by tiny valves controlling pressure from a small, but powerful, air compressor. Miniature heating elements provide an approximation of body temperature, and then finally there's the "lubrication management" system.

Garriott's responsibilities cover the gross mechanical engineering, including head and neck positions, the hand-tracking wings, and almost all the programming for the bots' internal computers. He also built the configurable seats they call "MetaChairs." Olya notes that while all these components seem to be working well, when run in real time, sometimes erratic, "maybe painful" behavior can result. Thus the software running in the devices' embedded brains is called the ErrOS, supposedly for "ERotic Operating System," but really a dig at the reliability of Garriott's code.

In fairness, his challenge is the most difficult. It's hard enough for two live humans to coordinate all the urgent motions of love, and the issues are multiplied exponentially when you insert two dumb robots into the mix. Olya explains that the team has found that people are very forgiving of sensory infidelity as long as *some* kind of rhythm is maintained. The dreaded "pop-out" in real sex must be avoided at all costs.

The iTeam combats this problem by having the large heads try to always maintain contact with the reflectors on their user's crotch. Internal to the heads one finds the appropriate sex organ, a mechanized vagina for Ginger and an adjustable dildo for Fred. As the male user enters into Ginger, she feels this and sends a message asking Fred to thrust out accordingly. Since the woman moves too, much of Garriott's massive code base is dedicated to hashing through data about who is doing what and determining the proper response for the robots.

Physically, Fred and Ginger are almost exclusively focused on points of genital contact. The exception is the "wings." These armatures provide a very rough sense of the rest of your partner's anatomy. They track the motion of your hands along the surface of your bedmate's virtual body, making no attempt to render subtleties like earlobes or nipples. They mainly just stand in for places you might be prone to hang on to: breast, torso, ass cheeks, and back of the head. The arms cover a large volume of space, but they also fold into a compact form that allows a single robot to be stored in a good-sized suitcase. The team planned for two more arms to allow v-lovers to feel the glide of each other's fingertips, but they've decided that the intricacies of that feature will have to wait for a future release.

Xan joined to create characters and animation, and she ended up with all of the demo's programming as well. But the iTeam's objectives have recently become more ambitious. They want a system that lets users all over the world come together using any skin they choose and start building their own scenes from day one. This is where I come in.

"James, the little ones tell me you are very good with networks."

"I've played around a little. I can't say I'm a 3D wizard though."

"I think this is okay. Maybe you have heard of NOD?"

I should have seen this coming. The whole reason I'm involved with these mecha-molesters is because a billionaire game maven seems unnaturally interested in them. Why should it surprise me that they'd use the same tech platform to pursue their deviant agendas?

Now that I think about it, NOD is perfect for the iTeam too. Being a feckless user-driven environment, it largely falls to the players to entertain themselves. The principal activity they've discovered is to copulate with all the frenetic energy and staggering variety one finds on earth.

More, probably. In NOD, you'll find everything from white weddings to gilded *scheisse* palaces. Bondage, age play, garment fixation, deformity adoration, and forbidden Orc-Ewok liaisons. But while this might seem exciting and new, it really boils down to spicy chat and some ribald but low-fi animation. Behind it is old-fashioned jerking off. Which, while amusing and effective, is perhaps in need of an update. This is the iTeam's mission.

"Absolutely. Nutting Over Data. I try to have all my sex there. It's cheap, hygienic, and nobody knows I'm a dog."

"A dog? Ah, you are kidding. But what you say is correct. Even more important, they are the only major world with the truly open-source software, so we can modify it to our, ah . . . specific needs. This is what you must now do: hook us up."

"That will not be trivial."

"Ya. So we give you four weeks."

The traditional absurd deadline. "What's the hurry?"

"We want to leak video then. So we can get TODD invite for formal launch."

TODD is a rapidly growing tech conference held annually in New York. The name stands for Totally Obsessed with Digital Depravity, and its founders conceived it as an antidote to the earnest nerdiness of the establishment's Technology Entertainment Design seminar, "TED." The target participants are dissolute digerati from all over the world, and the occasion tends to punch above its weight in terms of media coverage. Given their daily ration of boring cell phones and laptops, the tech press is notoriously receptive to stories with a little flesh tone.

"Formal launch. That implies you have a business plan."

"An artist is concerned about the filthy money?"

"They say it's the root of all evil. So if your filthy robots are going to enslave humanity, I suppose we'll need some pretty soon."

"But our robots will be very clean. Dishwasher safe, and they won't give you gonorrhea. The Dancers, we call them. The name is important. We want them to be elegant, classy. Like Fred and Ginger. Like iPhone. Expensive to make, but we get by so far."

"But eventually . . ."

"Eventually we need servants to peel our grapes, so yes, I have been talking to some people. You do not need to worry with this now. You worry about your work. We made the decision to start with a ready proto-type, so we keep more equity."

"Speaking of equity . . ."

"Ya, ya. What is your 'end,' yes?"

"A girl's gotta eat."

"Right. We must all sign the papers soon. When we get corporate structure set up. A business, it must be capitalized. So, with all that, we determine correct shares very soon. But I guarantee"—she leans over and caresses the back of my neck—"we make you happy."

We both know that signing up for a venture without having the business elements on paper at the outset is totally moronic. Is Olya just reflexively trying to manipulate a number-dumb video geek, or does she really think that brandishing her cleavage at me like it's a mind-control ray will make me do what she says? Excellent breasts have elicited from me a long list of ill-advised actions, but their allure tends to wear off after a few hours of coding.

"Well, I guess we're working for love, not money."

Of course, in the workplace, money is the only thing that actually *counts*. That's true often enough in the bedroom as well. People say that sex drives technology, but they're skipping a step. Money drives technology. Sex is just one of the few things people are reliably willing to pay for.

But I'm getting paid in any case. What she doesn't know is that I might get fired from my real job if I queer this relationship by digging in my heels over a fantasy fortune.

Olya flashes a feral smile. "That is the correct attitude. Welcome to our team, Mr. Pryce." She takes my hand in both of hers. "We'll enjoy having you."

II

THE KING OF HEARTS

22

After the meeting, I'd planned to spend the next twelve hours in bed, but the lure of Olya's challenge proves too strong to ignore. So instead, I go to my office to start downloading the NOD software developer's kit, the files one uses to create customized NOD worlds.

A text from Blake asking me to breakfast disrupts this plan. He's chosen Demeter, a painfully recherché cafe near his apartment that's advanced the recent farm-to-table obsession to the possibly satirical point of allowing diners to inspect online the genealogy of the chickens supplying their eggs. Hoping a $34 thoroughbred omelet can at least do something for my hungover stomach, I head toward SoHo.

Blake's idea of breakfast varies widely from mine. As I walk into the haute-country dining room, I see him already surrounded by food, conducting a meeting. A tall, svelte gentleman in an ostentatiously well-tailored black cashmere suit is delivering a heated lecture, jabbing his finger twice over the remains of his French toast. Blake gives me a "one sec" gesture and turns his blank business face back to his companion. I go in search of some coffee.

Who in the world gets to talk to Blake Randall that way?

When I return, the guy has vanished, and Blake waves me over. I sit, noticing the absence of a menu.

"So I'm not your first breakfast." I tilt my eyes toward the door.

Blake isn't fielding inquiries about the argument. He just says, "Fourth, actually."

"You must be a hell of a morning person."

"The empire of trade tends to swift decay."

"Right. I assume your sister told you that I think Billy has started another one of his experimental games?"

Blake nods.

I continue. "So if you follow the clues in the riddle he sent out, they take you to a private NOD sim that's a replica of the castle from Sade's *120 Days of Sodom*."

"What's the point?"

"I don't know yet. Do you have any idea why your brother would be particularly interested in the Marquis de Sade?"

"No. Though he seems to delight in torturing me. Whatever this is, that'll be his ultimate objective." Blake goes pensive. Then he asks, "Can you, given your skills, ah, make this thing go away?"

"There are steps we could take to obstruct him. But someone with Billy's resources, if he wants to put something on the web, it would be very hard to stop him. Also, I don't know why you'd want to do that. Right now, it's our only line on him. My advice would be to tread very lightly until we know more. If we start attacking his boxes, he might go to ground again."

"Understood. What else?"

"I've found a group of people at GAME that your brother's been spying on."

A neutral nod from Blake.

I ask, "It doesn't surprise you to hear that?"

"Nothing you could tell me about my brother's behavior would surprise me. Spying is not unusual for him. As a child, he had a mania for it. He'd gotten ahold of a video camera by his sixth birthday. The same impulse led him to become a hacker. He's always been obsessed with snooping around in other people's affairs. Trying to learn their secrets." Blake stops for a moment, recalling something unpleasant. He blinks and then asks me, "So you've found files he kept on these colleagues?"

"Not yet. But his arrest in Boston was due to a conflict with someone in the group, and Billy clearly had an abnormal interest in these people. I'm insinuating myself among them to find out why. They've picked me up for this thing they're working on."

"Thing?"

I'm not sure why, but I can't bring myself to tell him. The Dancers just seem like something I need to keep to myself for the time being. Beyond the trouble I have getting my tongue around the word "teledildonics," I just don't know how he would react.

"Yeah. They're working on force feedback gadgets for these virtual worlds. So you can see the connection to your brother's pursuits."

Blake looks up at the ceiling. "So I'm paying your firm three hundred dollars an hour for you to play video games and tinker with vibrating joysticks?"

I have to suppress a smile at how close he comes to the mark. "You're paying us because we're adept at finding hackers in hiding. If your brother were into bird-watching, you'd have people out in a swamp somewhere."

He screws up his face like his salmon cake has gone off, shaking his head minutely. Then he exhales and closes his eyes. I'm disturbed at my jolt of anxiety that he might not approve this iTeam infiltration, and I'll have to resign my new post. The Dancers have excited me well beyond their possible relevance to my assignment. Odd that last night's virtual tryst has inspired the first real passion I've felt in months.

A waiter arrives to interrupt Blake's consideration. Skinny and unkempt, the guy's wearing chunky fashion-nerd glasses and sports a very thick, slightly off-color handlebar mustache, a parody of the kind seen on jazz age French waiters.

His accent is equally preposterous. As he sets a silver-domed plate in front of Blake and says, "Dessert, *compliments de le maître!*" it occurs to me that both are fake. He whips off the cover. Too slowly I recall that this is not a French restaurant.

Then the smell hits.

Lying on that field of pristine china like a bloating mackerel is a prodigious turd. A garnish of parsley and lemon serves to emphasize the thing's foul menace.

Blake leaps out of his seat. But the horror only hits his eyes. By the time he's standing, the veneer of control has locked back into place. He opts for that ubiquitous word of disdainful reproach: "Really?"

The waiter appears nonplussed by this, as though his duet partner has wandered from the score. He lifts the plate toward Blake's face, offering it again.

Trying to forestall anything too disgusting, I lunge across the table, but I'm only able to get the tips of my fingers on the upper edge of the plate. The turd tumbles back onto the table and then falls to the floor, leaving most of its reeking mush on the linen. Other patrons catch the scent and gasp in outraged revulsion.

The waiter frowns at me. "*Merde,*" he says. Then he takes off running. When I move to follow, Blake places a staying hand at my ribs. I gather he wants to avoid any further spectacle.

Across the room, another scruffy dude pockets a small video camera as he slips out the exit. Blake nods at a concerned diner to indicate he's okay. Seeing several financial luminaries on their feet, I realize he probably knows half the people in here.

He smiles broadly, delivering a fine rendition of the pie-in-the-face-at-Davos good humor charade. He says to the room, "Please forgive the disturbance, everyone. Another one of our adoring fans, I'm afraid." This gets a few knowing chuckles, but much of the crowd is still murmuring with opprobrium. I see a tiny muscle under Blake's eye start to twitch.

Demeter's owner bursts out of the kitchen looking like she actually *has* eaten something repellent. A crack team of gloved busboys follow her and attack the table like a trained hazmat squad.

Before Blake steps off with the owner, he says, "James, find my brother. Do whatever you need to do."

23

The weekend is filled with all-night work sessions for the iTeam. That means I spend sleep-deprived days making gross animation in NOD to establish Jacques as an avid player of Billy's game. Having to choreograph such vile puppet shows while barely clinging to consciousness proves to be a form of torture that would warm Sade's heart. However, the positive effect of all this virtual vice is that I haven't once indulged my compulsion toward dangerous RL depravity since I met with the twins.

As I delve into the lecherous minutiae of Billy's hybrid world, I find his ultimate purpose has become even less clear to me. While Sade's book is pretty good material on which to base yet another piece of virulent agitprop, we've assumed from the beginning that he's working to seriously attack his older brother. The stunt at Demeter, though unnerving, seemed juvenile and used a fairly limiting medium. I'm sure he has a more harmful message for Blake, but for now, I don't see the stiletto in his garter belt.

Maybe what we need is a strip search. Perhaps Billy has concealed his real agenda under all these layers of virtual-world frippery. His game timeframe is unlikely to accord with mine, which puts me in the position of wanting to know the outcome of a game without having to play it. So there's really only one thing to do:

Cheat.

Today I will spend the morning compromising the virtue of an innocent server.

Doing so is the skill I have the longest practice in. Fittingly, given my new job with the Dancers, the first thing I ever penetrated for sexual reasons was a computer. Even for a twelve-year-old, hacking has in it something of the same thrill of a successful seduction.

As with a real seduction, there are many ways to tempt a system. Unfortunately, given the male-dominated ranks of practicing hackers, penetration lingo tends toward distastefully sexualized terminology. At Red Rook we call script kiddies necrophiliacs, since they are looking for zombie systems with brain-dead security. "Physical" attackers, who actually break into a facility, are rapists. The most common type of system compromise is the inside job. These people are onanists: they represent the organization fucking itself. Normal hackers are Rohypnotists, always trying to slip something dangerous inside you. I prefer the more civilized approach of convincing someone that they actually want to sleep with me. I like to be gentle about it too.

The host of Billy's *Savant* box, Scream Comm, isn't such a roundheels as to use social-plus-mom's-maiden for verification, but she does allow users to reset their passwords by answering security questions. The internet is refreshingly promiscuous in its development methods. When working on a site, you check what other people are doing and just take the code or procedure you need. This practice makes it easy and fast to get things up and running, but it allows bad ideas to spread like mayonnaise. In this case, the problem is the queries used to establish a user's identity: parents' middle names, city of birth, first car, first pet, high school mascot, favorite movie. I don't know where these questions came from, but almost everyone uses them. And they're not very good.

I have answers to all of them for Billy except favorite movie, and for that one, I have a strong feeling about *The Game*. In the end, his high school mascot, the lion rampant, gets me in. I quickly create a stealth admin account and reset his password back to the old one. A lightweight process copies an image of the hard drive to a secure Red Rook server. When that comes back complete, I start drilling into it.

But what I find is a dry hole.

Billy's been quite careful in making sure that nothing in this public-facing server points to his current location. The whole NOD install that constitutes *Savant* was uploaded two weeks before the GAME party from an open proxy in Taiwan. The disk contains no documents that might give a read on Billy's plans. All I have from him is the source code, which is spread out over thousands of objects and will take days or even weeks to untangle. And in all likelihood that process will be futile anyway.

His players, on the other hand, have left loads of material to sift through. There are thousands of nefarious cartoons, of course, but I also see several offerings containing live action. Some of these are from mainstream porn, including a stimulating clip from *Marquis de Sade* starring Rocco Siffredi's monster cock. The nastier vignettes degenerate into low-rent amateur stuff barely related to the source material.

However, some of the most recent submissions come from groups of people making original pornography explicitly for the game. Today there's a new video holding top billing for the "Dog's Breakfast" story. It stars two Great Danes, both naturals in front of the camera.

The segment has high production values: good video quality, nice candlelight, and even a gesture at period costumes. At first, I resist the notion that someone in the eighteenth century would adorn his animals in feathered tricorne hats. But the most cursory research convinces me that the urge to costume one's pet is fundamental to mankind.

These homemade videos, irrespective of their quality, share one thing in common: they've all been declared winners for their vignette.

Maybe Billy's sending a simple message by elevating those clips: in this contest, images of real people are preferred. He didn't set up this sprawling virtual infrastructure to compile a scrapbook of odious little films, he wants to see the stories *enacted*. So his players' formerly virtual activities leach into the real world. The Bleed in action.

Curious though that when Billy rewards his more creative players for their accomplishments, they tend to stop playing. Or at least they stop posting new videos and go silent in the forums.

Now, why would that be?

I think he must be graduating them into an otherwise locked part of his game. And I suspect Blake's breakfast is an example of how these secret levels play out. They're still enacting elements from Sade's despicable script, but out in the real world, and sometimes with unwilling costars.

Olya's disrupted necklace delivery is probably another example. Though the reference behind it eludes me at first. There are a couple of possibly relevant scenes, but I'll bet it derives from the way Sade's villains mark their victims for specific tortures by decorating their necks with different ornaments. A promise from Billy of future persecution.

What strikes me about that idea is that if you read ahead in the book, you quickly get into some horrible behavior. Right now we're still in the first month, and already the stories gleefully violate a number of state and federal laws, to say nothing of the dictates of hygiene. Once into the month of February, we're talking about mutilations and murder. And so the question becomes:

Where does it stop?

Maybe that's exactly what Billy wants to find out.

24

That afternoon, I remind Xan of the interview she owes me, and we end up in the back corner of a busy French bistro in Alphabet City.

"So for this documentary I'm working on," I say, "I wanted to get a better sense of Gina Delaney. You were already teaching when she enrolled at PiMP. But weren't you two both '03 at MIT also?"

"That's right."

"Were you friends?"

Xan stirs the martini she's drinking and sets aside the olives before tasting it. "Yeah, we were friends. Especially our freshman year."

"Did you have a falling out?"

"Not really. That spring she withdrew from school near the end of the semester."

"She was depressed?"

"Quite."

"Something specific bring it on?"

Xan nods vacantly. Then she recovers herself and looks at me sharply. "James, I'll tell you this if I must, but you can't go putting it in your docudrama."

"Okay. Deep background helps."

She takes a slow breath. "So Gina was raised as some kind of religious nutter. This hellfire church her parents belonged to. Not just strict . . . weird. There are more of them in Boston than you might think. But she claws her way out of their local slum and goes to MIT. She's a brilliant engineer. Not just smart, but someone even we Beavers think is a *freak*. But college isn't all work. Anyone who's raised that way is going to experiment a bit once they're at liberty. She doesn't take it *too* far, so things are just ducky." Xan takes an olive off her cocktail spear. "That is, until she meets the *boy of her dreams*."

"And who was that?"

"One of your lot actually. Maybe you know Blake Randall?"

I pride myself on my poker face, but I guess Xan is able to read the word "holyfuckingshit" in my eyes.

"You do know him," she says.

I put on a thoughtful expression. "Yeah. Two years above me. I saw him at parties."

"Hmm . . . ," she says, still observing me.

"So, ah, I take it something happened between him and Gina?"

"Right, so we get hauled over to one of those inane Porcellian parties—everyone wearing rep ties and talking shite about sailing and hunting." This makes me wince inwardly since I'd enjoyed many such occasions. The Beavers always have been barbarians.

She continues. "So Blake is there, and someone introduces him to Gina. She was a very pretty girl as you might know, and so they're quite taken with each other. Maybe he thinks he's going to score, but Gina doesn't really play that way. Fine. So this bloke starts to woo her. Boat rides up the Charles. Picnics at his country house, if you can imagine such bollocks. Treating her like they're in a Jane Austen novel. But that's just how she believes it's supposed to be. He's hot and rich, and probably has a whole line of girls, but he's putting in time with Gina."

"Doesn't sound so bad."

"No, it doesn't. Not until he gets impatient." She leans back, quiet now.

"Did she press charges?"

Xan waves away the idea. "It wasn't like that. She comes back to the dorm in a party dress and tears. One of those big black-tie dinners you all seem to insist upon. So she has a little too much champagne. Then a lot too much cognac. And then a fat cosmo for dessert. Wakes up without her knickers next to a Somewhat Distant Boyfriend."

Hearing this as an indictment of my gender, I try frowning to convey that I would never, ever even think of being involved in such an episode. Xan tsks at my display.

"Anyway, it's pretty typical. Gina is exactly the type of girl to get buyer's remorse. Little sophisticates that we are, her friends try to convince her that it's not a big deal. But she's different. For her it *is* a big deal. She doesn't blame him or anything, probably never told him she was a virgin. Anyway, he should have known. But what do you expect?"

I can only shake my head at the predatory nature of my brethren. I don't pull this off well, and Xan kicks me under the table.

"Oh, I know you're a pig just like the rest of them."

"So this messed her up enough to make her drop?"

"I don't think so. The problem was that her friends didn't understand. So she got the bright idea to talk things over with her mother."

"Yikes."

"Yeah. Her father showed up at the dorm that day, and she didn't come back. I guess some real fire and brimstone shite went down in the Delaney house that spring."

"And then she was back the next fall?"

"Yeah. Commuting from home. But I was in Barcelona my sophomore year. So we basically lost touch. I guess she lost touch with most of her friends. She went virtual."

"It sounds like she had some success with it."

"Oh yeah. Gina was troubled, but still a complete genius. That first start-up she joined, Ichidna Interface, was a one-woman show, wasn't it? But I'd have thought her greatest success would be getting out of that awful house and coming here."

"So she seemed better at PiMP?"

"Not at first. When I saw her at the welcome party, she was like a totally different person. Shaky, nervous . . . like she'd been too long in a space station and wasn't used to people."

Xan tells me how she reintroduced herself, and while Gina had remained as sweet as ever, she couldn't really look her in the eye. Xan asked about some of her well-known professional triumphs, but Gina seemed like she was yearning to escape her former work, or at least the isolation she self-imposed while doing it.

Gina said to her, "I looked up my new classmates, and they all seem so creative and interesting. I'm—I'm just excited to be here where I can maybe make some new . . . things. Ah, you know, work on my own ideas."

Recalling that pitiful sentence makes Xan stop her narration and squeeze her eyes shut for a second.

Xan stayed with her a bit more, but eventually she got pulled away to welcome other new students. But she kept an eye on Gina.

"The poor girl just stood there, fairly shaking with terror. She kept checking her phone like she had a preemie in the neonatal ward. I could tell she was mortified by her awkwardness. One of our friendlier lads tried to chat her up, but he didn't get past one-word answers. I could see Gina's eyes start to well up. Obviously she'd made some kind of death pact with herself to resist her shyness. So she just stood there rooted in place. Alone and miserable."

Xan tells me she couldn't bear watching it anymore and moved to rescue her old friend. But before she got there, she saw Billy stomp his way over to Gina's side. He put his fist up in her face and said something in a hostile tone. Xan couldn't make it out at first and rushed toward them to stop any kind of trauma this little kook might inflict. But she pulled up short when she saw Gina smile for the first time that night. Later she figured out what Billy said to her:

"Best of seven. Bet I crush you in four. I'm throwing rock."

As Xan tells it, Gina's eyes lit up, and she said, "Bring it."

Rock Paper Scissors. The child's amusement that obsesses geeks the world over, since it forms the conceptual underpinning for certain types of video games. Contests can become mental duels requiring Jedi-like powers of perception and dissimulation.

Billy came with scissors. Gina threw rock. Xan was relieved to hear her giggle. She decided to leave her in the hands of her unlikely savior.

A while later, Xan witnessed Gina actually drinking a beer and laughing with a group of her new classmates who had started a mini Rochambeau tournament. She noticed her exchange a secret smile of thanks with Billy. For his part, he seemed utterly in awe that fortune had blessed him with such a moment.

"So playing a kid's game isn't exactly the kind of brilliant wit that's going to get you invited to meet the queen. But any game is a sort of conversation. And I mean, the lingua franca of PiMP is Klingon, for Christ's sake. Anyway, because of Billy, Gina's suddenly no longer this schizoid loser on the verge of tears. She's *winning*. Both of them love games, and because of that, along with some luck, I think they won a little love for each other too. In Billy's case, a lot. Things got better for Genes after that. She seemed more comfortable eventually . . . When you could catch her offline."

"Offline?"

"Yeah, she was working a lot with NOD. Playing there too, I guess. That's where she and Billy would hang out." I flash to Nash's description of the pictures in her apartment. The family photos of avatars.

"Sounds like the makings of quite a romance."

"Yeah, we all thought so. But it seems Gina's mind was elsewhere."

"Really? Where?"

"Well, nowhere at first. But then, after a while . . ."

"What?"

"She started fucking Olya."

"You mean . . . ?"

"Yes, James. Hot girl-on-girl action. Close your mouth, dear, you look retarded."

"So—"

"Yeah, software aside, the main thing Gina developed upon graduating was Sapphic tendencies. It's not that unusual. The women here in New York are amazing."

"And Olya?"

"Her sexual persuasion? I'd say it's carnivorous."

"Like Catherine the Great?"

"More like a praying mantis."

"I guess an aggressive interest in sex is only appropriate considering our project."

"That's not really what I mean. But forget it. We can't be gossiping about our partners in crime, can we?"

"Were they, ah, *dating* when . . ."

"I don't really know much about it. I was in Hong Kong when it happened. Before I left, I heard they'd had a couple fairly public blowups. The rumor was that the relationship was flaming out. Gina was devastated. Olya can be cold as winter in Moscow—"

"And Russian campaigns don't end in parades."

"Exactly. Anyway, I came back early for the funeral."

"So did people blame Olya for pushing her over the edge?"

"No. We all knew Gina was a bit of a head case. There was talk, but you can't really blame a person for someone else's suicide, can you?"

"I'm sure it happens."

"Yeah, now that you mention it, I guess that's what started her famous row with Billy. But then he was a head case as well."

"Does Olya blame herself?"

"I wouldn't mention it to her."

25

Back at GAME, things do not go smoothly.

Xan pulls me into the iTeam's workroom, affectionately known as the Orifice. She needs a new data loop for debugging the sex avs, which are still twisting into positions not seen outside of particularly violent *Road Runner* cartoons. The session runs well until Ginger drops into a catatonic loop and begins humping my kneecap. Not for the first time, I ask myself whether we're doing the devil's work by making sex subject to technical difficulties. Or maybe God is as prudish as they say, and through us he's working a subtle sort of revenge against the unchaste.

Even outside of mundane moral categories, I have to confess that after my initial fascination abated, I began feeling some unease with the larger aims of our project. IT is a technology meant to address the eternal problem that you can't have unlimited sex with whoever you want. But as such, it introduces its own set of limitations.

For me, sex represents the zenith of human experience, and much of my mental energy has always been dedicated to endlessly rehearsing the act and scheming about how to achieve it. Nature has given us this profound ability to really *connect* with one another in a way that feels nothing short of divine when done right.

As technology marches ever onward, we immerse ourselves in more and more connection but accept compromises that reduce its finer qualities. A hurried cell phone conversation is, and will always be, a far cry from words spoken while gazing into your lover's eyes. The rise of email, chat, and SMS has robbed us of even the emotive color of our voices. And so, with our current venture, do we risk allowing some of the ineffable beauty of Eros to leak out along the phone lines?

Sex had seemed pristine in this regard. But now we're making inroads. Excavating the mysterious and secret shrine. As a lifelong technophile, I can't turn back any more than an archaeologist on the precipice of a tomb, but I have felt the occasional shiver of dread that we're setting out to defile something sacred.

In counterpoint to my uneasy reflections, Olya and Garriott start a round of gleeful sparring over the spec. This culminates in Olya throwing the 150-page document at him. The impact knocks his hand loose from its hold on one of Fred's retaining rings. With the air pressure on high, Fred's plastic member rockets into the wall and shatters just over Xan's head.

We're expecting a well-deserved freak-out, but Xan just sighs and says, "We're not building the bloody Panama Canal here, are we? I should like to live to feel the fruits of this grand endeavor. So let's be more careful with our private parts, shall we?"

Later that day, I check in with *Savant*. Already the number of players has jumped by a factor of ten since that first post about it in the NOD forums. The formerly rather idle Château de Silling now hosts a continuous stream of NODlings, from cyber-swingers looking to meet like-minded avs to machinima drones obsessively working their way through the available scenes.

Billy's conjured all these people to help him build something, but despite their labor, I can't make out the structure. I'm sure his game holds a story beyond the retelling of Sade's malignant fairy tale, but so far he's left me in suspense. Though if he's aiming to honor *120 Days,* then we need to shut him up long before he gets to the climax.

26

Though much of my life is lived online in domains defined by data, long experience has shown me that the human antennae, quirky though they are, can pick up signals invisible to any machine. To the extent that Gina's death is a significant flash point for Billy's hostility, I want to see where it happened.

So the next morning finds me standing in front of 301 Conover Street in Red Hook: Gina Delaney's last apartment. My secondary reason for coming here is that since I'm supposed to be working on this documentary, I should be able to produce a bunch of relevant raw footage if called upon. This is a pretty obvious choice for coverage, and so I'm trying to achieve arty framings of the semiconverted warehouse against the bright January sky. A small sign in front indicates that unit 4B is for rent and that interested parties should inquire with the landlord in 1A.

From the police report, I remember Gina lived in apartment 4B. Given the newspaper jammed in the building's entrance and the cloud of marijuana smoke coming from a ground-floor window, I'm guessing that the landlord won't mind if I just let myself in. At the top of a groaning spiral of stairs, I find the apartment door ajar as well.

The place has been redone. The walls painted, the floors reconditioned. The raw wood columns to which she attached those fatal pulleys have been sanded and covered with thick white acrylic.

After taking a couple photos, I start a shot that I hope will evoke spectral wandering. Midway through, I jump at a loud creak coming from the front door. A small black lady stands there, making no effort to conceal the joint she's holding.

"What are you doing, son?"

"Oh, sorry, I was just looking at the apartment."

"You want to rent it?"

"Maybe."

"But you taking pictures like one of them sickos?"

"Sickos?"

"People come because of the girl that died here."

I flash her a photo of Billy and a portrait of Benjamin Franklin. "This guy come here?"

"Oh yeah. He's a strange one."

"How so?"

"He came three days after. Took lots of pictures. Then he just stood there for a long time. It got late, so I come up to ask him what he's doing. He said he's 'conducting a séance.' But I seen a real séance in Flatbush, and that boy, he was just standing there."

After I thank her for the information, she lingers to watch me for a while but then departs.

I walk to the large bank of windows along the front of the apartment to take in what would, in a better neighborhood, be a million-dollar prospect of the Manhattan skyline. In the background is the mercantile majesty of the financial district, with a gorgeous front view of the Statue of Liberty standing off to the side, her arm outstretched as though she's hailing a cab on her way to some important meeting. In the foreground is the ruined beauty of Red Hook, presenting a stark contrast to the spider-eyed gleam of Wall Street. The decayed industrial port now bears clear signs of financial miscegenation. A tony coffee shop inhabiting a former loading dock here, a shiny BMW zipping past rusted hulks there. It's like a bleached coral reef spontaneously regenerating. And yet still dominating the area are giant loading cranes standing as though sentinels for long-forgotten gods of industry.

My camera feels drawn to them, and I reflect on the way that the once-packed shores of Red Hook, which sat quiet for so long as blue-collar activity fled, are slowly growing new factories filled with artisans creating things that exist somewhere on a continuum between idea and object. Figments fixed in our electrical web that you can see and hear, and maybe soon feel, but that would disappear if you tried to remove them. Gina spent her life in this fiber-optic dream catcher.

Beyond the windows, the crystalline winter day has lured people outside to enjoy the unaccountable warmth of the sun. Kids joyously traverse a huge piece of playground equipment. I wonder what Gina saw when she looked out onto this world. What was it that made her first retreat from it, and then finally decide to abandon it forever?

I know the answer is usually just malfunctioning brain chemistry. But I can't picture how all those misfiring neurons twisted her eyes. How could her filter have been so dark as to compel her to set her grisly machine in motion and make the last thing she saw her own blood spraying the wall?

27

Today Olya demands a "Stakhanovite" effort from the team, and we do our best to emulate the Soviet earth-moving hero, though as latte-sipping developers, the results are weak. But we beaver with a will late into the night.

Xan is the first to break. I notice a long period of silence from her fancy Dvorak keyboard and turn to find her asleep. The weight of my gaze wakes her, and without a word, she rises from the table and walks out of the room. Garriott's eyes follow her longingly.

A few minutes later, she bursts back into the Orifice, flushed and breathless, vibrations of panic projecting ahead of her. She drops a necklace-sized felt jewel case on the worktable.

Garriott asks, "Good lord. What's the matter?"

Xan takes a second to steady herself and then says, "I . . . these men outside—ah . . . grabbed me."

I jump out of my seat. "Are you okay? What happened?"

She wraps her arms around herself. "Yeah. I'm fine. I—I was just leaving, and there was this car parked on Suffolk with two creepy guys with cameras leaning against it. I walk past, and one of them snatches my arm and says, 'You need to give this to your friend Olya.'" She points at the case. "I ran back here and locked the back door. I think they might have been following me."

Olya steps over to the case. Before I can object, she flips open the lid, which blocks my view of its contents. Whatever it is makes her teeth grind together. She spins toward the door, and I have to move fast to get in front of her. She tries to push through me.

"Olya, no! Stop. Let me. I'll take care of it."

"Fuck off—" She keeps struggling.

"Garriott, get over here and hold her."

With that laughable suggestion, I race down the hall toward the stairs to the alley. I can hear what sounds like someone trying to yank the door open. There's a short burst of muffled swearing. I pause until they're really pulling hard, then slam the latch forward, and the door wrenches outward. The person on the other side is caught off balance, and a jerk on his ankle sends him toppling to the ground.

I vault up the seven steps, scanning for the partner, but it seems he's alone. I'm about to jump on him, but then I recognize the steel bone through his nose. He's just Goat, an authorized PODling.

He says, "What the fuck?"

"Did you run into two guys coming in here?"

"Wha . . . Uh, yeah. Going through the gate. They were—"

I'm already running to the alley's entrance. Looking right and left, at first I don't see anything. But then a black Dodge Charger peels out, heading the wrong way up Suffolk. The parked cars obstruct my line of sight, and I can't get past them quickly enough to see the plate as the car makes a screeching left on Rivington, swiping out the brake light of an innocent Audi.

They're bombing up Essex before I can make the turn. The Audi's alarm wails as I entertain the bleak thought that dealing with a single determined stalker is challenge enough. And Billy's called up a whole battalion of them to torment Olya.

Back down in the POD, Garriott brews Earl Grey while Olya rolls out the third degree on Xan, who has recovered enough to get irritated.

"I said I didn't turn around to watch them. I, being a meek little Asian girl, as you're quite fond of pointing out, was fleeing!"

"But you must have seen—" Olya notices me come in and inquires, "So?"

"They took off before I could get there. I scared the shit out of Goat, however. Maybe they bailed when they saw him coming in."

Olya lets out a long exhausted breath and cracks her neck. She gives
Xan a tender kiss on the cheek. "We're glad our Sashinka is okay," she
says. "Maybe late at night we have this strong man escort you home."
Then she leaves.

Garriott and Xan seem to be repressing a desire to look at each other.
I step over and pick up the case. Glued to the velvet backing is a horrific
mess of blood, bone, and metal. My mind takes a second to identify the
mutilated remnants of a human jaw with a large hole saw stuck through
it. Tooth fragments decorate the deep blue fabric like the pearls the case
was made to hold. The circumference of the bit is filled with some kind
of bloody meat. A reference to Gina of course, but within Billy's game
world, perhaps also to the *120 Days* vignette wherein a deranged libertine
uses a hollow drill to extract cylinders of flesh from his victims.

Attached to the sharp center point of the bit is a little sheet of paper
bearing a calligraphic scrawl:

I demand tooth for tooth still
So forever you will
Hear the sound of a drill

Though Olya rallied quickly, for a moment there, I think Billy's present
found its mark. I assume the bone is artificial, and the rest comes from a
local butcher. The display is gruesome enough without considering the
alternatives.

Garriott seems like he's about to say something but doesn't.

"Tomorrow we're going to have to talk about revving our security
here," I say.

They both just nod.

"I'll go check on her."

I slip into her office and shut the door behind me. Olya is gazing out her
window. She doesn't turn around.

"Why does Billy think you're to blame for Gina Delaney's death? What
does he want from you?" I ask.

"I don't think about what crazy little men want. He is not significant.
Like a mosquito."

"But we need to take certain measures. Aren't you concerned that he might come after the Dancers to get your attention? Or"—I think about Garriott's video of their fight—"do something violent?"

She gives me a long considering stare and then rolls her eyes. "Let's be real. Billy is an artsy *sooka* fuckwit, not a dangerous psychotic. And we make a slippery robot. Not a nuclear bomb."

"But, Olya, if I'm to believe the numbers you used to lure me onto this project, every time you walk through those doors with your silver cases, you're dragging millions of dollars behind you. What if he figures out he could use them to fuck with you?"

She turns down her mouth, acknowledging the point. "Ya. Zhimbo, you are correct. So maybe we get a safe."

But I think back to the look on Billy's face when Gina kissed him and then the photos of Gina's corpse. The message of revenge in this latest gift of jewelry to Olya tells me that Billy's rage is escalating. I don't think we have long before his next move.

And is it a safe the iTeam needs, or bodyguards?

28

Since the internet serves as high-test fertilizer for conspiracy theories, any game that harnesses the collective brain of an online community will have members who want to talk about what's *really* going on. With Alternate Reality Games in particular this tendency is overt. Solving the riddle of who's sponsoring it (and to what corporate end) takes on an importance that can supersede the game's actual story line. Given the obscurity in which Billy's cloaked his contest, I'm not surprised to find posts like this one:

| Anna_Lynne_Goss

Joined:01/09/15
Posts:047

Location:
In Deep | Let me put to rest all this nattering about what you have to do to "win" a vignette and get "promoted." Here's a list of current winners that haven't yet seen custom submissions:

Day 3, Scene 3 -- Romeo in Juliet [1971]
Day 4, Scene 5 -- Strapped [2009]
Day 7, Scene 2 -- Paradise Lust [1973]
Day 7, Scene 4 -- No Mercy [2000]
Day 8, Scene 1 -- Marquis de Sade [1994]
Day 11, Scene 3 -- The Whorestia [1972]
Day 15, Scene 2 -- Dante's in Fern's Hole [1974] |

. . .

And so it goes. Anyone see the pattern
here?

Like it's a coincidence that X-rated
literary adaptations from the early
seventies occupy half the top spots. Yes,
Ronnie seemed more interested in Sade
than his source texts. But please!

These rumors about the Pyros are total
bullshit. *Savant* is not an enlistment
site for an insane cult. It is not an FBI
sting operation. You don't have to do
anything violent or illegal to win. Just
pick the "right" porno and cash in.

This "game" is just a stupid marketing
gimmick to manufacture interest in
Exotica's back catalog. Let's not give
them the satisfaction. We're in NOD to
satisfy *ourselves*.

_Anna

For the most part, I have no idea what she's talking about. But one detail makes my hair stand on end: her line about "the Pyros." I should have known they'd come into this.

The Pyrexians are an urban legend, the demonic bogeymen of hardcore file-sharing rings. I first encountered references to them while assisting the FBI in penetrating a kiddie porn distribution network based out of Reno. The kind of low-rent psychos pushing that stuff often lead shifty, precarious lives. Any time someone in their circle disappeared, or an inexplicable tragedy struck, some credulous dolt would always name this shadowy group as the agent of fate.

Fans of torture porn, bestiality vids, and snuff films tend to obsess over their passions. Often, avid collectors call their compulsion "the Fever," another name for which is "pyrexia." Because supply is always severely limited, they constantly fantasize about abundant sources of new material. Seductive, then, to believe in the existence of this organization that possesses a massive reservoir of "the good stuff." That traffics in helpless victims while constantly turning out new ones, thereby controlling a global empire of sadistic violence. Of course, they're also very jealous of their treasure, and so you have to beware that certain material coming into your possession hasn't been stolen from them. If they catch you distributing it, you're marked for death. At once feared and revered, the Pyrexians represent a sort of Bilderberg group of kiddie porn.

At first, I thought the whole thing was a joke, one of many black fables from a marginal subculture. But in the crushed-anthill days following the Feds' first arrests, I discovered some genuinely worried conversations about them. Just as thieves fear each other more than the police, the same is apparently true of perverts.

From browsing the posts of early Château de Silling explorers, I can see wild theories cropping up that the place was a secret recruiting device for the Pyros.

But since the group is just a chimera from the folklore of the depraved, I decide to look into Anna's idea that someone made Château de Silling as a marketing stunt. While Billy's aims surely aren't commercial, if he's promoting players as a reward for such submissions, I should try to find out why. Which will require some diverting research.

I consult an online video service I belong to called Nutflux that specializes in soigné interface glosses on the Internet Adult Film Database. They also classify industry personnel according to everything from declared religion to "ejaculatory accuracy."

Four of the films she lists were all directed by the same individual, one Ronald Farber, a celebrated pioneer of modern erotica and I suppose the "Ronnie" that Anna tagged in her post. His detailed bio describes how in 1971, this lowly camera technician at a TV news station in Irvine, California, came out of nowhere to found Freyja Films, named after the Norse goddess of love. He created lush pornographic salutes to literary classics shot with the newly emerging video technology. His efforts, beginning with *Romeo in Juliet,* were well received. Freyja began minting money as the seventies porn explosion got under way.

Then in 1973, despite his obvious success, Farber took a large investment from the exploitation house Big Stick, run by "Big" Ben Mondano, a notorious industry asshole with reputed connections to organized crime. His product ran more to efforts like *Taste It, Don't Waste It,* parts 1–144, and so this merger of love and lust was a curious one to porn aficionados. The combined company was renamed Exotica Entertainment Enterprises, a.k.a. "Triple E."

Both Farber and Mondano died more than ten years ago, but Exotica has certainly thrived since then. The company is currently led by "Benito" Mondano Jr. and has become a diversified porn colossus. They're a huge blue-movie studio with a significant presence in the cable, pay-per-view, online, and mobile markets. They've got an adult novelty operation that sells everything from performance-enhancing herbal supplements to performance-obviating penile substitutes. They run the Amazone chain of high-end strip clubs, a sex education outfit, and even a political action committee.

Maybe I've let a specious forum post lead me off course here. I have trouble imagining why Billy might be interested in this specific porn company. Then I see at the bottom of their website that Exotica's headquarters are in New York above their Amazone flagship. Its location at Forty-sixth Street and the West Side Highway rings a bell. I check my notes and see that this is the address McClaren mentioned for the most recent of Billy's disorderly conduct charges. So maybe someone there was the last person to see Billy in the flesh.

29

At Amazone, Benito Mondano sits by himself in an aerie of leather couches commanding good views of the club's first floor. He's absorbed in a conversation on his cell phone, and a bouncer reads the paper on a stool next to the velvet barrier cutting off access to him.

I order a bottle of Michter's 25 from the bar and freak out the bartender when I take it from him as he's starting the tea ceremony prescribed for opening precious liquor.

Offering the bottle, I ask the bouncer, "Would Mr. Mondano like a drink?"

Without looking at me, the guy says, "He's got one, sir."

Mondano's eyes narrow at the label when I motion to him that I want a word. He gives a put-upon shrug to his security and hangs up his call. I walk up the short flight of stairs and introduce myself.

He looks like a sketch comedy cast member midway through a wardrobe change. Attired in the ugly suit and thick, too-short tie one expects from movie mobsters, he's adorned himself with bling-y D&G blue-tinted aviator shades and big diamond studs in both ears. Just the thing for schmoozing at Long Island nightclubs, but the kind of fashion choices that would provoke a capo of the old school to violence.

He lets me marinate in a decent Brando soul-stare for a while. Then he smacks his lips and in a much less accurate gravelly whisper says, "So . . . tell me, what can I do for you?"

A curious performance for someone not yet forty. I almost accord him a facetious "Don," but manage to resist. "Mr. Mondano, I'm working on a documentary—"

With a world-weary glance at the heavens, he says, "Please, my friend, let me stop you right there. You can't shoot in the club. Distracts the ladies and—"

"No, no. I just want to ask you a couple questions." I pull out Billy's photo. "This is my subject. He's an artist who designs these controversial games. Anyway, kind of an elusive guy. Right now I'm trying to track him down." He pretends to ignore the picture. "I heard he was tossed out of here a couple weeks ago. Maybe he was taking some unauthorized video himself?"

"Some douchebag comes in here with a camera, and we find him somewhere he's not supposed to be, he'll be lucky if he just gets tossed out. Very lucky."

Well, aren't you the tough guy?

In my research on the family business, I'd found out that when his parents divorced, Benito's mother raised him in Newport Beach, California, about as far away from Ozone Park as you can get. After his father died, the porn elements of the Mondano empire had been carefully extricated from his other shady pursuits and given over to non-Syndicate professionals. I'll bet anyone with pungent connections had been warned to stay clear. Thus, Exotica was preserved until Benito was ready to take the helm.

So despite his affectations, this guy has about the same level of authentic Mafia upbringing that I do.

"You mean he might get arrested?"

He squints, testing my words for sarcasm, but then just shrugs it off. "We handle our own business here. If he's still making a scene once he's off my property, maybe the cops show up."

"What was he shooting?"

Mondano's eyes sweep across the three sirens pole-humping on different stages and then settle on me to inquire whether I'm actually blind or just stupid.

"So he wasn't trying to plant a hidden camera to record, say . . . you?"

Mondano sneers. "*Paisan . . .*" I want to tell him what this word actually means. "That's real flattering. Maybe the kid, your friend, was a fruit. But if so, there are many better places for him in this city."

"But maybe he was interested in you for other reasons."

He shakes his head as though I've suggested the schools chancellor is going to mandate Stripperobics for P.E. classes.

I point at the picture. "Billy is working on a game that may have some connection to Triple E." I wait for a response, but he just stares at me. I try, "So you're not involved in any kind of game that he's producing?"

"The only game I play is the simplest one there is: You give me money, I show you naked girls. You crank it until you get off. Game over. Everybody wins. Why would I want to play a different one?"

"Maybe you wouldn't. But you're in the media business. A lot of companies use 3D worlds for promotions that—"

"You know, you remind me a lot of this fucking guy." He points at Billy's photo.

"How's that?"

"You both talk like you're broadcasting from Neptune."

I smile. "Fair enough. Do you remember what he said to make you think that?"

"Yeah. He said something like, the fruits from my plains would dissolve into smoke and ashes. As I said, we don't really serve fruits here. And because of that pussy Bloomberg, there's no smoking either." He smiles at me, fishing for acknowledgment of his wit.

"Huh. What do you think that meant?"

"It meant that he was a fucking lunatic."

"Have you seen him since then?"

"If I had, he'd be real easy to find now."

"How's that?"

"He'd be in the ICU over at Roosevelt."

He accompanies this statement with a practiced glower, implying that question time is over, unless I'm looking to warm up the hospital bed reserved for Billy. I want to laugh, but taking in the guys he's recruited as bouncers makes me think that maybe Benito's resurrected his father's violent business culture. One's sense of legacy can burn hot.

I thank him for his time and leave the bottle.

30

A mobbed-up pornographer represents perfectly the twin obsessions of humanity: sex and violence. But while certainly of a piece with the Sadean content of *Savant*, Mondano's precise role is unclear. Maybe he's supposed to serve as inspiration for Billy's players.

Though they don't seem to need much prompting. The next morning I find this blog post from Blue_Bella, a doyenne of cyber-kink chroniclers:

My deviant darlings:

Blue_Bella watches with delight the recent exxxplosion in
concupiscent creativity sparked by *Savant*. So kudos to
all you carnal cartoonists and video voluptuaries.

However, your sapphire seductress views with some
concern recent reports of material mayhem attributed to
our new hobby:

Item 1: We all heard about the house fire in Henderson,
NV, caused by an amateur video troupe (filming day 13,
scene 2) shorting out a battery pack when the barrel
tipped over. Our thoughts are with the lead actor as he
recovers from his "extremely unusual penile trauma."

Item 2: One Dr. Hans Vleiben, assistant professor
of French literature at Portland State University, was

arrested yesterday on charges of harassment and public indecency. Our hero followed a fetching young femme into the bathroom of a local church. There he unveiled for her appreciation no fewer than five full enema bags he'd sequestered in his waistband. A scene ensued.

Vleiben's lawyer maintains that the incident was a case of "mistaken identity" and that "discussions pertaining to colon health" are protected by the First Amendment.

Item the third: Miami's Lee_Cherry now seeks legal advice regarding the revolting rendezvous she had with a fellow Savant who proposed they reprise day 29, scene 2 (simulated necrophilia, natch). Something she takes pains to emphasize she's "very into." Once at his studio, however, he proposed certain measures to make the encounter "as realistic as possible." Was he actually aiming for a scene much later in the book? We'll never know, since our heroine clocked him with a handy shovel and fled. Poor etiquette, you say? Lee defends herself: "I'm not into *real* necro at all. Especially if I have to be the dead one."

Where are we headed with all this virtu-real xXx-pollination? No one knows. But your periwinkle paramour's sources high in the *Savant* hierarchy cryptically hint that this *February* will be the hottest on record.

Blue_Bella is not amused. She's all in favor of a little spanky-panky, but she thinks *violence* is vile, and the Fever is a *sickness*. A real Savant keeps her mind open, but also her eyes.

As with *NeoRazi*, Billy's courting a blitzkrieg of lawsuits. And if Blue_ Bella's *Savant* source is right, even worse is yet to come. But her sniffy reaction to his February comment felt like a non sequitur. Maybe there's more to it. Something that makes her relate his words to the Fever.

The case during which I first heard rumors of the Pyrexians featured a lot of obscure code names and references to sinister groups. Some of these shared a particularly dire profile, and we thought they might all be aliases for the same imaginary entity. The Burning Lads, the Wetmen, the Febrillians.

Something about that last one seems related. "Febrile" is another word for "feverish," but it also shares a linguistic connection with the month February. I look it up: the Latin word for fever, *"febris,"* refers to the purging of the body through sweat. Our second month's name derives from an ancient Roman purification festival called Februa.

Flipping back through my Reno case files, I find correspondence among some wealthy collectors of rare etchings depicting brutal child murders. They discuss an apocryphal club of Victorian eroticists called the Februarian Society of Ring and Rod. This was the oldest extant allusion to such a group we found in our investigations. The association's name was mysterious though. The best my team could come up with was that it derived from various pagan religions' propensity to sacrifice children on leap days.

Blue_Bella's post implies that Billy wants to exploit his players' interest in evil cabals by convincing them that the Pyrexians are somehow involved with Château de Silling after all. I guess my target has done his research on traffic in black-market media, and in his game world, this group's aliases don't refer to an abstract state of erotic fever, but rather to Sade's *120 Days*. February, of course, being the month in which the most horrific atrocities are perpetrated in Silling's dungeon.

Whatever Billy's ultimate aims are, he must know that he doesn't really have any control over what his players do. We're already seeing them turn from naughty exhibitionism toward real violence.

What's the point of all this? Why convene this dangerous game?

It seems unlikely I'll learn the answer by passively watching it unfold. I'm going to have to really start playing along with him.

When I called my friend Adrian Paulson, he suggested we get together at one of these secret through-the-phone-booth bars. Why New Yorkers, otherwise inviolable in their self-regard, submit to jumping through such hoops for a cocktail, I'll never understand. In this case, his choice is made even more eccentric by demanding I meet him there at noon, when the place is certainly closed.

And yet the trick door opens at my push. He's sitting alone at a booth cut into the amber-lit cellar. Seeing my arrival, he stomps forward and lifts me into a fearsome bear hug that makes my spine crackle. He follows that with a kiss on the mouth before I'm able to extract myself from his grasp. Adrian is a big, blond Minnesotan who took up highly decadent ways after fleeing a stark Lutheran upbringing. The most apt description of him I remember from school was "the Viking drag queen." Not so much for his fashion sense but for the fact that he oozed this quality of pansexual theater. Also a certain amount of violence. He was the only person I knew in college who both wore ascots and got into brawls. Now he's the closest thing to a porn baron I know.

He found himself at loose ends after Boom 1.0 collapsed and decided to turn his web skills toward documenting the thing he cared most about: sex. His site could have ended up a worthless pornado trap, but he brought an edgy intellectual style to Compleat-jerk.com and somehow developed a loyal readership.

Since the last time I saw him, he's shaved his head, grown a blond devil's beard, and has a runic tattoo spiraling up his neck. He sports a black Armani suit, so I guess business isn't too terrible. Adrian grins and waggles his eyebrows under purple-tinted wraparounds.

He gives me a three-syllable "Dude" and then asks, "How's the cocklodoccus?"

"Nearing extinction. Thanks for meeting me."

"Been way too long." Adrian reels off a string of what sounds like Creole French to the guy waxing the floor. He stops pressing on his buffing machine and hustles to the bar, returning moments later with a gigantic tropical drink decked with a Calder mobile of fruit for Adrian and a double bourbon for me. Adrian tongues a cherry.

"So, Ade, how's business?"

"Business? This is art, brah. If it were business, I'd jab this skewer into my brain and then set myself on fire."

"Why's that?"

"The pirates, man. We spend all day thinking of interesting substances to rub on our 'photo interns' and ten seconds after they're posted to our premium section, I find torrents of them all over creation. Our customers are good loyal hand jockeys, but it's getting to be a lot to ask . . . The personals section, now, that's booming. Even though those Craigslist fuckers are cutting into it. 'Course we do a good job of finding some real freaks that make the network valuable. Ooh, and we've started flavors."

"Flavors?"

"The one we just put in beta is Rednekkid.com. If I see another shot of a girl in a hayloft pouring buttermilk on herself I swear I'll—well, I'll probably call her like the last one. But I'm getting close to being tired of it."

"But you're still making videos?"

"Everyone and their stepchildren are making videos. That's another problem."

"Ever do anything on commission?"

He grins. "Pryyyycie! I hadn't figured you for someone with such refined requirements. You having trouble explaining something complicated to your honey?"

"Nope. It's for work."

"Work? You change jobs on me? What's it for?"

"Confidential. Of course."

"I'm just playing. Seriously, what did you have in mind?"

"A scene from Sade, *120 Days*."

"Ahh, a Sadistic Savant, are we?" He smiles like he's pleased to hear this, but then quickly runs through the implications and frowns. "Wait a minute, this wouldn't be on assignment for one of those crypto-fascist law enforcement organizations you consort with, would it?"

"No. Nothing like that. I promise. I need three to five minutes of high-quality video. Live actors, good lighting. I was thinking maybe—"

"King of the Hill."

"What?"

"Day twenty-three, scene four. In which a man can only get off from being savagely beaten with canes in front of witnesses in the second-floor parlor of a brothel. Just before he nuts, he makes them *defenestrate* him into a pile of dung sitting in the courtyard below. Only then can he climax. The Sadisticats love that kind of shit. I even know a stunt man with, shall we say, liberal attitudes toward personal hygiene."

"Um, okay. You, ah, seem to know the book well."

"True. By nature I'm a lover not a biter, but in this business, it pays to be conversant in the ways of the world. That filthy little Frenchman carved out a whole dark continent we've spent the past two centuries exploring."

"So . . ."

In a strange display of delicacy, Adrian writes a number on a cocktail napkin and slides it toward me. Then he says, "Cash, preferably. I'll have it for you this weekend. Assuming I can find some non-union livestock for the prop work."

31

Blake speaks out of the haze. "So has my brother gone with the dead girl or the live boy?" He's quoting a Louisiana governor's boast about who he'd have to be caught in bed with to lose an upcoming election. But Billy's preoccupation with Gina's death makes the joke ring off-key.

We're sitting in the steam room of the Racquet and Tennis Club, an illegal martini slowly warming in my hand. Blake prefers live meetings away from his office, as if we're old mates who just happen to be doing a series of work-related favors for each other. Since we're also not Ukrainian gangsters, this location seems particularly odd, but, as Mercer pointed out to me weeks ago, I can't quibble with our billionaire client over appropriate meeting attire.

"I don't exactly know yet. Given his literary inspiration, I'd have to say both. At any rate, we're looking at some ugly developments."

"How so?"

"Well, he's been trying to drag you into his world with these pranks, but we should prepare ourselves that another strategy of his might be explicitly breaking his silence on the topic of your family—"

"Has he sent something to the media?" This is the first time I've heard a quaver of stress find its way into Blake's voice.

"No. But I bet he'll invoke your name in this game of his."

"What's the point? If the little bastard wants to slime us, why doesn't he just bawl it out to Oprah? Or run an ad in the *Journal,* God forbid."

"Well, would you agree that at his core your brother is an artist?"

"At his core, he's a perverted baby."

I smile but realize Blake can't see me through the steam.

He continues. "But he does adopt the pose."

"So I suspect the instigation of all this was the death of his friend Gina. For whom he probably had romantic feelings. Can you think why he might connect her with you?"

"That's ridiculous. And anyway, Billy likes games, not girls. He may have been sad about his friend, but he didn't need her death as an excuse to fuck with me."

I'm annoyed Blake isn't more forthcoming about having dated Gina in college, but clients are often dissembling about something. Confrontation just makes them more defensive. So I change the subject.

"Do you think he might be jealous of you and your sister?"

"Of what? He's got the money to do whatever he wants."

"Yes, but he's not famous. He doesn't have your celebrity. A couple write-ups in abstruse art rags. But no one really remembers you two have a brother."

"He changed his name."

"Maybe because he felt cheated. Like his inheritance had been stripped."

"Bullshit. He—"

"It may be. But we're talking about how he feels. Perhaps he wants to amp up his profile enough to put his status on par with yours, and he's willing to trade on the most valuable thing he has in order to do that. His identity as a Randall. If he just dishes scandal to the *Post,* then he's the tabloid freak of the week, but if he's able to parlay the public's interest in your family into a groundbreaking work of art, then that's more like a career."

"And he thinks harassing me is going to help him achieve this?"

"That's an element. But I get the feeling he's trying to make an argument. The medium he's chosen is designed to get people participating, not just passively receiving a message. They can be very powerful experiences and are fashionable right now in gamer and media circles. But they're still mostly seen as trivial entertainments. Imagine someone putting together a game that revealed important secrets about the *real* world. One in which the efforts of the players had a significant impact on actual events. Maybe that's what he's aiming for."

"What kind of impact? What are these secrets, James?"

I don't know where Billy's going with his mishmash of Sade, cybering, and salacious cinema. But to Blake's question:

What do his arrest near Exotica and his indirect references to the company in Savant *have to do with the Randalls?*

Given that the haute porn director Farber and his gonzo partner Mondano Sr. both died while Blake was still in college, I'd be willing to wager that any connection Billy makes will be with Robert Randall. The obvious similarity is geographic, all three men having lived near Los Angeles.

An insight slowly takes form. The article on Ronald Farber said he "came from nothing" to produce an immortal classic of blue movies. But no one comes from *nothing*. He was a camera technician at an Irvine TV station. Right around the time Blake's father was starting to build his SoCal broadcasting empire.

Making my voice as neutral as possible, I say, "I'm not sure yet, but I think where this is heading is that your brother will try to link IMP and your family to the pornography industry."

I wish I could see Blake's reaction to this. There's a short pause followed by a snort that sends pretty Mandelbrots of vapor toward me. "That's it? That's his raw meat for the gossip sheets? That IMP benefits from pornography? Everybody knows that. Anyone with a cable box can see that pay-per-view is mostly porn. We provide internet access to two million people in this city alone. Do you have any idea what proportion of all the bits sucked into their apartments is porn? At least a quarter. Maybe a third. Regardless of the real number, everyone knows it's high, and nobody gives a shit."

"I think he's getting at something more specific."

"What?"

"Have you ever heard the name Ronald Farber?"

"Ronald Farber?"

"A dead pornographer. I think Billy will disclose he had some sort of relationship with your dad."

More steam whorls. "It's possible . . . my father was democratic in the company he kept."

"Blake, I'm going to have to play Billy's game if you want to know what's out there, never mind finding him. To do that, I may need to know these things. Maybe go pretty deep into your family history."

Blake grunts skeptically. "Okay. We'll get you whatever you need. But, James . . ."

"Yeah?"

"I'm sure you're aware that an enterprise like IMP doesn't get created without taking a certain number of . . . liberties."

"Naturally."

"So I don't need to explain that if we're to show you where all the bodies are buried, as it were, you'll need to exercise pretty flawless discretion, if . . ."

"If I don't want to end up buried with them?"

Blake's face emerges from the mist disconcertingly close to mine. He chuckles and slaps me heartily on the back. "Now, why would I say such a thing? You don't believe I make *idle* threats, do you?" He stands up and grabs a towel, then turns to me and says in a faux lockjaw, "Let's repair to the bar. This drink tastes like piss."

32

With three of the R & T's colossal martinis under my belt, I'm buzzed enough to convince myself that productive work might be possible, so I catch a cab downtown to GAME. I'd been hoping to slip into my office without a lot of commotion, but Garriott appears at my door saying, "Mate, you have to help me." Then over his shoulder, "I will not submit to it, you deranged Cossack!"

Olya barges in, reaching for his ear. She stops when she sees me. "Ah . . . Maybe now we have a real man."

The way she assesses me as though I were a hound of questionable pedigree sets me on edge. "What's going on?"

"Olya needs a dick."

"Yes, and better now I do not have to chase around this . . . this child."

"I was going to finish up—"

Olya shakes her head. "Mmm, but today we need to do the casting. We have new skin materials, new sensors. We need molds for anatomy. The pussy, it's a bottleneck right now. And the cock—"

"We've been using off-the-rack components," says Garriott. "There's no reason—"

"Andrushka, we are spending all this time like hospital surgeons cutting up Cyber Cocks and Pocket Pets. And it still feels like you're fucking the Cuisinart. If we have the molds, we cast silky silicone around your machines in twenty minutes. And the seams we have now—" She snarls with loathing.

I say, "I have to agree with her, bud. Ginger gave me quite a blister in the last test."

"You were too vigorous! Plunging away at her like she's a defective toilet!"

Olya and I share a look.

Garriott recovers. "Well, I won't do it. Your blister is nothing compared to what happened the last time she tried this on me."

Olya has had enough. "Listen to me, infant—"

"Okay, I'll do it," I say. "But what the hell are we talking about?"

Ten minutes later I'm sobering up and regretting my bravado, as I'm strapped pantsless into one of the MetaChairs with Olya standing above me wielding what look like electric sheep shears.

From behind me, Garriott whispers, "Don't let her do it. Back in November she wanted a specimen off me. Five days later, it was like I had the worst case of genital herpes in the history of primate intercourse." He pats my shoulder but shivers with abhorrence. "Ingrown hairs, mate. Thousands."

Olya shakes her head. "Maybe I was a bit rough with the razor. But you wiggle like hamster." She kneels in front of me and places a cool hand on the inside of my thigh, pushing it gently to the side. "But for you, I am very gentle."

And she is. Maybe it's her sly smile as she says this, or maybe it's the heavy buzzing of the clipper as she drags it slowly down my groin, but an awkward turgidity takes root. Oddly, the thing that goes through my head is that this is somehow unprofessional.

Olya picks up on my thoughts as though she's an alien empath. She softly brushes my tumescence away from her line of attack with the back of her left hand but looks up directly into my eyes. "Zhimbotchka, this is very good. Necessary for casting. But it is maybe a little early." She says this quietly, but I still get a glance from Xan, who's at the main table mixing up tubs of exotic pastel-hued polymers. Garriott turns away with a stagy sigh. He busies himself with the electronics to be cast into the "anatomy."

I get through the initial clipping, but as Olya leisurely spreads fragrant shaving soap around my nether regions, I have to resort to small talk to keep myself together.

"I take it you'll be representing the better half of our species? So I can have my revenge if you butcher me."

Olya picks up a safety razor and playfully brandishes it at me. "Ah, you want a chance at me, do you? I am sorry to say it, Zhimbo, but already I have the laser."

"You mean . . . ?"

"Yes. It's permanent. Very convenient."

Xan snorts. "Convenient for gratifying closet pedophiles."

Garriott adds, "Mate, she tried to make me do it too. But there's no way I'm letting a technician—they don't even have medical training, you know. No way I'm letting anyone near the wedding tackle with a high-powered laser."

Olya begins a long, careful downstroke, causing me to clench my teeth with pleasure. She says, "Little one, you seem very concerned about this body part that on you I think it's, ah, ves—" She starts reaching for the word while making a frightening circular gesture with the razor. "Mmm . . . like the appendix?"

"You mean it's small and filled with poisonous bacteria?"

Xan says, "She means 'vestigial.'"

"Ah, yes. You're so careful with this thing, yet you do nothing with it. Maybe this is why you want virtual girl?"

Garriott mumbles under his breath about the pounding he'd give any vodka-slurping whore mad enough to try him. I have to stifle a laugh at the image of the pair of them together. Like the mouse and the elephant.

Olya takes her sweet time with the shaving. Eventually Xan asks, "So we about done there? We're getting close with this silicone."

After a quick inspection, Olya's satisfied with her handiwork. "Ya. You want me to put it on?"

Xan bustles over, carrying a large vat of blue liquid rubber. She nudges Olya with her hip and says, "I suggest you get your knickers off. We don't want Fred getting lonely."

Olya looks disappointed, but she shrugs and reaches into a shirt pocket and extracts a yellow ovoid pill. "James, I would never question your manhood, but . . . it's very important that you, ah, maintain while the mold sets. Maybe twenty minutes."

I open my mouth and dry-swallow the tablet. Olya steps over to the

other MetaChair and starts tugging off her suede pants. This sight combined with Xan slathering me with Vaseline is more than I can bear. But
she expertly stops before anything disastrous occurs.

Next she presses home a cardboard box, one end of which is cut to
conform to my crotch. She then begins to pour, and I feel a refreshing
bath of cold liquid. I close my eyes and give in to the moment, reflecting
that a replica of my member may well end up in the Smithsonian. Or
more likely somewhere in Amsterdam's Rossebuurt.

This reverie ends when I hear Xan say, "Andrew, I'm going to need
your hands here. I've got to do Olya now." I'm no kind of homophobe,
but there's something about this bait and switch that makes me uneasy.

He winks at me, saying, "Believe me, mate, I don't like it any better
than you do."

I try to distract myself by observing the two ladies. Xan reaches for
the jumbo-sized tub of Vaseline, but Olya waves her off and makes an
adjustment between her legs. Xan then carefully positions a much more
complicated casting apparatus than mine. She asks, "That angle seem
about right?"

Olya squirms slightly and giggles. "Ya, but this feels like I am exam-
ined by the space people."

Garriott asks, "So when we decide Fred is going to need an arsehole,
will your rig serve for that as well?"

Xan frowns. Garriott turns back to me. "I'm sure you'll make a lovely
model for that part too." He blows me a kiss.

Suddenly my body seems to realize the following: that Xan and Olya's
interest in each other is purely professional; that I'm not likely to receive
any more Vaseline-related attention in the near future; and that I am in
too intimate contact with a fey Englishman who probably attended years
of public school and is making vague proctologic threats against my person. Aided by all the gin sloshing around my brain pan, my libido checks
out completely.

I guess Garriott can feel a drop in the upward pressure on the box. He
says, "Guys, we've got a problem here."

Xan looks over and says in what I regard to be an overly severe tone,
"James, dear, we need about fifteen more minutes."

Garriott says, "Xan, maybe . . ."

"I can't. We'll lose Olya's cast if I move."

The urgency of this exchange adds to my anxiety. Also making things worse is Garriott giving the box a tentative wiggle. I shake my head.

But Olya saves the situation.

With a luxuriant yawn, she says, "Aieee . . . little ones. Don't worry. The Cialis kicks in soon. But maybe it would be better if it weren't so hot in here."

The basement is almost freezing, but in homage to the time-honored stag film device, she slowly begins to unbutton her blouse.

She's got a diaphanous slip underneath, which exposes to remarkable effect her nipples' response to the chilly air. As though trained to the elegant absurdities of glamour poses from birth, Olya fans herself and lets a fingertip trail against her breast. Xan's eyes could not be rolled back farther in her head. Garriott has averted his gaze, embarrassed by the transparency of this display. I, happily, feel a twinge. Perhaps things are turning around.

Olya purrs with satisfaction. "That is better I think . . . You know, having the pussy cast is a very unusual experience. Pleasant, but, you know, maybe strange. It reminds me very much of . . ."

"What?"

"Mmm . . . Of the first time I ever come. Have orgasm."

Olya closes her eyes and a faraway smile passes over her lips. What follows is a scorching set piece, told in her dark molasses voice. It concerns her uncle's farm outside of Yekaterinburg, two albino lambs she saved from Easter dinner, a pail of spilled milk, and a subsequent vigorous spanking. During this I see Garriott miming a broad thumbs-up at Xan. I close my eyes to blot out his antics and focus on the alluring images flitting around in my head. Her story sounds like something out of *120 Days,* but gloriously free of blood or defecation.

As her account winds down, I'm brought back by Xan asking, "Garriott, can you throw me the paper towels?" I open my eyes, and she's squinting at me. "You people are quite ridiculous, really."

Olya's eyes are still closed. She stretches her arms slowly above her head, giving me a crowning view, before collapsing and starting to button up. She looks at Xan and says, "But the casts, they will be perfect, so what do you say? 'The ends satisfy the means.' James, you will be okay now, I am sure."

The Cialis has kicked in. My cock is painfully hard, and it feels unconnected to my normal arousal mechanisms, like it's no longer really part of my body. I suppose, soon enough, it won't be.

"Um, how long is this going to last?"

Olya grins. "The drug last for a couple days. It's too bad our robot children are not ready; what are you going to do with yourself?"

33

Around midnight the next evening, I'm sitting with Adrian in a werewolf-themed bar in the West Village. He's just screened on his laptop the final cut of his Sade short *King of the Hill*. I have to admit I'm impressed, and, despite the outré behavior being depicted, a little turned on. Something about his ivory-skinned princesses swanning about in giant Marie Antoinette wigs, but then gathering to viciously belabor the poor stuntman with knotted switches, tickles a previously unrevealed part of me. Its discovery is unsettling.

He can tell I'm pleased. "The ladies are panting to do a sequel. They like the wigs. Maybe we'll find a small role for the executive producer. Up for it?"

"Tempting, but I'm pretty busy with something else. You guys ever do anything with 'adult novelties'?"

Adrian studies me. I'm just full of surprises these days. "Do we ever. Oh, but you mean *selling* them. Why? You getting into indecent inventions?"

"You could say that."

"So spill it. I ain't a cheap date. You might as well take off the trench coat."

"Let's say I'm involved in a project that, ah, ups the ante in the sex toy business, well, pretty much all the way."

"The full teledildonic enchilada?"

"Let's say."

"The real virtual deal?"

"Uh-huh."

"No way."

"Just humor me."

"Okay, but this better not be true, because you know I would have to murder you and toss your apartment. You realize you're talking about the Holy Grail?"

"Indeed."

"Seriously. Men have been wanting this since boners were invented. I mean, it's mythic: from Eve to *Weird Science,* for Christ's sake! We'd be able to start getting rid of those infernal females." Adrian frowns. "To be honest, I thought the Japanese would get there first."

"But let's say you had this thing, and it, you know, *worked.* What would you do?"

"You mean besides making calluses on my dick? Hmmm." He plucks the straw out of his cocktail and sucks daiquiri from the bottom. "I guess I'd get insanely rich."

"How exactly? That's my question."

"Right, so who, other than everybody, would want something like this?"

"Yeah. So maybe we start upscale? An expensive, luxury personal-satisfaction appliance. Design it like an iPod. So it doesn't have that adult bookstore stigma—"

Adrian shakes his head. "Nope. First you make it as cheap as possible. Your early adopters are going to be 'sexual progressives,' otherwise known as perverts—like us, buddy! And we like that nasty aesthetic. Eventually, yeah, the crystal-and-lace crowd. But without a doubt, you will have knockoffs immediately. Since this thing is physical and maybe a bit of an investment, you've got a shot at locking people in. Then creating network effects. My advice would be to lose money on the machine early on. Maximize your user base. Which will be expensive."

"Yeah. That's another—"

"And don't forget you'll need a tongue farm in place on day one."

"Tongue farm?"

"Yeah, a customer service center. You don't want a new user to take his toy out of the package and have there be no one on the other end, right?"

"I was thinking a social network."

"At some point, sure. But short-term you need to seed the clouds with a bunch of people who know how the thing works. And you'll make an assload of dough. Charging by the minute. I mean, in this day and age, *phone* sex is still making billions every year."

"It just seems messy."

"Well the sex business ain't a church picnic. That's for sure. We can make all the Baudrillard references we want in our videos, but that doesn't change the fact that we need an army of hot nonsense to sell our product. You have to be okay with that, or you'll flub the money shot, and I'm telling you, someone else will be there to get it right."

"Yeah. I just didn't really see myself as the Madam of the Metaverse."

"If you had one of these things, would you use it to fuck your wife? That's ludicrous. Your customers will be lonely people sick of balancing a magazine on their lap. And now that I think about it, let's not underestimate the lovely ladies."

"Right. They're generally more comfortable with devices. My teammate was telling me that one of the first uses of steam power was a vibrating massager for the treatment of 'feminine hysteria.'"

"It goes back way further than that. One of the many failings of our gender is that when man learned to brew"—he looks sternly at his cocktail—"woman learned to whittle." He shrugs and downs the rest. "So what are you thinking about in terms of front end?"

"Ah, we've got a simulated penis—"

"No, idiot. I mean—"

"Oh . . . Right. I'm working with NOD right now."

He evaluates this. "Good choice. That LibIA cybering software's coming in handy, isn't it? And free too! Now you've got a small country's worth of Cy' Ber-geracs honing their skills."

"The stars are aligning. Who would you go to for the money?"

Adrian assumes a martyred expression. "Any time you hook up with a player in this racket, someone's going to get fucked. The Industry doesn't attract Boy Scouts and choir girls. But you can both get your nut if you keep at it. So you really need to make sure your partner doesn't have the Bug. Because it will kill your business."

"What's the Bug?"

"AIDS. But in the porn world it's mostly fraud—well, and AIDS too. You just need to worry about someone running games on you. Organized

crime connections are also bad. Not because they're not lovely, upstand-
ing people. Some of my closest friends and all that. But they'll be laun-
dering money, whether you know it or not, and that will bring down
heat. Even if you're innocent, heat is bad, because remember there are all
these anti-porn laws still on the books, and the Man can shut you down
pretty easy if you annoy him."

"What do you know about a company called Exotica?"

"Perfect example. On the face of it, they might seem good. Big, diversified porn conglomerate. They've got a novelties division, so they know
how to make and retail that stuff. But people think that the Mondanos
are mobbed up. Now, maybe that's bullshit. We get romantic about
the old days, and an Italian last name is probably enough to set tongues
wagging. But what's not bullshit is that Exotica is practically insolvent
because the IRS put a huge lien on all their accounts. God knows I hate
the IRS worse than rubbers, but as a businessman, I can tell you that it's
pretty easy to keep them out of your hair. So what's going on over there?
One thing you do know is that you won't have a fun time if you get in
bed with someone whose testicles have been nailed to the headboard by
Uncle Sam."

"Let's say you created this great system, but you want to make sure
your potential partners don't have the Bug. What would you do?"

"What would I do? Well, Jimmy, I guess I'd talk to me."

34

made sure to upload my submission from a computer at GAME that belongs to Don Lanier, an ARG enthusiast who doesn't already appear to be playing *Savant*. If Billy's watching to see who his serious players are, I don't want him associating Jacques with James Pryce just yet.

By the next morning, my offering is posted as the winner for that day in the Telling, and I have a message asking me to seek out Madame Desgranges.

In *120 Days,* Desgranges is the most senior of the storytelling whores, and by far the most bloodthirsty. Her avatar is, true to her description in the book, an ugly hag who is "vice and lust personified." As I approach her, she doesn't register my presence, so I assume she's another NoBot. I right-click to get her "touch" menu.

Just as my finger releases the mouse button, my cover cell starts ringing, causing me to catch my breath. I remember having surrendered a forwarding number when signing up, but I'm still amazed by the feeling of disjunctive anxiety produced by a game suddenly reaching into the real world.

The low, rumbling cackle that boils into my ear when I pick up does nothing to soothe my nerves.

She says, "Have we found one who seeks to burn?"

I say, "Yes."

"And can you keep the Secrets of our Order on pain of death?"

"Yes."

She continues. "You have studied the Book. Now write your own chapter. Innoculytes must withstand the full Course of their Fever over the Month of Purging. You must commit five crimes for each Degree until you're *consumed*. You will begin with a confession in the chapel. Do you accept this charge?"

Rushing to jot down what I just heard, I mutter, "Yes, I accept the charge."

The line goes dead.

That exchange removes any doubt that Billy's set up Château de Silling as a virtual recruiting post for the Pyrexians. I guess the "Course of Fever" Madame Desgranges mentioned is a series of trials one must undertake to gain membership. Our puppet master probably planted the rumors about the Pyros to begin with. So is he trying to import this legend into reality, using his game to actually *create* a lodge of risqué Rotarians to do his bidding?

Seeing that the first step toward initiation is ready to roll, I suppose I'll find out soon enough. Silling's chapel now boasts a series of previously hidden confessionals. Once inside, my voice-chat indicator lights up, and the Duke's voice says, "We're listening."

I sit there for a moment hesitating about what exactly I'm supposed to confess. Finally, I load a voice-processing program and improvise an overwrought tale about an unusually solicitous assistant football coach and a secret place underneath the bleachers.

A sickly giggle sound effect plays. Then the Duke says, "We are pleased. You are getting warmer."

Well, that was simple . . . if somewhat horrifying.

As I leave the booth, I notice that now a key is hung over the handle of the opposite side, where the priest would normally sit to hear his parishioners. I take it into inventory and then see that it opens all the doors on the row. I step into one of the other booths and immediately hear someone else reciting his census of sins. This one is about the speaker's recent tryst with his brother-in-law, and unlike most confessions, there's no note of repentance in his tone.

So recording my first "crime" gives me access to the submissions of my fellow players.

I have root on Billy's server, so I dig around until I find a few videos that look like they might represent more advanced crimes. The associated note cards tell me that the game's next step requires a live video of one-self engaging in a "solitary passion." The third demands a video of you perpetrating an "outrage" upon someone else. The first entry I find in this category is a video of a Japanese string bondage enthusiast delivering a lecture about the virtues of the Kikkou style over the Hishi while he ties an intricate pattern of cords over his "victim." I suspect he'll have to try again.

But others have done better.

The next one I check, entitled *Embroidering Celadon,* queues up a pi-quer fetish video: an adolescent boy having a wide variety of needles and other sharp objects jabbed into his buttocks. Mild examples of this genre resemble a naughty version of acupuncture. But given the array of instruments laid out on the table beside the kid, I doubt his vital energy is about to be rebalanced. More like the opposite.

I shut it off.

So Billy's warped hazing program has appropriated the "storytelling" mechanism of *120 Days.* It also shares elements of most pornographic file-swapping rings. You show me yours, I'll show you mine. The quality of the content you submit determines your privileges within the group.

But that's the first video I've seen in Silling that seems like it might end on the far side of the law. Of course, fetish filmmakers master the craft of making adult actors appear underage. And much can be done to maximize the apparent savagery of the action. Have these videos been constructed to seem worse than they are? Does Billy even care?

He can't be too worried. The Degrees feel designed to channel players along the Sadean progression of ever-greater horrors, like future serial killers mutilating their first cats. As Sade says:

    The more pleasure you seek in the depths of crime, the
    more frightful the crime must be.

35

Given the violence endemic to imaginary worlds, having placed myself on a giant game board with an army of demented Sade obsessives leaves me feeling unsettled. I'm not sure what the rest of the iTeam knows about Billy's game, but they've clearly learned enough from their GAME colleagues to make them uneasy as well. We're sequestered in our usual booth at Foo Bar, supposedly for a meeting, but in light of three quickly slugged rounds, it seems we've opted for pickling our anxieties over trying to work through them.

Even Olya, normally our productivity zealot, seems withdrawn. Watchful.

I join her in scanning the oddly boisterous Sunday night crowd. A cluster of progs from a social gaming start-up are downing shots in series and high-fiving each other. The spectacle screams "Series B round just came through." The organic-looking couple in the booth next to ours is alternately chugging beer and making out, like high school lovers who've ditched their chaperones.

At the bar, I notice three men sipping tequila who seem to be trying particularly hard to conceal their interest in our table. Two of them could be brothers, both with five o'clock shadow and similar spiky black hair. One wears a tight gray ski sweater with a red scarf, and the other a navy blazer and pink Thomas Pink button-down. With them stands a swarthy giant with unruly curls hanging down to the collar of a loud glen-plaid suit. I see that the bartender is watching us too. And the DJ.

Stop it. They're just admiring Olya's generous neckline.

Garriott's expounding on the thespian qualities of his favorite Fuck-ingmachines.com starlets, but I'm distracted when Xan gets up to refresh her drink. She reaches over the bar to signal our waitress, and that's when Pinky puts his hand on her shoulder.

I pop up instantly.

Xan starts at the contact and spins to face him. He leans in to say something, a sly smile on his face. Then the scarf-swaddled guy pulls a small digital camera out of his pants pocket.

I surge forward, pushing roughly through a knot of people, and grab Pinky by his lapels.

"Whatever the fuck you think you're doing, you better stop right now."

"Hey!" He jerks back awkwardly against the bar. Scarf grabs my wrist, trying to remove my hold on his friend. Plaid Suit steps around behind us to wrestle me away.

Olya's shoulder slams into Plaid Suit. She shoves her forearm across the neck of the guy holding me. "Get away from her!"

At first, her victims seem disposed to resist, but Olya's dazzling figure produces a severe primal confusion.

Pinky sputters, "What—what's your problem, man?"

"Whatever you sick bitches are planning, why don't you try it on me?"

"What are you talking about?"

I lean forward, renewing my grip. "Don't—" Xan's hand touches my arm.

Pinky says, "Look, psycho, I was just asking if she'd take a picture of us. It's my goddamn birthday."

I glance back at Xan. She nods.

"Guys, I guess I made a mistake. I'm sorry. Hey, ah, next round's on—"

They're not to be soothed. Plaid Suit shifts his bulk toward me and says, "Fuck you. Who the fuck do you think—"

Olya presses against him. "Eh, eh, eh. Maybe you let *me* buy you the drink. We don't mean—"

I don't hear the rest of her glamouring them because I'm thrown off by a movement in my peripheral vision. Back at our table, the guy that was sitting in the adjacent booth now stands in front of Garriott, shaking his hand. He puts his other hand on Garriott's shoulder and gestures at his date, who reaches over the back of the booth to greet him as well. The guy doesn't let go of his shoulder and bends down to say something else. I take a step toward them, not knowing exactly why.

Pinky grabs my elbow, evidently not done with our confrontation.

The woman next to Garriott raises her right hand. I'm horrified to see that her fist holds a steak knife. I try to yank my arm free, but Pinky's grip is tight. I call Garriott's name.

He can't hear me over the loud music. The woman cocks her hand, and anticipating the blow to follow, I set myself and twist my arm forward, breaking Pinky's grasp.

Too late, I think.

But then something strange happens. Instead of plunging the knife into Garriott, the woman pulls it back toward her own face.

And sticks the blunt handle all the way down her throat.

The resulting reflex delivers in one gushing eruption all four pints of beer she had consumed earlier, along with a full plate of macerated nachos and what might be a Greek salad. Garriott reels back in disgust as her partner lets go.

Another guy videos the incident from across the room. Rather than thoughts of vengeance, what enters my head is this simple observation:

Day 6, scene 3.

Olya gets there before me, and retribution *is* foremost in her mind. She stiff-arms the girl's head into the wall and then bashes the meat of her palm onto her nose.

In a low growl she says, "You stupid—"

I reach out to restrain her, thinking that nobody's really gotten hurt— yet. We can't have Olya getting arrested in a bar brawl. Unfortunately, the boyfriend also decides to wade in. I elbow him in the gut and jack him back away from the booth. Garriott composes himself by wiping his face with the corner of our tablecloth. He bears an oddly philosophical expression, like he's more disappointed than aghast.

I try to drag Olya off the girl, though she's literally spitting with rage. Just as I finally get them separated, I feel a hard jerk across my windpipe and am neatly ripped off my feet by someone with the physique of a bulldozer.

He says, "Not cool, James."

That would be Ray the bouncer, a former heavyweight wrestler. He hauls me fast through the door and hurls me, without undue rancor, into the gutter. As I lie there catching my breath, I see another bouncer politely but firmly escorting Olya out by her elbow. Garriott and Xan follow, upbraiding the bar manager on the way.

When I finally sit up, the Foo Bar staff has gone back in to deal with the other parties, though I imagine they've slunk out the back.

Xan kneels at my side and asks, "Are you quite all right, James?"

"Yeah, nothing a few more drinks won't cure."

Olya fumes, muttering to herself in Russian, no doubt detailing the hideous fate she has in mind for Billy. I could direct her to a few choice passages in Sade.

I edge upwind of Garriott. "You, ah, okay? That was pretty . . ."

Garriott musters the proper devil-may-care affect. "That? A little Roman shower? That's nothing, mate. I was a Wyvern at Cambridge, for God's sake. Not to say that'll stop me from pounding Billy's face into marmalade, if he ever has the stones to show it."

I'm glad Garriott can laugh it off, but Olya may well have broken that girl's nose.

And the Innoculytes are just warming up.

36

The next day I walk back from the corner deli through the icy morning sipping a cup of burnt, acidic coffee. It's not helping my tender head, which was already throbbing when I awoke. From my hard landing in the gutter last night? Or the unreasonable amount of Garriott's favorite Bordeaux we drank after escorting him home to change? I guess the group wasn't keen on traveling back to our respective apartments alone, because we tacitly decided to make a slumber party of it.

So this morning I'm exhausted and yet still anxious to get back to GAME and power through the bugs we left for today.

This intense impulse to resume work is alien to me. Am I feeling the first twinges of severe Stockholm syndrome? Maybe I need to take measures to get my personal shit together. Tamp down the Byronic passions I'm starting to feel for this tarted-up vacuum cleaner. Not to mention my paternal pride at seeing Fred make Xan or Olya go breathless.

On the other hand, the life I led before was tending toward the untenable. I was engaged in my work without being inspired. And my personal life after Erica resembled a speeding car in heavy fog.

At GAME, I've stumbled onto a project uniquely suited to my abilities and desires. Regardless of my qualms about the enterprise, in the past week or so, I've gone to work every day with a hard-on. Why? It's the difference between doing something and *building* something. While they're hard-won and all too rare, those flashes of triumphant creation satisfy like nothing else.

In combining them with the primordial lust I feel toward Olya—despite her obvious entanglement with the very target of my investigation—I've found myself creating a false identity I like better than the original.

Billy would be proud. Though when my job is done, I'm sure he'll want to see me bleeding in the more literal sense.

37

If Blake's SoHo spread seeks to frame its occupant with a discerning luxury, then Blythe's is much more of the "tremble now, all ye who come before me" variety. The very existence of a suite consisting of the top four stories of a seventies–and–Central Park West monolith testifies to an owner who controls things the rest of us don't even know about. I assume that's the message intended by this gym-sized foyer with carved-marble wing staircases sweeping upward toward an actual ballroom. The décor betrays an interior designer who recently visited Versailles and takes too much Xanax with her kir royales.

Not at all what I'd pictured for Blythe, something she acknowledges as she leads me into a cozy library for our meeting.

"Sorry about the place. I know it's gauche, but my stepmother forced it on my poor father when he was in no position to resist. She made him move to get away from his 'old life' in L.A., and all his stuff is still here. I know he was supposedly a corporate Antichrist, but a girl can still love her father, right?"

"No shame in loving a prewar penthouse either."

"I promise myself that one day I'll fill it with African war orphans to even the karma."

"I'm sure the co-op board will be thrilled."

Blythe had called me to ask if I could "swing by her place for a quick chat." It was eleven PM then, now almost midnight, and something in her voice made me believe she might be a little drunk. An exciting prospect.

The last time I'd seen Blythe get truly hammered was the night after I took her out of the Zeta house. The night she came by my apartment for a drink. The night, it is sad to say, that still stands as the clear apex of my life.

We'd powered through most of a bottle sitting close on my couch. Though at first she wasn't inclined to discuss it, after her third double, I brought the conversation around to the events of the previous night. I detailed my thoughts about exacting revenge on Novak, but she barely seemed interested, as though she'd already dismissed him from her mind.

"You're not angry?" I asked.

"Of course. But mostly at myself."

"Blythe, you can't blame—"

She puts up her hands. "James, I knew."

"What?"

"I knew all about Pete Novak. I knew his interest in me was . . . *profane*. It sounds so crazy, but I guess I wanted to see . . . Well anyway I never suspected he'd resort to such a cowardly cliché. I mean, a roofie? It makes no sense. The way he looked at me . . ."

She trailed off and stared contemplatively into space. I tried to survey the void with her while she collected her thoughts. But when I glanced back, I found myself transfixed by those unearthly green eyes.

"Was nothing like the way *you* look at me, James."

I racked my brain for something to say, but it had thrown a rod and juddered to a halt.

Blythe rose. I feared she was leaving, but she merely bent to pick up Novak's camera from my coffee table. She sat back down and regarded it thoughtfully.

I cleared my throat, but before I could speak, she said, "I want you to take my picture, James. I want to see what you see."

She offered me the camera. Her hand lingered on it before she let it go, the gesture saying to me, "I know I can trust you. That you'd never try to hurt me."

The images I made that night became for a long time the holy icons of my private cult, the same ones that years later drove away my fiancée:

A close-up of her glimmering eyes seeking mine through the lens.

A slightly tilted shot, from my shiver of excitement when she touched the first button of her blouse.

A profile of her lithe frame as she undid the front clasp of her bra.

A dark silhouette of her matchless figure as she leaned over me and undid my fly.

An extreme close-up of the appreciative quirk of her lips as she drew me out.

An unfocused picture of the ceiling that corresponds to my burst hydrant of a climax.

The curves at the small of her back as she rubbed her naked chest wetly against me.

A lascivious grin over her shoulder as she led me by the hand into my bedroom. Her body bare, but for those red pearls.

That was when I dropped the camera. It would never take another picture. But the memory survived.

Once inside her, my eyes snapped shut as I tried to parse the symphony of sensation played by her gently rocking hips. She smelled like the final dish of a twelve-course tasting menu. Some concentrated essence of citrus and vanilla cream that the chef had to consult a battery of chemists to concoct.

She grabbed my chin and said, "No. Keep looking at me, James."

I'd fantasized about sleeping with Blythe for more man-hours than they were wasting on the Big Dig. But I'd never imagined that the actual act could be better than all my fervid scenarios. Blythe was so in tune with herself, she was even able to make something of my amateur fumbling. She moved like she was a secret weapon the palace eunuchs trot out when the sexually ambivalent young sultan must produce an heir. Being a realist, I'm suspicious of over-the-top carrying on, but when Blythe subsided onto my chest with a self-conscious giggle and then bit my shoulder, I was so besotted I had to fight back tears.

But even then I knew the tears would come.

Only six weeks later, I was tracing her collarbone with my fingertips on a Tuesday afternoon. We'd both ditched class in favor of the coziness of her mammoth Chinese canopy bed, and we were listening to the ticking of snow starting to melt in the bright sunshine of late March. I couldn't imagine anything more perfect.

Yet true happiness had proven maddeningly elusive. I was unable to bask in the moment since it took all my energy to prevent myself from saying to her, "I love you." The words battered around my head like a thrush flown indoors, going frantic to escape.

This had been a problem for the past weeks, my finest hour made insufferable by my need to utter those three absurd words. I'd spent the better part of the previous four days creating a prop to help set the stage.

"I have something for you," I said as I reached for its hiding place under the bed.

A bouquet. Roses, yes, but not the hackneyed floral default.

They were heavy, hand-dyed stationery that I'd twisted into exquisite origami flowers. On each page I'd inscribed a love poem. Naturally, I spent dismal nights trying to compose my own, but the failure of that enterprise demanded that I let the masters speak for me.

The obligatory Shakespeare, of course, and Yeats. Her favorite, Byron, and mine, Dante. Lastly, Marvell's "To His Coy Mistress," to add a touch of plaintive irony, given the events of our first "date."

As I tendered them, Blythe's eyes flashed, instantly decoding their meaning. She studied my gift for a moment, then me.

Finally she said, "They're beautiful, but you know I'd rather hear it from you."

That sounded an awful lot like the invitation I needed. But the dare in her voice and some hint of amusement in her eyes frightened me. I was left speechless and miserable.

With her usual grace, Blythe rescued me by plucking out one of the roses. She took my right hand and wrapped its paper stem around my wrist. Then she tied the stem's other end around the carved framework of the bed.

"I have ways of making you talk."

Just as she started on my other hand, her phone shrilled us out of the moment. I tried to stop her from answering it but as always was no match for her. I'm not sure who had called, but he was certainly direct. After "Hello," she fell silent for a few seconds. Then she said, "No." And that single word bore the weight of a crushing loss.

When she hung up, she closed her eyes and said, "My father."

I have to admit feeling excited at this chance to show my empathetic mettle. I shook my hands free and gathered her gently in my arms, murmuring my consolations.

I said, "I'm here, Blythe. Anything you need."

She was stiff and disassociated, and I realized with dawning dismay that she was suffering this embrace for *my* benefit, not her own.

She said, "I need my father." I heard the "not you" loud and clear.

Of course, she called Blake. He'd already booked tickets home.

In her library I realize Blythe isn't at all tipsy and is itching to talk business. My hopes dashed, I say, "So you wanted to see me?"

"Yes . . ." She gives me a tight smile. "After I spoke with Blake about your most recent conversation, I just couldn't help thinking there were some issues I could, ah, elaborate on."

Interesting.

She turns and leads me to a small, book-lined reading room adjoining the library. There's an inlaid table upon which rests a stack of thick black binders. Blythe picks up a silver-framed picture lying on top. She hands it to me.

The shot shows the Randall family seated around a long dinner table. My eyes settle on Blythe in the full glory of her college years, her fingers brushing the shoulder of William Coles, her ex-boyfriend from the Bat. Billy slouches to her left. Robert Randall is beaming, with evident determination, at the head of the table. Blake sits across from Billy, and to his left appears Gina Delaney, smiling shyly a few degrees askew from the photographer, who I conclude must be Lucia Randall.

"My brother can be slow to trust, James. When you started asking about his connection to Gina, I think it surprised him. And when in doubt, his instinct is to withhold. I will try to get him to be less reticent. I certainly don't want these kinds of misunderstandings to impede your work."

"It's fine, Blythe. I already knew."

She cocks an eyebrow but doesn't ask me how. Instead, she seems to lose herself in the photo. "My father always tried to get his stepfamily together for Easter. Lucia, not unjustly, believed that our mother had poisoned us against her. And she didn't handle tension well. Billy of course absorbed tidal waves of stress from her. With my father insisting that everything was fine, well, let's say these were less-than-joyous reunions. Being the youngest, Billy was particularly affected."

She tells me how in that year, the twins decided that the emotional strain might dissipate somewhat under the view of outsiders, so they decided to invite their current significant others. Their idea turned out poorly. Lucia Randall took the innovation as a serious affront and was correspondingly rude to the twins, which precipitated a blowup with her husband. Billy, always terrorized by their fighting, suffered even more acutely in the presence of strangers.

Coles, "never a subtle creature," in Blythe's words, tried to take him aside and distract the poor kid with questions about sports, girls, and "partying." When Blythe checked on them, she found Coles looking at Billy like he was a three-headed porcupine, as her brother ignored him and played chess with himself. She could tell he'd focused on the game to keep from crying in front of a guest.

"I'd never seen Billy so dejected. I wanted to go to him and somehow comfort him. I don't know why, but he'd always flinch away from me like I was on fire. And my failed efforts just made things even more awkward between us. So, by that point, I'd almost decided that we should all just leave, whether my father liked it or not.

"But then Gina breezed into the room and took the seat opposite Billy. She cleared his chess pieces and started resetting the board. Without trying to meet his eye, she said, 'Best of seven. I'll bet I sweep you. Ten-minute games. I always open with the Latvian Gambit.'

"Billy was surprised, but ecstatic that he wouldn't have to keep talking to Coles. I believe what he said was, 'Bring it.'"

Blythe goes on. "She saved the whole weekend right there. Slowly got him talking about his alpha-gamer interests, and he was even laughing by the end of it. Gina was smart. She didn't let him win, which Billy would have hated."

She describes how he followed her around the next two days, obviously nurturing a Typhoon-class crush.

I smile and say, "In the right hands, I'm told the Latvian Gambit is irresistible." From what I've heard of the Delaney household, I can well imagine how it might move Gina to see a kid suffering from a poisonous family situation.

Blythe resumes. "It didn't stop there. Blake and I were blown away later that spring when Billy asked if he could come visit us at Harvard. A totally unprecedented request. Of course my father was thrilled to pieces. He hoped that his quarrelsome children were finally thawing toward each other. I had a feeling about Billy's real reasons for visiting. But we agreed anyway."

Blythe's eyes close in sorrow. "Imagine the catastrophe when he showed up at South Station to find that Blake and Gina had broken up. Blake snapped at him when he asked about her. Billy just marched back to the ticket counter and bought the next return without saying another word to either of us."

"Cherchez la femme." I hand the family photo back to her. "He must have been delighted to come across her again at PiMP."

She checks me for signs of irony to make sure I'm not a complete imbecile. Apparently satisfied, she props the picture on a nearby shelf and says, "Billy is like some kind of Terminator pit bull. Once he gets hung up on something, he doesn't let go easily. He needed that grad school like he needed an amateur lobotomy. But he is patient in pursuit."

Her phone rings. Glancing down at it, she says, "I have to take this. Those binders contain IMP's payroll records from before things were computerized. Feel free to flip through them. You'll find Ronald Farber in the earliest ones."

With that little daisy cutter, she leaves me alone in Robert Randall's archives.

Blythe has flagged the most important item: a human resources file on one Ronald A. Farber, an IMP employee for the three years prior to his founding Freyja Films.

So how does a lowly camera technician get the money to fund a high-end production company?

I'll check his tax returns for a rich uncle kicking off in '71, but I already know who Billy pegged as the silent partner.

From a chart of major IMP acquisitions that Blythe has helpfully included, I can see that the date of Robert Randall's bid for CalCast lines up almost perfectly with Mondano's investment in Freyja. So when he needed capital to take his shot, Randall had Farber take the investment from Mondano in order to buy him out.

If the CalCast deal represented Randall coming out of his chrysalis, then IMP was built squarely on a foundation of porn and mob money. Presumably, Billy thinks this tidbit might be of more interest to the general public than the fact that people jerk off in hotel rooms.

It wouldn't take much of a leap to suppose that some laws were broken or taxes evaded in one of these deals. If IMP expanded via financial fraud, that would be far worse than having grown from the fertile earth of heaving breasts and unimaginative dialogue.

That said, an allegation is one thing, proof another. I consider the disheartening prospect of having to gather evidence to support my theory. Melting the ice around transactions presumably handled by private banks is a pretty monumental task, like taking a blow dryer to an Antarctic glacier.

Then again, nobody asked me to prove anything. It doesn't really matter whether Robert Randall made shady deals with pornographers. What matters is that if Billy came to believe this, what is he planning to do with the information? Unlike his father, who tried to conceal his past, Billy wants to tell us the whole story.

Of course, people tell stories for many different reasons. Usually they entertain or enlighten, but some stories are meant to deceive or do damage. Others to scare or torment. And I think we know which kind Billy has in mind.

38

"Wait, James, there's more."

I'm back in the Orifice working with Xan. After the incident at Foo Bar, I'd proposed we set up an alternate site. But Olya's warlike nature doesn't admit such concessions, and she wouldn't hear of it.

I flip up my visor and back my MetaChair away from Ginger's insistent maw. "Sugar, any more will mean an hour cleaning our girl here with Q-tips. Garriott needs to figure out the wash cycle before I go insane."

"I thought you might like that."

"I do. But Xan, you know, you're way off spec here."

She frowns. Xan has been crafting demos to show off the capabilities of our wanton WALL-Es. We've just been through a scene involving a Puritan tutor and his comely but recalcitrant charge. I'm honestly stunned by what she's done. Xan has a deep understanding of the machines' attributes and how they can pander to all our manifold lusts. Like any virtuoso, she can be prickly with criticism, so I hesitate over how to put this.

"I mean, it's genius. You're the Orson Welles of the feelies." The "feelies" are a VR-like entertainment medium that appears in Aldous Huxley's *Brave New World*. Simulated sex is naturally a favorite activity in futuristic dystopias.

"Patronizing bastard."

"You won't think I'm patronizing when I electrocute myself again. The good thing about this medium is that appreciation cannot be faked."

"You really liked it?"

"Yes, but I'm hurt you're not using my new program." I'm talking about my software called e-Jax that we're supposed to be testing. It gives users an easy way to control the Dancers in order to set up their own sex scenes. But Xan likes to write custom code directly to the machines.

She gives me a guilty smile. "I know, I know. I just . . . It's a bit limiting."

"Right . . . We designed it that way. You know, simple, streamlined. Straight to the fucking. Not everyone who uses these things is going to have a computer science degree from MIT."

"But I think we can assume that someone screwing a robot will be a bit *technically inclined,* yeah?"

"That's the whole point. They don't want to screw robots. Look . . ." I step back to my laptop and pull up a site. "Here is a whole community devoted to 'aquatic erotica.' It started as people swapping stories about disporting with dolphins, but now they're in Second Life, Red Light Center, and of course NOD. And they've diversified into walruses and, hmm . . . anemones."

She leans over and points to a picture of an otter. "Ooh. I wouldn't mind taking a dip with that little guy."

Olya picks this moment to breeze in with Garriott in tow. "Why do you speak of animals? This is not in the spec. Always wasting time, you two—"

"And you're always interrupting conversations you know nothing about."

She laughs. "Zhimbo, you are so fiery today. XanXan, I think you are torturing him with your naughty schoolgirl?"

Olya's project-management style falls somewhere between the Dog Whisperer and Pol Pot, so her graciousness is quite a surprise.

"You're in a suspiciously good mood."

"Yes. I have very good meeting with a large potential partner, a company with very much experience in the sex business."

"Who is it?"

"Ah, Zhimbo, be patient. I tell you all about it when things firm up."

"Olya, come on, this is ridiculous."

She has the gall to actually ruffle my hair. "Zhimbo, just give me a couple days. Then you'll thank me. I promise."

I look imploringly at the other two, but they both shrug as if they've become accustomed to life on a Soviet mushroom farm. Olya grabs one of our test laptops and walks out.

Garriott clears his throat and says solemnly, "Working on this with you has been the greatest experience of my life. But I want you both to know that all the money"—he nods his head, coming to a momentous conclusion—"the money absolutely *will* change me." He closes his eyes and takes a deep, cleansing breath.

Then he says, "I'm going to become a vampire."

Frustrated, I step outside for a cigarette. The team seems quite lackadaisical about the legal basis of our partnership. Garriott, who has the very distant relationship with money found in real droid-druids, I can understand. But for someone as meticulous as Xan, this attitude doesn't make sense.

As I light up, I see Olya had the same idea. She's at the front of the alley talking softly into her cell but adding spiky emphasis with her freshly rolled cigarette. She observes my arrival and rings off.

From playing Billy's game, perhaps I've absorbed an "everything is connected" paranoid perspective that makes me stroll up beside her and ask, "So is it Exotica?"

Olya doesn't look at me. But from my oblique angle I notice her eyes flare slightly and her lips compress by a fraction. What am I seeing? The chagrin of learning that someone has guessed your closely held secrets? Or is she betraying some actual anxiety about the state of her enterprise? Maybe she's entertaining second thoughts about hooking up with a shady pornographer while Billy's stalking her over the death of her lover.

I can't decide in the bare instant before she's again mastered her apex predator insouciance. She takes a long drag and exhales leisurely. "So maybe you think you have ESP now?"

"Is it?"

"Zhimbo, I know the, ah, 'tenacity' is a very good quality for programmer. But, *milyi,* do not act like badger with me."

"Just how much do you know about the company, Olya? Are you sure they're the right people to be getting in bed with?"

"You think I'm not careful? You think I am a promiscuous woman, Zhames?"

"Well I have to question that, if you're proposing that we deal with this company. I understand that they know how to market. I understand they have distribution channels. I'm sure *you* understand how expensive it's going to be to tool up Chinese factories to make such a complex device. But did you know that your hot date is getting sued by the IRS? That their working capital has been frozen by a court order?"

She grabs my belt buckle and drags me close to her. "Eh, you listen to me now. I have not proposed *anything*. You are making bullshit assumption about what goes on here. How is it you know so much about this Exotica company? Are you a fan, Zhimbo? This is strange, that with all their interesting material, you take the financials to bed. Why is that, James? Why are you researching this company, when we've never discussed it?"

"Look—"

"No, you look. I know you want to find out what's happening. But this is my party. You come late but want to start telling the tune. You think I will sell our daughter to the first man who wiggle his dick at her? When I find Ginger a husband, he will be rich, respectable, and *committed*. He will put a kingdom at her feet."

"First of all, she doesn't have feet. And you think Bill Gates and Nelson Mandela are going to serve on the board?"

"Don't be stupid."

"Well, why don't you clue us in? Why all this secrecy? This isn't espionage."

"Ah, but our Dancers will be very famous when they are ready for the main stage. So it must be very secret now. Someone else copies our design and beats us into production? I will not allow this. With my first company the thieving bankers take it all. Russia, those days, there's not so much you can do. But that will not happen again."

"But we're on your team. You have to trust us."

"No, James, you trust me. Maybe I have trusted you too far already."

"What do you mean?"

"Let us be honest. You are too good a programmer for a video artist. You are too good a fighter for a Harvard pussy. So, you see, we all have our secrets."

"Wait, you think—"

"I think if you want to be private about your history, fine. I don't tell everyone my whole life either. But that means we take things a step at a time here. You keep doing such good work, and our team becomes very . . . intimate." She slaps me gently on the cheek. I almost think she's going to kiss me. But instead she flips open her phone. "I enjoy our little talk, but please excuse me. I have to call."

Dismissed, I head back into the POD. Olya's little wince of uncertainty when I brought up Exotica indicates a sore spot. I need to probe further to see if that was just a reflexive twitch, or if our otherwise thriving team has been infected by the Bug.

39

Late Tuesday night, Amazone is crowded with hard-core patrons, mostly financial players eager to take on the proverbial losing proposition. I actually have to wait for a minute to pay my cover. In the main room, I see Ben Mondano standing by the bar speaking with one of his bouncers, an older gentleman built like a septic tank.

Olya wouldn't expressly admit that Mondano is her secret partner, but I'm betting a little pretense can extract an official confirmation from him. And maybe some more information about their plans. In light of Adrian's warnings, I can't resist letting him know there's someone new on the team who will be watching him closely.

As I approach, his eyes pass over me without recognition. I sidle up next to him and say, "Hey, can we have a 'sit-down'?"

The bouncer stares at me and says, "I'll be with you in a moment, sir." He turns back to Mondano.

"I'd like to talk to you, Mr. Mondano."

He turns. "With me?" A slight slur tells me he's pretty much in the bag.

"Yeah. In private."

"Do I know you?"

The bouncer puts his hand gently on my shoulder. "Listen, guy, I'm sure I can help you with whatever you need here."

I ignore him and focus on Mondano. "We met last week. I was working on a documentary."

"Oh, yeah. How's all that going?" He hits 'that' with derisive emphasis, the booze having spared me from the solemn mafioso routine.

"It's over. I'm working with Olya now."

Mondano looks at me for a second, deciding whether to admit that he knows what I'm talking about. Finally, he sends his guy off with a sideways flick of his head.

I continue. "I wanted to ask you about a disturbing rumor I heard about—"

"Disturbing . . . you know, I find it *disturbing* to be seeing you here again."

"Why's that?"

"Well, you show up out of the blue asking me these questions about a missing fruit. And then I find out you've inserted yourself into Olya's project. That a coincidence?"

"Not at all. We work together."

"Yeah? Well I work with Olya too. She's handling any arrangement we might make. So if you have questions, you need to just talk to her."

"I could do that. But I don't think she'd be real happy to hear that you're not in any position to be throwing money around."

"I'm not, huh?"

"Exotica Enterprises? I hear the most exotic thing about your enterprise is its tax return. So maybe you can explain to me how you're planning to fund our space-age cybrator factory when you don't have the capital to back a hot dog stand."

Mondano stretches his jaw like a boxer preparing for the bell. "You're beginning to piss me off."

"Really? 'Cause I'm just getting started. Why don't you tell me—"

Mondano goes volcanic with rage. He yanks my shirt so our faces are inches apart. "I'll tell you this, motherfucker. Olya knows the money is not in doubt. I don't have to justify shit to you." He jerks me again. Out of the corner of my eye, I can see two bouncers walking toward us. He continues. "You're fucking with things you don't understand. This shit will get taken care of at a level way over your head. We are dealing with Olya. Only. You keep dicking around, she'll have your nuts. And that's not even close to what I'll do if you come back here. You understand me?" He jabs his index finger at my face.

Though I'm suspicious that I've just been subject to his best Joe Pesci impression, I set my feet, preparing to make him wish he'd kept his hands to himself should this run to actual rather than affected violence. I say, "What I understand is that you're not the only two-bit pornographer on the block. So I suggest you behave yourself."

The bouncers arrive and look at him expectantly. But he just stares at me.

"I think I can find my way out."

I wheel away from Mondano and brush past his security. He watches me go. His expression is now pensive but saturated with menace. Like he's sorting through a list of ways to dispose of my body.

Both of the bouncers follow me out to the street.

40

A stinging sleet falls as I search for a cab on Eleventh Avenue. The ice feels as though it's negotiating with the frigid wind to unite and form a full-blown fusillade of hail. Since precipitation instantly melts all available taxis, I resign myself to trudging the seven blocks to the Port Authority subway.

At home, I find that Red Rook Research has turned around my inquiries into the companies relevant to my investigation. The page on links between IMP and Exotica Entertainment contains only a rehash of the extent to which mainstream media companies benefit from adult content. They do. A lot. Who cares?

The next section deals with NOD. It lists a day-old post from a free-culture blog whose headline is "Four (w)Horsemen Fly." Underneath this is a series of progressively closer photos of four casually dressed young men boarding a G5. The post reads:

```
Repent, cynners! The signs of the coming infocalypse are
manifest!
   How else to interpret these photos we get by way
of Planespotting.org? Oh yes, the flying fetishists
caught the founders of the righteously anti-corporate
NOD Collective boarding that classic conveyance of
capitalists: the G5.
   And not just any G5. See that tail number N071MT?
```

Fellow cynners, that serial registers as the number of
the IMP! The plane is the dread flying chariot of the
devil himself: Blake Randall. Expect news of NOD getting
its 30 pieces of silver presently. Shall the faithful
NODlings be thrown into the fiery pit of "special premium
access accounts"? Judged for the cyns of gambling and
obscynity?

One thing is clear: the end is near!

In the closest shot, one of the NOD founders has spotted the photographer and attempts to hide his face with the leather portfolio he's holding. On that folder are printed the words GOBLIN CAPITAL, underneath which is a nicely embroidered logo of a toothy goblin. The creature was clearly drawn by the same artist who designed the IMP cyclops statue in Blake's apartment. Instead of a giant eye, the goblin has an enormous open mouth, tiny beady eyes, and a wild thatch of electrified blue hair. A beast geared toward consumption. Gobbling, I suppose, enterprises.

So Goblin Capital must be the acquisition arm of Blake's business development efforts. I've been trying to figure out why Billy's unearthed his father's relationship with the sex industry in the seventies. But now I see that all the ancient history is but a prelude to his main point, which I'm starting to think will be some form of:

Like father, like son.

A substantial portion of NOD's user base has sex on their mind when they're logging in, but you can say the same thing about the internet in general. Billy's indictment remains weak. There must be something else.

His other major endeavor has been antagonizing Olya. It can't be a coincidence that she's dealing with this guy whose father used to do business with Robert Randall. So how does IT relate to Billy's family morality play?

Let's try the skeleton key for unlocking someone's motivations: money.

Mondano said, "Olya knows the money is not in doubt."

Olya said, "When I find Ginger a husband, he will be rich, respectable, and *committed*. He will put a kingdom at her feet." That does not describe Exotica. So if Mondano's involved, he's either a junior partner or a front.

Where then is the money coming from?

I hear Blythe say: "I think the imp to which my brother seems most attuned is Poe's, not our father's."

Mondano said, "This shit will get taken care of at a level way over your head."

They've all been hinting at the same thing, and until now it *was* going over my head.

Over my head: like at the rarefied level of billionaires. Billionaires with grand visions who can assemble portfolios of companies in order to implement them. To lay a kingdom at Ginger's feet. Blythe isn't referring to her brother's self-destructive propensities. She's talking about his corporate strategy.

As obvious as it is in retrospect, I wish I could say I knew it all along. Maybe the idea was simmering in my subconscious, but it took this NOD acquisition to shove it into my forebrain.

Blake is the real backer behind IT.

I can see it: Olya decides she's going to reinvent sex. She initially contacts Mondano for help, and he pulls in Blake to provide the funding. They grew up within miles of each other and have been acquainted for years due to their fathers' business relationship. I make a note to check for common schools or peewee football teams.

So Blake hears about the IT project and likes the idea. He's aware of the conjugal genesis of IMP and sees an interesting parallel between his father and himself.

But the nature of the opportunity and the coming hearings on his sister's big merger prevent him from grabbing it with both hands. If he starts ordering industrial quantities of K-Y jelly from his corner office, it will not go unnoticed. So the operational aspect has to be delegated to Mondano, a man with a familial tradition of successful transactions with the Randalls.

But Blake *could* invest in the *idea* through clandestine subsidiaries like Goblin. So he starts buying up companies like NOD that will help create this vast new virtual playground.

I'll bet some digging will place Blake behind the LibIA cybering suite. The goal being to put sex on the brain of every avatar in NOD. A whole population just waiting for IT to be unveiled. Waiting for a product that finally lets them really jack into their fantasy world with the long-awaited *wet interface*. After all, why jerk off at your desk when for the price of a cheap dishwasher, someone else can reach across the country and do it for you?

Like his father helping fund the transition from stag films to adult video, Blake wants to midwife a new era of sexual commerce. While the knave tinkers with bits and bolts, the king builds an empire of Eros.

Thinking about Blake's schemes causes me to consider Billy's as well. I call Adrian, wanting to bring his netporn savvy to bear.

"De-Jim-erate! I knew you'd be back for more. Dirty pictures can be habit-forming, buddy."

"I'm well aware of that, but right now I've got another question for you. What do you think *Savant* is all about?"

"You mean besides child abuse and poop?"

"I'm just thinking that no one does all that work without an agenda, right?"

"Segmented marketing," he says.

"What?"

"Seriously. Learning someone's kink is more valuable than gold. I'll bet whoever's responsible is using Sade's carnal catalog to slice up the NOD user base by their fetishes. Extremely valuable information if you're trying to move product. Think about selling your sex robots. Wouldn't you like to know whether to show someone an ad featuring a man, a woman, or a donkey?"

Adrian's idea seems to fit. Billy must have found out what his brother and Olya are up to and decided to interfere. To "rain down fire" on his "festering Sodom." If he seeks to disrupt his brother's plans for the Dancers, maybe he wants to do more than just expose them prematurely. Maybe he's offering an alternative story line as well, one his players will discover as they tease out the purpose behind his game. Given Savant's initial video preferences, Billy's implying that Exotica is at some level sponsoring the game. So perhaps we're to conclude that Blake and Mondano are members of the Pyros, and that this Satanic Elks Lodge is developing the Dancers as part of a worldwide Sadean conspiracy to debase our culture. To that end, they've set up this monstrous game to cultivate and then harvest the secret desires of their future customer base. A fantasy, of course, but might it be compelling enough to color the way other people view our machines?

If Billy discloses Blake's investment through his game, then he's setting the terms for the controversy the Dancers will inevitably stir up. He'd be dragging his brother into his jaundiced fantasy world in a less literal but more significant way than his fecal effrontery.

Sadly, I can't test that theory on Adrian, so I say, "And I guess I could be confident that someone who's spent a lot of time with *Savant* is going to consider a sex robot about as scandalous as a StairMaster."

"That's for sure. The whole point of *120 Days* is that in matters of vice, you must always escalate. Same thing with technology. The eternal question: 'What comes next?'"

"And the two often come together."

"Since cave painting, dude. Any time we think up a new way to communicate, we use it for smut. Writing, photos, film, phone. Maybe even smoke signals. You, my friend, are walking a well-trod path."

"But teledildonics won't just be an incremental step. More like a giant leap. I fear for the children."

"Well, if everyone's fucking robots, maybe there won't be any more. But don't worry about the kids we've got. They're already irredeemably warped: the first generation who have all seen bestiality vids before their first kiss. With all their 'sexting,' they're used to making their own porn. Online they simulate all kinds of sex long before they get down to the real thing."

"Yeah, but I don't want to drain *all* the mystery from the real thing. I mean, what's it going to be like to lose your virginity to a machine?"

"Better than the town goat, Jimmy. Don't be going soft on us now."

When his cell goes right to voicemail, I say, "Blake, we need to talk."

41

But it was Blythe who got back to me.

I'm steeling myself for another meeting with her two hours from now when she texts me to reschedule. We'd planned to meet in Tribeca after a cocktail reception for the Women in Media roundtable she had to attend. That engagement has been canceled due to a carbon monoxide leak at the venue, so she asks me if I can head up to her apartment.

This is my second invitation in a week from a woman with whom I'm not supposed to be working. I wonder if her place has a steam room.

I'm just turning under her building's awning when a Mercedes Maybach with reinforced windows pulls up. Blythe slips out, riveting as ever in a pale blue cocktail dress. She tells me to stay with the car. She's just going up to change, after which we can go somewhere else to chat. Then she disappears into her building. A bell guy makes way smartly, darting a glance at her legs as she passes.

Disappointed, I follow orders and crawl into the car, giving a mopey salute to her bodyguard/driver Brooks, who's calling in a status update. He turns around to look at me and is about to say something when the left side of his face goes orange from a bright flash of light.

The sound hits with a breathy roar. We both duck instinctively.

"The fuck was that?" I yell.

Brooks lifts his head for a peek out the driver's-side window, squinting at the light. I conclude it's safe to look.

Across the street from us, high flames lick the frame of a car, spewing smoke thick enough that you can see it even in the dark. For an instant, Brooks and I are captivated. Then we hear a woman scream.

Both of us jump out of the car and careen across the street. Oncoming traffic has already stopped, and people are getting out of their cars to bear witness. Brooks runs right up to the burning vehicle to check for passengers. I hesitate, thinking about how bomb makers love to plant a small preamble charge to draw a crowd before the big one hits. Then I hear the scream again and see that it's coming from a large Hispanic woman lying on the sidewalk a couple feet away. Dropping my cowardly calculations, I run over to her, where I'm quickly joined by two bellmen and the security guard from Blythe's building. We're all yelling questions about where she's hurt in what must be a confusing clamor.

It turns out she was screaming mostly with terror. Also that she'd dropped her leash, and her dachshund, Tupac, had elected to get the hell out of there. One of the bell guys rushes off to search for him. While she's bleeding from a couple scrapes she suffered in hitting the deck, I can't see any major injuries. I'm relieved at the sound of approaching sirens.

Brooks comes over to render assistance, having found no one in the car. The flames are dying, and really there wasn't much of an explosion at all. The frame is intact, and I notice that it's an eighties-vintage subcompact, an unusual specimen in this neighborhood. While flames are still billowing out the open windows, there's not even any glass spread around.

The glass.

If that was a real car bomb, this lady would have been peppered with glass from the exploding windows. But she's not. Implying what? That the windows were rolled down and the windshields . . . removed? Which means someone took care that this car fire wouldn't hurt anyone. Which means—

Blythe.

I sprint back across the street, dodging an oncoming phalanx of firefighters. I'm expecting a hassle from her building people, but they're all out watching the commotion. An elevator stands open, and I hammer the button for her floor until my finger jams.

As the numbers tick by, I bounce with tension, furious at myself for being taken in by one of Billy's spectacles. My fury turns to fear when the door opens on Blythe's apartment. Her alarm rings loud. It must have sounded in the lobby, but I didn't pick it out from all the sirens outside. Even above the grating blare, I can hear a rough voice straight ahead of me. I bless the low-level persecution complex I've absorbed from *Savant*, since it's prompted me to start carrying a pistol around.

"—that behind every great fortune is a great crime, dear sister. Maybe both of you will find your fortunes turning because of his crimes."

Holy shit. This isn't one of his game slaves. Billy's finally come calling in person.

"What are you doing here? This is our life, not some cruel game. Don't—"

"Cruel? That's fucking rich. You know you can't keep his secrets locked away anymore."

"Please calm down. You're scaring me, sweetie."

"You should be scared, Blythe. You keep this picture up like nothing ever happened. Like you don't know what he put her through."

I come around the corner and see Blythe standing in the doorway to the reading room where she showed me her father's old records. Directly in front of her, Billy holds a full messenger bag on his hip and a short but nasty-looking crowbar in his left hand. Behind him, a carved wall panel hangs ajar off a set of bent hinges. There's a hidden space behind it, now empty. His other hand thrusts at her the silver-framed picture Blythe showed me the last time I was here.

I draw my gun and advance quietly.

Blythe takes the picture in both hands. "Billy, you can't blame Blake for—"

"The pieces are coming together, Blythe. One more and Blake will face the consequences of what he's done. He calls *me* sick? We'll let the world judge that. Soon enough, everyone will know him for exactly what he is. Maybe then he'll suffer like she did."

I can't get a clean view of him through Blythe. Close now, I step to the side to try for a better angle. They're both looking at the picture.

Blythe sighs and says, "Can't we just try to work this out? For me?"

"Fuck you!" Billy lifts the crowbar.

I jump forward, angling my gun over Blythe's shoulder for a shot, but she throws herself backward, knocking my arm into the doorway. The crowbar slams hard into the picture she's holding, shattering the glass and mangling the frame. I hook one arm around Blythe to drag her away. But Billy lunges at us. He's tiny, and his bull-rush should be in vain, but my legs tangle with Blythe's, and even his slight impact is enough to send us down to the floor. My gun fires into the opposite wall. I brace for the blow from Billy's crowbar, trying to cover Blythe's face, but it never comes.

Billy dashes down the hall toward the exit.

Blythe rolls off me and jumps back to her feet. As I stagger up, I fight the urge to just collapse on the floor. But this is Blythe standing in front of me, her hand covering her mouth from the shock of what just happened.

"Are you okay?" I ask.

She nods wordlessly. I take off after Billy.

I rip open the door to the stairway and hear nothing, so he must have caught the elevator. It's a slow old-fashioned one, but it's also twenty stories to the lobby. I don't see any alternative, so I start rumbling down the stairs at ankle-breaking speed. On the way, I call McClaren and tell him to get his people to cover the exits.

"We're already there," he says.

A couple flights down, the building's fire alarm adds its staccato screeching to Blythe's system. Billy must be trying to engineer a crowd to help cover his escape.

A heart-pounding eternity later, I bang out of the stairwell to find a wide variety of firearms pointed at me. Through its open door, I see the elevator stands empty.

McClaren waves them down. "Well?"

"You guys don't have him?"

"He wasn't in the elevator."

"Well he wasn't on the stairs."

McClaren squints at me. "Please tell me you did not leave Blythe alone in that apartment."

The elevator ride back up is one of the longer minutes of my life, my head throbbing in time with the sounding klaxon.

But Blythe is fine, quietly crying to herself. When she sees us come in, she takes a deep breath and says, "Please, just give me a minute." Then she walks down the hall to her bedroom and shuts the door behind her.

McClaren grips my shoulder. "So where the fuck is our boy?"

"I guess he got down before y'all arrived."

"Impossible. My guys were there when you called. So—wait a sec." He presses a finger to his earpiece and mumbles something into the mic. "They just checked the security tape. The elevator didn't stop at any of the floors. And none of the stairwell doors have been opened in the past half hour, except floor three, which was some old guy leaving his apartment."

"So—"

We both hear a sound at the same time. The low thrum of helicopter blades nearby. Out the two-story window above the ballroom, we see a news chopper flying by, presumably to get footage of the car fire, or maybe some more important eruption of civic disorder.

McClaren gets it just before I do. He knows the building has a decommissioned helipad. "*Up* the stairs, James. He just went a couple flights up."

"You've got to be kidding me. I didn't even think you could fly a helicopter in the city."

"Kid's a crazy billionaire; he ain't going to rob his sister and then figure on escaping by bus. Got to hand it to the little bastard . . ."

McClaren turns on his heel, barking into his radio. I assume he's trying to get a trace on Billy's escape vehicle. Probably a waste of time.

I jog up the stairs and inspect the door to the roof. Its latch is alarmed and locks automatically from the inside. So not a viable way in. But once Billy got inside Blythe's place, it would make an ideal exit provided you could fly off the roof. How did he get a helicopter to land there? A licensed charter claiming temporary mechanical difficulties, maybe. The pickup quick enough to escape the notice of air traffic control.

I admire the elegance of the way his route flows in one direction through the building. Like the work of a good level designer making sure his player never has to retrace his steps.

— — —

I knock on Blythe's door and step into her room without giving her a chance to rebuff me. She's slouched on her grand canopy bed, and as I enter, her hand snaps up to wipe at her eyes. She realizes the futility of the gesture and relaxes with an uneven breath and a forced smile. I set a double Laphroaig on the nightstand and sit down beside her.

"Just thought I'd check on you."

She hesitates, but then grabs the drink and takes a hard swallow. "Thank you."

I notice she has a bloody towel wrapped around her other hand. She sees me look at it and puts it in her lap. "It's fine. Just a cut from the glass."

"Blythe, I'm sorry."

"You're sorry? What are you sorry about?"

"He shouldn't have gotten so close. We should have been . . ." She's frowning at me. "I think I've executed a very nice clock in your library."

Blythe laughs, though it's a sad little thing. "We'll inter it with full honors. I . . . I'm just glad you didn't . . ."

"What did he want?"

"I don't believe he meant me any harm. He . . . well, I think he took some, ah, family things."

"Family things?"

She looks away.

"Blythe. Come on."

She's crying again. Trying to pull herself together. After a moment, she says, "Some home movies. Private. That's why they were kept in that cabinet. Most of them were his anyway. Confiscated by my dad over the years. He could have just—well, I don't . . ."

"Home movies?"

"Yeah. We . . . Why don't I just show you?" She slips into her room-sized closet. I can hear her opening a safe. She emerges with a tiny black memory stick and slides it into her laptop. "Before he died, my father had all his records digitized. These were a few things I had pulled from the archive. Billy just took the originals." Sitting back on the bed, she turns the screen toward me.

— — —

The shot starts on the face of a maybe seven-year-old Billy, who has just turned on the camera, which rests on a bureau above his bed. He drapes a piece of clothing over it so that an edge of plaid fabric obscures the top of the frame. Billy then scampers down and secures himself under his blankets. He feigns sleep.

A few seconds later, his mother sits on the edge of his bed next to him. You can see the resemblance between the two. Dark coyote eyes. A sort of smoldering energy. She's wearing a sheer, light green negligee. She rubs his cheek gently and says, "Billy. I need to speak with you for a sec."

Billy slowly opens his eyes. He yawns, overplaying it.

"Sweetie, I heard you come into our room. You know you're supposed to knock first."

"I know, Mom. I'm sorry."

"Now, Billy, if you saw anything that maybe frightened you . . . I need you to know that everything is okay. You don't need to worry."

"But . . . was he hurting you?"

"No, honey. It's like a game Mommy and Daddy play. You'll understand when you're older. But what's important is that you know that your mommy and daddy love each other very much, and he would never really hurt me. Okay, cowboy?"

"Yes, Mommy."

She reaches to hug him. The motion twists her torso so that her back moves into the cone of light from Billy's bedside lamp. On the pale plane of her nightgown, stripes of blood have seeped through the fabric.

Uh-huh . . . Just another quiet evening in the Randall household. Jesus.

Blythe was never disposed toward confession, so her showing me that video is surprising. Is it supposed to *mean* something to me? Maybe she's trying to illustrate the emotional stakes involved in this confrontation between her brothers. Far from a mere fraternal tiff over corporate politics, Billy's looking to exorcize some very real violence he absorbed growing up in his father's household. A secret dark enough that I suppose Blake might resort to equally harsh means to suppress it.

My question from the beginning had been: what are the Randall twins so afraid of?

In showing me this video, Blythe is starting to make that plain.

I reach for something to say. Sadly I arrive at a brittle joke. "So I guess we know where his interest in Sade comes from."

Her eyes fill with tears again. "My father . . . My father wasn't . . ." But she just shrugs helplessly and dissolves into a racking sob.

She presses her face against my shoulder, and I hold on tightly. I'm ashamed to admit that even now, the touch of her skin suffuses my body with a warm narcotic feeling.

"It's okay," I whisper. "It'll be all right."

But some kind of dam has broken in Blythe and she starts speaking desperately. "But my father's not the reason. It's Gina. She's behind all of it. He blames Blake for her death. He only knew her in college, but Billy thinks that he did something to her. He won't tell me anything more. You know how he talks in these ridiculous riddles. But I know it's all about her. They say in her last words, she's talking about Sodom or something, and that's where all this shit comes from."

I can feel her tears melting into my shoulder. I say, "He was in love with her."

"But it's more than that with Billy . . ." She pauses to regain her voice. "He's only loved two women in his life. His mother and Gina. And they both killed themselves. Can you imagine?"

Leaving aside the grisly details, can I imagine losing my mother and the only woman I'll ever love? Yeah, I can.

"Blythe," I ask, "is it always going to take a crowbar to get you to open up?"

She shakes her head. "I should have told you all this . . . I'm sorry. I know our secrecy makes it hard for you. But it's just that . . . there's so much pain in our family. We've learned to bury it deep. And now poor Billy is digging and digging. You know what that's like? My brother, he's going . . ."

"But Blythe, you know that I . . . that of all people, I'd never do anything to hurt you."

"I know," she says, squeezing harder now. She lifts her head slightly so her cheek brushes mine. "I know that, James. That's why we called you."

Suddenly, I feel her pull away from me. I don't need to turn to know who I'll find rushing through the door.

"James, I need a moment alone with my sister," he says.

42

I had no desire to linger as Blake took in the sight of his wounded twin. Their voices were just audible through the door. Quiet but edged with fury.

Blythe's apartment has filled with serious men conducting themselves as if at a crime scene. Someone is checking the door for tampering, someone else photographs the damage to the reading room cabinet. None of these people are police. I doubt if anyone not directly accountable to the Randalls will ever see the inside of her home.

I look at the shattered remnants of the picture lying on the ground and think back to what Billy said to Blythe: "The pieces are coming together."

What "pieces" is he talking about?

Well, he stole videos from Robert Randall's hidden cache, and *Savant* is a game wherein the primary currency is video clips. Recordings of one's crimes and outrages. It stands to reason that Billy's planning to deploy his morbid home movies in some way. But he said he needed "one more" before his brother would be held to account.

Does he mean one more video?

Blythe said Gina Delaney's death is driving Billy's actions. Detective Nash told me that she videotaped her suicide. Which Billy blames on Olya, though according to Blythe, perhaps he's implicated Blake somehow as well.

So is Billy planning to use Gina's death video in his game?

Publishing an actual snuff film seems extreme, though he hasn't shown any tendency to flinch from strong content. He'll want his players to see Gina's sickening final moments and, by following his slowly unwinding narrative, come to blame his enemies for them as he does. I already assumed it was Billy who tried to buy the video from Nash's bent crime scene tech. And that implies a crucial detail about his agenda:

He doesn't have the video yet. And that means I can get a step ahead of him.

I start typing an email to Detective Nash.

I'm too charged up from my encounter with Blythe to sleep, so I decide to console myself in the immaterial arms of my digital dalliance.

Around one in the morning, I head back to the Orifice and find the place abandoned.

After spending some time to synch up to Xan's latest updates, I'm bending over to plug in our Ginger simulator when I get that shivery feeling that someone's watching me from behind. I turn around to see Olya silhouetted in the dim light of the doorway. She looks like she's just rushed away from an awards show after-party, wearing the kind of dress you have to use industrial adhesives to keep on. She glares at me with such rage that a ripple of fear runs through my guts. Like I'm a small child who has done something unmentionable and is about to receive the full wrath of my evil stepmother.

"Olya, hey . . . what's going—"

Two long strides bring her near. I can see her wind up from over her left shoulder, but I just watch, fascinated, as she unloads on me with a vicious backhand that hammers into my face. Her rings dig long welts in my cheek. My hand flies up to cover the damage and feels the slickness of blood.

"What the fuck?"

She's not listening. I barely get my arm up to deflect her forehand follow-up. She takes this in stride, grabbing a handful of my shirt at the shoulder. She steps in close, her foot just behind mine, and then uses all her weight to shove me backward over my chair. I sprawl disgracefully on the floor.

Olya seems ready to bolster this treatment with a good kicking. Maybe it's her heels, or maybe my abject state, but she decides against it and just looms over me.

"Who the fuck do you think you are?" Her voice is a fearsome hiss.

Trying to lever myself up against the wall, I say, "Look, I don't know what—"

This infuriates her enough that she bends down, plants a knee in my crotch, and grabs me by the hair. "Don't fucking lie to me!"

This time I'm better prepared. I take her hand and twist it back so she has to let go. Then I snatch her other hand and force it across her chest, so she can't hit me again. She fights it all the way, and I'm dismayed at how strong she is.

"Olya, you need to stop this shit now!"

She writhes violently, and I push her off me. I get up slowly, examining my torn cheek again. "What is your problem?"

She stands, and I check my guard since it doesn't look like she's finished. But she straightens her posture, composing herself. She says, "You think you can take this over? You think this, Zhames?"

"Would you calm down?"

"I spoke with Benito. You go and start making threats to our partner? How stupid a man—"

"Olya, relax. Let's talk about this."

"You want to talk? You don't talk to anyone but me. You're nothing. How could you think to do this?"

"Listen, I understand why you're upset. I'm sorry. It was a mistake."

"Oh, you make mistake?"

"Well, did you ever think maybe you were making a mistake?"

She closes her eyes. A long susurrant exhale is followed by, "I know what I am doing, James."

"Are you really sure about that? I know about Blake as well."

Her expression darkens again. She's about to deny it but then shrugs irritably. "So what? We will need lots of money. He has it. And he owns half the media in this shitty country."

"Well, let's leave the good old USA out of it. But Blake Randall is the leader of a public company, and so if he has to invest through this shady porno proxy—"

"Exotica knows the industry. Their experience is essential."

"Exotica is a mobbed-up filth factory that sells giant black dildos called 'the Negro Problem.' You want your brilliant invention competing for shelf space with that?"

"Ugh. Zhames, you think you're not working on a sex toy? What is this stupid saying? Ah . . . 'It is what it is.' Now you are getting romantic about a cow-milking machine." She steps over and grabs Ginger by her neck and drags her toward me. "So this is going to be your lovely new girlfriend? No. You will hide her under the bed."

"I thought we were going to challenge that impulse by injecting some class. Like Fred and Ginger, remember?"

"You are naïve. We could spend years making fine design. Nice packaging, but this is still a sex toy. The only thing you inject is *spermu*."

She moves closer, pulling Ginger with her. I put my hands up. "Olya—"

She bats them away irritably but without her former violence. "I show you."

Lots of things about Olya have amazed me to this point, but the new pinnacle is the dexterity with which she has my fly down and my dick out before I can react. She stretches across me and dips her fingers into one of the tubs of Ginger's special lubricant. It's sharply cold as she applies it. Exciting. Then Olya jams Ginger's mouth over me. Without the heating elements and wiggling air bladders, it feels plastic and alien.

"Eh, Zhimbo? It's like fucking a Barbie, no? You will not make love with this. You will never use it with a lover. It will be strange bitches who talk dirty and disappear, and charge you for the arm and leg. Exotica knows how to do this. Make you play with this plastic toy."

"You, ah, have to turn it on."

"No, Zhames, you cannot turn this on. It is a machine. It does what we tell it. And not very much at that. Just this." She jerks Ginger's head back and forth roughly. "*Da,* you like that?"

"It feels fucking great. That's why we're doing it. I don't know why you want to let them make it cheap and tawdry. Ugly, like all that other shit."

"Oh, do I insult your girlfriend? Please. You must know that this"— she raps Ginger's head with her rings—"is not at all like this."

She takes my hand and places it under her dress.

Had I been asked, I would have bet that Olya doesn't wear underwear with formal attire, but it's nonetheless shocking to feel bare flesh under my fingers.

"She will never be like a real woman, Zhames." She's close to me now, whispering in my ear. "You forget what one feels like?"

My head is still pounding from our earlier altercation, and I'm not entirely sure when this changed from an interrogation to a seduction. But it makes sense to me that Olya would operate this way. My blood was up before I got here, and I don't need to be asked twice.

Ginger goes hard over sideways as I lunge at her. Olya steps back and I get a twitch of panic that she's retreating. But the heavens open and hurl a bolt of sweet elation into my brain when she props herself on the table and seizes me with her legs. I go instantly inside, like our bodies are precision-milled parts finally snapping together.

It doesn't take long. She makes very little noise, just an occasional quick intake of breath. But as we recline, she's pushing against me with an urgency that I take to be a challenge.

For a few luscious moments I know nothing but the animal imperative to thrust for all I'm worth. Olya shakes so violently that my grip on her shoulder slips, and my knuckles thump painfully against the table. She convulses in a way that's borderline distressing. Like she really can't breathe, and it goes on for longer than I thought possible. Maybe I'm discomfited and hesitate, because she gasps, "Don't stop." I'm shaking right along with her moments later.

The end comes as suddenly as it started. She covers her face with one hand for a second. I take my weight off her and start to straighten up while remaining inside, because I can't bring myself to leave just yet. As I shift, her right leg flashes by my face. But she's not attacking me again, just stretching with her usual flamboyant aggression. Her lips twist slightly at my flinch, and she puts her foot on my chest and slowly pushes me out.

I gaze down at her breathtaking chest and see what looks at first like some horrible attack of hives spreading all the way up to her neck. But then I realize it's just an uncommonly intense sex flush. I reach out to trace the boundary of her inflamed skin, marveling at the depth of sensation that it must take to cause this. Her body feels like cooling lava.

When I glance up at her face, her eyes have turned dark, and she says softly, "We have so much to do."

43

We're at it again the next day. By unspoken agreement, Olya and I both show up at the unheard-of hour of six AM. I don't get so much as a "good morning." She just steps into my office, hikes her skirt, and beckons with a peremptory flick of her fingers. I start to say something, but she presses her hand over my mouth and unzips my fly. Olya's rule number one is no talking. Rather suspicious that our relationship flowered just as I started asking her uncomfortable questions. But for the moment, I'm more than happy to keep my mouth shut.

She's pretty indifferent to foreplay as well. I start trotting out what few lovemaking niceties I possess, but before I've even made a single circuit around her earlobe with my tongue, she's got me inside her and is hammering on my ass with her heels.

I've never been confronted with such naked physical need. Her eyes clamp shut, and I'm certain they won't open until she's done. Right now, my identity as a fellow human is of zero consequence to Olya. She's totally consumed with her own body, and all she needs from me is a strong rhythm and mammalian heat. In this, she's the opposite of Blythe, my only other experience with a goddess-level bedmate. For Blythe, ecstasy was a hollow thing if it wasn't shared and mutually reveled in.

I might feel depersonalized by Olya's sexual trance, but instead I find it incredibly liberating. There's no trace of anxiety about timing, performance, or emotional synchronicity. I'm left with the sheer joy of drowning myself in her incomparable flesh.

She comes hard, fast, and, as near as I can tell, automatically. During our second attempt she completely clears my desk. But a broken monitor is a small price to pay for the memory of this woman panting and writhing in my arms.

Last night she'd unsettled me with her dismissive talk about the robots she normally refers to as her children. Previously, I entertained certain doubts about our project. But finally having real sex after all this time has freed me of any ambivalence.

What I'm feeling with Olya now is a living dream.

This particular dream we've been chasing together for weeks now through a digital fantasyland. Far from being an alienating, sterile technology, the Dancers have fostered a sense of erotic ease among the iTeam. They've been a safe sandbox in which we've gradually gotten comfortable with each other. Not only Olya, but I'm beginning to see stirrings with Xan as well. Our dream world may even be working on Garriott's congenital shyness.

I wonder what Olya's like with other, normal lovers. Does she whisper endearments, stare longingly into their eyes? In a sense, she's already *had* sex with me any number of times, and she feels totally entitled to treat me like I'm a machine. Which may sound unfortunate, but in practice brings pure bliss.

People tend to be at their best when they feel empowered. And there's nothing like the malleable magic of virtuality for inciting that sense of possibility. Liberated from our corporeal prisons we feel superhuman, not ghostly. You can try anything, since mistakes can be wiped out with the click of a button. And that lets you do things, explore emotions you would never consider in the squalid permanence of meatspace. In NOD there's no conversation that can't be had. No activity too risky. No thing you cannot do.

Is it perfect? No, far from it. But the Dancers are powerful in this way, and I want other people to feel it. Not to adopt them as any kind of replacement, but to use them to explore. This sense of adventurous communion they can encourage seems to diffuse into reality. As evidenced by the glory of the current moment.

− − −

Just as I'm starting to worry about my endurance, Olya emerges from a decisive series of shudders and pushes me away. She steps back quickly and looks at me like she's awakened to find a stranger in her bedroom. Her eyes close as she takes a deep breath and cracks her neck. I get a veiled smile and an ambiguous, "Hmm . . ."

Then she walks out.

At nine fifteen AM, I get a message that the RAT embedded in the email I sent Nash last night has been activated. The text had simply requested that he download a voice sample of Billy and ask around if anyone had fielded inquiries from this guy about Gina's death. As hacks go, this one hardly deserves the name, but infecting someone when you've established a trusted relationship is always pretty easy.

Nash emailed me back, tersely saying he'd look into it, but by then, using a brand-new flaw Red Rook found in Microsoft's Media Player software, my file had already released its toxins, and I'm now busy dumping his hard drive and installing keystroke loggers. He doesn't have a copy of Gina's video, so I'll have to wait until he logs into the NYPD's digital evidence vault to get it.

44

Back in *Savant*, I find a message from the Duke congratulating me on reaching the Third Degree. To do so I've had to satisfy an ever-more-egregious series of commands. Sourcing abominable porn has been fairly easy due to my contacts in law enforcement, but four of the "crimes" have required that I personally appear in the videos. Though I seem to have no problem with robot sodomy, when it comes to Sadean levels of pain, perversion, and paraphilia, I'm simply not varsity material. Fortunately, the genre permitted me to wear a mask in each of these cases.

My most recent chore required that Adrian hook me up with a local role-play specialist to spend a couple hours reenacting a weird armpit frotteurism episode from *120 Days*. While probably not fulfilling the stipulated quotas of bodily fluids, we put enough vigor into it that I thought it might suffice. And it saved me from having to violate any health codes.

Normally, a new quest is transmitted right after completing the previous one, and today is no different. Though the tasks usually come as messages from one of the Friends, here I'm confronted by a NoBot called Madame Champville, who was another one of the storytellers from the book.

She hands me an envelope that contains a note written in flowing cursive with little pictograms substituting for certain words:

Gather the 🌹 *from the* ⊤ *in time*

Leave at the ▮ *, and please know that I'm*

Observing your courage or noting its lack

So make sure in this case that you never look back.

So far, the orders I've received from Silling's inmates have been quite explicit. But this one is in code. As my tasks tread the line of legality, a criminal organization like the Pyrexians *would* start encoding their commands. I suppose anyone seeking to join them lusts after forbidden images and is therefore familiar with the methods one uses to conceal them.

This particular code seems fairly simple. The image files standing in for the words "rose," "table," and "grave" are unusually grainy. I could spend hours scouring them for information, but Red Rook has a whole department dedicated to this kind of image analysis work. So I zip them up and forward them to our Stegosauri.

Half an hour later, I get a response:

```
From:  denigma@redrook.com
Sent:  Saturday, January 23, 2015 0:45 am
To: prycesryght@redrook.com
Subject:  Re: Lost my decoder ring


Mr. Pryce,


Please note that you sent these images to Red Rook's
Steganography department. Steganography means "hidden
message," not "message advertised by preposterously
sloppy enciphering." In this case, an insultingly
trivial high-density LSB encoding on the carrier files.
Your payloads are enclosed, but in the future, please
```

```
send such work to Red Rook's "dallying with dimwitted
dilettantes" division.
```

```
-DeNigma.
```

Though wanting in professional courtesy, I can't argue with our Cryp-tiles' results. Attached to the note are three new, even-lower-resolution files.

The rose holds a portrait of a skinny girl who looks about seventeen. She has caramel skin and green eyes set off with too much eyeliner. She's wearing a tight pink baby tee with the name "Rosita" spelled out in gangster-Gothic script. The pattern I've seen with the Degrees is that for any names that come up, Billy always picks some variation on a child victim from the book. In this case, Rosita is a Spanish version of little Rosette, the general's daughter kidnapped from her mother's house in the countryside.

Needless to say, she does not fare well.

The wooden table's image shows a different kind of table: here the schedule board at a train station. Given that it lists Metroliner departures to both Boston and Washington, DC, I assume that it's Penn Station. Only an Acela from DC currently occupies a gate. One of those red time stamps, the kind nobody uses anymore, sits in the lower right corner of the photo. The date reads "01.24.15 12:47 AM," which would mean that the picture was taken tomorrow night, a revolutionary advance in digital photography.

Finally, the headstone file contains an image of a graveyard, though the flowering riot of tulips and overhanging redbud tree give this one a dis-tinctly cheerful cast. I'm further cheered by the ease with which this par-ticular graveyard can be identified. The building filling the background has a granite façade inscribed with the words AMERICAN STOCK EXCHANGE. That would place the shot at Trinity Church, which lies just at the foot of Wall Street. The time stamp on this one shows two AM, about twenty-five hours from now.

Substituting these new images into my original orders reveals pretty clear instructions: pick up this Rosita woman from Penn Station at the specified time. Leave her at the Trinity Church graveyard an hour later.

For Jacques, Billy's game so far has been purely virtual. It's located in NOD and deals with digital objects: avatars and video images. But now I've finally caught up with the elite players, and *Savant* seems primed to start hemorrhaging into real life.

45

The train is right on time. I see her step off the escalator and start scanning the station.

"Rosita?"

She examines me, a little startled, as though she hadn't expected to be met. In case someone is monitoring this exchange, I've disguised myself in a woolen cap with tinted glasses. A real human-hair mustache rounds out my "I drive at night until the art world evolves enough to understand my work" look.

Rosita's dressed in a dissonant combination of a nice suit, a casual blouse, and fuck-me heels. She seems young and nervous underneath it. Like she's going to a business meeting, but no one's ever told her how to dress. The way she squints at her surroundings tells me that she hasn't been to Penn Station before. But she marshals an edgy smile and puts out her hand.

"Rosa de la Cruz," she says. She's carrying a beat-up duffel bag, which I move to take, but she shifts away and says, "I got it," her accent second-generation Hispanic. We assess each other for a moment. She says, "You're with Sweetest Taboo?"

Her question resolves in my head too late to prevent me from saying, "What?"

"The Sweetest Taboo" was a hit single from the British-Nigerian singer Sade Adu. Her name is pronounced Shah-day, but the connection is clear. Rosa rocks back on her heels, reconsidering me.

I try to recover. "Oh, right. Yeah. I'm just the driver."

She thinks about this for a second and then hands me her bag. "So where are we going?"

Her second query also throws me. Unless Rosa's the consummate actress, she honestly doesn't know the answer. I can't bring myself to say that I'm taking her to a graveyard in the middle of the night, so I go with, "Downtown."

She relaxes somewhat in the front seat of my rented Lincoln Town Car. As I drive her down the West Side Highway, I wonder what happens once we get to our destination.

I start with small talk about her trip. Whether she's ever been to New York before. She gazes avidly at the bright skyline. I ask what brings her to the city.

"Business."

"You look a little young to be doing business. How old are you?"

"Twenty-one." She doesn't hesitate, but she paints her answer with an emphatically blasé shade that destroys the realism. "I'm a fashion designer. Your company wants me to do a line for them. That's why they invited me up here."

"A whole clothing line?" I take in her tone-deaf outfit. "For real?"

"No, man, it's virtual clothing. I design for NOD avatars."

"Oh, like one of those video games?"

"It's not a game. I get paid real money. Here, I'll show you."

She extracts a sketch book from her portfolio, flipping to a section pasted with color pictures taken from NOD. Rosa's designs range from belle époque confections of satin and lace to fanciful barbarian marmot brassieres. They're good enough to make me want to commission some RL pieces. I give her a soft wolf whistle.

She brightens at the compliment. "Yeah, I like that stuff. But Taboo's new store is on this island where all the *desviados* hang. They spend a lot more money than normal people. So . . ." She fans through several pages. They contain drawings of buxom women wearing unicorn blindfolds, the business ends of which are circumcised to match their dildo-spurred boots. She's got supervillain men with tentacle hands and some animal outfits that flip by too quickly for me to make sense of. Again I see that for fauna fetishists, the beast itself isn't always sufficient. We have to go one better and put Bowser in a latex nun's habit.

I tilt my head at her. She shrugs.

"I'm saving up to go to the Fashion Institute of Technology."

"Your parents know you're here?"

She gives me a hard look. "My dad is in Afghanistan. I've been all over the world. This is no big deal."

Of course she'd be an army brat: Rosette, the daughter of a general. I glance at her as she stares out the window, arms crossed over her chest. A trail of holes runs down the edge of her left ear. Evidence of a rebellious stage? But oddly her ears aren't pierced in the normal place. Instead a short vertical scar notches each lobe, as if she once wore earrings but . . . had them violently jerked out. Then the torn flesh was stitched back together. Maybe this one is a fighter. Or maybe she's been abused. I notice she didn't mention her mother.

I decide to risk trying to slip past the fourth wall. "Ah, this may sound crazy, but let's just say that you weren't really going to a meeting."

"What?"

"Just bear with me. Let's say that someone offered you some money to come up here and pretend like you were going to meet with this company." Her frown deepens. "All I'm saying is I know some people who would pay you a lot more if you could provide any other information about why you're here."

She shifts away from me, her hand inching toward the door handle. "Man, what are you *talking* about?"

I back off. "Nothing. Don't worry about it. I must have you confused with someone else. Forget I said anything."

She eyes me warily. "I thought you said you were just the driver."

"That's right. I am."

"Then why don't you just drive?"

Our arrival at the graveyard goes more smoothly than I expected. While a lot of New Yorkers find Wall Street's emptiness at night spooky, Rosa just sees a bunch of nice buildings, any one of which could be a hotel. I park along Trinity Place across from the Amex building. The church is perched on a knoll right above us. A hoary, now eccentric brick wall lines the embankment. An archway is carved into it midway down the block, and a steep stone stairway leads to an oak door that doesn't look like it's been opened in the church's four-hundred-year history. Tonight we find it unlocked, and the door loudly protests our disrupting its repose. The gloomy climb up into the churchyard finally breaks Rosa's composure.

She jerks on my sleeve. "Hey . . . Where are we? Why'd you take me here?"

I pretend to check something in my cell phone. "This is the address I was given. I think someone is supposed to meet you."

"No. That can't be right. This . . . This place is a *graveyard*."

"It's right. Trust me. Someone's coming to get you. Just sit on that bench over there. It'll be fine."

"Wait. Where are you going?"

"Well, I was just told to bring you here. So now . . . I have to go."

She can't believe what I've just said. "You're leaving?"

I relent. "Look, I have . . . my orders. I'll tell you what." I write my cell number on a twenty-dollar bill. "Stay here for fifteen minutes. If they don't pick you up by then, call me. I'll come get you, and I'll check you into any hotel you want. The Ritz-Carlton is a couple blocks away." I give her the twenty and walk briskly back toward the stairs.

"The Ritz . . . Wait, no, don't leave." She trails after me. "Hey man, don't leave me here." She's on the verge of tears.

But my orders are clear: "Don't look back." I shut the door and hear it latch.

"Come back . . . Please." The last word is a high-pitched cry.

I get into my car and head slowly down the street.

My instructions implied that I would be watched, but I can't see how he'd pull it off. The street around me is empty, no cars, no pedestrians. I make a couple quick turns. Billy could have stationed someone in a building with a view of the churchyard, but there's no way an observer could see to the adjacent streets through the cluster of skyscrapers.

Don't be an idiot. You're buying into his absurd atmospherics. And no matter how well-run his game is, you cannot leave a scared teenage girl alone in that grave-yard at two in the morning.

I swerve right up Liberty Street and then dart the wrong way down

William to head back toward Trinity Place. Turning right, I park on Pine Street two blocks above the church. After slinking down another block among the columns of a temple to commerce, I take refuge in the entry to a Citibank with a good view of the churchyard. I'm hoping Rosa sat on the bench, because then I'll have a perfect view of her through the statuary.

But Rosa is gone.

I survey the area, but there's no trace of her. Other than her bag sitting abandoned on the bench. That doesn't seem good.

Stop it. This is just overproduced street theater. She's gone because Billy can't have his audience follow the actors into the wings.

But I can't help thinking about the awful fate visited upon poor Rosette in *120 Days.*

Come on. She'll be fine. They're probably taking her out for dinner tonight.

All the same, Sade's infernal images have colonized my head.

46

That uneasiness makes me log back into *Savant* as soon as I get home to see if I can discover some clue to clarify what just happened. But I merely wander around the eerie castle battling the creeping, sub-rational feeling that I've done something terrible.

Maybe that's why I start so violently when I hear a familiar voice say, "Congratulations . . . Jacques."

The voice is right behind me, and I spin around so violently that my knees bang into the right trestle of my desk. But there's no one there. Just my rear channel speakers. I realize the voice must have come from *Savant*. Run through my audio system, it sounded like he was in the room with me.

It dawns on me that I didn't have NOD's voice chat feature turned on. For some reason people generally prefer regular text chat to voice. And yet someone just started a session with me without my permission. In NOD, the only person who could do that would be the guy *who owns the sim.*

I mash keys to turn my av, and at last I behold the virtual alter ego of Billy Randall.

But I can tell right away that's not quite right. The av in front of me is a dashing rake in all the finery of a pre-revolutionary aristocrat, and Billy has made him tall, athletic, and extremely fair. A faithful image of his brother Blake. And now I know why the voice was familiar. It's a spot-on impression. Confirmation that Billy's virtually impersonating his brother to place him as a member of his fake Pyrexians.

His NODName, Fedor_Sett, stumps me at first, but eventually I work out "Feed Durcet." Of Château de Silling's four Friends, Curval the judge and Durcet the banker have the most pronounced appetites for ingesting filth. If Billy's assigned Blake the latter role, then I can see why the freelance waiter at Demeter looked surprised when his offering was rejected.

I take a deep breath to settle myself and say into my desktop mic, "Ah, thanks. I'm glad to finally meet you." While speaking, I start a trace on the IP address from which Billy's av is connecting.

But Fedor_Sett doesn't respond. With an impressive flourish of animation, he extracts a card from his jacket pocket. This av is merely a messenger.

I'm surprised Billy hasn't masked the originating IP address for his NoBot, which comes back as 192.0.2.133. The first domestic one I've seen from him. But those numbers feel familiar as well . . .

Because he's spoofing the connection record to appear as though it came from IMP. So Billy's impersonation goes even more than skin deep. When I take the item he's offering, the NoBot rezzes out.

The card reads:

For the favor you've done
From our collection here's one
So to discharge our debt
Please enjoy this vignette

Fedor_Sett's "vignette" link leads to the first of the videos Billy stole from his sister. A clip that stars him and the twins as young children. Blake sits on top of Billy, force-feeding him a dark mushy substance that sadly does not look like chocolate pudding. Billy repays Blake's culinary exertions by vomiting all over him.

A charming childhood scene that should really appeal to the Sade fans' interest in bodily fluids. The video makes clear where the roots of Billy's rage against his brother were planted.

So this is how Billy's planning to expose his family dirt. He's mixed his awful childhood mementos in with a trove of reward videos for his players. I'll bet he's assembled a record of Blake's crimes that covers everything from youthful cheating at Wiffle ball to his recent indecorous investments. Since the videos have to get progressively worse, he probably intends the climax of these atrocities to be Gina's suicide video and will then detail his reasons for laying her body at his brother's feet. Billy must think that as people start digesting his gumdrops, the pressure on Blake will ratchet to a point where he'll start to envy her.

47

I'm far from the only one helping to pump *Savant*'s poison into the real world. Judging by the series of news reports sent from Red Rook's clipping service, Château de Silling has turned a wave of its inmates loose on the streets.

Several online crime blotters have noted an uptick in sexual misdemeanor cases in certain metro areas. One put together an interesting montage of cuffed men in police cars wearing full powdered wigs.

Sex worker boards are filling with alerts defining archaic terminology. For example, this one on *The Erotic Review*:

Ladies, if someone asks if you allow "fustigation," the answer is "No," or "Fuck off." It means beating you with a stick. And red-flag him for your sisters. Has there been a full moon this past week, or what?

Then this appeal from a woman posting to the main *Savant* forum:

Thread: Reward for Information

Frantic_Mom	Please help me!!!
Joined:2/01/15 Posts: 1 Location: Los Angeles, CA	My son has been missing for four days. I got into his computer, and I know he spent a lot of time playing this game.

> I don't care what he's been doing, I just
> want him back.
>
> I have $5,000 for anyone who can give me
> information to help find him. No questions
> asked. He is only sixteen.

Attached to the post is a picture split in halves. The left is a yearbook photo of a spindly, nervous-looking teen. The right shows a screen shot of his burly leather-lord NOD avatar.

I guess these days one picture isn't enough.

Blake finally got back to me later that evening.

He left a voicemail asking to meet at an unfamiliar address in Brooklyn, a small bar called Paul's that is more or less the inverse of the Racquet and Tennis. At six PM, the place is dark, dusty, and deserted. Paul must be going through a long-term identity crisis. Woefully maintained Irish accents are muddled by pictures of Mexican national soccer teams from the 1970s.

Blake has secured us a pair of martinis, and he tips his glass as I take the seat next to him. He says, "I didn't suppose the little bastard would ever have the balls to attack my sister. Think this might add some urgency to your efforts?"

"Do you really believe having him committed is going to prevent people from finding out that you're building a virtual sex empire?"

My question was meant to jar him, but it fails miserably. Blake beams a satisfied smile at me, like his prize pupil has just solved a complicated proof. "Virtual sex empire. I like the sound of that."

"Think your board will? What about your sister?"

Blake just shrugs as if the questions, or at least the questioner, are of little consequence. I try a different approach. "You know, my work would have been a lot easier if you'd told me all this at the beginning."

Blake sips his drink and says, "True. But I needed to know what you could find out and how you'd go about it. I won't mention the fact that *your* disclosures on this topic were, shall we say, less than candid?"

"Fair enough. But I'm trying to help you, and you're making that more difficult."

"Okay. Absolute honesty henceforth." But his eyes sparkle mischievously. As if mocking the whole concept of veracity. "What would you like to know?"

There's a lot I'd like to know. Why does Billy blame him for Gina's death? Does he really think his brother is crazy? What's he going to do if he finds him? But all these give way to my real concern: his intentions toward the Dancers.

I ask, "Why are you backing IT? With this huge merger coming up, why give your brother the ammunition? It doesn't make any sense."

"You have any idea why I wanted to meet you at this shithole?"

Exasperated, I shake my head.

"Good. Let's take a walk."

Five minutes later, we've stepped across the street to an anonymous red brick warehouse. Now we sit in a conference room, empty except for a pair of odd contraptions. While I'm used to mechanisms with human orifices, these things look like the open mouths of giant robotic squids. Each has a steel center ring five feet in diameter around which stand a series of eight spiky robot arms. In the center of the ring are two segmented beams bristling with heavy-duty motors. They terminate in what seem to be extraterrestrial ski boots with soles supported by large air cylinders.

"Welcome to Project Holy Duck," says Blake.

He walks up to the first machine, slips off his shoes, and steps carefully into the boots. A rack hanging from the ceiling holds a pair of HMD goggles and a foam maul. Something about its fat cylindrical head attached to a thin plastic handle sets off hazy recognition signals.

Leveling his now sightless gaze at me, he says, "When I said 'let's take a walk,' I hope you didn't think I meant just across the street."

Blake gestures at the other machine, and I climb aboard. A series of bladders inflate around my feet, and I rise a couple inches on what feels like a cloud of air. As if I've strapped on a pair of Mercury's winged sandals. Then the visuals rez up, showing almost the reverse.

I stand in front of a polished brass mirror in an underground burrow. Tree roots meander along the dirt walls. My reflection shows that I've become a garden gnome, complete with bushy white beard and red conical hat. I wiggle to test out the body tracking. It's seamless. I look over to see that Blake's assumed the form of a tiny fluttering fairy.

He says in a voice processed into a squeaky chirp, "Hurry, Gwilligur! Our burrow is under attack!"

With that, he sparkles open the room's door and flies out. Without thinking about it, I follow him. Only as I cross the threshold and enter a long, torch-lit passage do I fully realize what I'm doing.

I'm walking.

Perhaps the most crucial problem with this kind of simulation has been the lack of a natural way to move oneself through space, which tends to ruin the illusion of presence. Here I'm not pushing my av around the screen with a joystick, but actually walking like a normal human through a fantasy world. Just to try it, I turn and walk in the other direction down the hall. Blake's mechanized boots handle this without a hitch.

He's got a working omnimill.

Technically you'd call it an omnidirectional locomotion interface. Most of these have been developed for the army, and various labs have tried everything from motorized roller skates to giant spherical hamster balls, with varying degrees of success. But Blake's system represents a real breakthrough. The complete gestalt.

My thoughts are interrupted by a trickling of dirt down the wall in front of me. A hole opens, and out of it emerges a small but demonic-looking purple mole. Its giant claws and pulsating star nose remind me of something from a fifties creature feature. It calmly steps out onto a nearby root, takes a tiny crossbow off its back, loads a bolt, and fires.

I'm startled almost to the point of panic when I feel a sting on my chest where the arrow hits me—the snap of a rubber band fired from close range.

Can Blake's machine actually be firing BBs at me?

"Ow. That hurts."

His fairy grins at me. "Well, what are you going to do about it?"

Just then I feel another much more painful sting on the left side of my neck. Instinctively, I lash out at the horrible mole with my maul. I'm expecting an airy visual damage metaphor, but instead I get a sharp twinge in my elbow when my mallet impacts with an unbelievably delightful crushing sensation. Right then I realize what's familiar about this setup: it's a thirty-years-overdue update of the classic carnival game

Whack-A-Mole. As the most tactilely satisfying game of all time, there's no better app for Blake to show off his next-gen VR system. This game lets the player stroll about and whack moles, not in a restricted little box, but all around him.

And the moles can fight back.

Blake flutters over to inspect the green goo dripping off my war hammer. "I give you Walk-A-Mole." He pronounces its name like the avocado dip that bears a strong resemblance to the remains of the creature I just pulverized.

Suddenly, there's a huge cascade of dirt from the surrounding walls, and a regiment of mutant moles begins unloading on me. Mass slaughter ensues, and three minutes later, after a desperately fought running battle, I stand victorious. Out of breath and sweating, I contemplate the single most compelling digital experience I've ever had—save of course my first date with Ginger. But what Blake has done here is even bigger. He's finally put us all the way into the machine.

I flip up my HMD to see him standing to the side of his omniboots, watching me.

I look him in the eye and say, "Holy fuck."

He bows. "Thus the name. Derived from the word 'holodeck,' but we soon realized it was refreshingly apropos."

"So . . ."

"So my brother's not the only one who swallowed the blue pill." Blake turns his back to me and lifts the hair at the nape of his neck. He uncovers a small tattoo: just a dot with a circle around it.

But clearly a jack.

We're seated in a small chamber behind some one-way glass watching several of Blake's technicians work on the consumer version of the military-grade system I just test-drove.

"Had I known the difficulties," he says, "I would have never started this. But here we are, and now I've got over a hundred engineers worshipping the Duck."

"Shave my head and dress me in robes. That thing is insane. It's also insane that your board was avant-garde enough to back the development effort."

"Ah, well that's just it. They didn't."

"What?"

"Yeah. I pitched them an earlier version of the project, and they barfed all over it. Not a core competency and all that. I decided to do it anyway."

"So you diverted the money? Wait, let me guess . . . From Goblin, which was supposed to be venture capital for squashing future competitors."

"Right. Soon the department will start showing 'material losses,' and the board will start shitting Yorkshire terriers."

"And the Dancers are going to glide in to provide a distraction?"

"Not exactly. When I found out about Olya's opportunity, I knew that, regardless of whether people really want to copulate with machines, the *announcement* would generate a certain amount of heat. And one can profit when the animal spirits are stirred. Now, IMP couldn't invest in IT directly, but I could use some of my personal money to prime the pump. And Goblin could benefit if I bought support companies that might see immediate returns as Money realizes the implications of real virtual sex."

"That's why I'm doing this turbo NOD integration."

"Yeah. And why beforehand we funded the development of LibIA, so that we have a cybersexual ecosystem already in place for when we release the Dancers into the wild. Goblin cashes in on the buzz, and I get time to finish Holy Duck. Once it's a fait accompli, the board will fall in on the marketing." Blake's voice segues into ironic soliloquy. "Holy Duck will be a huge hit, and I become the visionary who is going to lead IMP into the twenty-first century. Then there will be no one to stop my evil plans."

"But in the meantime, you're walking a fine line. If the board finds out about all the money going into Holy Duck, or that you're the one behind our plastic fantastics—"

"They could unravel the whole thing."

"To say nothing about what your sister might do if all this causes the snake handlers in Congress to queer the pitch for her merger."

"She'd take steps to ensure I never experience the kind attentions of your femme bot." He sighs. "I don't want to cross the Princess of Hearts."

"Wait . . . Lady Di?"

"No, Lewis Carroll. Her nickname in the cable division. Comes from her tendency to solve problems by saying, 'Off with their heads!' Very much her father's daughter in that respect. But ultimately she's of a typical 'pipes' person, who wants nothing more than to provide bandwidth efficiently. I prefer to imagine the wondrous things at the end of those pipes."

"Like your father?"

"If he'd shared Blythe's perspective, IMP would never have existed. His empire was built by exploiting novel technology faster than others. New media always lends itself to adult content, and my father had the sack not to shy away from that."

Blake stands to pour himself a cup of coffee. He continues. "My great-grandfather supposedly made a fortune publishing French postcards during the First World War. Lost it all in the Depression, but smut peddling is something of a family tradition. Few people in the world are lucky enough to have a clear sense of destiny. I do. And it's thoroughly informed by my father's legacy. Part of that legacy is the strength not to let the petty prejudices of others prevent you from exerting your will."

"Which is what your brother is threatening to do."

"Right, but we have you to make sure he isn't successful."

I brief Blake on the state of play with Billy. I tell him that, aside from his recent RL provocations, it looks like his brother has set up this Sade-themed file-swapping ring that encourages players to record themselves committing acts of progressing indecency and then share with the group. Given his theft of those awful family videos, I suspect he plans to trickle out the worst material to his players. Who will leak it to the press in this irresistibly lurid context. Which he probably hopes will embarrass IMP's board enough for them to disenfranchise Blake, just as they'd done to him years ago.

Blake agrees that scenario sounds like his brother. While he still favors my pursuing Billy through his game, he's impatient. He wants more action. Billy knows we're stalking him, and his attacking Blythe has soured her twin on stealthy recon as a strategy.

We talk about the brute force option: a herculean program of cracking, bribery, and extortion against several international ISPs in an attempt to trace a physical location from which Billy is connecting to his *Savant* server. He doesn't blink at the price I ballpark him.

I imagine Mercer will kiss me on the mouth at our next meeting.

Which will be sooner than I'd expected, because the next item on Blake's agenda is me.

He says, "So now that you've been initiated into the mysteries, are you ready to take the brand?"

I had a feeling something like this was coming. Now that I know his secrets, Blake wants to bind me more tightly to him. He wants me under his control. A new knave for his suit.

"What did you have in mind?"

"I originally hired you to look into my brother's disappearance. Since then you've proven adept at working your way into some of my most important initiatives. Given the level of trust we've built—"

Except that we haven't. Blake has been evasive from the beginning. He only confirms things I learn independently. And I can sense that there are cavernous pools of information he's still not sharing.

"—I'd like to formalize our relationship. I want you to come and work for me full-time."

He pulls out the contract he's proposing. I let the folder sit on the table between us. I can tell there's something else to this.

Blake searches my face for a while. Then he says, "Were you to join the team, you'd be working for me *exclusively*."

Ah, so that's it.

My stomach sinks.

"So of course there'd be no reason for you to keep meeting with my sister."

Blake has always seen me as strictly servant-class. Like Olya and her robots, he wants only a prince for his sister. So he's asking me to choose between the Dancers and Blythe.

Through the squall in my head, what finally emerges, plangent and raw, is that moment on a gorgeous day in May that Blythe euthanized those few of my hopes still clinging to life.

The Randall twins didn't come back to school until just before exams. I'd left Blythe messages that tried to strike the right note of mournful support, but I received no response. I explained her silence with the notion that such a profound woman would grieve deeply. Without an invitation, pulling the trigger on plane reservations proved impossible. I was plagued by the image of Blake answering the door.

When I finally learned that Blythe was back, it was through a girl who took a bit too much satisfaction in telling me that she was accompanied by a boy.

That "boy" was none other than Graham Welles, then the leading man for a popular twentysomething soap on one of their cable channels. In fairness, they'd starred together in Exeter's production of *The Tempest*. He was an old family friend who'd really "been there for her" during her desolation. He and Blake got on like bandits. And he was hypnotically handsome.

I couldn't even bring myself to blame her. I didn't want a big fight or anything like that. I don't know what I wanted, but I felt like we had to talk. So I staked out her apartment until I caught them coming in.

Welles saw me first, and I had to give the guy credit; he was cool about it all. He shook my hand and smoothly remembered a pressing need for the latest issue of *Variety*. Blythe's soft expression let me cherish a split second of hope that the circumstances were other than what I imagined. Then she said, "You must think I'm completely evil."

"No. Not at all. I just wanted to—"

"I know. I know. I'm sorry. I kind of collapsed. I— I just wish none of this had happened."

"None of it?"

"Oh, honey. You've given me nothing but precious memories. I'm sure you'll hate me now, but—"

"No, Blythe. I'll always—"

As usual, she already knew what I was about to say. So she covered my lips with hers in a gentle, lingering, and even maybe a little passionate kiss. But I could taste the wistful finality of it. Part of me wanted to wrench away in hurt and indignation. But that part was summarily beaten down. I needed to make our last kiss as good as possible.

Any time I'm lying in bed and the episode once again invades my mind, the seething embarrassment of what I said next guarantees I won't sleep until the sun comes up.

As she walked slowly up the stairs outside her apartment, I called out her name. She turned and smiled at me sadly. Then, in my desperation, I said the unthinkable:

"We can still be friends, can't we?"

I think she was surprised that I'd so completely abandoned my dignity. "Oh, James." She shut her eyes and gathered herself. "James, we were never friends. I don't think either of us will be able to settle for that."

A cold and merciless thing to say? Maybe. But she was right. As it was, I could lick my wounds without constantly being faced with the opportunity to create fresh ones. While I spent the summer staring at Blythe's pictures and drinking myself nearly to death, I never even tried to call her. Seeing that person I became in her presence had hurt enough. The drunk that came after wasn't so great either, but at least his pain was endured in private.

And besides all that, she remained in my imagination too perfect to blame. I always absolved her with the refrain that she never made me any promises. She still hasn't.

But her brother, it appears, will.

And really, why pretend you have a choice?

Blake has me cornered. If he removes me from the case, I won't be casually ringing Blythe for cocktails. The whole basis of our reacquaintance is that we're working together to find her crazy brother.

She only invited you to solve a problem for her. She never made you any promises.

The Dancers, however, hold all the promise of the future.

I reach over and place my hand on the folder.

"I accept."

48

Susan Mercer's office is frigid at twilight, suffused with the azure glow of the evening magic hour. I'm exhausted, and nervous about the meeting. Exhausted because I saw little sleep last night while I rattled through a comprehensive proposal for Blake's assault on the internet. Nervous not just because I'm afraid of displeasing Mercer with my news; I'm more worried that she'll amplify my concern that this move is impulsive. That I'm following my testicles into a dicey situation. But with my younger and more beautiful mistresses Olya and Ginger whispering inducements, I gird myself to tangle with the Norn.

At first it seems that she's not there, her desk showing only a vacant circle of orange light streaming from an antique lamp. I hear a faint creak over in the shadows beside the bank of large windows at the far end of the room. She's slowly rocking next to a small table bearing a steaming tea service. Her eyes are fixed on me, her hands, as always, busy with a complex textile.

Eventually she says, "A bittersweet moment."

I try on my own regretful face and take a seat in the weird miniature chair opposite her. "I meant to speak with you about this first, but I see Blake has been impatient."

Mercer shrugs. "Had I known this assignment would be your last, I'd have sent your irritating colleague Mr. Holley."

"I'm sorry. I love it here, it's just—"

Mercer cuts off my apology with a magisterial wave. "Your simple reconnaissance has devolved into a great deal of *unsavory* business." She pats a thick document lying on the table next to the tea. It's bound in red, signifying a services contract. But something in her emphasis bothers me.

Has she found out about the Dancers? Is she aware of my newfound mecha-philia?

If so, she doesn't let on.

She continues. "You know your new employer had the gall to offer us an 'employee referral award,' as if we were an impoverished tribe selling our children for millet."

"You should take it."

"Maybe the partners will. And I shall be forced to blot my tears with ill-gotten specie. Not a position I'm unused to. But what about your tears, dear boy?"

"My eyes are clear and dry."

"Such a hasty marriage . . . What if your groom should disappoint?"

"You assume I'm the wife in this arrangement."

She picks up the invoice and fans through it. "This, while no doubt an amusing expenditure for someone like Mr. Randall, feels like a bride price."

I nod in acknowledgment of the point. At least she's characterizing me as a wife rather than something less charitable. I think about the subtext of my deal with Blake. While returning to a state of Blythelessness may have been the natural result of completing my work for them, he had to make me formally accept it. To choose it.

She offers a wan smile. "I'd just advise you to remember your Tenny-son—in general, a sniveling romantic, but wise in writing, 'He will hold thee, when his passion shall have spent its novel force / Something better than his dog, a little dearer than his horse.'"

At this, she stands, and shockingly opens her arms wide, gesturing me inward. Her embrace is awkward—perfunctory and unpracticed. I can feel her gazing past me, at the city, when she says, "Do know that we'll always have a stall here in our stable for you. Remember that before you go trotting off to the glue factory."

49

If I worried over the source of the foreboding Mercer conveyed, she doesn't leave me hanging for long. On my desk sits a thick stack of time sheets for my work to date on the twins' behalf that Billing wants me to initial. The paperwork is generally in order, but someone has "mistakenly" appended a number of forms for various other Red Rook employees from the same client code, but a different case number. I almost just toss them in the burn bin, but one of the entries stops me. Listed among all the opaque acronyms for our shady activities is inventoried six hours for a system penetration of someone code-named E10_Vinyl. Nothing unusual there; we do it every day. But among all the enciphered identifiers is the confirmation line for the computer that got penetrated, which includes its IP: 192.0.2.112.

That's the internet address for *my* home computer.

My brothers in arms have turned their knives on me. Of course one's own medicine always tastes the bitterest. But after taking a panicked inventory of my actions over the past couple weeks, I conclude that they've been mostly innocent with respect to Blake. Since I'll still be working closely with Red Rook in my new position, the philosophical perspective seems best. Besides, leaving a known penetration in place can accord you a stronger position than the person who put it there, since you now have control over a trusted information source.

Perhaps I adhere to some quaint notions of company loyalty, but I'm a little shocked that Red Rook agreed to instrument one of its own employees. Though I guess a cold warrior like Mercer would approve of "watchers watching the watchers" involute security schemes. Since there's no way these papers ended up on my desk by accident, I conclude that at least she had the good grace to give me a heads-up. What motivated her to do that? Occam's razor leaves me with the words: she likes me.

Thank God for that.

An hour later I finally get a message from one of *my* RATs indicating that Nash has logged in to the NYPD's evidence repository. I wait until he signs off for the day before starting my search. Because he was the principal investigator, I have full access to download the file on Gina Delaney's death.

Along with the sundry reports and morgue photos, there's a digital video with a default name from the camera that shot it. Once the transfer finishes, I run a program called MephistoFilese that corrupts the original beyond any hope of redemption. My adding an erroneous storage location entry for the camera's memory card and then switching its status to "item lost" should make retrieving the original nearly impossible. Now I've got the only accessible copy.

I pull up the video on my laptop.

Gina's pale face fills my screen. Tears flow freely past her closed eyelids and down her cheeks. There's a low whirring sound that must be the drill behind her. For a moment, her head sways unsteadily on her neck, and then she opens her eyes. Their sparkling amber is now dilated black, as though she's taken a heavy dose of tranqs. Her gaze rests on a point just above and to the left of the camera. She inhales haltingly and then starts to say something, but her face contorts as she tries not to cry. She jerks her head, the movement restricted by the cords binding her to the garrote. She lets her neck go slack and sobs.

After a few seconds of this, she makes a clear effort to calm herself, taking deep trembling breaths. She closes her eyes. When they open again, she's found a certain stillness.

She says in a nearly inaudible voice made husky by her tears:

I guess you thought
I'd play the daughter of Lot,
But I will not.

The extreme close-up makes it hard to distinguish what happens next. The restraints bite more deeply into the skin of her neck and chin, like she's pressing forward against them.

Then there's the short scraping sound of a cigarette lighter.

The right side of Gina's face receives a warm, flickering light. This seems to wake something inside her. Her eyes become less glassy and start darting around. Maybe she's making a last-minute inspection of her setup. She rotates her head slowly to the right, perhaps testing the tautness of the line. Then back to the left. She repeats the process more quickly, and then I realize:

She's shaking her head.

Her eyes are bright now with panic.

The drill bursts through her mouth, spraying the camera lens with drops of blood. Her body goes limp from the huge hole torn into her spine. I have to close my eyes.

When I open them, Gina's face is still there, mutilated by the razor-toothed hole saw, which spins on with mechanical abandon. The video rolls for another twenty minutes, and by the end of it, I know I'll see that image for the rest of my days.

50

Acquiring Gina's suicide video finally gave me a good card for my hand. But I still need an opportunity to play it. I check in to see where the rest of Billy's gamers are.

Savant's forum has come alive with controversy over a post by someone named Clay_Media proposing that Big Ben Mondano was a member of the Pyrexians. An idea that would unify, as good conspiracy theories do, the two primary strands of speculation concerning the party backing *Savant*. Initially, I assume this is Billy again seeding the story behind his game, but I become unsure, since the post mostly inspired an effort to comb Exotica's back catalog for Pyrexian imagery: black candles, red rings, antique medical equipment, coded messages inscribed on their victims. I suspect this line of inquiry will actually lead them *away* from any kind of connection to Robert Randall.

That said, I'm worried that the *Savant* players' growing numbers and organization will eventually allow them to find their way inside Billy's gingerbread house. And that will complicate my work. I contemplate a subtle disinformation campaign, but before I can solidify any ideas, my duties to the Dancers call.

Olya's discovered a new vibration in Fred's corpus spongiosum, and she and Xan are at loggerheads about whether this is a bug or a feature. I've been called to help Garriott investigate, but perhaps more importantly to procure late-night fuel for the team.

– – –

On my way over, McClaren pulls up and invites me into his Town Car. His news is that Charles Delaney, Gina's father, had called the NYPD out of the blue to demand a copy of his daughter's suicide video. Nash put him off with some claptrap about "evidentiary sequestration" and phoned McClaren. They ran Delaney's bank accounts, which showed two recent deposits of just over nine thousand dollars apiece. The conclusion: Billy is trying to use him to get the video, the "final piece" he mentioned to Blythe. McClaren orders me to Boston to see if he can be bribed into leading us to Billy.

Garriott and I finish our urological procedure on Fred more quickly than I'd anticipated, allowing me to leave GAME at three AM. Needing to sleep on the way, I opt for a train that gets into South Station five hours later.

Somerville is a suburb north of Harvard's Cambridge that's been transformed into a postcollegiate Eden, filled with organic cafés and bars thronged with recent grads. But if you wind up on the wrong side of McGrath Highway, you'll find a neighborhood whose residents didn't all get the "inexorable gentrification" memo: East Somerville. It's only about two miles from the neoclassical halls of MIT, but as with most old Eastern cities, you can span whole galaxies just by crossing a street. I'm amazed Gina made the transition.

The Delaneys' house stands on a blighted block of slumping three-story railcar tenements framed by giant denuded elm trees that look like they were last pruned by WPA employees. Despite the hopeless aspect of the block, there's a yellow Mustang with dealer's plates parked askew at the curb.

Eleven Cross Street is a small rectangle of leprous brown shingles. Its only gesture at decoration is rusting steel bars on the windows, which seem to have been bored into the building's surface at random.

I ring the bell and wait a long time before someone starts wrestling with the warped wooden door. At first there's just a thin gap into the dark of the vestibule, but then the door swings open on a woman who begins the painfully slow process of climbing down a short cement staircase to open the metal security door in front of me. I think she might be in her midsixties, but she has the sick thinness and carriage of a woman well into her eighties. She's draped herself with a worn housedress, and her dull gray hair listlessly crowds her face. Her eyes speak of sleepless nights, and her breath speaks of a seven AM encounter with a gin bottle.

"Mrs. Delaney? Hi—"

"You're here about Geenie?" she asks in a reedy whisper.

"Yes, ma'am."

Before she can continue, a deep voice booms out from behind her. "Ruthie, get your ass back in here. I'll take care of this guy. Go finish your breakfast."

Ugh. I can tell I'd prefer sharing her kind of breakfast to dealing with the owner of that voice. Mrs. Delaney scuttles off without another word.

Charles Delaney is scrawny and unkempt, with a large flat head framed by patchy stubble that in some places aspires to be a beard. He's wearing greasy jeans and a plaid flannel shirt, underneath which a moth-eaten T-shirt proclaims, OBAMANATION: WIPING OUT AMERICA, ONE BABY AT A TIME. He looks me over with a jittery scowl but eventually says in a cigarette-scarred bray, "Well, get yourself in here. It's colder than ass out there."

Against my better judgment, I put out my hand. "James Pryce, it's nice—" But he's already walking away from me down a narrow hallway.

I almost take off. Charles Delaney is disturbing. You see him and think base-head. You smell him and think opossum. His wife's clearly hanging on by her fingernails too. If his daughter suffered from mental instability, the genetic component has certainly been confirmed. The grim abode tells me that her environment wasn't helping anything either.

I follow him down the hall. What I first took for a limp proves to be a stagger. Like his wife, the guy is drunk as a lord at nine AM. He heads straight back to a flimsy door with a Yosemite Sam "Back Off" mud flap stapled to it.

It opens onto a den obviously meant as an off-limits refuge for the man of the house. The room has a sixties basement quality, with artificial wood paneling adorned with outdated Boston sports posters, a beat-up Naugahyde couch, and a giant duct-taped recliner. The low coffee table is covered with Natural Light tallboys dragooned into service as sloppy ashtrays. I'd expect to see an old TV set with a jury-rigged antenna, but instead there's a brand-new sixty-inch Sony LCD inexpertly bolted to the wall. A badass surround-sound system sits in boxes on the floor.

Delaney collapses onto the couch and takes a swig out of a bottle of Midleton Irish Whiskey, which stands in glaring contrast to the dead cans of discount beer. He doesn't offer me any. There's evidence here of an epic Home Shopping Network binge: a lacquer stand of samurai swords, a wall full of valuable Red Sox cards mounted in mahogany frames, and two leather gun cases, which I'm hoping do not contain actual weapons.

I sit on the recliner and start with, "Thank you for taking the time to meet with me."

He snorts as though I've said something idiotic.

"So your wife might have mentioned that I'm working on a documentary that in part deals with the work your daughter—"

"Yeah, I know all about you and your 'documentary.' You want to dig shit up about Geenie. So go ahead and ask your questions. I'm a fucking open book."

"Well, first of all, my condolences on your daughter's death. You must have been shocked—"

"No, I always knew my girl was heading for hell."

"Hell?"

"Suicide is a mortal sin, ain't it? You can't just go picking out the parts of His Holy Word that you happen to like, right? Not like those Episcopal faggots."

"I guess it depends—"

Suddenly heated, he leans toward me. "It don't depend on shit. The Word is the Truth. You better fucking believe that. Yeah, I can tell you don't like me saying that shit about my own daughter. But I don't need you judging me. That's for the Lord, not someone like you." Then he takes a long pull off his bottle and relaxes back into the couch. "But you know . . . I'll probably end up joining her there. Way things have gone for me."

"Faith can certainly be a great comfort. Ah, did your daughter share your commitment to the church?"

"If she did, she wouldn't be burning in the fiery pit right now."

"Did she seem depressed at all before? Did you notice any signs—"

"What I noticed was that she moved to Jew York to be with all those communistic dickheads."

I know there's never been any love lost between New York and Boston, but this is an odd perspective for someone living north of the Mason-Dixon line and in this century. I try, "I understand she went to study at NYU."

"Yeah, all that techy shit. You know computers are the tools of the devil? Once they get their hooks into you, Satan himself can mainline poison directly into your brain."

Here I think he has a point most people would agree with.

He continues. "And those people who went to her school. You wouldn't believe the kind of faggots showed up at her funeral."

Now we're getting somewhere. "Yeah, I was told that one of her class-mates created a commotion there."

His enthusiasm at holding forth on the communists and faggots van-ishes. "Well, I don't remember much about that. I was dealing with a lot of shit at the time."

"That's understandable. Let me see if I can jog your memory." I pull out an eight-by-ten of Billy. "I heard you might have had words with this gentleman. A friend of your daughter's. That maybe he was taking pictures. That he tried to put something into your daughter's casket. You wouldn't by any chance know what—"

"I don't know that boy from Adam," Delaney says quietly, without looking at the photo.

"Are you sure?" I wait for a while and then push Billy's picture toward him. "Because I was given to believe—"

His earlier rage rushes back. He shoots up and leans over me, poking my chest with his finger. "'Given to believe'? What kind of shit-talk is that? Why don't you just call me a liar to my face?"

I put up my hands to placate him, mentally measuring the distance to all the weapons in the room. "Mr. Delaney, I didn't mean to in any way—"

"Fuck you!" He's still yelling. I feel a fine spray of spittle on my fore-head. "Whoever the fuck you are. Yeah, I know you're no fucking film-maker. He said you'd come sniffing around. Well I'm not telling you shit, so you can get your ass off my chair and get—"

"Mr. Delaney, maybe we could come to some arrangement, if you'd just listen to—"

"No, you listen to me, you shit-sucking—"

Clearly the interview has gone off the rails, so I snatch his finger and roll it back toward his chest until he's forced to subside onto the couch. I don't let go but say softly in his ear, "When you see our friend Billy again, tell him that I have the only copy of that video, and he needs to come to me if he wants it."

I let go and take a step back. Delaney's gaze settles on his new swords. I shake my head. He rubs his sore finger and stares hate at me.

"I'll see myself out."

As I walk back up the hall, I glance into the kitchen. Mrs. Delaney hunches at a battered wooden table with a coffee cup in both hands, letting the steam bathe her face like a child. Her eyes rise to meet mine, and I read in them a nervous question. Her lips open, but she doesn't say anything, and eventually looks back into her mug. I want to walk over to her, but then I hear something crash in her husband's den. I run through the likely consequences of dragging her into this, and my conscience won't sanction the risk. Instead I just take a card out of my pocket and place it on a stack of newspapers sitting against the wall. She makes no acknowledgment.

I slip out into the lacerating Boston wind.

51

Being a dropout, I can't explain why I'm still so attached to my alma mater. But I let the existence of an Acela departure to New York three hours from now convince me that I might as well head toward the river and look in on Fair Harvard. It's after eleven by the time I find parking for my rental car, and I decide that a nice long lunch at the Bat would be a fine antidote to the infectious misery of the Delaney household.

But just as I'm pouring the bourbon over ice, a 617 area code rings my cell.

I answer and hear a small, hoarse voice say, "Can you come back to the house?"

By the time I get there, the yellow Mustang has departed from its place at the Delaneys' curb. I wait through another long pause after knocking, but then Ruth opens the door wearing a worried expression. Without preliminaries, she holds out two items in the palm of her hand. The first is a four-inch figurine of a woman. The second is a Sony memory stick.

She says, "I . . . I saved these. Please take them."

I gently put them inside my jacket pocket. "Thank you, Mrs. Delaney. This is really—"

She puts up a hand. "I thought . . . I thought maybe your film . . . Maybe you could tell me something. She never said anything, and . . ." She stops, at a loss. "I—I just don't know."

With that, she shuts the door firmly in my face.

On the train home, I turn the figure over in my hands. I've seen plenty like it around GAME. One of the touchstones of geek culture is collectible figurines. The ability of 3D printers to crank out custom miniatures of one's online alter egos has only intensified our passion for them. This figure is clearly a NOD avatar. Though representing as a blond, blue-eyed anime vixen, she has Gina's playful elfin features. She's wearing a set of billowing purple robes reminiscent of a kimono, and her hands are joined in front of her at waist level holding a large red gemstone. The only label left on the figure is a name inscribed on the base. It reads: Ines_Idoru.

Could this be another one of Gina's NODNames?

I slip the memory stick into my laptop and see that it contains photos of her funeral. The thumbnails follow a trajectory that confirms Garriott's story. Some introductory shots of the graveyard, then images of a group of maybe forty people gathering around the open grave. Finally a couple of Gina's father stomping over and reaching for the camera.

Running through them again, I see a sequence where Billy focuses on two attendees at the periphery of the group as they're walking in from the parking lot. The first picture shows Blythe Randall extending her hand to Xan. And the next shows Xan taking it.

52

That night I get my chance to ask Xan about the photo.

I slip back into my office under the pretense that I've been "working from home" all day. The team is properly derisive of this excuse, but they don't care to spend the effort scolding me since they want me to put the final touches on the Dancers' voice-recognition abilities. I'm not sure why we're adding this obvious next-rev feature, but Olya demands that the Solo Control mode function without having to balance a keyboard on our chests.

Given the complexity of voice input, all we've been able to implement are simple commands such as "Fuck me" to initiate sexual contact, "Keep going" to prolong it, and of course the ever popular "Faster" and "Harder."

Xan and I are lying in the MetaChairs facing away from each other, both breathing deep from a robust test of the evening's progress.

"I can't believe we get paid to do this," I say with a contented sigh.

She looks over her shoulder. "What, someone's been writing you checks? All this work on my back, and I've yet to see the first shilling."

"You know what I mean."

"Yeah. But our Dancers have yet to prove themselves in front of the public."

"Are you worried? Olya probably told you by now the money's coming from Blake Randall, so—"

"I know. I'm still here, aren't I?"

"What about Blythe?"

"What about her?"

"Do you know her at all?"

"I met her at the same party where Gina met Blake. But no, not really."

"Have you seen her recently?"

"Why do you ask?"

"Just curious."

"You're 'just curious' about Blythe Randall, are you?" She sighs and stretches her back. "Yeah. I saw her at Gina's funeral. We exchanged condolences. I was surprised she was there, but I guess she'd met her through Blake."

"So you were just being polite?"

"James, what are you asking me?"

"Nothing. I remember her from school, and I wanted to see if—"

"Let me suggest that you keep your mind and other body parts on your robot overlords here. You can think about her all you want once we're sailing around Sardinia."

At ten fifty PM, my GAME email gets a message from the spoofed address louis_markey@savant.net. My pulse thumps as I realize that my Boston gambit worked, and Billy wants to meet.

On short notice, it turns out. His message reads:

```
Have a Rabbit Hole at Apothecary by 11pm tonight.
```

Apothecary, a posh downtown bar, publishes a cocktail list so esoteric that it has attracted the attention of both the *New Yorker* and the New York Health Department. A Rabbit Hole must be one of their signature drinks.

As cocktails go, this one sounds treacherous, but if Billy wants to meet for a drink, then he can sure as hell call the round.

53

The bar lies on the border of the Lower East Side and Chinatown. It's unmarked save for the customary mortar-and-pestle glyph molded in wrought iron on the building's side gate. Behind the railing, a steep staircase leads to the basement. Apothecary's interior maxes out the medical history theme with specimen jars of preserved animals, organs, and ambiguous polyps mixed in among the liquor bottles.

A little out of breath from having jogged over, I take a second to text McClaren about this, though I doubt he'll have time to arrange a shadow for me.

Inside I find a man with a stringy beard and beady eyes who has the mien of a Renaissance Faire staffer. Someone who lives by stringing together a patchwork of marginal gigs well on the outskirts of conventional theater. He's polishing the marble bar top with a studied diligence that I've never observed in a real bartender.

Where does Billy find these people?

Of course he'd never make things easy by just meeting me at the bar. Though if I had Blake for a sibling, I would handle one of his agents with a snare pole as well.

I sit down in front of him, and he looks into my eyes with sugary solicitude. *"What* shall it be?"

His delivery makes me want to punch him, but I stick to the script. "I'd like a Rabbit Hole."

I can tell he wants to ad-lib theatrical flourishes but has been warned against improvisation. So much so that he places a beaker in front of me and pours a stream of muddy brown liquid into it from a cocktail shaker. The pre-mixed beverage seems obviously wrong under the circumstances. And Billy is exactly the kind of guy who has a Kool-Aid recipe several lines longer than it should be.

I lean over to smell it. "I don't suppose there's anything unusual in here?"

"Like what?" He makes a visible effort to suppress the phrase "pray tell."

"A sedative would be traditional."

He grins like I've just nailed a Daily Double. "No sedative in there." He reaches into a pocket of his dirty apron, pulls out a large light-blue capsule, and places it on the napkin beside my drink. "There is in this though."

"You want me to take a pill?"

This is too much for him to resist breaking character. He bugs his eyes and smiles. "Just like *The Matrix,* man."

"What if I don't?"

He frowns. "Then I guess we can have a nice talk. May—" He wants to say "mayhap" but stumbles over it. "Mayha-be . . . I can regale you—"

The prospect of being regaled depresses me enough that I pop the pill and wash it down with the suspicious drink. It tastes like a black rum and cider fusion with some odd herbal tones. Delicious really.

The guy tilts his head toward a green velvet couch in the back. "You might want to lie down, sir."

54

As was only to be expected, I wake up in a cage.

A cage packed into a reinforced crate. I'm curled up in a ball, but the space is tall enough for me to sit Indian style in relative comfort. Feeling around in the darkness, I learn I'm surrounded by a grid of iron bars covered over with planks that smell of new lumber. I sense the quiet vibration of motorized transport.

Taking me somewhere.

Also, I'm completely naked. Not that I fear for my safety, though I am concerned about splinters; my nudity just highlights how bizarre my job has become now that I find myself so frequently disrobed in the line of duty.

Those concerns are interrupted as the truck stops and my crate rolls down a steep ramp. I'm wheeled around with teamster brusqueness until I bang gently into a wall. Then I wait for what feels like several hours.

Someone prying off the front side of my crate yanks me back to alertness. I'm in an abandoned construction site well lit by the cool blue glow of an almost full moon. Billy Randall squats before my cage. He's holding the same crowbar with which he attacked Blythe. He raps it against the bars.

I wouldn't have thought it possible, but Billy looks worse than when he was electrocuting himself. His hair has grown longer and now sticks up in greasy dinosaur spikes. The bags under his eyes stand out like makeup, but the eyes themselves reveal a manic fire that makes me start to worry a little. He's sweating profusely.

"I can't believe you actually took the pill. Seems foolish for you to assume I'll be gentle."

"I'm foolish? Your game will have you exchanging your glass house for a concrete cell. When your lunatic horde really hurts someone, it'll be your fault."

"Amazing that my brother's rent boy has the gall to lecture me about morality."

"Rent boy? You've got our relationship all wrong. Think of it more like the one between your marquis and his valet Latour."

Billy coughs out a chuckle. "Really? How's that?"

"It's true I do errands for him. But under the right circumstances, I'm also willing to fuck him."

"And what happens the morning after?"

"He won't know what happened. He's unaware I've got your friend Gina's farewell address. I know you need it. Though I have to ask, would she really want to star in your sophomoric melodrama? Seems like the last project you cast her in had some unfortunate—"

"You better watch your fucking mouth."

"Fine. But if you ever want to see the sequel she made, you'll stop patronizing her demented daddy and deal with me."

"What do you want?"

"A hundred thousand in cash. Delivered by you. In person. No one else and no more games."

Billy considers this for a moment. His lips twist into something resembling a smile. Then he slams the tapered end of his crowbar down into the juncture at the hinges to the door of my cage. Splinters graze my forehead.

"I'll be . . . *in touch*."

He leaves the crowbar, allowing me to begin the long, blistering process of prying my way out.

55

Billy showed unexpected courtesy in also leaving my clothes, so I'm able to ooze home without making an undue spectacle. I arrive at my door exhausted, but assuming that Blake doesn't look kindly upon well-rested employees, I again choose my coffeemaker over my bed.

To follow up on the figurine Ruth Delaney gave me, I check to see if Gina's Ines_Idoru account is still alive. I pull up NOD's sign-in page and enter her NODName, hitting the link for the password hint, which comes back as: d@d.

That seems obvious enough that I should be able to finesse it quickly. I have a program called [p]ass_crack that will spit out intelligent variations on a given string of characters. For example, when I give it "Charles Delaney," it tries "CH@r135 D3!@n3Y," among many other combinations. But none of them are right, so I open up the parameters to include leading and trailing numbers and feed it his birth date, her birth date, and both social security numbers. Still nothing.

Knowing her father's personal deficiencies, I suppose it's unlikely that she'd have wanted to bring him to mind each time she logged in. So let's take the avatar itself: Ines_Idoru. *Idoru* is the title of a William Gibson novel, about a holographic person that a Japanese progressive rocker is planning to marry. Acting out fan fiction is a favorite NOD activity, though most of the energy flows to space opera and X-rated anime. But it makes sense that an intellectual like Gina would name-check a character from one of the classier sci-fi authors. So maybe her hint meant the *idoru*'s father.

The web has only poor plot summaries, so I torrent a copy and start skimming. I gather that Rei Toei, the virtual woman in question, was created by a media conglomerate, not a specific person. I try jamming the corporation name and a number of characters and places from the book into [p]ass_crack. It chugs for a while, but again I get nada.

Frustration warring against fatigue, I check her av name to see if she turns up on any NOD blogs that might give me a clue. Nothing comes back but hits from some Cyrillic language I don't recognize. I'm about to pack it in for the evening when I notice Google asking if, by chance, I might have meant "anesidora" rather than "Ines Idoru."

I didn't, but mindful of NODlings' penchant for wordplay, I click through.

The name, I'm informed, is an alternate spelling for the woman whom Eve displaced as the most significant female ever: Pandora. She of the fabled box that when opened brought everything evil into the world. I pick up Gina's figurine and realize that what I'd blithely assumed was a kimono is actually a stylized ceremonial toga. The jewel-like container's placement over her pelvis refers to a common feminist interpretation of the myth: Pandora's box represents the womb, and the tale is a crude expression of male sexual anxiety.

So who was Pandora's dad? A little reading tells me that while the creation of Pandora was a joint venture, with several deities bestowing various gifts, Hephaestus, that ugly god of fire, blacksmiths, and of course technology, gets the primary credit.

Seconds later, a NOD scene graph is rezzing, and I'm entering the world in Gina's skin.

But Ines_Idoru is a big disappointment. Like a newborn, she's almost completely blank. No inventory, no friends, no favorite places. No evidence of the woman who made her.

Did Gina scrub Ines before she died? But then why would she leave the account alive? Or if this was just a random alt that Gina never really used, why would Billy pick this av to place in her coffin for all eternity?

I'm about to give up in disgust when I notice the box that the av is holding. It doesn't show up in Ines's NObject inventory because she's actually wearing it as an accessory. I select it and bring up the thing's property page. That's where I hit pay dirt. Contained by this box is a list of scripted NObjects. The first lines read:

```
20140203_F0001.215
20140206_M0000.9.3
20140207_F0002.215
20140209_M0000.9.4
20140211_F0003.0
20140213_M0001.0.0
```

They look like successive entries for two objects in an ad hoc version archive, which could be this alt's only purpose. While Gina wanted to obliterate even online traces of *herself,* perhaps she liked the idea of a little bit of her *work* surviving in a forgotten corner of NOD. Maybe this was her last project and held some kind of significance for her, so that she couldn't bear to drag it with her into the void.

I teleport to my private dev sandbox and block-rez a bunch of the NObjects out into the world. When they all finally appear, I'm reminded of that spurious diagram called "The Ascent of Man" that tries to explain how we changed from chimpanzees to Homo sapiens. They're a series of 3D sketches that show a clear evolution from the barest glimmer of a design to two fairly polished mechanisms.

The experience is like seeing baby pictures of your fiancée for the first time. I'm looking at snapshots from the childhood of the Dancers. The last examples show Fred and Ginger very nearly in their current form.

The create dates on all the objects start in early February of last year, and they end four weeks before Gina killed herself.

Five weeks before Olya called the first iTeam meeting.

56

At ten AM, Olya's not in her office or the Orifice. When I call her, I'm surprised to hear that she's working out.

The room on the top floor where I find her is beautiful in the way of ruins. A former dance studio with crumbling brick walls and worn oak flooring. The far side is a huge mirror that has a barre running down its length. The glass is violently cracked, perhaps from the meltdown of a high-strung ballerina. Olya has installed herself in the cool morning rays coming through a mansard window. She's wearing a pale pink halter-style ballet dress and is *en pointe* doing leg lifts. She sees me enter but doesn't stop.

"Zhimbo. What did you want to see me about?"

I watch her for a while, getting lost in her rhythmic movements. Finally I ask, "Our Erotobot operation here was your idea?"

"Idea? They are my children."

"Yeah, but who conceived them?"

One thing I love about Olya is that she catches on quick. You don't have to waste a lot of time with the initial *stupid* lies. She squints at me and snaps out another couple leg lifts. "You know, I wish you'd spend as much time thinking about our glorious future as you do wallowing like a pig in the past."

"Olya, did you steal Fred and Ginger from your dead girlfriend?"

That irritates her. She turns and says, "What is this you're asking? Did

I work with Gina on this? Yes, of course, but it was *our* project, and she's not here anymore. So what do you want me to tell you?"

"Just tell me all of it."

I'm expecting an angry defense, but what comes out is more like an elegy. It's revealing to hear Olya speak without aggression, outside of the imperative case. Her voice is slower and softer; she closes her eyes as if she's really trying to call up the past.

Olya says, "Gina, she is very pretty and nice, and at NYU everyone *likes* her, but she doesn't have any friends. Other than this shit-head Billy, who uses her for his stupid videos. He takes over her apartment for days to make that thing. He forces her to act like this high-tech whore on camera. And then she keeps that horrible torture device afterward to give her dark thoughts. All this because she doesn't know how to say no. I used to see her every day during lunch sitting by herself at this tiny café. I don't know why I care, but it starts to drive me crazy. A woman with these gifts, you know? I decide that we will be friends. I want to help her. So I start sitting with her at boring coffee place."

Olya relates to me how Gina eventually began asking her abstract questions regarding her specialty in exotic materials. Ever direct, Olya soon ferreted out that she was dancing around the idea of simulating flesh, and it became obvious what this inhibited prodigy had in mind. Gina was an *engineer*. She was looking for a material solution to problems residing in her mind. But being a pathologically shy girl overwhelmed with religious guilt, she couldn't take the first step.

Olya sure as hell could, however. When they graduated, she convinced Gina to accept a GAME residency. Their cover project was to create tactile games for blind children, but really they started working in earnest on what would become the Dancers. Gina already had the basic idea and much of the design mapped out. So over the summer, they started prototyping.

She describes how after weeks of searching fruitlessly for a trustworthy source of start-up capital, Gina rolled in and laid a cashier's check for forty thousand dollars on her desk. She said it was from an "anonymous patron," but of course Olya forced Billy's identity from her. She yelled at her that this asshole could not be a partner in their enterprise. But Gina replied, "No, it's a grant. He doesn't even know what the project is." Then she blushed and said that when the Dancers were done, she was going to surprise him with them.

Olya says, "Ginushka goes red as beet. With this silly man she is again acting like a prostitute. But this time for real. I do not like Billy, but this is a lot of money, so I think, *We must be practical.*"

But while Olya couldn't abide the thought of Billy as a long-term partner, she also couldn't help but wonder about the source of his seemingly unlimited wealth. In researching its origins, she figured out who his siblings were and learned from Gina of the estrangement between them. And rumor had it that Blake was an easy touch when it came to new media.

"I think, *Why not?* I have a unique product, maybe he will understand. So I go to his office. You maybe understand that I can get meetings with most men easily. Blake has this very bitchy secretary, so I sit in his waiting room for a long time. Then I see him walk by. She tries to stop me, but for a bitch, she is only a Chi-hua-hua. So I take his arm and say, 'Maybe I know a very good way to torture your little brother.' Blake is interested, so we come to an arrangement."

They worried that Billy knew too much about the project, but they eventually concluded that he probably wouldn't want to mess up their plans out of loyalty to Gina. So he'd be furious he'd been displaced, but impotent—a prospect Blake had found especially appealing. In the end, they decided it didn't matter what Billy did. Blake said, "I can handle my brother."

Everything seemed perfect to Olya.

"So I set up surprise meeting with Gina to tell her this very great news that we finally have a good investor. I think she will be happy, maybe to get rich. She is from poverty, you know. Blake when we meet is smooth, but Gina . . . she is crazy. She says nothing and runs away. I apologize to Blake. He told me before they have this history. Maybe they fuck ten years ago. I tell him I'll talk to her and make everything okay. It's no problem.

"I go back to her place. You know what she is doing? She's in the bath, drunk like a moose. And she is sawing her wrists with a knife. The water is bloody, but they are . . . not deep cuts. She babbles all this religious shit. Verses from the Bible, I think. This is all from her parents, you know. I can understand nothing, so I haul her out and bandage her wrists. I put her in bed . . ."

Olya falters here in her story.

"What?" I ask. But Xan has already told me what's coming.

"And then I make love to her."

She closes her eyes, playing back the evening in her head. Her lips seem to want to tug upward. Then she shrugs. "Ai. It sounds very bad maybe, but I think it works. Gina is not like normal person. She doesn't care about food, clothing, money, where she lives. All she needs is hard problems for her head, and a little love for her heart. But you know, she's so strange, she doesn't get much of that. And she is a wonderful girl. I do love her in certain way."

Olya tells me that in their new relationship, Gina blossomed like a hothouse orchid. She became vivacious, and her newfound energy fed into her work. Gina went from sulking in coffee shops playing *Spore II* to spending all her time in the lab playing Pygmalion.

And Olya knew that her need for Gina was just as strong, because she'd caught the holy fire for teledildonics. "Zhimbo, I think maybe you feel this way, but it's like I was born to do this. When I work, I feel the angels next to me. Maybe they are really devils, but I don't care. So we can't have deal with Blake. Fine. We scrape by until we find someone else."

But while they were building their electrosexual ambitions, Gina's real project morphed into a towering passion for Olya. One that demanded a grand gesture.

"She wants us to move in together. Make all these commitments." She shakes her head at the absurdity. "I find out, the girl, she goes and buys me a ring. She's thinking when our children are ready to be born, we should get married. In Massachusetts." Olya pronounces the state's name as though it's a rarely observed asteroid.

And Olya wasn't the only target for Gina's declarations. Intoxicated with this mad love and resolved to permanent rebellion, she decided to tell her parents. She thought one decisive stroke could free her from a lifetime of resentment against her awful family. Then she could begin building real happiness with her soul mate.

"I don't know what happens when she goes to Boston. I am sure all this seems very unnatural to her parents. But when she comes back, she's like a zombie. She won't work. Doesn't do a thing for a month. She's fucked-up all the time. I try to help her, but she keeps talking all this Bible shit about butt-fucking."

"Sodom?"

"This is butt-fucking, yes?"

"Among other things. So what happened?"

"After weeks of this, I invite her to dinner at this stupid Chuck E. Cheese place she likes. Obsolete video games and rat robots; this is just how she is. I want to try to cheer her up, you know. But she doesn't come. Won't answer her mobile. So I go to her place to look for her."

"And?"

Olya glances down sadly. "And I find her in the bath again. Bleeding." She takes a deep breath and lets it out.

"The cut is again nothing. Used dull scissors. She's not really trying. It's just her craziness. Better if it were like the last time. I make love to her, and everything's all right. But this time she attacked our project. I can't believe it. She cut all the Dancers' wires and then set the laptops on fire."

"What did you do?"

"I took hammer and put a hole in the tub."

I must look dismayed. But Olya doesn't get defensive. Just gives a weak, melancholy shrug.

"Sometimes people need a shock. She's crying like a beaten dog. I don't know half of what she's saying. It's like 'Can you forgive me? Can you forgive me anything?' But I don't want to forgive her for damaging our children. I want her to stop being this crazy bitch. She keeps saying, 'I won't do this anymore. I can't bear it.' I'm tired of her acting so conflicted all the time. So . . ."

At this point in her narrative, Olya pauses for a long time, playing the scene back in her head. Finally she says, "Well, I guess you know I have a very great temper . . . Also, I have not had the easiest life, and . . . I have learned how to hurt people."

She finishes this with a catch in her voice. Her eyes are brimming. I'm astounded that the ice queen is about to melt with only me here to witness. Olya takes a long blink.

I didn't think it was possible to recall tears back into their ducts, but when Olya opens them, her eyes are dry.

"The next night she was dead."

I move to comfort her, but she spurns this and turns back to the barre.

"You can blame me." She shrugs. "Other people do. I knew she was depressed, I put all this pressure on her, I say terrible things to her, and now she's dead. And so it's my fault."

"Olya—"

She puts her hand up. "But I ask, what about her family? I only knew her a year. They had her whole sad fucking life." She flicks her fingers with distaste. "So they tell her she needs Jesus. I say she needs Prozac. But Gina? She decides what she needs is nothing."

"Maybe a little unconditional love would have gone a long way that night."

"Yeah? Or maybe a little less vodka. Or a little less bullshit religion. But too late for that now, is it not?" She slowly rotates back to look at me in the mirror.

I come very close to saying it, but some instinct for self-preservation stops me.

Convenient that she died, isn't it?

But this echo of Billy's question to her sits uneasily. If it's convenient for Olya, it's doubly so for me. If Gina hadn't died, IT might have been in production by now, and I'd just be jerking it at Fleshbot as I wait to find out when I can order one.

I take a different tack. "Thanks for the confession. You have any other revelations about our intellectual property?"

Olya, her face divided crazily by the cracked glass, fixes me with an unreadable expression. "Well, Zhimbo, you think we're being unfair to poor Gina's estate? You should meet her father. Maybe we put him on the board?"

57

My talk with Olya shed some light on Gina's final days. After her death, Olya assembled the iTeam, and of course went back to Blake for money. His initial rejection as a suitor had further piqued his lust. Olya thought she had things under control. "But," she said, "now this *svoloch* Billy is making shit for everybody."

I can also better piece together his state of mind. When Gina dies, he knows enough to have theories about her reasons. And he knows who to blame. He tries to bury with her a figure not of her main av, but rather the one she used to store her Dancer mock-ups. He asks Olya, "Are you happy now?"

Thinking about how I started to unravel this story brings to mind the other party whose grief over Gina seemed as keen as Billy's: her mother. I feel like she deserves to know what I've discovered.

I'm relieved when she picks up the phone, and after thanking her for the figurine and memory stick, I say, "I just wanted to tell you that I acquired the video your daughter recorded of her death. I don't think you'll want to see it."

"No, I guess not." She pauses for a long time, fighting to control her voice. Finally, in a high, plaintive tone, she asks, "But why did she record it? Does she say anything?"

"She says, 'I guess you thought I'd play the daughter of Lot, but I will not.'" I wait to see what she makes of that, but only silence follows. "I could tell you what I believe she meant, to see if it accords with your—"

"No, Mr. Pryce." Hearing her daughter's last words is too much for Ruth Delaney. Her voice breaks as she says, "I've heard enough."

Then she hangs up.

So I'm left to interpret Gina's death for myself. What exactly did she mean by that laconic rhyme? She obviously shared an interest with Billy in Genesis 19: the chronicle of the Lord spending his utmost wrath upon sexual deviants. Lot's virgin daughters were to be sacrifices to a throng of Sodomites. So perhaps Gina identified with them in that she felt she was being forced into serving, through her invention, the lusts of the mob.

But I'm puzzled by her close identification with the Dancers. Why would she have equated Olya's commercialization of them with *her* being savaged by the masses? One hears self-aggrandizing artists talk about the sales process as a form of rape. But that's not a perspective native to engineers. Also, if she truly abhorred pandering to the global umma of perverts, why didn't she just destroy the things? Instead she damaged them superficially and focused on destroying herself.

She knew from previous attempts she didn't have the force of will to drive the blade home. So, like she'd done all her life, she built a mechanism to solve the problem. She looked around for the right materials, and her eyes lit on Billy's garrote. Maybe she recalled the video they made together. Might release from her strangling desperation feel akin to that burst of ecstasy her character achieved when the jack popped into her neck?

Yet the record of her last moments shows the opposite happened.

I doubt I'll ever know all the reasons behind Gina's sad demise, but clearly Billy feels like he understands them well enough. He holds his brother and Olya responsible for her death, and now he wants to put them under the same level of mental strain they placed on her. By making himself the Genghis Khan of cyberbullies with his game.

A game that will be rolling through embarrassing family revelations just as public scrutiny heats up on Blythe's deal. Billy surely knows that in attacking Blake now, the blow will really fall most heavily on Blythe. He would hope the damage then multiplies even further in the pain-reflecting echo chamber of the twins' relationship.

But to complete his oeuvre, he needs the record of his heroine's swan song, something only I can give him. So if Billy wants to play games with it, he's going to have to come to the table.

58

The final words Billy spoke through the slats of my crate were, "I'll be in touch." Thirty-six hours later, I'm driving myself nuts with the worry that I've completely mistaken his need for Gina's death video.

Just as I'm starting to brainstorm new "operational concepts" for a surely unpleasant meeting with Blake, his brother finally deigns to make contact. But he's not reaching out to me; his message comes to Jacques.

In NOD, I find orders for the next *Savant* Degree sent from Madame Martaine. As tired as I am of this nonsense, which has yet to produce any concrete lead, I still open it greedily. The virtual parchment says:

Searching for service to the Duc de Blangis?
Please look at my pictures, *and soon you will see*
Just what you can do to be helpful to me.

The word "pictures" links to a server hosting a huge library of images.

I zip up all 14,400 and forward them to Red Rook's code quarry. Then I dig in myself.

The unifying theme: women doing violence to other women. Of course, most are lesbian bondage shots, and I'm distressed to see such lovely anatomy so thoroughly abused. Intercalated among all the pinching and probing, I find other categories. Stills from the recent YouTube craze for brawl videos of teenage girls, mothers slapping daughters, soccer harpies dragging opponents to the ground by their hair, and morgue photos of the rare woman murdered by another female. They're Billy's bitter comment on Olya and Gina's relationship I guess.

My cypher-punks return disappointing results: none of the files hold encoded information. So cracking this puzzle won't be as easy as the last one. They're seeking other avenues, but the inquiries will take time. Which leaves me to stew over the images.

I know they carry some kind of message, and Billy probably designed this kind of challenge to frustrate automated analysis. Maybe he wants to force his players to really immerse themselves in his assemblage of gyno-lence.

They click by for hours as I make detailed notes. But not only do I fail to determine a pattern beyond the obvious, I can't even see a method by which I'd ever find one. How can one be expected to trace all the possible connections among such a mass of complex photographs?

I return to my starting assumption: these files must be telling me something. But what if the individual pictures are relatively meaning-less, and their secret resides only in the *collection*? How do you view a series of images collectively? You place them on the table and then stand back.

But that raises the problem of how to arrange them. A linear layout seems unlikely. So how, then? What's the best way to organize 14,400 files? How could one determine the right structure a priori?

I look back at Martaine's message, but there's no hidden verbiage there. Just these thousands of shots mocking me with their intractable quantity.

But that's just it: their *quantity*. The *number* of photos describes the only correct form: a square. 14,400 is the square of a particularly relevant number. Once again, Billy's riddle provides a self-validating solution. The number that multiplied by itself equals 14,400?

120.

A couple minutes using a photomosaic program to make a square of files 120 to a side leaves me with a picture composed of Billy's photos, each one representing a single pixel. Together they reveal the sublime visage of Olya Zhavinskaya.

My new target.

— — —

The crypto department comes back a bit later having determined that if you source Billy's images from the web, you find that the first letters of the file names for each one combine to form an acrostic text.

The message is 165 characters followed by meaningless garbage. It reads:

Our prey resides at 290 Grand second floor
So this evening be sure to keep your eyes on her door
Report when she leaves and observe where she goes
And the Divinest of torments will be mine to impose

Billy's demanding that Jacques assist in his attempt to spoil Olya's evening stroll.

Getting this order right now sets off internal warning bells, but a quick scan of the *Savant* box reassures me that Jacques was probably chosen for his skills, not because Billy's identified me as his player. Assuming he'd select someone from GAME to surveil Olya, he's got forty players to choose from. Only ten of us enjoy Innoculyte status, and six have completed RL missions. Of those, two seem to have quit the game shortly after, and one deleted his NOD profile entirely. With Red Rook's help, I tend to solve puzzles the fastest among the remaining four, so it's no surprise that Billy might call on Jacques if he needed someone to tail Olya.

I'm sorely tempted to ignore the directive, but the last line of the poem implies Billy's going to take a very personal interest in this exploit. Might he even show up himself for the most severe humiliation yet of his favorite target? I can't risk losing a chance at him.

Thinking it through, I realize there's another risk I can't afford:

Telling Olya what's about to happen to her.

I had expected Billy's maniacal minions to do their worst on the way over to GAME. But Olya arrived for her evening work session without incident. Luckily it's cold out, so with sunglasses, a scarf, and my parka hood, I can obscure my face enough to avoid recognition should Billy actually show up. I monitor the exits from the bodega on the opposite corner, sending periodic status updates back to Madame Martaine.

Since my first real break came from following Olya back to her apartment, wouldn't it be just perfect if I finally caught up with Billy after trying it again?

At midnight, she emerges from the rear alley and takes a right. I follow well behind her. Every pedestrian out this evening looks sinister, each glance broadcasting malice until they move past. Twice over the seven-block route I break into a run as some kind of van pulls up next to her.

But nothing happens.

I watch the door to Olya's building shut behind her. What went wrong? While Billy's assets are certainly amateurs, his gross little productions so far have come off quite well for him.

You're missing something.

I pull up her number on my phone but can't quite think of what to say.

A light comes to life in her second-floor apartment. The tall windows are obscured by a translucent shade, but they allow me a view of her silhouette stepping forward to draw together the heavy inner curtains. Only . . .

Only it's not her silhouette.

The contours of Olya's shadow would easily merit an R rating, and I just saw the mundane lines and angles of a skinny man.

I run across the street, dismissing the idea of the police right away. I can't be sure she's in any real danger, and she'll kill me if in trying to help her, I end up getting her deported. I hurtle down the alley on the short side of her L-shaped building and see a rusty fire escape dangling from its back. I have to climb a chain-link fence and carefully navigate a slack coil of razor wire, but from the top of the fence, I can just leap to catch the bottom of the steel walkway.

My first view of her apartment shows a cavernous industrial space held up by exposed brick pylons. The room is layered with luxurious fabrics and filled with low, bed-like furniture.

A motion catches my eye through the window at the far end of the fire escape. I creep over for a better look and see four men in Olya's sitting room arrayed as though on the set of some gonzo porn production.

Two of them are pressing a gagged Olya face-first into a column. A heavyset South Asian with a wolfman beard is trying to handcuff her to a chain thrown over a high wall sconce, but he's only secured one hand. His partner is a grizzled biker wearing a sleeveless leather vest to display his welter of violent Nordic prison tats. He slices at the back of Olya's shirt with a large butterfly knife. Naturally, Olya is *resisting*.

The other men are setting up the gear. A skinny geek with an atrocious grin and Manson bug-eyes has trouble suppressing his excitement as he rigs a hi-def video camera. To his left, a tall guy in a black trench coat with waist-length brown hair done up in a topknot types into a laptop resting on Olya's coffee table. At his studded belt dangles a cat-o'-nine-tails with thick leather straps knotted at the ends. Not the modern prop of safe-and-sane naughtiness but a tool designed to rend flesh.

On the laptop's screen I can see a video feed of a man's face. The window's too small to tell for sure, but I'm distraught to think Billy's decided to witness this via teleconference. Topknot takes out his whip and turns to observe his comrades' struggle with Olya.

Prison Tats has her shirt ripped up its length from the bottom, but the collar has presented difficulties.

Topknot flicks the leather whip against his opposite hand.

Olya wrenches violently, causing Prison Tats to lose patience. He presses his blade hard against her neck. A line of blood smears her throat as she writhes. I have to move.

I charge down the length of the fire escape and pull my jacket up over my face at the last second before I hurl myself into the window. The glass crashes inward, and I'm able to roll as I hit the floor.

Which would be great, except for my Glock jarring loose from my waistband. It flies across the room, caroms off the bottom of a bookshelf, and then slides behind Olya's love seat.

There's no time to mourn its loss. Everyone breaks into furious motion as the split-second shock of my arrival vanishes. Despite seeming the fiercest of the group, Topknot grabs the laptop, tears open the front door, and runs from the room.

I've regained my feet and lunge toward the South Asian guy, slamming my forehead between his eyes. He goes down with a girlish screech.

Prison Tats is a lot faster. He drops into a passable knife-fighting stance and aims an overhand slash at my face. But my first opponent falls awkwardly against his legs, so his swipe gets my jacket, rather than me. He nimbly steps over his colleague while he reverses the stroke.

I'm about to be stabbed to death.

What neither of us anticipated is Olya's right leg arcing up in a perfect roundhouse. Her foot slams into the guy's mouth. That staggers him enough that I'm able to grab his knife hand and ram into him. He drops his blade as he hits the floor, and I kneel on his ribs to drop an elbow into his eye. Olya unhooks her chain from the light fixture.

A piercing, tremulous scream stays my follow-up blow.

"Stop! I'll blow your motherfucking brains out!"

I'd assigned the Geek such a low threat priority, I nearly forgot he was still in the room. Now I'm shocked to see him standing by the couch jerkily pointing my gun at me. Beads of sweat appear on his forehead.

I throw my hands up and stand. Prison Tats rolls over groaning. The South Asian man takes the opportunity to stumble from the room, cupping his broken nose.

The manic glint in the Geek's eye makes me imagine a man who never had the guts to take out his homeroom, but now relishes the feel of a loaded gun in his hand. His chance to take charge.

I say, "Hey, everything's going to be fine here, just—"

He shouts, making an effort to deepen his voice. "Shut up! Who the fuck are you?"

"Eh! Tiny Dick, who the fuck are you? In my home!" Olya yells back. She's leaning against the corner of the column, but I can see her right hand slowly reach for something behind her. Prison Tats spits blood and tries to get to his feet.

"Shoot this fucker," he hisses to the Geek.

I say, "Look, man, I don't know what you've been told, but please listen to me. The police are on their way, and you need to get out of here. This is *not* a game."

Awful choice of words. My last phrase is the very mantra of the Alternate Reality genre.

Prison Tats picks up his knife and advances on Olya. "Now get that shirt off before I have to cut it off. And I ain't going to be so careful about it this time."

The Geek adds, "Do it, bitch!"

Olya glares at him but then slowly tugs at the button to her collar.

Wanting to force the issue, Prison Tats bellies up to her and jerks at the front of her blouse with his free hand. Olya leans in so the tip of his knife is just past her left shoulder. Then she brings her other hand around fast. A liter vodka bottle from the bar cart behind her shatters into the side of his head. He takes two drunken steps back before collapsing.

The Geek twitches the pistol at her, but she pays no heed and marches toward him, brandishing the bottle's jagged neck.

"Shoot me, *goluboi!*"

The Geek considers it.

I place my hand out to stop her while I desperately try to think of the right button to push with him. "You're going to fuck your real life forever if you don't leave now. Things can't be nearly as bad as sharing a cell block with guys like that." I gesture toward Prison Tats lying inert on the floor.

"And also I cut off your balls," Olya adds, pressing closer.

He turns the pistol sideways. Breathing heavy, working himself into a lather.

I step in front of Olya. "This stupid game is not worth it."

Again, probably the wrong thing to say. His face sets as though he's made a decision. He flicks the safety.

A moment of pure terror. His knuckles go white on the trigger.

He's squeezing.

Harder than necessary, I realize. Since I had the safety off when I burst in, the Geek has actually disabled the gun.

I charge at him.

Though the gun failed to fire, I fail to appreciate that it remains a weapon. The Geek throws it hard into my face, nailing me above my left eye. The explosion of pain makes me stumble to one knee. He runs out the door.

Olya goes after him but pulls up lame after leaving several bloody footprints on the way to her door. Glass shards from the broken bottle. I wipe my eye and try to catch up, but the Geek skids down the final stairs and out into the night before I've made the first landing.

Back upstairs, I find Olya ignoring what must be severe pain to stomp on Prison Tats's fingers. He remains unconscious. I embrace her and gently lead her away. She places a hand over her mouth, breathing in deep gasps as the event catches up with her.

I rub her back and whisper soothing nonsense. Olya submits to this for longer than I'd expect. But suddenly she draws back and skewers me with a calculating stare. Her eyes narrow.

"Zhames. Why are you here right now? How did you know to come?"

I don't have a good answer for her.

59

Over coffee the next morning, I cast around for something positive about the events of last night. Since tossing me out after my avowal that I'd happened to drop by in hopes of romance, Olya has ignored all my calls. I have to assume my entrance last night was recorded, so now Billy must know I'm the player behind Jacques_Ynne. Leaving me right back in the tedious position of waiting for him to make a move.

His first sally comes at six PM. I'm about to log off from NOD when Jacques gets a message from Louis_Markey that says:

> I have to conclude that you wanted to see
> What I had in store for the evening's Plan B.

Below that is a NObject link that gives me a short video file titled She Loves Me Not #1.

Rosa stands naked and shivering, her back pressed up against a filthy green-tiled wall. She's bound spread-eagle with rusty chains to a steel framework. A bright light washes out her skin to the tone of a cadaver. She squints, a strip of duct tape across her mouth. From above dangle more chains, each of them terminating in a wicked hook, like something you'd find at the end of an amusement park pirate's arm.

A hissing voice from off camera says, "Let us hear her."

Two men wearing black velvet executioner's masks and long rubber gloves step to either side of her. One rips the tape off her mouth.

Rosa begs. "Please. Please. I'll do anything you want—"

The man on her left kneads the flesh of her shoulder as if seeking to comfort her.

But then the other one sinks in the first hook.

Rosa screams herself hoarse.

I force myself to watch until the end, when they hoist her into the air by the six huge hooks they've stuck in her back. Her flesh pulls into grotesque Vs, and she leaves a trail of blood as she's dragged up the wall.

This can't be real.

But . . . the close-ups on the hooks' insertion. The way she screams. They go out of their way to *demonstrate* that it's real, and I can't see how Billy could fake it.

And if it's real, then Billy truly has gone bug-fuck. That he'd take out his rage at my disrupting his plans for Olya by punishing Rosa in this way defies comprehension. His brother has been constantly talking about how crazy he is, and I'd always put that down to fraternal rancor. But now . . .

Did Gina's death really damage him so much that he's actually drowned his former self in this Sadean cesspool? That he's let his noxious experiment infect his own imagination?

Given Billy's previous manipulations, I can't completely trust what I've just seen. But clearly something awful is happening.

60

Rosa's video demands that I make inquiries to the DC police's missing persons department in a futile attempt to figure out who she is. Though I'm racked with equal measures of guilt, helplessness, and doubt, I cling to the hope that Billy will have no choice but to contact me again.

While trying to think of ways to bait him, I swing by the Orifice to see if Olya's shown up. There I find Garriott head-down on a worktable, a section of his bangs being slowly singed to carbon by a soldering iron he's left on. Perhaps Olya hasn't yet told our partners about last night's events. Which gives me time to get a better story together.

I think to wake him, but he needs his rest and will probably see his style by fire as a badge of geek honor.

On my way out of the building, I get a text from Louis_Markey:

```
Center fountain in Washington Square Park. One hour.
Bring an iPod with the video on it.
```

My fingers nearly spasm with excitement as I put in the call to McClaren.

Fifty minutes later I'm sitting on the edge of the giant circular cement fountain under a gray sky trying to spot either Billy or components of McClaren's "executive" team he's had standing by for the past weeks.

I've just met some of the principals. Three intense, wiry gentlemen in forgettable business casual, but with very expensive sunglasses. McClaren explained that my role was simply to show Billy part of the video and then demand the hundred thousand dollars. They would handle the rest, and one of them even insisted on confiscating my gun as a "potential distraction." When I raised the issue of witnesses—morning commuters crowded the park—the team leader said, "Sir, you will not ever see us. We are very good at this. We could pick him up right in front of the NYPD, and no one would notice."

He was right. Looking around at the mass of humanity traversing the wide plaza, everyone seems suspicious, but no one particularly stands out.

I take a moment to gut-check my role in this "involuntary commitment." At first, I thought that if Billy was crazy, his madness was the high-functioning sociopathic kind, not the delusional "danger to self and others" type normally required to treat someone against their will. But the turns his game has taken lately point to the latter.

Now I'm thinking that if Billy's such a fan of the Marquis de Sade, then an asylum will be the perfect place for him to gain a better understanding of the man's work.

Billy is late. My ass is getting sore from the concrete, so I stand up and stretch. My phone starts vibrating from a text:

```
[C12@192.0.2.117 ProSoap Alert]
Cam 12 - Unrecognized - conf .89
```

I'm about to ignore the message when I remember that camera 12 is the one in the alley at the back of GAME that leads into the POD. The only people it ever sees are GAME residents, and I've only gotten a handful of alerts on it. I pull up a low-res stream.

It's no wonder the face comes up unrecognized. The person standing in front of the doors is wearing large wraparound shades and has a black baseball cap pulled low. But what stand out are the guy's high cheekbones and extreme pallor.

It's Billy. He's decided not to make our meeting. He brandishes a security card at the camera and runs it through the reader. Then he bends down and picks up two items lying beside him. The first is a small gray duffel bag, and the second is a comically large sledgehammer with a short but very fat cylindrical head. He's traded his crowbar for a post maul. I'm sure Billy chose the tool for its aesthetic properties: the proverbial blunt instrument.

He hefts it and then takes a lazy swipe at the camera. The signal goes dead.

Oh no. Our plan is falling apart. Looks like Billy had a different one.

I radio McClaren and tell him the news. There's a brief silence, and then he says, "Okay. Sit tight. We'll get him."

I feel deflated, like the starting quarterback getting unaccountably benched before kickoff. It occurs to me that Garriott is probably still in the Orifice. I'm not sure what Billy's intentions are—though the presence of the post maul provides some insight—but it's worth warning Garriott to lock the room and stay there until we get this under control. I try his cell, but it goes right to voicemail. Concerned, I pull up the bank of camera feeds from one of our tracking systems. Front_Cam_B shows a wide shot of the Orifice. To my dawning terror, Garriott's not there, but Ginger is. She's sitting right in the middle of the worktable. In his sleep-deprived delirium, Garriott must have forgotten to put her in our safe before he stepped out. I picture Billy's hammer coming down hard on her head.

I take off toward the southeast corner of the park, thinking about the odds of getting a cab during rush hour. Then I see a hippie walking toward me with a beat-up ten-speed. I careen up to him and grab the handlebars.

"Buddy. I need your bike. It's a matter of life and death. Take this."

I flip my money clip at him, and he catches it with his free hand. Seeing a hundred-dollar bill wrapping the outside, any thought of resistance leaves him, and he steps back, allowing me to mount up.

I hear him say, *"Vaya con dios,"* as I sprint away.

I'm amazed at the time I make. It's just over a mile from Washington Square Park to GAME, and pedaling furiously, I'm halfway there in less than two minutes. Normally, riding the way I am, I'd have been mowed down by a bus before I hit Lafayette. But as fate would have it, traffic is completely gridlocked the whole way.

I jump off the bike in the alley behind GAME and check myself briefly at the cellar doors Billy left open. The crushed wreckage of the video camera reminds me that I am unarmed, and that it's often best to treat a man with a mallet delicately.

I grab the top lip of the entrance and swing myself down without stepping on the noisy metal staircase. I sink behind a large bank of rusting industrial detritus and listen.

A motor whines along with a high-frequency scraping sound. I see Billy kneeling at the door to the Orifice using a handheld angle grinder on its edge. His choice of tools is commendable, because the noise will cover my approach.

I slink down the hall. Billy doesn't look up until I wrench his grinder away from the door.

I say, "I take it you're going to want to reschedule."

He grins. "Yeah. There's been a change in plans."

Seeing him smile at me in triumph when it's quite clear that I'm going to kick his ass and then hand him over to the dubious care of his brother tells me he really is living in another dimension.

"What did you do with that girl? You little—"

Then I feel something to my right. I don't know if it's a slight shift in the air, but I start turning too late. There's a soft click, and the muscles along my vertebrae seize up in succession like a row of toppling dominos. My entire musculoskeletal system ceases functioning. The sensation is not unlike having your man die in a first-person shooter. You don't always notice the shot that takes your life bar to zero, you just find suddenly that your guy is no longer responding to your input, and then the camera crashes to the ground.

I hit my head hard on the doorjamb on the way down. The last thing I see is the man who gave Olya the necklace sneering at me from above. His lips move in some vindictive epithet, but I can't decipher it. In one hand he's got a sparking stun baton. In the other, a liquid-soaked rag that he's bringing toward my face.

61

McClaren appears above me with a terrifying expression of concern. "Are you all right?"

I run through a system check. My head confirms that it hurts like hell. I can see and hear. Basic mental functions seem to be in order. I can feel my extremities, but—and here's where some triple-distilled horror pours in—I can't move them.

My answer: "No."

McClaren sees me trying to wriggle into a position where I can see what's wrong with my arms. He puts calming hands on my shoulders and says, "Let me untie you, killer."

Before McClaren sent me to the emergency room, I established that Billy made no further attempt to get into the Orifice. So Ginger remained intact. The break-in was just a ruse to get me down there and out from under McClaren's security umbrella, so that he could steal my iPod, and with it, Gina's suicide video. While things are well shy of good, at least the worst case didn't happen.

I'm even able to spare a little admiration for Billy. Since disappearing, he's been hunted by a team of trained professionals, and so far he's run circles around us with his illusionist's ability to make us look the wrong way while he pulls off the trick.

I go home and sleep for a blissful two hours before I'm roughly shaken awake by McClaren. I stutter out a question about why he can't ring my fucking doorbell, but he interrupts. "Get up. Your boss wants a debrief on this morning's tscrewnami."

I've worked with Blake for a month, and this is the first time I've been in his office. He begins with, "Do you want to tell me how the fuck this happened?"

"I'm sorry. Events got out of hand. Your brother engineered everything from the beginning. Our meeting was a ploy." McClaren had filled in the details on the way over. "He used traffic barriers to create a circular detour that snarled traffic all around the Lower East Side just so our team couldn't get down to GAME. Even the guy I got the bike from was probably a plant. We should have been prepared for something like this. Setting up carefully rigged scenes is, after all, what Billy does best. We need to determine how he knew about the team we had in place."

"No, you need to *determine* whether you're capable of doing this job."

So here it finally is. The imperious master lecturing his deficient servant. We're not old college buddies anymore. I want to reply that I was the only one of his underlings who was able to locate his brother in the first place. I'm tempted to offer my resignation, but then I think about the Dancers and stifle the impulse. Luckily, Blake is winding up for a diatribe that doesn't require any input.

"You take off half-cocked into a situation where you're not in control, and without backup? We have a team of ex-SEALs on retainer, and somehow my little brother *subdues* you, and now we've lost the only real leverage we had over him. This is your progress over the last several weeks? Forgive me if I sound less than thrilled."

"Blake, I told you at the outset—"

"You've told me a lot of things, but my brother is still out there fucking with me!"

I'm almost relieved when I hear the strains of a smooth jazz cover of Metallica's "Master of Puppets" issue from my BlackBerry. I'd selected the song for alerts that Billy's av has appeared in *Savant*. "Looks like he wants to join the conversation."

I lean over Blake's laptop and log in to NOD.

Louis_Markey is standing at Château de Silling's gate. He's got audio chat turned on, so we hear him say, "Hello, James. Sorry about our mis-understanding earlier. But these things can happen when you make your-self the plaything of monsters."

"Monsters? Where's Rosa, Billy?"

He ignores my question. "And speaking of which, I take it my brother is there with you?"

How could he know that? Probably tracing our IP to an IMP domain. Or maybe just a good guess after the day's events. I hesitate to answer him.

But Blake presses on. In a faux conciliatory tone he says, "I think it's time we sat down and talked, Billy. Resolved our differences. Let's straighten things out once and for all."

This draws a distorted laugh from the laptop's speakers. Billy adds, "It's too late for that, Blake."

"It's never too late for a new beginning."

"Actually, I think an ending is long overdue. See Blake, I know ev-erything now. I know what you've done. And it's time that you received judgment."

Blake snaps, "Jesus Christ, Billy. You *are* a delusional little poseur. You don't even believe in God."

"But I believe in retribution. And where better to find inspiration than the Good Book? Are you prepared to be judged, Blake? To feel the flames of righteous vengeance?"

"You really played too much Dungeons and Dragons as a child."

"Blake, you're a seeker of strange flesh. Get ready to suffer for it."

"These threats won't look good at your commitment hearing."

I'm not sure Blake should have openly declared his agenda like that, but Billy's already gone.

Blake pushes away from his desk in nearly terminal frustration. He starts making crabbed "You see?" gestures. But then he subsides back into his chair. We stare at each other for what seems like a long time.

He lets out a tired breath. "You have any idea what he's talking about?"

I think about his question. "Well, this is coming just after he saw the video of his friend Gina's suicide. He believes you bear some responsibil-ity for that."

"That's ridiculous."

"Even so. How exactly were you connected with Gina?"

"I'm not."

"Blake, I know she invented the Dancers. So there's no point in hiding the truth here. I'm on your team, remember?"

"Okay. She helped in getting the project off the ground. But I was just brought in as an investor through Olya. Gina was the engineer. I only met with her once."

This is a Blake I never knew in college. This Blake is uncomfortable. On edge. Given his earlier severity, I'm disinclined to make things easier for him. "But you knew her before that. Didn't you?"

He starts to answer, but we're distracted by sudden motion on his laptop. In *Savant*, apparently the world is ending.

The meteors come screaming in from a high angle in the western sky. They're beautiful: startling confections of flame effects and smoky particle systems. His graphics card gives a hitch of admiration as the screen fills with fire.

Then they're upon us. The first clips one of Silling's towers, smashing it and sending stones and masonry into a small group of avs who are watching the spectacle. The meteor buries itself into a nearby mountainside, causing a massive explosion. The ground quakes as two more hit, one much closer to Jacques, and then the whole world vanishes in the inferno.

With the chaos of fire, ash, and airborne earth, visibility shrinks to a few feet. Still, I can see several avs remain standing. All of us are on fire, our avs' clothes and hair incinerated almost instantly. We're treated to the abnormal sight of people watching themselves combust, saying things like "Kewl" and "WTF!?!"

Eventually my avatar freezes. I rotate the camera around him and see that poor Jacques has become a charcoal cinder, now rapidly eroding in the raging winds. Moments later, he's completely gone, and all I can see is the fire and, through an occasional gap in the haze, the ruins of Billy's chamber of horrors.

Quite a show. But what does it mean? Why all the wanton, albeit virtual, destruction?

And more destruction follows. NOD suddenly crashes, but not back to the desktop. Sitting there on a black screen is a lonely blinking cursor.

I try to restore Windows, but Billy seems to have formatted Blake's hard drive as a Parthian shot. And that means he must have compromised his brother's laptop some time ago. Which would be an easy way to monitor Blake's activities. But why would Billy scuttle such a valuable asset? Perhaps, like he said, he really thinks he does "know everything."

I say, "You're going to need a new laptop."

But Billy's just getting started.

Blake's office door opens to reveal Blythe. She looks over her shoulder and then back at us. "What's going on, Blake? What did you do to him?" Her voice is low and freighted with tension.

"What are you talking about?"

"I'm talking about *that*." Her arm shoots out toward the frosted-glass ambient display on Blake's bookcase that indicates movement in IMP's stock by changing colors. It's turned a bloody crimson and has started pulsing ominously. "*That* is our stock collapsing!"

"What? Wait . . . Why do you think it's my fault?"

"It's Billy. He's trying to dump his entire trust into the open market. I've called Ger. He's going to have the NYSE suspend trading for the rest of the day."

The red globe begins flashing more urgently. Blythe closes her eyes.

She says, "We'll discuss it later. Right now, you need to call your bankers and get liquid. You and I are going to step in and absorb some of this or we will have panic selling come Monday."

"Wait, Blythe, I can't really—"

"You can, and you will. I don't need to tell you what this is going to do to our deal with TelAmerica."

"Now, let's just calm down a second."

Blythe makes an exasperated "please the court" gesture at his stock indicator. "Let me ask again, what did you—two—do?"

Blake falls into aphasia. "I . . . I—"

I've never seen Blake at a loss for words. He's rattled. His brother is getting to him.

"I have to testify in front of Congress next month with this shit going on? I can't work while I'm always worrying about one of you exploding a bomb under me. I can't live like this. Blake, please"—here her voice breaks—"is it never going to stop?"

Blake is up like a shot, taking her in his arms. I assume this is my cue to leave. On my way out, I see written on Blake's face a plan to exchange every tear shed by his sister for a liter of Billy's blood.

Blake stops me with a sharp, "James."

"Yes?"

"I'd hate to think you've been subject to conflicting priorities recently."

I squint at him, not sure what he means. Is he talking about the Dancers?

He adds, "Find my brother before the bell on Monday. Or we'll need to find someone who can."

62

Billy still isn't done.

I soon learn that his virtual firestorm was but a fitting prelude to the digital mayhem he's unleashed.

Only a few minutes after I leave Blake's office, an emergency email alert arrives saying that Billy's hacked an IMP server. I have a couple of their tech people pull me a disk image. Live for only minutes before they shut it down, the box is filled with the stuff of IT personnel nightmares.

Billy had reconfigured the server as his own NOD node. I set it up on a clean machine and rez in Jacques to find a duplicate of Château de Silling after the meteor blitz. Only the blackened shell of the castle remains.

However, that leaves the dungeon intact.

And the dungeon has changed. Rebuilt as a prison for the avatars of Billy's players, each of its cells contains the skin of someone who signed on to the game. Since his labyrinth now stretches hundreds of levels into the bowels of Silling's mountain, I gather that nearly a quarter million people have at least dropped in to check out his creation.

I walk through the dank halls, taking in the vast array of avs he's captured. There's something wrong with these skins. Billy has removed all privacy protections on their users' underlying profiles.

Even worse: all of the avs' RL names and addresses appear convincing. I punch a few into the Experian credit bureau database, and they each come back current and accurate. As does phone number, marital status, and occupation. Billy has tied real identities to all these avatars. Looks like *Savant*'s special NOD plug-ins contained some nasty surprises.

Nastier still are their inventories. They're stuffed with way more text, image, and video files than one normally picks up in-world. An aggregation of dirty data that seems to represent anything untoward these people have ever seen online. Billy must have developed some kind of automated system to sift their hard drives for the "naughty bits." Maybe he's reversed one of the flesh-tone and bad-word filters kid-friendly internet companies use to exclude adult content.

Browsing through the videos, I find a mix of *Savant* creations, amateur porn (including some hidden-camera stuff), and genre porn: fetish, bestiality, torture, child. The volume and variety would astonish even the Divine Marquis. I dredge up note cards containing lewd chats with mistresses, employees, and even a babysitter. There's evidence of infidelity, abuse, and some serious crimes.

To refute any claims of innocence, Billy provides links to forensic support, including full hard drive images. He instrumented his hapless victims' computers with all sorts of system monitoring: browsing histories, screen capture, and keystroke logging. The first selection I check shows a Kansas City paramedic logging out of her wedding website. Then she punches in a password to Adultfriendfinder.com. Next I look for my own name, and I'm relieved to see that Red Rook's custom security suite has prevented Billy from completely defiling my system. But many, many others haven't been so fortunate.

Ms. Charlene Sweatmon, of Champagne-Urbana, IL, mother of three, created a series of lush videos of *120 Days* vignettes, including the notorious "sticky toilet seat" interlude. Dave Loeffler's Little League team might like to view his NOD wedding video in which he marries a ten-year-old boy. Glenn Ricardo of Tempe, AZ, is a middle school English teacher who likes commanding (in very colorful language) amputees to coat themselves with tapioca pudding. Ernie Lemuel seems to have a regrettably close relationship with his Labradoodle. Just by dipping my toe in this torrent of twisted video, I can tell that many of the worst offenders are the Pyrexian Innoculytes.

Trusting that I have a pretty good sense of Billy's dramatic instincts at this point, I pilot my av to the bottom of the dungeon.

True to form, he's tricked out the lowest level as a sort of antechamber to hell, complete with stalactites dripping blood and a fiery lake. In the middle is an island on which two avatars are seated in gilded skull thrones. The Duc de Blangis, the leader of Sade's Friends from *120 Days,* is represented by Dr_B_Longey, a handsome re-creation of Robert Randall at his predatory peak. Next to him is Fedor_Sett standing in for Blake.

Dr_B_Longey has a single video file in his inventory. Billy has spliced together a concise summary of his father's dubious business deals along with an account of his many crimes against his family. Among others, there's the clip of Billy's mother displaying the dire effects of their bedroom activity. A kitchen argument that degenerates into his beating her with a spatula and then coming after the cameraman. A particularly harrowing episode of his stuffing Billy's face into a toilet.

Blake's profile contains his personal information (for "occupation," Billy cheekily entered "Malefactor of Great Wealth") but no media. He has a single note card, which reads:

```
One day his plagues will overtake him:
   death, mourning, and famine.
He will be consumed by fire,
   for mighty is the one who judges him.
```

That turns out to be Revelation 18:8 with the gender of the pronouns changed. The original passage refers to the Whore of Babylon, a typically subtle dig at Blake. His use of "one day" implies that, though he seems intent on judging his brother for his crimes, Billy has started the trial by granting him a continuance.

Why would he do that? Is it simple showmanship, building suspense for his audience? Or maybe he believes Blake is liable to commit even greater villainy than his father, and Billy simply wants to wait until all the evidence is in.

My friend Eeyore sees the biblical dimensions of Billy's leak as well. He texts me:

```
Pornaggedon draws nigh.
```

I call him to see what he's learned.

"You think a lot of innocent perverts are going to be spraying their morning coffee all over their computer screens?"

"James, I've just determined that our congressman collects crush videos. Women in high heels mashing insects mostly, which is a relief. The attorney general of Delaware has footage with, ah, various mammals."

"How did you rez in?"

"No, James. Not NOD. I'm using the web database our target has helpfully provided. A nice Flash interface for the casual browser."

I pull up the link he sends me and can't resist trying a few searches to get my head around it. After sorting by occupation, I'm not too surprised to see several state reps, a judge, seven clergy, two semifamous actors, and a child welfare specialist among those indulging some peculiar tastes. Though I'm sure these people *will be* surprised to have their private delights so publicly exposed.

Eeyore says, "He's even got pictures of most people. And linked their addresses to Google Maps."

"I'm glad I finally have some icebreakers for when I see the neighborhood celebrities in the deli."

"If you can fight through the camera scrum."

I check the magnitude of the disclosure. Billy has just shy of a million people pinned to his digital Styrofoam. Like a collection of exotic insects he neglected to suffocate before display, their legs still twitching. That's a far bigger group than just his *Savant* players, and there's something else strange about the data.

"Eeyore, how can this database be *growing*?"

"We don't know yet. Probably some kind of worm. Maybe he's got black hats on the payroll. We have the trawl nets out."

"Money is no object."

"That's true more and more these days."

I sit, remembering the terror I felt the first time I was too reckless online and found my laptop at the mercy of a Czech cracker co-op. When you get infected, you worry first about your bank passwords, then about your files, and finally you deal with the notion that your secrets have been exposed to prying eyes. But most crackers just want your bandwidth and couldn't care less that you spend too much time at MILFmonitor.com. Billy's worm is different, however. Here, exposure is the sole purpose. If his *Hell Is Other People* experiment sought to explore fear, then this turn in *Savant* is clearly meant to explore *shame*.

Anonymity is the lifeblood of the frenzy of raunchiness that followed in the wake of the internet. I can't think of a better way to kill a sex-related business than to start revealing personal details about its clients. What chaos might be created for Blake if his investment in NOD blows up from being implicated in a privacy scandal? He mentioned his board shitting Yorkshire terriers over material losses from his VR project. If Billy's successful here, I think we'll see them trying to pass a mastodon.

Assuming he has one, Billy's larger artistic objective must be to remind *everyone* that while the internet affords us our aliases and avatars, the same technology also makes it feasible to record all our purchases, conversations, and actions with frightening ease. In most cases, our beloved disguises are distressingly fragile, and the volume of secrets that can be disclosed is greater than it's ever been.

McClaren calls me two hours later.

"You have any hot ideas for getting this genie back in its bottle?"

I'd been assessing the possibility of containment just before he called. A couple net-crawlers I sent out searching for sample file names told me Billy already has his NOD shard up on another server. It will only be a matter of hours before his dungeon reconnects to the main grid.

"Well, since he's distributing child porn, I'm sure the ISPs will move fast to shut down his backups. In the meantime, you can have Red Rook hose down sites as they crop up." I'm suggesting he mount a denial-of-service (DOS) attack to cripple any servers found hosting the files. "So if not back in its bottle, maybe we can wash it down the drain."

"Yeah, our guys thought of that. But looks like Billy has alternates in quite a few uncooperative lo-calities. And he's crammed Google's results with pages that link to mirrors. So attacks won't buy us much time before they get impractical."

Billy came prepared. Even if Blake authorizes an internet-scale reprise of his Whack-A-Mole game, I doubt it's one he can win.

McClaren asks, "Anything else?"

I say, "He's probably got a kill switch. If we could find him—"

"Yeah. I'll bet we could talk some sense into the boy. You can imagine the boss is getting a little—"

"I know. I'm doing everything I can."

But I feel a ramping sense of futility. A person with the brains, devious nature, and unlimited resources of Billy Randall can stay hidden from his pursuers too easily. Our only recourse is to track him down, despite that for the past month, the entire Randall security apparatus has failed to do so. They can't expect that I, working more or less alone, will be able to locate him before this stuff storms across the internet.

And yet . . . My mind won't quite let go of the problem. The hallmark of a good hacker is machine-like persistence. The numb commitment to the belief that there is always a way in. You just have to keep swinging your pick.

63

When confronted with what seems like an impenetrable wall, one studies it carefully for even hairline fissures. I bet the faults in Billy's fortifications will radiate from the impact of Gina's suicide. Her death demands this twisted tribute from him. Her memory makes him emotional and precipitate, maybe less careful. Indeed, I first found him through her.

And what do we know about his most recent actions?

Watching that video must have really multiplied his anger at Blake over her death.

But why?

I force myself to endure it several more times. For the life of me, I can't find anything new in that tight head shot. Billy said, "I know everything now." As though watching the video provided some last, essential piece of information. So is there something in the video—a dog-whistle code that only he can hear—that makes him want to train his guns on his brother?

Maybe a dog whistle is a bad metaphor. Maybe it's something that I *could* hear if I just knew what to listen for.

So how do I find out what I'm missing?

Of the two people who could answer that question, one is in hiding and the other is dead. But then I recall something I've learned about Billy's research: the curious way he described his visit to Gina's apartment to her landlord.

Maybe it's time to conduct a séance.

— — —

Virtual world builders are usually very mindful of security since they often have convertible currencies on which their users rely. So they face an economic holocaust if some enterprising cracker finagles himself keys to the mint. NOD keeps their boxes' software locked correspondingly tight.

Breaking in will take a bit of setup. I start by hunting through a bunch of NOD forums for email addresses of company employees. For all but the most senior, they have an enforced "first name underscore last name" convention. I spend a few minutes with Spemtex, a delightful spammer's tool that sends a test email to thousands of combinations of common first and last names at a given organization. This gets me a list of seven people responding with out-of-office emails.

One of these, a database administrator named Zach Levin, is kind enough to provide in his auto-reply the information that he's part of the team at the Massively Metaversal Media conference currently under way in San Jose. Running the names of the subset of other employees whose spam didn't bounce through Dice, the Ladders, Monster, and Career-Builder yields five résumés from active NOD employees. Two of these are low-paid off-hour IT support drudges who are likely to be on duty Saturdays. One of them, Matt Jones, is a recent hire at NOD's satellite office in Austin and simply hasn't yet taken his résumé down. New employees make good targets because they're not as familiar with the company's security policies, they aren't likely to know a lot of their coworkers by voice, and they're generally insecure in their position and eager to comply with well-framed requests. As a final bit of icing, he's included his cell number.

The plan is simple: I pay eight hundred bucks to rent a well-distributed botnet to intermittently DOS the NOD world domains as well as the corporate servers at their main Menlo Park office. One of these boxes is an internet telephony system. Attacking it will cause havoc in their comms. Then I send an email to poor Mr. Jones spoofed to look like it's coming from Zach Levin:

```
Hey,


Sorry to hit you with this out of the blue, but I'm sure
you've heard we've got some problems with the Menlo
```

servers. I'm here at M3 with some guys from Second Life
who say they got nailed last week. They tell me it's just
Chinese script kiddies screwing around. There'll be a
CERT coming out on it soon.

   Anyway, Jack Fisher [VP marketing] is meeting with
IMP about some biz dev stuff, and he needs this report
from the main server for background. Traffic stats,
etc. . . . I tried to log in when the thing was going
down and managed to lock myself out. I can't get ahold of
the Menlo techs, so can you reset my password and leave
the new one on my voicemail? You'd really be saving our
ass up here. Thanks.

—Zach

A key strategy in establishing credibility with a mark is to make predictions that are then confirmed by "independent" sources. So twenty minutes later, I send him a fake report from Carnegie Mellon's Computer Emergency Response Team confirming my story. CERT maintains an email list to which most webmasters subscribe to tell them when giant worm infestations are eating the internet.

I let that marinate for an hour and then lob in a call. I'm counting on the fact that these two people don't know each other well enough for instant voice identification over the phone. I throw on a little cell static just in case. "Jones," he answers.

"Hey, man. Zach Levin. You get my email about the password reset?"

"Yeah. I just put it through."

"Great. Hey, I'm on my cell here. I think there's something wrong with the exchange in Menlo. Can you put me on hold and try one of those lines?"

He clicks off and comes back a minute later.

"Yeah. Seems like it's down. It's not ringing through."

"Right, so I can't get into my voicemail to get my new password. So can you reset it again and tell me what it is?"

"Well . . ." You never give passwords out over the phone.

"I know you're not supposed to. But we're in kind of a bind here. Tell you what, can you put your manager on?"

"He's not here."

"Hmmm . . . Well, I don't know what we should do. It's really starting to hit the fan. Jack is on the warpath, and I'd hate to be one of the Menlo IT guys tomorrow. You could be a real hero by helping us out. I'll write you an email right now authorizing this. Hold on."

I send him another email copying a couple people high in the tech hierarchy. All of whom work in Menlo and don't have access to their server right now.

Finally, he says, "Okay, it's one five bravo tango seven kilo kilo zero four six."

"Thanks, bud. I owe you one."

Five minutes later, I'm deep in their network. I've got some bent Linux libraries on their database server, and I'm silently sucking a copy of the two-terabyte hard disk across their hosting facility's rocking fiber-optic line.

While her physical remains are well beyond my necromantic abilities, perhaps one of Gina's digital selves can be resurrected. I'm hoping this undead Gina will retain some spectral connection to Billy.

Of course no avatar ever really dies to begin with, they just enter a limbo of inaccessibility. Now we can be so carefree with memory that you almost never destroy data, you just redescribe it as "deleted." So I'm betting that Gina's primary av can be exhumed from her plot in the database I've just stolen.

64

---

ike people, avatars tend to bloat as they age. Rezzed on 9/07/2003, during NOD's beta-testing period, Joanne_Dark had grown gargantuan. Her bulk appears not in the Audrey Hepburn contours of her av, but rather in her possessions. She stores huge amounts of gear for role-playing sims based on *Star Wars, Star Trek, StarCraft,* and *Battlestar Galactica.* J. R. R. Tolkien and George R. R. Martin each get folders. As do C. S. Lewis and Lewis Carroll. But I want to find the places where her NOD life intersected with her real one, and I suspect these fantasy games will only lead me farther afield.

I scroll through her in-world buddy list looking for Billy, feeling my way through her data like a newly blind man trying to recognize a familiar face by touch. If I can find the av Billy uses outside of *Savant,* I may be able to catch him in NOD using a connection I can trace.

Gina has 552 names in her buddy list. A thorough search through all their profile data might take days, but Billy is a kind of artist, and most artists regard anonymity as a deadly poison. He wouldn't neglect to brand his personal avatar. By now, I should be able to spot him from a mile away.

I spend a couple minutes writing code in NOD's scripting language, which they call nVerse. It populates a large area on my server with the primary skins of all of Gina's friends. The assembly looks like a parade formation of the guests from a Halloween party at the Playboy Mansion.

I run through the ranks, first deleting all the Furries. Then the stereotypical fashionistas, stripperellas, goth girls, and superheroines are cashiered along with their male counterparts. Plain Jane animals and their mythical cousins are sent packing as well. I reject a couple avs for their too-obvious monikers, like Ben_Dover or Mike_Hunt.

A couple hours later, I'm left with a company of uglied-up humans, some scary children, a couple clones of famous dictators and serial killers, and monsters of various persuasions, including five renditions of the devil himself. Overrepresented in the top ten of these are what I'd call "freaks of nature." A six-legged Chernobyl horse fetus, an African albino covered with human bite marks, a repulsive sex troll, and a two-headed crow.

I think Billy would rep as something more fearsome than a carrion bird, but there's something about this one's dual black heads and beady crimson eyes that imparts a feeling of menace. Not to mention that its creator has given it a gigantic schlong, which is surely nonstandard equipment for any creature dependent on aerodynamics. Still, I'm about to dispel it when I pause over its handle, A_Ross_Fowles.

I'd initially dismissed "Fowles" as the dumbest possible self-referential name, but the key attribute isn't that the little monster's a bird, but rather that it has two heads. Of course, bicephalic birds have been common symbols throughout world history, used by everyone from the ancient Egyptians to the modern Masons. But I've encountered one of these more recently.

Where was it?

I mentally rehearse everywhere I've been over the past weeks. Finally it dawns on me that since I'm looking at something in NOD, it's not where *I've* been, it's where *Jacques* has been. And he's spent time almost exclusively in one place: the Château de Silling. And a two-headed bird, really an eagle but rendered to look more like a crow, is the first thing you see upon entering. The Sade family crest carved in stone over the castle's gate.

That insight solves the name for me: A_Ross_Fowles reads as Eros Fouls, a natural choice for a man who in real life renamed himself "Coitus Defiles."

But in finding Billy's digital embodiment, I've only uncovered another corpse. My crow's account was closed two days before he disappeared.

I suppose even the dumbest fugitive would abandon his usual online haunts. Or at least he'd use a new avatar.

I can't quite believe that Billy has dropped NOD cold turkey. Since he's forced to keep a low profile while on the lam, what better place to express himself than a virtual world where he's securely armored in a plastic identity?

Beyond that, I've been berating myself that I didn't think of this search strategy before now, but in fairness I'm not sure I could have. I didn't understand until I really got into NOD how attached people become to their virtual world of choice. While players may try on identities like so many party dresses, they often think of the *place* as a sacred homeland. That's why I'd bet my whole stack that Billy is still logging on.

I spend a long time browsing the profiles of A_Ross_Fowles's buddy list. I see that Billy, disagreeable enough in real life, when unburdened of basic social constraints in NOD, becomes intolerable. Almost devoid of "real" avs, his list is populated by corporate mascots and sex workers. More interesting is the series of "friends" that he's made but who have then revoked friendly status within a couple weeks of meeting him. This wall of shame is complemented by an extraordinary number of venues that have banned him, including Fran's Fecal Funhouse.

What could one possibly do to get kicked out of there?

Despite all this information, he's been savvy enough to obliterate any direct trail between his old and new avs. So I face the daunting prospect of having to seek out his new identity in the sea of almost ten million active NODlings.

At least his mutant crow has given me a police sketch to use in my manhunt.

He probably came to life within a week before or after Billy went off the grid. This alone will filter out nearly all of the avs but still leaves me with something on the order of sixty thousand. A couple more filters include avs who have visited servers with *Savant*'s former IP address, NODlings with more than three location bans, and finally people who are registered in any of NOD's developer programs. Sadly, these criteria still yield an army of 7,461 possibilities. Doable, but not on my time-frame. I drum my desk, mulling how to proceed.

I'm resigning myself to just getting on with it when I remember an innovative data-mining package one of the Red Rook librarians was flogging a while back. I find the old email and download the test version of CogneTech's Cut_0.87 data-slicing tool kit.

Once I get it installed and eating from the NOD data trough, the software lets me put in all kinds of free-form search information, including all my previous filters. The algorithm offers to consult the internet to gather data helpful in forming "metaconnections," whatever those might be.

Cut ponders for twenty minutes while I shower. When the software's window resumes focus, I'm presented with a ranked list of avatar handles that it thinks I'll most enjoy meeting.

The results are both amazing and depressing. While I'm nearly floored by the eerie intelligence of the software's choices, I can see immediately that the first results aren't going to be Billy. The top prospect, Tad_A_ LaPhille, lists his real name, and he's a former PiMP classmate of Billy and Gina's. The second is a minor player in the Jackanapes' circle. The third is the av of their dead friend Trevor Rothstein.

After a couple more misses, I find Lillie_Hitchcock, who is unique among Cut's selections in that she's so pedestrian: the off-the-shelf Barbie av of a complete noob with the default T-shirt-and-khaki-pants outfit that everyone ditches immediately upon rezzing in. Her player has only replaced the T-shirt's texture with a set of wide red, white, and blue stripes.

I'm disposed to disregard her, since Billy designs avatars with exacting craft. But what keeps me interested is that I can't tell why Cut selected her in the first place. I flip to the dialogue that explains an item's ranking, and it tells me that her placement was based on a high relevance score for the av's textures to the search term "double eagle." I inspect Lillie for tattoos or anything about her that refers to birds. There's nothing, so I impatiently check the links for an explanation.

Never before have I been so possessed of a desire to kiss a piece of software, my work with the Dancers notwithstanding. And what is the valuable nugget it sifted from a flood of worthless internet nonsense?

The Russian flag. Not the pernicious crimson hammer and sickle. The broad white, blue, and red stripes of the new Russia, which first lived as a flag of the Russian Empire. The other flag in use around that time was yellow, imprinted with a black double eagle from the Romanovs' coat of arms. Nearly identical to the one on the Sade family crest.

Knowing I have my man, I ask Google to unravel her name. Billy's skipped the usual verbal trickery, opting instead for just an obscure reference. "Lillie" and "Hitchcock" are the first two names of the philanthropist who commissioned the famous landmark that looks over the city of San Francisco. Her last name: Coit.

And this av is not only live, but I see she's logged in recently.

I wrap up by inserting a routine in NOD's database scripts that will message me any time Lillie_Hitchcock logs in. So the next time Billy enters NOD, I'll be waiting for him.

I check in with my Red Rook colleagues regarding their suppression efforts. Billy's database had recently propagated enough to stay live for over five hours before they were able to disable the servers, and I sense a growing pessimism among the team. Meanwhile, Eeyore forwards me an entry from the NOD forums describing the Silling firestorm and the poster's subsequent exploration of the dungeon. He details in vehement terms his feeling of betrayal at seeing his hard drive mirrored online and expresses his desire to, appropriately enough, torture Billy to death.

There are nearly a hundred responses, mostly in the same torches-and-pitchforks vein. Though one complains that he found out his daughter's pediatrician had gone pretty far along in the Course of Fever, and he laments the downed server due to the loss of his ability to check his zip code for "shit-eating Sade-freak pedophiles."

The controversy has already been picked up by a couple of the nimbler tech blogs. Blue_Bella renders this verdict: "Such a breach of privacy, some have called it the *Unmasking*, is frightening to closeted exxxplorers, but it could be for the best if it exposes how much we all like this stuff but just refuse to talk about it."

Slashdot is running an article quoting anonymous porn sources saying traffic to their sites has fallen off a cliff. Meanwhile, drive-formatting freeware hosts are currently offline due to unheard-of traffic spikes.

HoseDown has an item headlined:

Netphomaniacs scurry in the glare of sudden sunlight.

Soon I suspect they'll begin to sizzle.

65

illie_Hitchcock logs in at four PM the next afternoon.

A short query to the NOD central server gives me what we've been after for over a month now: an honest IP address for Billy Randall.

I'm tempted to send this straight to McClaren's team and go buy myself a bottle of small-batch. But from long experience, I know that I need a solid physical address, or else there's a good chance that they'll wind up SWATing a midtown Starbucks.

I treat the situation gently. A light scan shows his machine is as tight as one might expect from someone with Billy's technical skills. Of course, I've already planned an attack. His Achilles' heel is that he'll have the NOD developer's kit installed on his machine, and I've had plenty of opportunity to assay it for flaws.

There aren't many, but I did find a trapdoor buried in their testing tools. A poorly designed function allows one to load outdated versions for some of the program's components. These contain errors that let me order his current NOD session to silently run any program I might specify. Even if Billy were watching closely, it just looks like NOD has started another of its many processes. But in reality, I've sliced a fatal hole in his system by uploading a tiny RAT designed to mimic a common security application.

Now I have to be circumspect. Not wanting to risk tipping him off, I decide to lie back. In the meantime, I write up a triumphant status report to McClaren and hope that getting into Billy's machine will suffice to prevent Blake from firing me tomorrow.

— — —

I wait until four AM Monday morning to risk firing up my Trojan. I start by creating myself a shadow admin account. After that, I install a program that lets me discreetly spy on his sessions. Then I start copying down his hard drive. I browse through the software he uses: all the Apple media shit, Eclipse . . .

Oh, what's this?

He's running his own remote-access app called Mesmer, which lets you control your desktop from any smartphone.

Billy's phone, that's what I'd really like to crack.

Instrumenting someone's cell used to be a huge pain in the ass. But now that your phone is really a fully functional computer, it's become a perfect surveillance platform. With one program I can listen to your calls, download your texts and email, grab your Facebook password, turn on the mic to listen to your live conversations, take pictures or video, and, most importantly, learn your location from the built-in GPS receivers.

I find several devious hacks in the Red Rook exploits database and rig Billy's system to execute one of them the next time he syncs his phone.

Before signing off, I start his webcam for a quick peep. I'd love the opportunity to spy on Billy at home. But all I can see is an unfocused view out of a large bank of windows, the city lights forming an amorphous constellation.

I set up a script to have the camera wake up periodically, record a couple frames to an external server, and alert me if there's any motion in the images. Then I log off and start poring over my copy of Billy's hard drive. I see immediately that it won't give him up. He's thoroughly stealthed his system. I can hope that by watching his live sessions with it, I'll catch him in a mistake, though that will be chancy and time-consuming—and I suspect Blake won't be satisfied with any kind of long-term digital stakeout.

While things are bad enough now, I'm sure Billy has even more fireworks in store.

Since I left her apartment, Olya has completely ignored me. I decide to check GAME and see if I can find Garriott or Xan to determine what they've heard from her. Neither of them are there.

Actually, almost no one is. Last night, a burst pipe on the third floor caused a team of emergency plumbers to shut off the water for the entire building. This morning they commenced a multimovement symphony of power tools and pipe banging, which has driven away what few of GAME's inhabitants remained. At eight AM, I decide to take my laptop to a coffee shop around the corner on Clinton Street so I can work in peace and avail myself of a functioning bathroom.

I'm still rummaging his files when I get a message from my RAT on Billy's computer. Interestingly, the event wasn't initiated by Billy himself. A server somewhere has stimulated a background program to spawn a window showing a low-res video feed that looks like an abstract photograph. It's all black except for a faint gradient highlighting a square shape in the lower right-hand corner. Nothing happens for a second as I check the title of the program. It's Brimstone. That's an ominous name, so I run through his project files and locate the underlying code.

It begins with simple motion detection on the video feed. When a specific recognition event triggers, it sends a text to a given phone number. Then the program pops up a button that, when pressed, relays a bunch of commands back to the device that's transmitting the video. I skim rapidly through the instructions, until my head almost shorts out as my understanding catches up with my eyes.

The function handler reads:

```
_OnButtonClick () {

    sendCommand(CO_BOX_ADDR, _release_valve1);
    sendCommand(CO_BOX_ADDR, _release_valve2);
    sendCommand(CO_BOX_ADDR, _ flow_accel);
    sendCommand(CO_BOX_ADDR, _ignite);

};
```

The word "ignite" is what grabs me.

What is this? Another one of Billy's faux incendiaries?

Then two things happen in rapid succession. The video image

changes: a wedge of light opens at the bottom, and an arm enters the frame. It flips some switches, which illuminate a familiar space.

It's the Orifice, shot from above. And the arm belongs to Olya.

She enters the room, followed by Blake. A graphics square flashes briefly over his face.

Olya says, ". . . don't know why you want to meet me here. You only should be finding this *govnyuk* brother of yours. You promise me his head. But where—"

"Wait, I wanted to meet? You emailed me."

"I email you yesterday about—ah, never mind. We're here now, so . . . ?"

Blake steps closer to her. "So . . . ?"

They embrace.

Pointless jealousy dilutes my apprehension until I see the Mesmer service awaken. Billy's password scrolls into the key log.

I jump up so fast I upset the table, and my laptop crashes to the floor behind me.

66

slam into the door of the Orifice, but Olya's got it locked with the inside latch. I bang on it frantically, bruising the meat of my hands. Finally, she jerks it open. Her clothes are disheveled, an irate glare on her face.

"James! What—"

"You need to get out of here. Now!"

Blake steps forward. He looks tired and irritable. "James, get ahold of yourself."

"No. You don't understand." I slide in and grab Olya by the arm. "There's—"

She wrenches it away. "Ai. Don't touch—"

"—a bomb."

Both of their faces go slack as they recall their confusion over who asked for the meeting. I assume Billy wanted them together for this and spoofed their email to that end.

Olya squints. "You think I'd believe anything—"

Behind her, we hear a metallic snap. I flinch away in raw panic. But nothing happens. There's a small sputtering sound coming from above us, where the camera's mounted.

As if to mock my hysteria, the room's sprinkler turns on. Blake and Olya look at each other, negotiating a reaction. Far from a bomb, but something is happening here.

And the water is . . . wrong.

I can't immediately tell what it is. A strange scent. Something like a place I remember . . . or is it, what? Matches. It smells like a box of matches. Then I remember the place that came to mind: Yellowstone National Park. The smell around the hot springs:

Sulfur.

Brimstone.

"We need to get out of here," I say.

The flow from the sprinklers increases, and a new smell wafts in. This one is easy to recognize.

Gasoline.

Blake jumps toward the door. Olya seems transfixed by the sprinkler head. She must have gotten some of the fluid in her eyes, because she blinks them shut and puts her hands up to rub them. I dive to tackle her into the hallway.

Not quite soon enough. As I'm in the air, there's another soft click, but this one is followed by strong wind in my face and a burst of light. Then pain.

First is the shocking collision with Olya, who is not a petite woman. Then the crunch of my kneecaps on the hard cement floor of the hall. I wrench my face away from her hair, which is now on fire, and start batting at it. The heat at my back intensifies. I spastically rip myself out of my jacket, rolling off of Olya, allowing her to flip onto her back and quench the flames licking at her hair. She staggers up and leans against the wall, smothering the flickering fire at her calves before it can ascend her legs. I get my jacket off and glance at her to confirm that she's okay, but she's not looking at me.

She's looking back into the blaze.

Her face has a transcendent focus. A tendril of flame starts climbing again up her leather pants. But she doesn't even twitch.

She steps toward the door.

It takes me a second to understand that she's going back to rescue Ginger. And that with gasoline-soaked clothing, she's not likely to emerge. And that I have to stop her. Suddenly I'm running into the fire as well.

She gets two steps into the room. The Orifice looks as though it's been painted with fire. All the tables, chairs, and computers are still recognizable, but they're outlined in roiling blue and orange flames. The smoke is building, the ceiling now covered by a dense gray cloud. I reach for her arm, but she senses this and pulls it from my grasp. She takes another step forward, grabs Ginger by her neck, and tosses her out the door to skid across the hall into my office. Then she turns to scan the room for other valuables. She pauses long enough for me to get my right arm around her neck. I'm not sure of my ability to wrestle her out.

That's when the real explosion happens. I register a microsecond of surprise when the back of Olya's head impacts my mouth, smashing my lips. Then there's a gap in time, and I find myself lying back in the hall, my head partially buried in the drywall opposite the door. Olya and I have switched positions, with her body now sheltering me from the flames spreading out from the Orifice.

There's a violent cloud of white, and I can't breathe anymore. The last thing I think is:

I can't believe that fucker killed us.

67

I come to in a cool, clean room with luxuriantly breathable air. A hospital room. Things are vague, and I start my "what happened last night" checklist. Then I notice the bandages on my left arm. A beautiful woman sits beside me. It's Xan.

Seeing her makes everything come back, but I can only whisper, "Olya?"

Xan looks at me quickly but then buries her face in her hands, opening in me a black fissure of dread. Tears streaming freely, she says, "She's in the ICU. Surgery."

"Blake?"

Xan tips her head like she might have misheard me. "Blake? What about him?"

This confuses me. I'm not thinking clearly, but I have a specific recollection of his being there. Running back through my traumatized memory, I conclude that the white explosion was a fire extinguisher, and Blake must have discharged it on Olya and me and then disappeared before the firemen showed up. I want to ask Xan about all this, but another question demands precedence.

"Me?" I ask.

This elicits a fragile smile through her tears. She says, "You're going to be all right."

I suspect she might be lying. A body wiggle confirms that my spinal cord is still intact. I'm incredibly stiff, like how a veteran demolition derby driver must feel on the day of his retirement. I gingerly pat myself. Parts of my skin throb like they've been worked on by the Stasi school of cosmetology, but I don't find any stitches, so things can't be too bad. Then I think of Olya and start looking for the morphine button.

Xan is good enough to push it for me.

I wake up alone and in an entirely different frame of mind. I must have slept for long enough for the anesthetics to wear off, through the night probably. The pain from my burns is worse, and I feel unsettled. I reach for the button but can't grasp it. My irritation flares into anger.

Take it easy. You're just coming down from the drugs.

But then I find a target for my fury.

I forget about the button as the feeling crystallizes. This aberrant ass-hole blew up Olya. The thought of such an unrivalled beauty scarred by one of Billy's dangerous pranks fills me with rage.

How did he even pull it off?

The plumbers of course. He probably flushed a cherry bomb, precipitating the maintenance crisis, and then slipped in with a fake beard and coveralls. I'll bet back at GAME they'll find a storage room directly above the Orifice with its floor ripped up and a remote-controlled flame-thrower resting in the crawlspace, its nozzle disguised as a sprinkler head. Funny that when we upgraded the security of that room, I changed the locks on the big steel door and patched the hole in the wall I came through that first week, but the idea of death from above never occurred to me.

On the chair Xan occupied I see a small duffel bag. In it there's a set of clothes, perhaps pulled from the GAME lost and found. More importantly, in a side pocket, I find my phone.

I rip the bandages off my left hand and start typing.

Minutes later, Blake picks up my call. His voice has an uncertain timbre.

"James. Jesus Christ. I—"

"They say Olya's in intensive care."

"I know. I can't believe . . . I can't believe she—"

"Yeah. Thanks for, uh, extinguishing us."

"Oh. Right. Look, I'm sorry I took off, but it didn't seem like there was much more I could do. And, well, I didn't want . . ."

"I understand."

"You do?"

"Yeah. It will be better if no one knows you were there."

"Uh-huh." Blake's tone is wary; perhaps he was thinking he'd have to sell me harder on the virtues of forgetting his presence. Now he tests how far he can push it. "So I guess the police may want to speak with you. This is very serious, but if I could just—"

"I won't be here."

"Wait. What do you mean?"

"Blake, call McClaren. I know where your fuckhead brother is."

68

Slipping out of the hospital without the normal exit processing is liable to raise some questions, especially when my injuries were sustained in a pretty noteworthy case of arson. And since I was just here after being Tased, maybe I really should stay put to make sure there aren't any parts coming loose. But catching Billy seems more important, so I devise a rickety plan to blame my erratic behavior on PTSD and make my escape.

At first I was puzzled that Billy had holed up in Washington Heights, but on mapping the GPS coordinates spit out from his phone, it made more sense: he's not at a new apartment, he's at the Cloisters.

As good a place as any to contemplate the enormity of one's crimes, the Cloisters is a branch of the Metropolitan Museum of Art dedicated to medieval-period pieces. Set on a hill in Fort Tryon Park and overlooking the Hudson River, it stands as one of the most serene and beautiful places in the city, possessing all the enchantment of an actual medieval abbey. I recall finding in the folder where Gina stored her own NOD models a lovingly detailed replica of the entire complex. Maybe a favorite place of hers. Maybe even the site of a rare RL excursion with Billy.

My GPS fix is good enough to tell me that he's in a gallery in the North Cloister that houses an impressive set of illuminated manuscripts. One of the most famous has a lovely depiction of the destruction of Sodom and Gomorrah.

After a brief stop at home, I hurry uptown. Blake wanted me to wait for instructions from McClaren confirming that his extraction team was in place. But despite having sent two messages, I've yet to hear anything back.

I arrive to find Billy striking a reflective pose on a bench facing the water. His attitude makes me question whether he knows the outcome of his fratricidal attack. A tree on the other side of the path provides a suitable screen as I settle in to wait.

Several minutes pass. I send increasingly shrill messages to McClaren, but they're flying into a void. I get antsy.

Billy fishes his phone out of his jacket pocket, presses some buttons, and reads. He doesn't like what he sees and shakes his phone as if he's going to chuck it into the water. But he restrains himself and just slams his fist into the bench's wooden slats. He then shoots up and casts around as though he's not sure where to go. He elects to return toward the galleries, and I decide I can't take any more of this.

The wind is loud and the clouds prevent any revealing shadows, so I'm able to stalk right up to him and seize him by the shoulder. He freaks, wrenching himself away so hard that he falls down. Gone is the smug hipster who grinned at me when I fell for his tricks at our earlier meeting. Now he's a skinny geek looking up in naked terror. I squat over him, making sure he sees the pistol clipped to my pants. To ensure docility, I hammer my fist down on his nose.

"We're going to start with that," I say.

He yelps, his eyes filling with tears. He takes a second to recover and tries to blow out the blood filling his nasal cavity.

"Where the fuck is Rosa? What did you do to her?"

"No. No, man. She's fine. That's her *job*." This answer is so preposterous I hit him again. But he continues desperately. "Dude, she's a *body modder*. They hang her up like that at tattoo conventions. I swear to God." He starts coughing again while I think about this. Something about it actually seems credible.

Of course: the ripped earlobes. Sewn-up holes from extender plugs.

I can't spare the time to beat myself up for being taken in, since now that I have him, Billy has a whole litany of other crimes for which to answer. I ask, "How do we shut down the *Unmasking*?"

He gasps, "You don't. It's out there. And it's not coming back."

I press my hand over his mouth. "Wrong answer. You're going to fuck with someone you just set on fire?"

He starts coughing blood out his nose. I release my hand.

He says, "Look, man, I didn't know you were going to be there. By the time I saw you, I'd already set it off."

I slap him hard across the face. More blood pools at the corner of his mouth. "You might have killed Olya, you little twat."

"You should thank me. She was—"

I grab him by his shirt and rap his head against the ground. Then I pull his face close to mine. "Are you so nuts as to believe that *they* are responsible for your friend's death? They deserve to die because Gina acted out something from one of *your* sick little movies?"

Billy's eyes had jammed shut on impact, but now they pop open. He gapes at me like I've informed him that headless ogres are rampaging through Central Park.

"Wait . . . You mean . . ." He shakes his head, trying to clear it. "You're telling me you don't know? You *gave* me the video, man."

"You stole it."

"But you've seen it. How can you not know?"

I drop him back to the ground. "Know what?"

He props himself up by his elbows, an incredulous look on his face. "They killed her. G never did that to herself, they tied her up . . ." He trails off, suddenly focused on something behind me.

I twist around for a quick look, see nothing, and turn back to him, thinking he's trying to distract me. But he's still staring north up the pathway. He tries to scramble to his feet, a new sense of panic in his eyes. I let him up but grab him by the hair so he can't run.

Something isn't right. I glance behind me again, and this time I see it: two shadows off to the right of the path moving toward us.

Finally the cavalry show up.

But immediately I know I'm mistaken. These guys aren't McClaren's people. For starters they're both too big: one looks like he's six foot six with a giant head, goatee, and leather Kangol cap, wearing a black Adidas tracksuit, for Christ's sake. The other is shorter but proportioned like a kettle bell. He's got on dark sunglasses and a leather trench coat, underneath which he's carrying something long and unwieldy. Surely not a shotgun.

Who the hell are these guys?

Billy has concluded that whoever they are, they mean him grievous harm. He tries to hurl himself away from me even though this results in a fistful of his hair ripping free. I snatch his right arm and pin it behind his back. Billy is physically weak, but he flails around like a gaffed shark. I wrench his arm upward, which freezes him briefly. He whines, terror-stricken, "Please, not yet. You don't understand . . ."

I only half notice this because my mind is going a mile a minute. I can't escape the conclusion that Goatee and Shades are a hit team. I never had any illusions that Billy was going to be forgiven for trying to kill his brother. He's in for some rough treatment.

But gunning him down in a public park? This was never part of the plan. It's insane.

They're within twenty yards. Goatee is smiling at me. He reaches into his jacket.

Does Blake really want his brother dead? There was a symbolic, mad-scientist quality to the GAME fire. Olya was really only injured because she went *back into* the room. If he'd used a normal bomb, which would have been easier than his napalm sprinkler, all three of us would be dead.

All that aside, could Blake possibly want a police investigation into his brother's public murder?

Shades pulls his coat away from a sawed-off twelve-gauge.

Do I?

No way. This cannot happen.

I push Billy as hard as I can so that he topples over the low wall separating the path from an overgrown slope. I then turn and pray I can clear my Glock before they start shooting. Their reactions are slowed by disbelief, but Shades gets his shotgun trained on me first.

I'm fucked.

Thankfully Goatee has read the situation and swipes his hand under the barrel, knocking it up away from me. I've got my gun out but decide not to risk pointing it at anyone.

Instead, I ask, "Who the hell are you?"

But Goatee ignores me and runs over to the wall, searching for their target. Billy has disappeared into the trees.

Shades has his gun trained on me again, looking like he's dying to use it. But Goatee stares at me with amused contempt, and maybe a little bit of relief. "You just *fucked up*."

69

That turns out to be Blake's perspective as well.

Shades detains me while Goatee converses briefly with an irate Mondano. They then drive me down to Amazone, empty at this hour, and install me at one of the tables near the main bar.

I simmer through twenty minutes of cheek-chewing tension before Mondano and Blake walk in. As he flops down on the seat next to mine, Mondano smirks like he's going to relish this. Blake just looks bewildered. All over he's showing signs of deep strain. Dark bags under bloodshot eyes combine with jerky movements to signal nervous exhaustion. To be expected, I guess, when, while all this is going on, he's trying to run part of a major conglomerate. The effort must be costing him. I'd have given myself over to bourbon and barbiturates long ago.

He shakes his head like he's trying to understand a misbehaving child. "James . . ."

I'm a little bewildered myself. This is the second time I've been responsible for losing his brother, and yet I feel like I've saved Blake from a catastrophe and don't deserve his scorn. I decide on aggression.

"Blake, if you want to murder your brother in cold blood, think maybe you could do it when I'm not standing right next to him in a public park?"

Mondano says to Blake, "I told you this guy was a fucking fruitcake." I notice he's abandoned his world-weary Mafia boss shtick in front of

Blake. Someone who knows him from the old yacht-basin neighborhood.

"So your guys were just there to check out the tapestries? And they needed a shotgun in case, what? They were attacked by squirrels?"

"They were there to take control of the situation, which you then intentionally fucked up. That little prick offer you more money?"

"Actually, he offered to spare all three of us a twenty-to-life sentence at Sing Sing."

"Already planning to rat on us, Jimmy?"

"Well, Benny, I'll need someone's ass to rent out for cigarettes, and I can't think of anyone better suited to the work than you."

That's too much for Mondano, and he lunges out of his seat. Like many supposed tough guys, he can talk hard but isn't much of a fighter. As I jump up, he aims a looping roundhouse at my head that doesn't have a prayer of connecting. I think, *This is going to feel incredible,* as I pivot to send a debilitating kick into his testicles. I wonder who he'll turn into with his nuts squashed into jelly.

But my kick never gets off the ground. I find McClaren, who's gotten inside on me before I even know he's there, standing on my foot. He catches Mondano's punch, twists his wrist, and pushes him back into his chair.

He says, "Now, gentlemen, that's no kind of attitude for a team. Ain't any sense trading paint here when we've all got the same color stripes, right?"

I shrug and look down at my foot. He lifts his off of it, and I sit back down. I ask, "Where have *you* been?"

"I've been far afield protecting Ms. Randall, who we can all agree is our first priority. James, I had no idea you'd be so efficient after getting toasted. You seem to have a real knack for locating Billy. It's hanging on to the slippery bastard that's the problem."

"Y'all can handle that without me this time." I point at Mondano. "I'm not working with this clown."

"Oh, you think you can just walk out?" he asks.

"Watch me."

I trudge from the room with Blake calling at my back.

— — —

McClaren sidles up beside me before I get my cigarette lit.

He nudges me with his elbow. "Quite a diva routine you put on in there."

"It's not an act. You weren't there. And *I'm* not going to be there when it all goes tits-up."

McClaren nods sagely. "Yeah, I'll admit it seems our fearless leader might have had a lapse in judgment. Billy's sites are back online. Your boys don't seem to be able to shut them down. So he's under a lot of stress. Sometimes in ex-treem-is we listen to our baser instincts, in this case represented by our Eye-talian-American friend."

"Uh-huh."

"Anyway, I understand you're kind of burnt out. Why don't you spend some time getting your blow-bots back together? That'll be important to the boss pretty soon here. Since you flushed him, we've got some new leads on old Billy we can run down."

Not sure what I'm going to do, I keep quiet. McClaren pats me on the back and continues. "It's been good working with you, Jimmy. You're a real prince."

As always, my conversation with McClaren was troubling. I suppose his grossly premature order to stand down is a sign of Blake's loss of trust in me. But the way he put it sounded like I was due for a medal, and that the whole thing was essentially wrapped up. I try to prevent my frazzled brain from overloading his last comment.

He said prince, but did he mean knave?

In my voicemail, I have messages from a GAME administrator wanting to know what in the world is going on, Officer Aiden Rosedale asking for a statement about the fire, and the hospital trying to determine if I'm planning to pay my bill.

I call Xan.

She's holding vigil at Olya's room with Garriott, whom she puts on speaker.

She says, "James, you didn't see fit to let the poor nurses know you were tired of their care and wanted to go and seek infection for your wounds?"

"Thanks for the concern. But I'm okay. Glad y'all are keeping an eye on Olya."

"While you avoid helping the authorities apprehend the man who did this."

"I'm working on that. What did you tell the police?"

"That Billy was stalking her and finally lost his mind."

"Right. Good. Did they find anything that made them ask what went on in the Orifice?"

"No. Everything melted down to sludge."

Garriott asks, "Do you think it's a good idea to be, uh, messing about with the police? Maybe they'll need the whole story to find that prick."

"Believe me, we'll have Billy in a rubber cell soon enough."

There's silence on the other end of the line. Then Xan asks, "James, what's all this really about?"

A plausible fiction comes to my lips, but I decide my friends have a right to know what's going on. "Billy thinks Olya and his brother killed Gina Delaney. He wants revenge. So for the time being, we need to take some more safety measures. Xan, I want you staying at my apartment for the next couple days . . . Garriott, you can crash there too."

"Hardly, mate. I'm not afraid of that ponce. Just let him come near me."

The idea of Garriott and Billy in a physical altercation is so amusing, I have to bite my tongue. But on the other hand, Billy has almost killed the indomitable Olya, so my levity is short-lived.

At home, I don't have to search much to gauge the level of media hysteria Billy's *Unmasking* has generated. The entire national press corps must be reaching for their Ritalin to help them pump out the necessary yards of coverage. While more financially serious exploits have occurred in the past, the prurient purity of this one has captivated the journalistic tribe:

```
Porn worm spreading rapidly. Experts decry one of the
"greatest privacy breaches in history."
                                        —Associated Press
```

Local archdiocese investigating "computer misconduct" by
several officials revealed by "hacktivist."

—*Washington Post*

Black sheep Randall heir exposes dark family secrets.
Many others compromised.

—CNN.com

Is your kid's teacher making virtual child porn?

—*New York Post*

Governor Bryant's spokesperson offers no comment on
allegations concerning the use of office laptop for
"inappropriate chat" with government employees.

—*Idaho Statesman*

Almost none of Billy's victims are making statements at the moment.
Except Layton Mayfield, an Oakland police officer caught with videos he
made exhibiting some appalling racial bondage scenarios.

He jumped off the Golden Gate Bridge.

70

The stress of the day and the large weeping burn on my forearm convince me to permit myself some painkillers, which in turn convince me to allow myself a few hours of much-needed sleep.

When I wake later that night, McClaren still hasn't left any messages. Changing my bandages, I reflect that Billy has no doubt disappeared back into the ether.

But it's not in his nature to stay totally hidden. Midway through my rewrap, I hear the tone for a critical message on my phone:

```
[Script_Alert: Av_Stalker_07]
Lillie_Hitchcock @NodULE: http://nod.com/ule_find/
dev:143.365.186
```

I would expect Billy to opt for the sterility of a new av, but here he's reusing the very means of my penetration. He must want to talk.

Checking out the IP of his datastream leads to his usual double-buffered open-proxy hell. So I just fire up Jacques_Ynne and teleport to the location in the alert. It's in one of NOD's test sims, and he's left the area in its blank default state, just a flat white plane floating in the perfect blackness of a binary vacuum. Until now, Billy has carefully curated his surroundings, and I'd imagine he's got thousands of dramatic settings, from caves to sky palaces, in which to conduct a meeting. His av stands unmoving in the center of the space.

Though he doesn't turn to face me, he can tell I've rezzed in. A dialogue bubble forms over his head.

Lillie_Hitchcock:	Still think my dear brother is innocent of murder?
Jacques_Ynne:	With a sibling like you, I'm not surprised that there's domestic violence.
Lillie_Hitchcock:	And yet you were an incompetent accomplice to my assassination.
Jacques_Ynne:	You're welcome.
Lillie_Hitchcock:	Why?
Jacques_Ynne:	Why what?
Lillie_Hitchcock:	Why did you let me go?
Jacques_Ynne:	Practical considerations only.
Lillie_Hitchcock:	No. You did it because you believe me.
Jacques_Ynne:	I believe that you need a straitjacket.
Lillie_Hitchcock:	I can prove my brother and his whore spilled Gina's blood. Just make sure you're not standing next to him when he reaps judgment for his crimes. But then . . . I'm not

```
                              really the one you should
                              worry about.

Jacques_Ynne:                 Meaning?

Lillie_Hitchcock:             He knows you know. Do you
                              think he's going to let you
                              live?
```

Billy disappears with that baleful question literally hanging in the air. I pan around the void surrounding my av. Has the close call in the park stripped away all the baroque effects from his punitive fantasies? Are we now dealing with a more efficient and dangerous Billy, one who's finally stopped playing games?

I write McClaren a short note about this most recent contact, but I don't send it.

What am I waiting for?

Slowly it dawns on me: I'm waiting to see Billy's proof.

71

Though he was masking his NOD connection, Billy most likely logged on from a computer somewhere relatively nearby. I'm sure it will be pointless, but I check the state of my tentacles into his laptop. As I suspected, it's gone dark, probably permanently. Once your machine has been infected by a real hacker, you can't ever trust it again. He'd have figured out we located him through his phone and assumed his computer was compromised as well.

I check my server for the webcam images it was transmitting. The shots are all the same incoherent blur until the final one, taken just before my RAT went offline. The image still shows the view out of a wide bank of windows. But either the lighting has changed or his laptop got moved, because I can see through them now.

And the view makes high-voltage spiders crawl around my scalp.

I grab the image and blow it up as far as it will go. The place must be pretty far south, because you can see a lot of open water in the background. I notice a distant figure emerging from the waves. It's out of focus and yet unmistakable. The stern visage of our Lady Liberty. And there's really only one place in the city from which you get a clean look at her face.

I've seen a similar vista from Gina's former apartment building.

Appropriate that Billy would relocate near the scene of Gina's death to plot his revenge. His sentimentality gives me another chance to find him, but I'm not sure what I'd do with him if I did. He deserves harsh punishment for burning Olya, never mind the lives being shredded by his *Unmasking*. That said, I don't want to be party to a summary execution if I deliver him to Blake and Mondano. At this point, Blythe is probably his only friend, and that's not saying much.

But at least I can rely on her to deal with Billy rationally.

I whiz through the area in Google Maps' Street View until I see the statue from the area I'm targeting. The green space facing Billy's window is too indistinct in the webcam shot to figure out exactly where it is. I find three candidates and select the one whose windows best match the inside framing of Billy's place.

I print out a map and jog downstairs to hail a cab.

The neighborhood around 120 Ferris Street is deserted. Wanting to approach undetected, I tell the cab driver to let me off a block early. Billy's place is three tall stories of corroding brick with an assortment of boarded-up arches for windows. Bits of wire and the crazily sloping remnants of a fire escape decorate its skin, which shows scars where gutters have been stripped off for scrap.

The back of the building, away from the street, will be my safest bet. There's a line of large but sickly trees along the alleyway between the building and the vacant lot next door. One of them has a thick branch leading up to a window whose boards have mostly rotted away. I scramble up the tree, make a hole in the glass with a diamond-tipped cutter, and insert a stiff wire to flip the window's antique lock. I have to climb down a set of empty cable brackets attached to the back of a huge open-air atrium that runs from a deep basement up to the roof.

The interior of the old building is a wreck. The walls down in the basement sprout disused pipe connections and mounting hardware testifying to machinery ripped out when its former occupant was liquidated by creditors. The kind of place that drives architects to suggest "accidental fire" as the best motif for a redesign.

At the far end of the basement is a wide spiral of cast iron stairs, which I follow up to the ground floor. Billy's living room consists of a green velvet couch and a shattered seventy-two-inch LED television. A bachelor kitchen, which appears never to have been used, opens off to the right.

I've been exploring the place in sepulchral silence, but now I become aware of a sound floating just at the limits of my perception. It's a single, unvarying, high-pitched tone, obviously made by an electronic device, but it doesn't have the alternating quality of an alarm.

Another steep spiral staircase leads up to a studio area. As I climb the stairs, the sound gets louder. It confirms my impression that no one is here, since I doubt if any normal human could tolerate the incessant ring.

On gaining the third floor, I see four large workbenches on the left side of the room, each littered with tools, materials, mechanisms, and scraps of clothing. There are three ripped-open workstations and a crushed laptop strewn around. The place looks like a Tokyo gadget market after Godzilla waltzes through.

One of the tables holds what I take to be a severed limb until I see the titanium ball joint projecting from its humerus. Nearby on the floor lies the former owner of that arm, an exceedingly lifelike rendering of a small boy that's been hacked apart. "Drawn and quartered" would be more accurate. Blood from internal bladders, still an artificially bright red, has pooled on the floor around him. I assume this gross display represents a beta version of a prop intended for when Billy reaches the limit of what he can hire body modders to do to themselves. There's a tag on his ankle that reads SAPROPHYTE STUDIOS, which is a Pittsburgh FX operation best known for making fake snuff films so realistic that a Kentucky man spent almost two weeks in jail after police found a copy of one in his apartment.

Toward the back of the room, two more of these mechanized grotesques hang from the wall. One is another little boy, the name "Giton" scrawled in black marker beside him. The other's skin dangles in shreds, as if someone compulsively slashed the latex with a box-cutter. The name beside it, though mostly obscured with blood, seems to be "Augustine."

On either side of the stairwell are small rooms made of pristine drywall. The tone is emanating from the one on my left. I step up to the door and turn the knob. The door catches on its frame at first, and I have to bear down with my shoulder until it pops open with a suffering creak.

Terror starts boiling inside me before I can make sense of what I'm looking at.

It's the smell: once again, brimstone.

Instinct makes me fling myself out of the room. I almost tumble back down the stairs, but my shoulder bangs into the curving iron banister. As

I scramble back to my feet, my mind has a moment to process what I'm seeing.

A bank of monitors surrounds an unmoving human shape seated on a large, high-backed wooden chair. Several plastic blocks rest at his feet. I take a deep breath.

It's just another one of his stupid gore puppets.

I try to get ahold of myself and flip on the light switch by the door. The scene gets worse.

It's a re-creation of the suicide video Billy sent to Blake. But taken to a new level of repulsiveness. The body slumped in the electric chair looks as though his skeleton has been reduced to fragments, held up only by the rusty iron band at his head. Around this are deep lacerations, blackened by the intense current. Below the cuts, one eye has popped out of its socket and dangles to the side of his nose. The other eye is just a red void, the border decorated with a clear jelly. A long, dark stain issues from his mouth, which is shut tight. I refrain from thinking about the state of his tongue.

Finally, there are discolored pockmarks all over his chest and arms, which I can't figure out at first. Then I glance down at the row of car batteries at his feet. Many of them are distended, and a few show cracks in their cases. I guess that would account both for the damage to the body and the smell of brimstone in the air. Many car batteries use lead and sulfuric acid to hold a charge. If one shorts them too quickly, they become very hot and explosive gases can build. Sometimes they rupture, spraying acid everywhere. The last thing I notice is the screen above the body's head. It's a heart monitor, with an unbroken horizontal line traversing its center. The source of the tone I've been hearing.

I don't know what makes me realize it; maybe the barely detectable stench of burnt hair and early decomposition, but suddenly I'm certain: this isn't one of Billy's atrocious mannequins.

This is Billy himself. In the flesh.

72

Back at my apartment, I peer down the neck of a half-empty bottle of Hancock's President's Reserve—a rare treasure I looted from his otherwise indifferent liquor cabinet—and ruminate on William Bennett Randall and his (now vindicated) paranoia. The question that has me slugging it down at three AM:

Do I believe him?

That he was killed in his struggle against his older brother, I have no doubt. His death is obviously rigged for a suicide determination. A verbatim reenactment of his *Jacking Out* video, both continuing the unfortunate Jackanapes suicide rash and making him another victim of his family's yearning for oblivion. I can just see Blake looking despondent, saying to an officer, "We were so worried." True, in its way.

But the Billy I'd come to know this past month was a fighter. He had plans for retaliation, and there's no way he'd fall on his sword without taking another whack at Blake.

My conclusion: Mondano and his goons somehow found him and did this to shut him up forever. I'll bet the batteries were well drained before the lethal jolt from inquiries about how to shit-can his porn worm. Given what he said at the Cloisters, that would have been a bleak exercise. At least whoever planned it came up with a more creative package than a twelve-gauge in broad daylight.

They meant to suppress the climactic reveal in Billy's arcane tour de force: that his brother and Olya murdered Gina Delaney to get control of her invention. I'd love to roll my eyes at his allegations and chalk them up to his deranged game narrative, but he's denied me the easy escape of willful disbelief.

Billy left evidence.

My bourbon bottle now sits next to the lone intact electronics left in the place. And it wasn't easy to find.

From searching the wreckage of all the computers in Billy's studio, I found that each of their hard drives had been meticulously wiped, presumably by whoever had meticulously wiped Billy. They'd even done a careful job destroying the processor boards and flash memory residing in his robotic voodoo dolls. I assume they intended this action to simulate the artist burning his life's work before joining it on the pyre. But after all that, they still missed something. Something only I could see, having been subject to Billy's codes and symbols for the last month.

I'd already completed one round of searching the place. Retossing each room. Pulling open tools. Checking the innards of his electronics. Anywhere he might hide some final communication. I was walking by his animatrons on my way to make a more thorough inspection of the room in which his corpse reposed, something I'd been avoiding for the past couple hours, when the shredded remains of Augustine grabbed my attention. Her silicone body molding had been mostly torn away, but still attached to a small chunk at her left arm socket was a ragged scrap of purple fabric hanging loosely over the shoulder. Something about that particular rich hue, and the way the fabric bunched, brought forth a memory.

That remnant was the same color as the purple toga worn by Gina's av Ines_Idoru.

Despite the thorough dissection, I could tell right away that they'd missed her vital organ. The large gear casing sitting right between the aluminum tubes of her legs. The place at her center of gravity: her womb.

I picked up a screwdriver.

It took quite a bit more surgery to take apart the gearbox. But as I suspected, at its center were the guts of a compact smartphone with a live connection to Verizon's wireless network. I plugged it into my netbook and saw that Billy had a custom script in the scheduler. If he fails to check in for more than 48 hours, it sends a video to a long list of email addresses, including the NYPD, the FBI, and several national news outlets.

This was Billy's version of letting his demons out into the world. As such, the video's a masterpiece.

We begin with Billy's argument for the prosecution in the case of Gina Delaney's murder. It's pithy, well produced, and certain to captivate his audience. Especially when you have the freshly mutilated corpse of the author to add sanguinary interest.

Documentary in style, it starts with a reprise of IT's progress, complete with stills of early versions of the Dancers. He identifies Gina as the real inventor of our system, gives a little background information on her, and then there's a cut to black.

Billy's voice narrates mournfully:

The New York City medical examiner's office ruled Gina Delaney's death a suicide two days after she was found. The primary basis for this determination was a videotape taken of her death, discovered by the responding officers at the scene. Here is the video.

And again I watch Gina's harrowing final minutes. But this time, framed by his forensic inquiry, I'm watching through Billy's eyes. The video takes on the cast of subliminal witchery one finds in the ice cubes of liquor ads.

At the end, we freeze on the shot of Gina's hideous demise, and Billy says, "If you look closely, this video proves beyond a doubt that she was murdered."

Then he starts his assault. His leading elements are reminiscent of those late-seventies Zapruder reconstruction "documentaries," trying to establish that JFK was assassinated by time-traveling Martians. Gina couldn't possibly have lifted the meteorite ballast. The light patterns on her face indicate fire traveling *toward* her. The ME's photos show conclusively that her wrists were recently bound. Some nonsense about the blood spatter being the wrong shape.

The case is meretricious: Gina had plenty of mech-E from MIT and could figure out how to lift anything; there were any number of reflective surfaces in the apartment; her wrists already looked like uncooked funnel cake; and the right combination of model parameters could get Billy's "expected" blood spatter to form a portrait of Mao.

But like a true showman, Billy saves his best for last. And here's where he makes me sit up and take notice. Now he just looks closely at the video itself. A part of it I've seen but never really scrutinized, since it occurs well after Gina is clearly dead.

About three minutes after she dies, her body shifts slightly. Maybe from the drill's vibration. Maybe her muscles relaxing in death. The movement causes her head to tilt slightly to her right. Billy freezes there on a single frame. The video is high def, so he's able to zoom extremely close on Gina's left eye. So close that I can just distinguish the reflections on its glassy surface.

And for me those tiny glimmers have the power of a collapsing star.

There's an old legend that says the eyes of a murder victim will capture the face of his killer. This belief was held widely enough in the early twentieth century that forensic photographers devoted a whole branch of their nascent art to the detailed recording of a corpse's eyeballs, and in some cases even attempted to "develop" images off the deceased's retinas through some rather gruesome means. The idea is lunacy of course, but exactly the sort of thing that would appeal to an artist like Billy. Maybe the concept sprang to mind when he was confronted with Gina's agonized eyes at the time of her death. I can just see him examining them minutely, since that image was the last remaining evidence of the now impassable pathway to her soul and its tragic mysteries. At some point he must have noticed the subtlest motion. Then he realized that in combining a high-res camera with the half-mirror of her eyes, he had a situation where the superstition actually proved true.

They're tiny, picked out in pixels of lightness against the deep black of her pupils. The outline of two figures standing side by side. Her head must have come to rest at just the right angle of reflection from some light in the room. There's not enough detail to get a very clear picture, but one attribute stands out: they both have blond hair. Almost white.

Billy slaps up a frame counter and lets twenty seconds tick by. During this, you can see the couple's heads turn toward each other. The man steps forward until he's directly in front of the body, perhaps touching it.

Then he moves back, and they both walk off to the right until they disappear at the margin of her pupil.

Billy can run all the hypotheticals he wants, and I'm unlikely to pay much heed. Lawyers consistently show that, much like statistics (or people), you can torture models into saying anything. But now he's showing me something I can see with my own eyes. An image recorded on video. And what it means:

Gina wasn't alone when she died.

Not content to rest his case there, Billy wraps up with a seductive reconstruction of his theory of events. There were two people with Gina that night. They drugged her, bound her hands, placed her in the chair, set up the lighter fluid, put a lighter by her hand. She revived slightly and spoke her last words. Not addressing the camera; addressing them. They stood just behind the meteorite and lit the cardboard tube on fire.

When certain she was dead, they unbound her hands and left the room.

As stand-ins for the murderers, he uses these indistinct wisps from Gina's eyes. Then he focuses on them for yet another unmasking.

Gradually, the foggy pixels begin to coalesce into more specific visages. Of course, he chooses his blond bêtes noires. Olya Zhavinskaya stands there directing half-closed bedroom eyes at her accomplice, Blake Randall.

He asks, "And what was their motive for this crime? Why not hear it in their own words?"

An audio loop begins. The sound is slightly muffled, but I can understand the words pretty clearly. Blake must be closer to the mic, since his voice is loud and instantly recognizable.

He says, ". . . why she still feels that way. It's unfortunate. Do you think you'll be able to bring her around?"

Olya's voice is less clear but identifiable from her accent. "She can refuse me nothing. I make things very unpleasant."

"Ah . . . 'The way to a woman's heart is the path of torment. I know of no other.'"

Olya says, "Eh? I don't know. G is very difficult. I think maybe the right path is through her rib cage."

"A bit unsubtle, darling, don't you think?"

"Mmm, but I'm tired of petting her always."

"Well, be patient. I'm sure you'll be irresistible in the end."

Blake's intonation on his line about "a woman's heart" suggests that he's borrowing the words. I guess their source even before searching for it.

So was this conversation what stimulated Billy's whole jihad against his brother? Blake glibly quoting Sade's dating tips?

It explains Billy's use of the marquis's words in his electrocution speech. When did he record this? An early jewel from his surveillance at GAME? Or he could have been listening through the mic on Blake's compromised laptop. Regardless, in the context of all his other evidence, the dialogue plays like a confession.

We fade back in on a shot of Billy himself addressing the camera. He's sitting a few feet away from where I found the video. His face bears a glazed, sorrowful expression. He's wearing the same clothes as yesterday.

Your viewing this video means that I am dead. Murdered. I've never been one to apologize for my art, but I'm afraid this fact may be cast into doubt by my recent endeavors. My death will be seen in the context of suicides both in my family and among my colleagues at GAME. My communications with my brother will be used as evidence to support these lies. I regret that I've given them the weapon. But that cannot be helped now. Here is the truth, for those willing to listen.

Upon receiving evidence of my friend Gina Delaney's murder, I could not proceed any further with my artistic response to her death. I had to take action against the perpetrators. My intention was to finish Savant *with evidence of two final crimes: the one you just saw, and a companion piece showing my revenge against my brother and his whore. But I suppose that has not come to pass.*

I don't argue that my hands are clean. I have never claimed to be innocent. But I cannot abide the idea of my brother standing before the world pretending to virtue. He is a grotesque fiend and must be known as such.

He is aware that I've begun to discover the truth about him, so for the past several days, I have been evading men he has sent to silence me. Abetting him in this have been the pornographer Benito Mondano, Blake's security goon John McClaren, and their mercenary James Pryce. There are others as well, a whole black mob of them, but you will find that these are the principals in my execution.

My only desire now is for the world to hear this shred of the truth I've been able to uncover. The truth about IMP, the truth about my family, and the truth about the horrible murder of at least one innocent young woman. Whether you believe it is up to you. But the facts are there, and I hope that this testament makes it impossible for my brother to keep them from the light.

The screen cuts to black.

I look out my window as I collect my thoughts and notice lights going on across the street. A garbage truck pings as it stops on its way up the block. Billy's case spins through my head. Most of it isn't too compelling: the weight of the rock, the ephemeral light analyses, the marks on her wrists distinguishable only to him . . . Something about that snags my train of thought.

The marks on her wrists.

Billy's phantom binding marks would be hard to detect because of Gina's real scars, put there by her repeated suicide rehearsals. Yet Olya had told me that Gina had cut herself in the bathtub the night before she died. Though the wounds weren't deep enough to be life threatening, there would have been serious cuts that should have shown up in the morgue photos. But they exhibited no recent damage. So why would Olya tell me a story like that?

Unless she was trying to make it seem like Gina was recently suicidal.

I can feel myself start to integrate into Billy's theory all the little discontinuities and suspicious details one observes in an investigation. I force myself to stop.

I look down at the viscera of Billy's last connection to the outside world. In the dim predawn light filtering into my apartment, I can see reflected against the wall a blinking glow from the phone's indicator LED. The sedate pulse tells me that it's connected to the net. In ten hours, Billy's orders will send his story into the public domain.

There's a part of me that just wants to let the program run, come what may. It makes me grind my teeth to realize it, but Billy's video has seeped into me. God help me, but I believe him.

But you just had to name me, didn't you?

I bring my bottle down hard on the fragile electronics. The light goes out, leaving the room still and dark.

Billy's created enough bedlam with his *Unmasking* already. A ring of privacy activists have started combing databases and news accounts to assemble a literal postmortem on the incident. The tally so far stands at forty-one arrests (mainly for the people caught with kiddie porn and not fast enough to wipe their drives before the police barged in), fourteen civil lawsuits, eighty-nine divorce filings, seventeen emergency custody hearings, five resignations of public officials, almost a hundred terminations "for cause," three more suicides, and one domestic murder.

Of course, another ghost rattling her chains is Gina. But if Olya and Blake are really guilty, what then?

The police would be one option, but how does that play out?

I walk into Nash's office with the story that one of his suicides was actually a murder, and I know this because of a secret multimedia game created by another dead artist. Billy's death was clearly effected with professional élan, and his killers left nothing incriminating except his video about Gina. While intriguing, it would be pulped into pixel soup by any reasonably sober attorney—never mind the kind of legal firepower Blake Randall could deploy. The video Gina shot is compromised as evidence, since I personally corrupted the official copy. I can't imagine, in a country where Phil Spector remained free for half a decade, that Olya and Blake wouldn't walk. And I suspect neither could a prosecutor with half a brain.

Billy must have made a similar calculation. Is this what pushed him into the role of self-appointed avenger, or failing that, what prompted him to make sure his case reached the public?

And what about his case? If what he says is true, that means, Jimmy, that you're in business with people who murder innocent girls. And, knowing this, maybe your life is in danger as well.

Like Billy said, "He knows you know. Do you think he'll let you live?"

73

M ate, you realize you sound totally daft." Garriott is looking at me
like I just ripped off a *Mission: Impossible* mask.

"I know, Andrew. But I'm completely serious."

Xan's eyes sweep over to mine, and she asks coolly, "You want us to
get on a plane?"

"Yeah. Just until I get a better handle on things here."

We're standing in her office up at PiMP an hour after I called them
from a brand-new cell phone. I have to assume all my normal comms
have been compromised by Red Rook. And it wouldn't do to have Blake
apprised of my new plans.

I rolled in tired and just beginning a crushing hangover, not the best
state for what I'm trying to sell them. They'd been reluctant to leave the
hospital, but Olya was scheduled for a long, delicate skin-graft surgery
and wasn't expected to be conscious until the next morning.

Garriott says, "Really, stop fucking about."

"I wish I were."

"So you're telling us you think we're in danger because of some family
tiff between the Randalls?"

Xan helps me out. "Garriott, shut up. He's serious. Listen to him." She
turns to me and says, "So?"

I sigh, calculating how much I can reveal. "I think we may be at risk.
When Olya told me about our partner Mondano, I had some friends in
law enforcement check him out, and he is certainly a violent criminal.

I've come by some evidence that . . . well, that Billy's allegations about Gina may not be completely false. Whatever the case, we don't want to be in business with these people. They're dangerous."

"Billy tried to kill us. You can't believe anything from that nutter!"

Xan says to Garriott, "You're telling me you don't think there's been something off about this from the outset?"

He lowers his eyes.

She continues. "I've never worked on a tech project with a casualty rate before."

"But to mothball the Dancers? Flee to California? It's what that dick wants."

Xan ignores him and asks me, "What do you propose?"

"Look, we can debate the merits of our partners later. But I get the idea that they prefer to negotiate with corpses. So right now, we need to take that off the table. Once we're somewhere safe, we can worry about the long term."

Garriott says, "Yeah, let's have ourselves a merry vacation while everything we've worked for goes down the shitter."

Xan asks, "What about the police?"

"We may have to go that route. But first I want to establish exactly what happened. Bear in mind, if all this gets out, it will mean surrendering control of the Dancers to the legal system. We may have to do that, but I think maybe there's another way."

"So where do we go?" she asks.

"We can stay with an old friend of mine at his beach house in L.A. He's actually in the business. If we're nice to him, and introduce him to the Dancers, we may get a new deal out of it."

Xan stares at me for a long moment before nodding. She directs an imploring look at Garriott, who closes his eyes irritably. "Does it have to be L.A.?"

I say, "Garriott, get Fred and Ginger. Xan, maybe you can zip up all our source code and transfer it to a new server. I'll meet you at JFK in two hours."

We stand there looking at each other. Then Xan turns and walks out.

— — —

I hurry from PiMP back toward my apartment and spend the trip on the phone making arrangements with Adrian for us to crash at his place.

I hang up as I'm turning onto Bond from Lafayette. The street is busy with its many construction crews. I'm walking behind a pair of Mexican carpenters, and we have to squeeze past two guys in business casual and hard hats on the way into the wooden passage that takes us under the forest of scaffolding blocking the sidewalk. One of the men in front of me nudges the other and gestures back behind him. The other guy turns to look and shrugs, smiling. I check for an attractive woman or something, but all I see is one of the hard hats putting a radio to his mouth and the other rolling up the plans they were examining.

The Mexican guys I was following duck into their site. Ahead of me now are two men in hard-worn Carhartt overalls carrying tool bags. They're at the end of the block slowly coming toward me. Both are white and clean shaven. On the other side of the street is a pristine gray van with tinted windows. Its engine starts.

I go from hungover plodding to red alert. Just past my left shoulder, another pair of guys walk gradually in my direction on the other side of the street. The two close behind me are still chatting amiably, not making eye contact.

What is it? What's wrong?

There are too many pairs of fat white guys all converging on me right now. I come abreast of my building and notice vague human shapes through the frosted glass of the lobby door. I pause for a second, fishing for my keys.

Hmmm.

The van starts rolling forward now, but it's cut off by a speeding cab coming from the Bowery. This seems like a sign, so I plant my hand and vault over the cement construction barrier into the street right in front of the cab. The driver, a turbaned Sikh, screeches to a stop and lays on the horn. Which gives me time to yank open one of the passenger doors and jump inside. The driver stops yelling when I extract a wad of cash from my pocket.

"Take me to Astor Place fast. A hundred bucks if I'm there in less than a minute. Go!"

He punches it, and we take the corner of Lafayette in a squealing drift.

A number of faces turn to track our progress, and I can see curses form-ing at some of their lips.

We blaze up Lafayette, fortunately hitting a string of green lights. Looking back, I see the gray van rounding the corner five blocks back. I jump out of the cab and rush into a Kmart across from the main subway entrance. Behind me a black SUV and a beat-up delivery truck pull hastily to the curb.

Christ, that's a lot of people.

Mondano isn't messing around with a skeleton crew. I doubt I'd still be at large if these were McClaren's guys. Either way, how did they know I was planning to bolt?

There's a security guard at the door, so I walk in smooth, but then as I get past the checkout lines, I switch to a light jog. The escalators are clear, and I hustle down to the store's underground exit. I'm hoping that my pursuers won't know that there's this opening directly to the subway. Maybe they'll just cover the aboveground exits and wait, planning to get me quickly into the van rather than contend with store security raising hell. This Kmart's location on St. Mark's demands heavy vigilance against shoplifting punks.

My prayers for a train go unanswered. I hesitate, bouncing on the balls of my feet. The tension is too much, so I check both tunnels for lights and then jump down onto the tracks, nonchalantly, like I've every right to be there. The trip to the other side is a dirty business, but none of the people waiting seem to notice beyond an elderly gentleman pointing out my antics to his grandson. I go to the exit at the extreme end of the sta-tion and hide partway up the hallway that leads to the stairs. From here I can still see the entrance to Kmart.

Within seconds, two beefy guys, different from the ones I'd seen before, rush onto the platform where I came in. One pinches his temples and raises a walkie-talkie. I want to break for the surface, but I'm nervous that they would have much of Astor Place covered by now. A beautiful rum-bling sound holds me in place. The 6 train comes up the opposite track and stops with its usual squealing protest. The two guys either get on or go back into Kmart, because they're not on the platform when I look again.

I'm still feeling exposed, since it's probably only a matter of time before they check this side of the station. Thankfully, the northbound train arrives before they do. I hop on, careful to check that no one joins me at the last second. Once we hit Union Square, I've lost them.

On arriving there, I race to the L westbound.

Just making that train gives me a chance to think. How did they know to come after me now? I'd have spotted a tail from Mondano's people when I left Billy's. But static surveillance is a lot easier than sticking to a moving target. And Billy's place was fairly isolated on his street. I'd never notice if they were watching with a telescope from half a mile away to see who showed up. After the Cloisters, Mondano would consider my loyalties suspect. So when I didn't go to Blake immediately after leaving the murder scene, he'd know something was up. Were I them, I'd want to neutralize me and take control of the Dancers. Which means they're probably going after Xan and Garriott as well.

I get out at the last stop at Fourteenth Street and Eighth Avenue, grab a cab heading downtown, and dial Xan. My call goes straight to voicemail. That scares me, but there could be plenty of reasons for it.

Garriott, however, picks up. "What is it?"

"Hey, they know what's going on. Can you see anyone strange on your street?"

"What?"

"Look out your window and tell me if there's anyone loitering outside. Sitting in a car. I don't know. Someone walking a dog around the block that you've never seen before."

"Um, okay." He pauses for a second. "There's no one on the street."

"What about in the cars?"

"I can't really see from here. But I don't think there was when I came in."

I decide it's worth it to risk a pickup. There's no way Garriott could even spot a tail on his own, much less shake one.

"I'm going to be there in three minutes. When I call you, I want you to run to the corner of Greenwich and Charlton. I'll be in a cab."

"But—"

"Don't worry. We'll get you whatever you need. Just bring the Dancers. Now I gotta call Xan, so just wait for me."

I dial Xan, but it goes to voicemail again.

My driver has a real third-world enthusiasm for urban Formula One, and we barrel down Seventh Avenue at an inordinate rate. Rounding onto Charlton, our starboard side threatening to lose contact with the road, I call Garriott and tell him to go.

Near the corner of Greenwich, I get a jab of panic and yell for the driver to stop. Right in front of me is a tall bearded guy in tinted glasses reaching into his jacket. I burst out of the still-moving cab and blindside him. My elbow explodes in agony as it hits the cement, and I hear metal skittering along the sidewalk as something slides off the curb underneath a parked car. I hope it's his gun.

Garriott is walking toward me from the door to his building. Focused on my dramatic arrival, he doesn't notice the two men who step out from behind another apartment's entrance to his right. A blue van is speeding toward us, its side door sliding open like a raptor's third eyelid. I call out, but the men behind him move fast. Garriott starts running, but doesn't turn until one of the guys tries to torque the handle to Ginger's rolling case out of his hand. The other jams a small pistol into his ribs to encourage cooperation, but Garriott doesn't see it. He just reacts to the pressure by letting go of Fred's case and trying to push away the barrel of the gun.

When people describe moments like this one, they always say that time seems to slow down. It feels to me like the reverse happens. The next thing I know, I'm standing in the gutter dry-firing my pistol at the van now careening up Greenwich.

I turn. Behind me Garriott lies crumpled on the sidewalk, a bloom of crimson growing next to his head.

74

I run as fast as I can down Vandam toward Sixth Avenue, sirens converging behind me. I don't feel too bad for running since the EMTs will be able to do a lot more for him than I could.

Flashing through it in my mind, I think it went like this:

Garriott grabbed at the gun. The other guy saw his partner losing control of it and slammed the butt of his piece down on the back of Garriott's head. He went limp, pulling his assailant down with him. I opened fire at the one still standing. Being a notoriously poor shot, I missed three times before he dropped Ginger's case and brought his own gun to bear. I guess I should be thankful that the bearded man I had just tackled returned the favor by knocking me down into the space between two parked cars. I hit my head hard, but recovered enough to fire at the guy trying to pick up Ginger's case. These gentlemen probably weren't expecting to get shot at, because he abandoned it, and I heard someone shout "Go!" All three piled into the waiting van. I squeezed off my whole clip, and I think I might have hit one of the tires, but that didn't stop it.

I rolled Garriott over. He had a terrible gash almost down to his neck, and blood was pumping out at an alarming rate. I called 911 and spent a second trying to revive him. The pistol in my waistband meant that I couldn't be there when the police arrived, unless I wanted to wind up in jail on a gun charge. I grabbed the Dancers' cases and took off.

— — —

A cab crosses the intersection in front of me at speed, but I whistle loud enough to get it to pull right abruptly. Not knowing exactly where to go, I tell him to keep driving.

Then I call Xan.

Any relief I felt at getting away dissolves instantly when she answers.

"James. So glad you called." She's tentative, completely artificial.

"Xan, what's going on?"

"Yeah. We've had a bit of a change of plans here." Maybe it's the pronoun, or maybe it's the stress saturating her voice that warns me. She's in danger. I picture her with a gun to her head.

"Who's there?"

A shifting sound as if she's put her hand over the phone's mouthpiece. I hear what might be a male voice. Then she says, "I'm not going to be able to make our meeting."

"Right. Okay, what do they want me to do?"

"We all need to get together. I hope you can bring our special friends."

"Fine. Where?"

"There's a warehouse in Secaucus."

New Jersey. One of Exotica's local distribution hubs. Mondano's turf. I don't like it. I say, "How about the McDonald's in Times Square?"

Xan inhales. "Uh. No. It has to be . . . this other place." The terror in her words makes me want to rip someone's face off.

"Fuck. Fine. Tell your friends they need to be careful starting now. And principals only. I see one of these guys from earlier today, things will get very ugly."

"Um . . . Okay, principals only. We, ah, hope things go smoothly."

"When?"

There's a short pause. "Immediately. We'll have a car sent for you."

"No way. I'll be there in ninety minutes." I start to hang up, but she stops me.

"James?"

"Yeah?"

"We may need to demo the products. And we don't want any surprises. Nothing shocking, right? So with Ginger, be sure that you . . . Well, you know how she is. So we'll see you soon."

The line goes dead.

What was Xan's incoherent addendum all about? I can understand that they'd want to confirm that we haven't sabotaged the Dancers. But what does she mean by "nothing shocking"?

"So with Ginger, be sure that you . . ." The words I'd use to complete that sentence are: "Don't come."

She's telling me to bail on the meeting. But I can't bring myself to pull out now.

I have the cab drop me at a twenty-four-hour karaoke place in Korea-town. One of their private lounges serves as an office for twenty minutes while I, taking a cue from Billy, compose an affidavit summarizing recent events. I bundle this with his final testament and attach everything to an email. I set my mail program to send it to my entire address list twelve hours from now.

In less than a day I've gone from suppressing his message to poten-tially acting as Billy's press agent. The threat of violent death has a way of changing one's perspective. As a cadaver, I suspect I'll be indifferent to being accused of involvement in his murder. So, like a video game pala-din, I'll be walking into this engagement clad in armor wrought purely of information.

With that thought weighing on me, I decide to spend my remaining time making sure that the Dancers are ready for a memorable debut.

75

Mondano's warehouse looks like a modest operation from the street. A run-down, one-story brick structure topped by a faded sign whispering EE LOGISTICS. But behind a screen of businesses installed in lots fronting the road hulks an enormous steel-sided warehouse.

I walk through a narrow gap in a chain-link gate topped with a triple-stranded overhang of barbed wire. The tiny parking lot is lit by a pallid green security light. The building looks dark and deserted. As I approach the dented metal door, Blake Randall swings it open. He adopts a rueful expression intimating how sad it is that things have come to this. I just brush right past him.

A reception area holds a bank of cast-off airport chairs opposite a tall counter like you might find at a car rental agency. Fake plants and inspirational posters round out the décor. The banality of this foyer is meant only to camouflage the eruption of carnal oddities beyond.

Blake buzzes me through a security door and into a reprobate's fantasy land. I stand on a thin catwalk overhanging a huge space filled three stories high with pallets of adult novelties sourced from nations spanning the globe. Hanging signs organize the aisles according to some innovative scheme of Dewey Decimal depravity. I can see a section containing enough rainbow-colored dildos to fill every orifice in the tri-state area. A miniature Library of Congress of pornographic DVDs. There's an area where remaindered magazines are collated into "value paks" unlikely to satisfy anyone: *Mature Foxes* with *Barely Legal, Footsie's Petites* with

Rump-A-Dump. Under different circumstances, this place would provide for an amusing couple weeks.

Blake leads me down the catwalk along a series of offices with glass walls commanding views of the warehouse floor. At the end is a long conference room equipped with a ten-seat table. The walls are decorated with promotional posters for storied Exotica releases.

Mondano and Xan sit at the far side of the table. Xan seems unperturbed, but she makes a tsk of exasperation as I walk in and set Fred and Ginger's cases in front of her. Mondano stands slowly. He's got a pistol tucked in the front of his pants.

He catches me looking at it and winks. That little gesture frightens me more than any of his earlier gangster posturing. In contrast to Blake, Mondano's become progressively jolly as events have spun further out of control. He's no longer acting like some kind of Lucky Luciano manqué. Here he's exposing the burbling molten plastic of his unhinged personality. After the Cloisters, I knew I'd underestimated him, but seeing him now makes me think I misinterpreted him entirely.

Slowly, with the exaggerated motions of a street mime, he takes his gun by two fingers and lays it gently on the table. He nods at his piece and grins, inviting me to do the same.

I do, and there's another thud at the end of the table where Blake's positioned himself.

So he came strapped too. Will the wonders never cease?

In front of him lies a U.S. Army standard-issue Colt .45 auto. In service between World War I and Vietnam, if I'm not mistaken. Call it his dad's, or maybe even grandfather's, gun. Reaching for his legacy even now.

Blake assumes the seat at the head of the table and begins. "So this situation is unfortunate. But as long as we all keep ourselves together and stay, ah, courteous, I'm sure we can work this out."

"Is knocking out our partner your idea of courtesy?" I reply.

"Garriott? Is he okay?" asks Xan.

Blake's eyes ignite. He says tightly, "I understand he attempted to disarm one of our employees."

"He was shitting his pants, Blake. He wasn't 'disarming' anyone. I'd be happy to stick my pistol in your ribs and see how you react."

"Now, James, I don't think threats are the way to go here."

"No? How are we supposed to interpret assault and kidnapping?"

Mondano leans forward and levels a spastically wagging finger at me. "If you hadn't started fucking around, he'd be sitting in that chair having a scotch right now."

"Oh. Does the chair have high-voltage lines attached?"

Blake jumps in. "Careful, James. We need to come together to find a—"

I'm about to protest, but Xan saves me the trouble.

"You expect us to 'come together' after you send this shit stain"— she points at Mondano—"to my flat trying to mouth-rape me with his gun?"

Mondano licks his lower lip. "I'll do better than that, *luv*. I've got—"

Everyone jumps as Blake slams his hand against the table. "Enough!" A tortured silence prevails as he collects himself. "Look, we can all walk out of here—"

"I know *we're* walking out of here," I say. "Your roll-up didn't work. So you must know that if Xan and I aren't swilling mojitos at Foo Bar by happy hour, you two are going to be under heat that will melt your skin. Maybe *you* want to try to beat it with an army of lawyers. But maybe cash-poor Benito here doesn't want to spend the prime of his life rimming his ink-faced Latin King cell mate."

Mondano chuckles like that might be a rare delight, but Blake eyeballs him skeptically.

I continue. "And, Blake, I'll bet that if the DA doesn't have your ass, your sweet sister—"

"You say another word about Blythe, and this meeting will end badly."

"I thought you didn't make idle threats, Blake. You're not going to kill us. You have too much to lose. And you won't be able to cover it up this time. I've been more thorough in my preparations than your brother was. So here's how it's going to be. We're going to leave now. You can hang on to the Dancers as insurance. Once we get to a safe place, we'll contact you about the files. It won't be cheap, but maybe we can make a deal. But we're not going to play ball with a gun to our heads. Because we know the gun isn't loaded."

Blake says, "Okay, James. All I ever wanted was for this project to succeed."

And your brother's head on a stick.

Mondano leans forward in his chair. "Wait. These things don't do us any good if dickface here lobotomized them." He leers at Xan. "Maybe our little geisha can show us how they work with a horizontal pussy."

Xan just looks through him.

"Fine," I say.

Is this actually going to work out? Are the Dancers really all they want?

Xan and I configure them in silence for a few minutes until everything is connected. I start up the ErrOS test package on my laptop.

As I'm doing this, my fragile hope that this meeting might remain civil is shattered. From watching Billy's video, I must be sensitized to moving shadows. It's slight and happens very fast, but in the far left corner of the back wall I sense motion. The smallest flicker in the profile of light coming through the glass.

Someone is peering around the corner. I force myself to continue what I'm doing. Then an almost subaudible scuffing sound, this time coming from the right.

Tentacles of acidic fear grip my stomach. There are people surrounding the conference room. Our partners have decided to continue politics by other means. I glance at Mondano, who leans back in his chair with reptilian complacency. Blake, on the other hand, is clearly on edge. Expectant.

I type a few runtime parameters into Fred's system. Xan starts Ginger's software, and we put the Dancers into a test mode that dispenses with the visuals and associated body tracking. The setting makes the machines just a simple sensor/actuator loop, taking them back to their most primitive form.

I say, "Since you're both so excited to see them in action, why don't you guys do the honors?" They both look askance at this suggestion, so I add, "Just use your hands, and you can tell that they're working. We don't have the gear to do full-service here."

Xan is quick on the uptake and grabs Blake's hand to guide two of his fingers into Ginger's opening. This would normally cause Fred to thrust outward a corresponding distance. But he stays in his plastic shell like a frightened turtle.

Mondano smiles up at the ceiling. "What—the—fuck?" he asks in an unnerving singsong.

"Relax," I say. "Maybe he's just having some performance anxiety with our new friends here." I see Mondano catch Blake's eye and shake his head sorrowfully. I take a small Allen wrench out of my bag and open the side flap of Fred's head that allows us access to the hardware. I make a minor adjustment.

"Try it now."

Again Blake slides two digits into Ginger. Again nothing happens. Mondano laughs like we've finally come to the punch line. "You think we can't fix this? You think we need you to make this work?"

I open Fred's hatch again, and while I'm twiddling, I rotate his base slightly counterclockwise.

Blake leans across the table and says, "James, this is very disappointing. What did you think was going to happen here?" Right behind him, I see a flutter in the light from the window. Mondano's men responding to his raised voice. Checking on their boss.

I guess it's now or never.

"Well, Blake, from recent experience, I figured you were going to try to"—I incline my head toward the mic in my laptop—"fuck me."

"Fuck_Me," of course, is the voice prompt that stimulates Fred to action, and so I used it here, but with modified orders.

A soft click sounds as Fred releases the latch restraining his manhood, and there's another louder one as he shifts the cylinder on his primary control valve. During the minute we've been waiting, I let the air pressure build up to over 250 p.s.i., quadruple its normal value. So Fred's plastic member shoots out of his pelvic casing and impacts with the force of a pro fastball into the right side of Mondano's mouth.

He's flung hard to the ground behind the table, so I can't see the exact effect, but I suspect a team of oral surgeons will send their kids to college on the proceeds from repairing the damage.

At the same time, Blake cries out at the surprise I installed for Ginger. All of her internal air muscles inflate to their maximum extent, trapping Blake's fingers in a vise-like grip. Her head then rotates while pulling down hard, hopefully placing his wrist in a painful position.

I dive over the table to knock Xan to the floor. Mondano is screaming, a strangled whistling sound, and his men will be coming in fast.

Xan and I hit hard next to Mondano, who's trying to go fetal under the table. I roll over and thrust my leg up into its underside with enough strength to topple it over so that its opposite edge rests on that side's row of chairs. It forms an incomplete barrier between us and Mondano's men. The giant glass wall explodes from the blast of a sawed-off shotgun. I nearly lose control of myself. Pistols are bad enough. But a shotgun in close quarters is a recipe for slaughter.

Through the gap under the table's edge I can see two sets of legs move into the room. I missed the chance to grab my gun as I vaulted over the table, but Mondano's slid down with me, landing right next to Xan's head. I snatch it and fire at their kneecaps. A startled shout indicates I hit someone, but I know it's not going to be enough.

The men will be on us before I can stand, so in desperation, I grab Mondano by the back of his jacket and turn him so that his body is mostly covering mine. I'm just bringing my pistol up when I see the face of Shades from the Cloisters emerge over the edge of the table. He's looking down past the barrel of his shotgun. He takes in the situation and hesitates. With a handgun it would be an easy shot, but his pellet spread would take a large chunk of his boss along with me. It's just enough time for me to squeeze off two shots into his chest, and he disappears from my view, firing into the ceiling as he falls.

There's still at least another shooter, maybe disabled, but probably not incapacitated. But I can't see him through the table. I roll into a squat and jerk Mondano up onto his knees. He tries to grab at my face, but he's wild with agony and can't mount much of an attack. I lurch forward with him, my adrenaline-saturated muscles just able to propel him up over the lip of the table. I'm right behind him, again using his body as a shield. A muzzle flash from the floor just to my left, and Mondano's head snaps back, spraying my face with gore. I empty my clip in that direction, but I can't see shit with my eyes full of blood. Mondano becomes dead weight and slumps forward onto the edge of the table.

I duck back down, frantic about what I'm going to do now that I'm out of ammo. I listen to try to get a sense of what's happening, but a horrible silence has enveloped the room. Xan levers herself upright beside me, her breath coming in sobs. I put a finger to my lips. She holds her breath. The air is heavy with the acrid smell of burnt gunpowder. Then I hear a muffled thump to my left, maybe against the far wall. Someone is still moving. My brain seizes with terror.

And then I see it. Mondano's lifeless body hanging over the edge of the table has caused his pants to ride up enough to uncover an ankle holster. I grab the gun and rise, looking for targets.

It's Blake leaning against the back wall. One of his hands is bent around at a disgusting angle, the wrist obviously mangled. I suppose that happened when I kicked the table over. Ginger would have come flying off with Blake's hand attached. Despite what has to be unbelievable pain, his other hand is steady. It holds his gun, and is pointed straight at my chest.

On seeing this, I almost start shooting immediately. But something holds me back. Mondano and his help planned violence from the beginning, but throughout, Blake has seemed legitimately shocked by what's happened. He is someone I *know,* and regardless, there shouldn't be any more bodies coming from this. My dreams from the past weeks of a triumphant demo are cruelly mocked by the blood drenching the room's walls. Our unnatural vision of love replaced with this gory nightmare of war.

I have to swallow hard to get my voice to work. "Blake, let's just—"
But then he fires.

I guess I saw in his eyes the hysterical equations he was processing reach a solution. Maybe I noticed him adjusting his aim. Because as I hit the ground, I know that I got off a shot as well, and we both went down.

I can't say it hurts too much, but I know it's bad. Partly because I can't really move my head. In fact, I'm rapidly losing control of my whole body. I see Xan's face swim into my line of sight.

Her mouth opens in what must be a scream.

III

THE QUEEN OF HEARTS

76

My cocoon goes from pleasant darkness to a brighter reddish brown. A light has been turned on, and if I open my eyes, I could find out why. I keep them closed.

Hazy days pass in a swirl of numbness and pain. A surgery I think. I have a dim recollection of being moved onto a rolling stretcher. Some forms thrust at me. McClaren's face close to mine, saying my name. These are only a few among some far more outlandish memories, so they may be nothing but the residue of a fever-fraught, opiate-laced dream.

The next thing that seems definitely real is a soft feminine voice speaking words I can't quite hear. Then an entrancing smell of cigarette smoke. My chest clenches with must-have-right-now urgency. I open my eyes to assess the possibility of getting one.

At first I'm optimistic. The mahogany furniture, impersonal floral wallpaper, and decorative molding place me in a premium hotel suite. But my hopes fall as I take in the adjustable bed, IV stand, and nearby heart monitor, which is reproachfully recording my nic fit. I try to lever myself up, which makes me realize that I've also been shot just over the right hip. Combined with my chest wound, this makes almost any movement excruciating.

I lie still, but a section of my brain is pumping out some sensational anxiety messages. I look around for clues to their cause.

In a sunny alcove off to my right, I see Blythe Randall chatting on her cell. She's wearing a gauzy dark-gray suit. And despite the setting, she's smoking. I'm struck by how beautiful she looks. But then I remember my recent history and conclude that maybe I should be afraid.

Thinking of my email bomb makes me start wishing I hadn't survived. My phone sits on a table next to me just within reach. A few clicks reassure me that it never went out.

Now, how could that be?

I guess Red Rook was farther up my ass than I imagined.

My sigh of relief gets Blythe's attention, and her phone flips shut. I test her attitude by placing two fingers sideways at my lips.

She shakes her head, but the crinkle at her eyes conveys "What are we going to do with you?" not "I'm going to strangle you for shooting my brother." She steps over and places her cigarette between my lips. I inhale deeply, ignoring my suspicion that a coughing spasm might kill me.

Blythe sits next to me and says, "You've had us a bit worried."

I have so many questions, it's hard to know where to begin.

"Where am I?"

"Well, you're not in Secaucus bleeding to death." Her cool tone implies, "Though that could be arranged."

"Good . . . But—"

"We thought after . . . everything, you might need a break. So you're at a private clinic on Long Island. Where you'll receive the best medical care known to man. For the *full duration* of your recovery."

Does that mean I'm effectively a prisoner? Do I care, as long as they keep the Fentanyl flowing?

I'm just amazed Blythe isn't ripping my eyes out.

"What about—" I realize belatedly that I'm heading into dangerous territory.

Blythe is a step ahead of me. She takes some papers off the nightstand and hands them to me. "We're going to need you to confirm this as soon as possible."

I take the pages warily and start skimming.

The document is Xan's statement to the police. She's given them a background précis very close to the truth, but substituting in place of the Dancers some crazy porno NOD build Mondano and Blake wanted to set up. We'd gone to the warehouse to discuss ramping up security on the project due to Billy's attacks. Halfway through the meeting, Blake shows up and starts screaming threats at Mondano about something having to do with his little brother.

The key paragraphs read:

```
In response, Mr. Mondano produced a firearm from his
waistband and pointed it at Mr. Randall. At that point,
the two security personnel [Unknown #1 and Unknown #2]
appeared outside the room, both armed as well. Their
arrival seemed to surprise Mondano, who called them
"worthless traitors" and pointed his gun at them. I
gathered that Randall had co-opted these men and arranged
for them to intervene in case of any altercation. Randall
then drew his own pistol and aimed it at Mondano, who
reacted by pulling Mr. Pryce out of his chair and
stepping behind him. Randall fired his weapon, hitting
Pryce in the chest and hip areas. Mondano shot at
Randall, hitting him in the chest.

    Mondano kicked over the table, blocking my view of
subsequent events. There were a number of shots fired, and
I believe that Mondano shot both Unknown individuals. But
when Mondano moved to inspect the room, one of them shot
him in the head. I then fled the premises.
```

The first thing I realize upon absorbing this is that Xan has lied extravagantly to protect me. In her account, I have been made into an unarmed bystander.

What about my gun? Is it possible that Xan had the presence of mind to get rid of it?

I reach to remember what really happened. No, I never fired it, so there won't be traces for ballistics. The only guns I fired were Mondano's.

But they would have my fingerprints on them, wouldn't they? Is it possible that Xan wiped them and then ran them back through his hands?

What about the Dancers? They're not mentioned, so she must have hidden them as well. Not hard to pull off in a warehouse full of sex toys.

And why would Xan do this anyway?

I think back to that picture Billy took of her shaking hands with Blythe at Gina's funeral. Xan had said she was just offering condolences, but what if it was more than that? What if they struck up an acquaintance? That led to a business arrangement. Could Blythe have asked Xan to "keep her informed" like she did with me?

So when things blow up at the warehouse, Xan calls Blythe, and she sends McClaren to perform triage. They concoct a tale for the police, and the responding officers buy it.

The sickening second insight follows on impatiently: for Xan to have felt free to deliver such a fabrication, there must be no other surviving witnesses. And that means that Blake Randall is dead. I glance cautiously at Blythe, once again wondering if I'm next in line.

She looks at me steadily. "My brother's been laid to rest, James."

I clear my throat. "You seem—"

Her eyes flash. "I am *shattered* with grief for him." She takes a long breath and calms. "But I saw more clearly than anyone how dedicated he was to reliving my father's life. And that couldn't have ended well, could it? I mean, consorting with a psychopath like Mondano?" A hint of bitterness creeps into her voice. "The way Blake would rail about our 'crazy half brother.' When all the time, he was the one losing touch with reality. The Randall family curse." She brushes the corner of her eye with the back of her hand.

"I'm sorry."

"I had hoped you might be able to protect him. Though I'm not sure if anyone could have by that point. He was so bent on . . . Well, anyway, Xan tells me he shot first. And I'm inclined to believe her."

"I'd thought it was over. I don't really remember pulling the trigger."

"I think you'd better forget it. He was a big believer in destiny, and he reached for his fate with both hands. You had the bad fortune to be present at the reckoning."

"And your other brother?"

"After the police found him"—she shudders slightly—"it didn't take them long to piece together what they'd done to him and why."

"Are Xan and Garriott okay?"

"They are. Garriott's here. Recovering nicely. Maybe you two will find yourselves on the shuffleboard court soon. Xan is fine. You are indebted to that woman."

She adds a sharp glance at the papers I'm holding, commanding me to endorse this fantasy for the police. That feels dangerous. There are dead bodies here, and lying about what happened, if it unravels, would be a good way to get a murder jacket rather than a shot at justifiable homicide.

But the tale has already been told.

I'm holding the official version in my hands. If mine should deviate, I not only lash myself to all four corpses, I also make Xan a perjurer. She may not be completely innocent in this affair, but she must have made her statement for my sake.

Easy choice.

"I know. She saved my life."

We sit in silence. Blythe gives me another drag off her cigarette. I watch her smoke for a moment. She French-inhales, which makes me think of someone else.

"And Olya?" I ask.

Blythe's nostrils flare at the name. "That one remains an outstanding issue. She found the strength to check herself out of the hospital well before anyone would have thought her able. Head injuries can be like that, I'm told. We have people looking for her, but she seems adept at covering her tracks. Our best information is that 'Olya Zhavinskaya' isn't even her real name. McClaren tells me there are some unsavory Russian gentlemen trying to locate her as well. Something to do with a previous enterprise. Even so, there's no telling where she went, though I understand statuesque blondes can find all sorts of diverting work in Kuwait. But with the burn scars . . ."

I close my eyes, remembering her.

"No doubt men all over New York are tearing their hair that she's gone. But you'll heal. I'm sure next year's model will be even better."

"So what happens now?"

Blythe waves toward the window framing a priceless view of white sand and sparkling water. "For you? You'll understand that your relation-ship with IMP can't continue, but I'm prepared to offer generous sever-ance."

I shoot her twin brother, and she's offering me severance?

My surprise lessens as she continues. "After such a tragedy, I'm sure I don't need to say the word '*plomo*'? With all these nasty perforations, I suspect you've had your fill of the heavy metals."

Disconcerting for Blythe to pose a question immortalized by the hall-of-fame kingpin Pablo Escobar: *Plata o plomo?* Silver or lead? A joke, but an edgy one.

She glides a finger just above my chest wound. "What happened was awful, but one day I'm sure you'll treasure these scars. There's something so attractive about a man with the power to stop bullets."

77

After my release from the hospital, I'm tempted to slink back to Red Rook, but that doesn't feel quite right. Blythe bore the cost of patching me up, so I figure the least I can do is spend some of my separation pay to fix the two parties who helped save my life. Ginger's neck is broken in several places, and of course Fred needs to be remasculated.

I try to recruit Garriott and Xan to help, but they seem fairly traumatized by what happened and want no further part of the roborotica business. And they aren't going to have Blythe Randall pulling strings for them forever. We agree that they'll keep their shares of any new company, but otherwise I get free rein.

Though it turns out Blythe is pulling strings for me as well.

Something I find out after fielding a call from my old poker buddy William Coles. He begins by saying, "Dude, I'm totally into fucking robots."

He's taken a page from his father's playbook and gone into currency trading, though his company, Philosopher's Stone Financial, works with virtual currencies. Spinning gold out of silicon. Blythe tipped him off to my new enterprise, thinking he might be an ideal investor. We set up a meeting for a demo.

He closes the call by saying, "And at this meeting I want to fuck

Whitney Houston. Like pre-Bobby? No wait, an octopus! No . . . Uh!
All three Olsen twins! Wait, can what I'm fucking change in the middle?"

I then call Adrian to convince him to work with me full-time on
bringing Fred and Ginger back to life. He quickly agrees, saying, "The
margins on manufacturing virtual snatchola are going to be obscene."

A few weeks later, I pass a newsstand on my way home. The front page
of the *Journal* shows a picture of a black-clad blonde emerging from a
limo into a crowd of photographers: Blythe Randall returning triumphant from the closing of her TelAmerica deal. The article lauds her
"iron resolve" in getting the transaction done after it was plunged into
uncertainty in the "amazingly brief" period of chaos at IMP caused by
the deaths of both her brothers. While Blythe has never addressed the
press, the article quotes from the statement made by an old Randall family spokesperson:

> Ms. Randall is deeply grieved by these developments and
> asks that the media respect her privacy in this difficult
> time.

Of course, the media is not in the business of respecting privacy. From
my hospital bed, I'd read some of the coverage in the weeks after Blake's
death. You could hear the reporters gnashing their teeth as the police
conducted their investigation with unusual dispatch and discipline. They
quickly concluded that Billy had been murdered by Mondano's two dead
henchmen, and that the warehouse shootings stemmed from a fight that
escalated to a lethal pitch. This determination relied on the testimony of
two eyewitnesses whose identities had to remain confidential for fear of
reprisals. All those suspected of violence were now deceased, so the case
was closed without the glorious spectacle of a trial.

The verdict on Blake was, "Rich kid, under too much pressure from
an early age, cracks. Tragic consequences ensue."

Two weeks later, Israel reinvaded Lebanon, a photogenic toddler was
kidnapped, and an earthquake re-destroyed Port Au Prince. The story
dissipated.

Billy's *Unmasking* stayed with us for a bit longer. There were trials to cover, public disgrace to bestow, and tearful confessions to extract. But once the worm was contained and the source of new victims dried up, the sex scandals, being primarily virtual and involving mostly regular folks, lasted no longer than they usually do. Remarkable more for their simultaneous disclosure than anything else.

While there was a short and sharp drop-off in certain online activities, and perhaps a quicker uptake of browsing anonymizers, Lucifer quickly reasserted control over the world's computer screens. I came to agree with Blue_Bella's prediction that Billy's trick would produce more eyes opened in wonder than it did heads hung in shame.

I had little doubt that the Dancers' reception would be a warm one.

78

Ten months later, I'm starting to question whether they'll be received at all. There's a critical bug we can't seem to stamp out.

The problem is that Ginger can have exactly eight orgasms in a session, and then she inexplicably dies. We want to have test units reviewed by a group of influential Sex 2.0 bloggers, and we can't send them out until we squash the bug.

At ArrowTech, our "erotic technology" company, my team has been bickering about it nonstop. Since thirty hours have passed without a solution, I tell them I'll take it over.

Eight hours in, all I can think is that I'm not even supposed to be doing this. Though I'm in charge of our tech efforts, I haven't openly picked up a screwdriver or written a line of code in six months. The last time I tried, it caused a vitriolic argument with Adrian about my wasting time in the weeds. He said that whenever I'm tempted to do anything useful, I need to pick up the phone and tell our HR coordinator to hire someone to do it for me. With the lavish funding from Thrust Capital, Coles's new venture fund, I've already conceded the "get erect fast" argument. But this whole time I've been secretly indulging an urgent need to get my hands dirty. Which is why I'm here at two in the morning hunting this pesky critter.

We started by establishing that the bug exists in the original version of the Dancers' code, in Fred's orgasm-detection routines. So I've been poring over Garriott's old files to see if we missed anything.

After a long time searching, I begin to feel another presence in the code. In a few places, generally the most complicated parts of the program, the ones you can't quite understand upon first seeing them, I find some constructions that don't seem like Garriott. Like someone is speaking with a different voice. A coder whose head is altogether closer to the machine: lots of complex class structures, fancy recursion, and elegant bit manipulation. Garriott is a very good engineer, but his code gives the impression of a rigorous proof. This stuff looks like poetry.

No one would ever write sample code like this, so where did it come from?

The answer's obvious: Gina.

Reading her syntax elicits a welter of emotions. Sadness that I never got to meet this tortured genius mixes with creeping guilt over my exploitation of the project for which she was murdered.

I'm trying to parse a particularly thorny section when I get a feeling of déjà vu. This code is distinctive enough that I must have seen it before. I do a global search and find, in a totally unrelated library, an almost identical function.

My screen-burned eyes finally focus on the difference:

Function 1 is called: `O_fill_packet`

Function 2 is called: `O_fi11_packet`

Only a couple of shifted pixels separate the lowercase L from the number 1 in most default programming fonts. A discrepancy so easy to overlook that the names must be intentional. We hackers often use such lettering tricks when trying to disguise files or processes on a target's machine.

The only difference between the two functions is that O_fi11_packet has a single line allocating a variable that creates a huge memory leak.

Someone intentionally put a bug into the system.

I restrain myself from immediately stomping this guy, and instead I check the value of the wayward variable when Ginger goes into her postcoital depression. It reads:

```
This little death I exalt \n
For I'd rather halt \n
```

```
Than make a pillar of salt \n
Gina Delaney \n
03.21.1980 - 10.29.14 \n
```

Gina put in an Easter egg.

The practice of embedding hidden treasures into software has a storied history. There's the Hall of Tortured Souls in Excel '95 wherein, by executing an obscure series of keystrokes, the user can enter a *Doom*-like 3D world. The infamous "Hot Coffee" pornographic cut scene in *Grand Theft Auto* actually prompted Senate hearings, with Hillary Clinton, of all people, acting particularly aggrieved. But generally Easter eggs are credit reels for underappreciated programmers.

Strange for Gina to put hers in a critical bug. This critter has caused enough ill will that any normal coder would remove it immediately. I fix the memory leak but decide to leave her secret memorial. She deserves it.

The word "memorial" sticks in my head. Gina's statement weirdly evokes her final words, and the lifespan notation at the end makes it look more like an epitaph than a signature. Knowing her history, I'm not surprised that she would focus on the connection between death and orgasm. Or that she'd program her bots to actually "die" after experiencing a certain amount of pleasure. But the "halt" she mentions can't mean Ginger, since the next line refers to Genesis 19, just as she did in the video of her death.

Then it hits me.

How could she correctly guess the date on which she would be murdered? And if she didn't put it in, who did?

This section of IT's code base was Garriott's responsibility. But the file history shows he never changed it. So Gina must have added it. Which means the line really was her epitaph, and she hid it in the DNA of the project that came to define her life. If that's true, then she knew the day she would die.

My mind recoils from the logic. I try to clear it by standing up to stretch. But my gaze keeps returning to the verse sitting calmly in my debug window.

If Gina placed these words in her magnum opus, then either she was clairvoyant, or she *selected* the date of her own demise. She could only know it would be October 29 if she chose that date.

And if that's true, then Gina wasn't murdered after all.

79

Her message goes to work on me that night.

Why do I care so much about what happened to this poor girl? I feel like over the past weeks, I've come to know Gina well. In fact, my now gleaming future is really a gift from her.

It was Lot's wife who turned into a pillar of salt, so is she saying here that she'd rather "halt" or die than share the fate of her mother? Billy had assumed Gina's death related to her work on the Dancers, as did I, but here she's invoking her wretched family.

Thinking it might be helpful to review a few details of her case, I lob in a call to Detective Nash, leaving a message that I just want to "tie up some loose ends."

Then I call Ruth Delaney. Having delivered her daughter's last words to her, I guess I owe her these as well. And she may be the only person who can help me decode them.

But the Delaneys are now represented by a "please check your number" message. Charles probably burned through Billy's largesse in a hurry, and now maybe they're having trouble with the bills. I search for an alternate listing but can't find anything.

I know I won't be able to give this up until I talk to her, so the following morning I catch a train to Boston.

— — —

Standing at the corner of Cross Street and Blakeley, I stare with amazement at a vacant lot where the Delaneys' wilted house used to be. Did the city mercifully elect to put it down?

No. A quick look around reveals traces of debris from a fire. Chips from burned timbers still leach black soot onto the sidewalk in the cold Boston drizzle. A few remnants show where the brick chimney fell and fractured across the back of the lot. I find a mud-covered scrap of yellow safety tape from the fire department.

Eventually a neighbor, a balding man with an impressive belly not quite covered by his yellowed T-shirt, shuffles out to get his paper. He darts a suspicious look at me but doesn't retreat when I walk over.

I ask, "When did it burn?"

He replies in thick Bostonian, "Back on the first day of February. Two o'clock in the goddamn morning."

I run this through my mental calendar. That was the night I called Ruth Delaney.

"You know what caused it?"

"Yep."

"What?"

"The wife."

"How do you know that?"

"Well . . . I ain't a fire-ologist, but they can tell stuff by the way the gasoline was spread around, or so they said."

"The fire department said this?"

"Uh-huh. Charlie being stuck to that couch of his with a samurai sword through his gut probably helped them figure it out."

"Wow."

"Yeah. I got the feeling the guy was hard to live with."

"And Mrs. Delaney?"

The neighbor looks a little pained. "I guess she didn't want to live with herself either."

Ruth Delaney burning everything the same night I spoke with her is way too much of a coincidence for my heathen mind to process. So I turn to religion.

She heard something in her daughter's words that I couldn't. I pull up the entire chapter of Genesis 19 on my phone, and this time I read to the end. It details what happens between Lot and his daughters after their mother transforms into a condiment:

```
And they made their father drink wine that night also:
and the younger arose, and lay with him; and he perceived
not when she lay down, nor when she arose.
     Thus were both the daughters of Lot with child by their
father.
```

While incest may have been the order of the day in Biblical times, in 2014, being impregnated by your father might start a girl on trying to find a way out.

Is that what Gina meant? Is that why Charles Delaney objected so fervently to an autopsy? Had he received a revelation of what they might find?

I recall Olya's chronology of Gina's final days. She went back to Boston to tell her parents about her new love. She came home depressed and spouting Bible verses about Sodom. Might her grand declaration have set something off in her father? With his frayed sanity, I can imagine Charles deciding that his daughter had surrendered herself to the Sodomites, and that somehow justified him in doing whatever he wanted with her—to her.

So he rapes his girl, maybe reverting to an old habit that Gina thought she'd escaped. Her personality is probably consistent with someone who had been sexually abused growing up. She returns to New York the broken woman Olya observed. Her despair deepens over the following months, enough time to miss two periods. She goes to a doctor and has it confirmed: she's pregnant by her own father.

Like the daughters of Lot.

It stands to reason Ruth Delaney would have a better working knowledge of Old Testament stories than I do. Thus the vacant lot.

Incest would also explain the bloody bathtub the night before Gina died. I'd thought Olya was lying about that incident, but thinking back, she never actually said that Gina slit her wrists again. She just said she cut herself. I pull up Gina's morgue photos from my private server and see it immediately: a ragged scratch moving horizontally between her hips about an inch or so below her belly button. Perhaps she was working up to a freelance hysterectomy the patient was not expected to survive. But Olya finds her first. Gina asks if she can forgive her anything, says she "can't bear it." She looks for redemption through her lover. But Olya lashes out, rather than comforting her.

For a certain breed of computer scientist, symbols are of the utmost importance. So upon learning of her pregnancy, and that Olya cared more for their robot babies than she did for her, Gina might have felt the keystone supporting her life had cracked. That her great project, her Jack of Hearts, had brought her to ruin. I can see how she might want to expunge it.

And so Gina gets busy in her workshop, and the next night she jacks out.

While incest is far more common than people realize, it remains so taboo that even when it's staring one straight in the face, most people won't see it. Social workers have to be specially trained to tweak their antennae. The tragedy here is that if anyone could understand the toxic emotions that spew from a gothic upbringing, it should have been Billy. But he sought an explanation for Gina's misery in his own fucked-up family, instead of hers. Once taken with the idea Blake was responsible, he was predisposed to believe later that he'd actually murdered her.

So did he conjure all his proof out of thin air? Sharpening digital artifacts until they looked like something sinister? Could those two blond apparitions have been summoned by Billy himself?

Whatever the source of his evidence, he was wrong. If there was one person responsible for Gina's fate, I'm now sure it was her father. And Billy ended up dying for his mistake.

I get a call from John McClaren at nine AM the next morning. He's full of his usual hail-fellow irony, but there's an undercurrent of irritation. He wants a meeting. Now.

On the way over, I try to figure out the significance of this appointment. Nash must have informed him about my call. The two had known each other before I ever got involved, and I start to wonder about the basis of their relationship.

— — —

At McClaren's office, I get an overhand shake and a slap on the back. He tells me to sit and spends a moment inspecting me. Finally he says, "So, bud . . . you must be hella busy with your *twatomata*."

"Yeah. It's getting hectic right now."

"Sure, sure." He tilts his head to the side. "That's why I was surprised—I'd say amazed, even—to hear that you've been bothering the local con-stab-ulary with interview requests."

"All work and no play makes Jack a dull boy."

A mirthless chuckle. "So are you planning to blow up the Overlook just for a little excitement?"

"No, I've seen enough fire for the year." I smile back at him and reach for a tone of idle curiosity. "Something came up that muddied my understanding of recent events. Just wanted to mop up a couple details."

"Jim, cleaning is my job. And I just dealt with a very big mess that you were involved in making. Everything's fine now, but what I don't need is you tracking in more shit."

"Things don't look as clean as you might like."

"Uh-huh . . . But remember, you've been read into this situation. So what you see isn't what everyone else sees."

That line pops the bubble of uncertainty that's been swelling in my head. I'd been asking myself: why did Billy see something so different from the police when he watched that video? Most of his voodoo forensics were unconvincing, but what about the pale figures in her pupils? No one who watched the recording, including me, ever saw them before he got it. As if they represented a hidden message intended only for him.

I feel an itch deep in my brain stem. How uncanny that in both *Getting Wet* and her suicide video, Gina's eyes would transmit recondite information. Life imitates art.

Too perfectly, I think. More likely that detail is a product of the same artifice Billy used in *Getting Wet*.

How do I know the copy of Gina's suicide video I took from the NYPD server was anything like the original?

I've been overlooking the crucial attribute of that file: chain of custody. McClaren could easily have gotten Nash to upload a different version. Those tiny ghosts could be the result of a couple hours with After Effects. A capability well within reach of someone who works for one of the biggest media companies on earth.

Relieved by my newfound certainty, I decide to push it. "Is that because you had Nash swap in a doctored recording of Gina Delaney's suicide, knowing that Billy would eventually get ahold of it?"

McClaren laughs. "Buddy, you don't seem to understand that nobody
cares anymore about your questions."

"I think after what happened . . . that I deserve to know the whole
story."

"You're just killing me here. Look, the only 'story' you should be worried about is your own. Right now you're getting a happy ending. With
your line of work, you can probably have as many as you want. Billy?
Now, Billy's story is a very, very sad one. You don't want to get caught up
again in that kind of story."

"You want to make that threat explicit?"

He watches me, his face shut and barred, bonhomie doused like kids
pissing on the coals of a campfire. My mind is still racing.

*Why would McClaren want to give Billy a doctored video? To make him believe
that Blake murdered Gina? Could it have been a scheme to enrage Billy to the point
of recklessness?*

If so, I guess it worked, but not before endangering Blake's life and
risking that this fraud would be discovered. As a strategy, that would
be akin to defusing a live artillery shell with a hammer. I remember
the look on Blake's face when Billy started dumping his stock. If that
video was a key piece of some plan hatched by his own employee, why
did Blake act so surprised when his brother's actions then spiraled into
violence?

McClaren sighs as though he expected better of me. "Threat? I'm
not making any threats. The only threat we're discussing is the one Ms.
Randall might see in you going around trying to dig up the family cem-
etery for some ridiculous nonsense you got banging around in that head
of yours. You should chew over the possibility that maybe things won't
go so smoothly for you if she has to withdraw her helping hand. If I was
you, the last thing I'd want is for that hand to become a fist. That's just a
little friendly advice. Me to you."

Helping hand? My stomach drops as I realize what he's talking about.
Blythe called Coles about my new IT enterprise, and I thought that was
the end of it. But isn't it interesting how quickly a currency quant was

able to raise venture funds? Coles is loaded, but he wouldn't have *that* much just lying around.

Christ, is my company built once again with Randall money?

As the thought settles, it starts to make even more sense. Blake was many things, but he wasn't stupid. Most of the infrastructure he built to profit from IT is still in place. Blythe has already won the contest for control of IMP, so why not appropriate Blake's idea as well?

Which leaves me once again a legionary serving the IMPire. That's a hard thing to swallow right now. But there's nothing to be gained by acting out with McClaren. I need time to think about all this.

I stall. "So that's how it is?"

McClaren makes a hospitable gesture at the space between us, as if to say, "We serve only the finest of fecal foodstuffs. Please enjoy." He looks inquiringly at me.

I have to bite. I'm not prepared to start a rebellion here and now. "I absolutely never meant to cause Ms. Randall any aggravation."

"You haven't yet. That's why we're talking. So that you don't."

"I wouldn't dream of it."

McClaren gets up and puts a hand on my shoulder, giving it an ungentle squeeze. He nods at me solemnly.

"Thanks so much, Jimmy," he says. "You're a real prince."

80

Susan Mercer has lunch by herself at the Sichi Zhilu teahouse in Chinatown at noon nearly every day. Many of my former colleagues believe she secretly owns the place. I find her pouring herself a cup at her regular table.

"Now, James, if you wanted lunch, you could have called my girl. I believe your new vocation is impinging on your sense of decorum." She says this with a smile, but it still throws me.

"I, ah, Susan—" I hadn't expected her to bring up my new job.

"Please, dear boy, no need to blush. Perhaps I'm not the withered old prune you imagine."

"No, of course, I—"

"You came here to discuss something else."

"I just met with John McClaren."

"I know. Johnny and I go way back. I take it you've developed questions that he declined to answer."

"That's right. But he implied that my asking them was dangerous, which leads me to believe there's some truth to their premise."

"You want to know why he set about manipulating certain information."

I nod.

"Let me suggest the traditional follow-on: *cui bono?*" She sits back to let me ponder that.

Who benefits?

There's only one answer to her question: Blythe. She ended up with all the chips.

Supporting evidence: isn't it funny she didn't fire McClaren, despite that for a security specialist, he failed utterly in protecting Blake?

For that matter, Blythe acted suspiciously forgiving of me, the man who *actually killed* her brother. She explained her lack of malice by saying she believes that he brought his fate upon himself. But she can't claim to have done much to stop it. I had always framed the battle of the Randalls in terms of the brothers. I never really placed Blythe in the action.

Mercer sees the light go on in my head. She shrugs. "Consider that while old John is certainly formidable, he's not nearly so formidable as his boss."

"You were working for her. From the beginning."

"We both were. Your Blythe is a student of history. She knows that if you wish to be emperor, you must entice the Praetorians to your side. And we all know the value of picking the right side in a civil war."

A civil war with a faction the other two combatants didn't know they were fighting. The Randall brothers had been openly at odds since Billy had his supervotes yanked. Through it all, Blythe played the appalled bystander to the hilt. But at the same time, she was contending with her twin in the friendly competition for control of IMP. Surely she saw that Billy distracting Blake redounded to her benefit.

"So she planned all of this?"

"I think that would be impossible. But . . . Well, perhaps you know that her twin brother was given to dismissing her as an unimaginative 'pipes' person, while presenting himself as the family visionary. But in my estimation, Blythe is better seen as a *network* person, a weaver of webs. Someone who thinks not only about information itself, but how it's distributed. Someone who understands that you can get a person to accept even the most ridiculous proposition when you present it in the right context."

So how did she ensnare her brothers?

Blythe sets feelers on the shaking strands of their lives. Eventually, she sees this shared pursuit of the male Randalls reemerge: Gina Delaney. Billy's bipolar love interest, and now Blake's conflicted money shot. She watches, pretending to dampen their burning enmity with one hand while secretly mixing nitroglycerin with the other.

Gina's death provides the spark.

Blythe intuits that Billy's terrible grief can, with a judicious reframing, be focused, amplified, and turned to rage aimed straight at Blake. She makes sure he gets a warped view of Gina's last moments and leaves his dark paranoia to do the rest. Like a Soviet spy who only believes information he steals, Billy trusts the video's authenticity because he lifted it from me.

"She used Billy's own puppet-master techniques against him."

Mercer says nothing, but her eyes twinkle with satisfaction that I'm finally getting it.

"And yet she seemed so hurt by everything that happened. After her brother broke into her apartment, she cried . . ."

I think back to that night. Billy knew Blythe was attending that Women in Media panel. Remarkably unlucky that a freak carbon monoxide leak sent her back to the apartment to surprise him. She winds up bleeding in her twin's arms.

Was that the incident that finally did it for Blake? Or was it her sobbing as Billy sold his stock and then asking him, "Is it never going to stop?"

For a woman who supposedly wanted peace between her brothers, she shed quite a few tears in front of Blake. Tears she must have known would inflame his hatred for Billy.

Mercer says softly, "Will no one rid me of this troublesome priest?"

So Blythe wasn't lamenting, she was recruiting. And she found eager volunteers in Blake and Mondano. Then I get stuck again. How did they ever locate Billy? They'd shown no ability in that regard before, and suddenly he winds up dead before I get to his apartment?

Maybe "old John" already knew where he was. That day when he showed up at Amazone after ignoring my calls for over an hour, he told me he was "far afield" protecting Blythe. But I'll bet she adheres to the "good offense" school of security. Let's say she ordered McClaren and his surveillance teams to monitor what Blake and Mondano were going to do at the Cloisters from a safe distance. They see me release Billy, and so McClaren sends a detachment to follow him. Later that day, he "discovers" Billy's whereabouts and passes that information along to her brother. Blake in turn passes it to Mondano's people, who then pass a lethal jolt of current through Billy's brain.

If all this is true, it's a hand well played. Using Mondano, McClaren, and me as the fuel, the brothers incinerate themselves in their feud, leaving Blythe to cool their ashes with her tears.

Weeping, but standing alone on the field.

I say, "Okay, Billy I get. But Blake wound up dead too. Was that just luck?"

"Well, you pulled the trigger. What did it feel like to you?"

I light a cigarette, still thinking. Mercer surprises me by reaching for one as well.

Standing there, facing off amidst all the blood, I remember both of us being dumbfounded that things had gone so haywire.

Mercer continues. "I think we taught you well enough to appreciate that one can never plan everything to the last detail. Chaos will reign. But that doesn't mean you can't devise scenarios that tilt the odds to your advantage. That put others in impossible situations."

So if Blythe was an even better puppet master than Billy, might she also be a better social engineer than I am?

After that initial meeting, I'd asked myself, "Why me?" The answer: Blythe knew I'd be especially easy to beguile into serving her aims. Thinking back through the past weeks, I see how she used each of our encounters to deploy a specific technique we Soshes use to worm our way into the good graces of our victims. *Establishing trust.*

At our Harvard Club chat she delivered the classic *appeal for help,* while providing *privileged information* about her brother Blake. She then offered me *special assistance* with her father's records, at which point she also directly contradicted a few of Blake's lies and evasions. She said he was "slow to trust." The message I took to heart: "You should not trust him. Trust me."

"We both trusted Blythe, but not each other," I say.

"And why didn't he trust you, his faithful janissary?"

"I met with the iTeam instead of going to him after finding Billy's place."

"Why did you do that?"

"I was scared. Seeing the body was upsetting, but I more or less knew that was in the works. I was scared for *myself*. The night he died, Billy warned me. He said, 'He knows you know. Do you think he's going to let you live?'"

"He said that to you?"

Wait . . . No, that's not right. He didn't say it. I read it.

"We were chatting in NOD." Which is odd, since he had used the voice system in our previous meeting. Also wrong was the undecorated blankness of the space. The still, zombie-like avatar, a stark contrast to Billy's previous showy animations.

"Dear boy, that could have been *anyone*."

Who was it then? One of Blythe's people, maybe McClaren, trying to condition my interpretation of events and turn me against Blake.

"But why?"

"Look at what happened," she says.

I freak out and try to take off with Xan and Garriott. Blake and Mondano move to prevent that. Since they've just murdered Billy, it's not unreasonable to conclude that violence could ensue. Blake might be implicated in a crime serious enough to neutralize him. Maybe Blythe had been preparing me for the time when she'd ask me to help her do just that.

If true, then her plan worked better than she might have wished. Blake and I ended up pointing guns at each other. Had he been fed disinformation about me as well? Something that moved him to pull the trigger? Would I have gotten my shot off if I weren't disposed to believe that he really meant me harm? Was it Blythe's whisper in my brain that added just enough pressure on my index finger to see her brother dead?

I'm amazed at how my new picture of Blythe's actions so closely mirrors Billy's game. They both seeded cancerous information about their family within distracting spectacles. In his case, *Savant*; in hers, this break-in at her apartment. He used an avatar to represent as his brother, while she impersonated him. He *tried* to deploy Gina's video to antagonize the twins. She *succeeded* in using it against him. He taunted Blake with a fake electrocution; she made sure that image became a reality. Whatever moves Billy made, she played right back at him. Even the idea to distort the reflections on Gina's pupils derived from Billy's *Getting Wet* video.

I look at Mercer. "So what do I do now?"

"I would recommend a stiff drink to fortify yourself for the realization that the game is over. Please don't indulge the self-important notion that it's your responsibility to ensure 'justice' is served. Indeed, where is the crime here? Maybe something petty like bribing a police officer. Perhaps some flavor of conspiracy. But let's be honest, these are things *we* do every day."

"There are five dead bodies here. Including both her brothers."

"But she didn't fire a weapon. You were the one who did that. James, you must assure me you won't do anything rash. I trust you can see that should you involve anyone else, they may have a less than sympathetic view of your participation in all this. Of course, you remember the cardinal rule of our business?"

"Never make yourself a soft target."

"And don't forget what you've learned about Blythe Randall thus far."

That she is a dangerous woman, to be fucked with at your peril.

Mercer sees the acquiescence form in my eyes before I actually come to a decision. She stands and brushes a lock of hair off my forehead. "Do come see me when you've spent yourself on this new . . . enterprise of yours."

In parting, she plants an adder strike of a kiss on my cheek.

The next day, an invitation arrives.

Blythe is having cocktails at her apartment to celebrate her promotion to CEO of IMP. A little more than a year after her brother's funeral. The minimum decent mourning period.

Written on the embossed cardstock in red pen are the words:

```
Perverse? Perhaps. But I suppose serving the Imp runs
in my family. Anyway, I'll bet nothing shocks you these
days.

-B
```

81

When I first saw her ridiculous ballroom, I thought it far too large to ever be filled. But tonight Blythe has made a fine effort to do so. The bulk of the crowd consists of executives from IMP with a contingent of up-and-coming actors from their studios to provide the requisite astral element.

I notice Blythe across the room immediately. She's alight with plutocratic joy, laughing and gesturing broadly. Her beloved scarlet pearls gleam at her neck, and I can't help thinking that the strand has grown a bit longer. I'm burning to speak with her, but the conversation will require privacy, so I scuttle out of her line of sight. Biding my time.

Luckily I find a group of old friends from school huddled in a corner of her aircraft carrier of a balcony. I sequester myself among them, as I field questions probing how I've risen in the world enough to score this invite.

I'm astounded at how the night melts away. My watch suddenly reads three thirty AM. When my opponent passes out, I emerge from the billiards room to see that the party has breathed its last gasp. I spare a glance into the ballroom as I pass by. The only signs of the earlier throng are several sticky puddles reflecting the light coming through the windows from a giant moon. Under that moon is a slender figure leaning, hands spread wide, against the balcony's rail.

Blythe.

I can tell from her posture exactly where she is right now. Outside on a perfect night, after a rocking party, celebrating something special. I know the feeling: you want to be by yourself looking down at the sleeping world and take some time to simply *rejoice*. Though Blythe is the kind of person who's probably already making new plans. And I'm afraid some of those plans include me.

I'd agonized about coming tonight. Her sub-rosa investment in ArrowTech meant that I'd have to constantly watch her and worry about her latest agenda. That seemed untenable. So while I may not have the courage to go to the police, at least I want a divorce. The question was: how to serve the papers?

That made me think of the last time I presented her with special papers. Back then my purpose was nearly the opposite, but reprising that motif felt like the right way to close the circle.

I slip through the balcony doors and watch her for a moment. "Blythe . . . Are you starting to feel lonely at all?"

She shuts her eyes and inhales deeply. Then she takes her purse from the balustrade and fishes inside it. I entertain the possibility that she's thumbing a radio that will signal black helicopters to descend and whisk me away, but she merely extracts a pack of Nat Shermans. I light one for her, and she hands it to me. Then I light hers. She sends a long plume of smoke out over the city. I'm about to repeat myself when she looks at me and smiles slyly.

"You ever think about tattoos? As a form of self-expression?"

"I asked you a question."

She ignores it again. "We live in an inspiring age. Human freedom is erupting across the globe. And people embody this by doodling on their skin. Little pictures we use to define ourselves."

"And?"

"So poor Billy and his unfortunate friends decorated their bodies with their obsessions. One of them even crafted her demise around her sacred symbol."

"Billy's demise was 'crafted' that way too."

Blythe nods equably. "You'd seen Blake's right wrist? The Suicide King? He got it shortly after our father passed away. It doesn't take a genius to unravel its meaning. But most people didn't know that he had one on the inside of his left wrist too. His watch band covered it. The Gemini glyph. That was for me, of course. Our birth sign is Aries."

She takes another long drag. "When people looked at us, that's what came to mind: the Gemini. Two, that are in some unnatural way really one. Identical. Copies of each other. Obviously we're fraternal. Male and female. Maybe an even stranger pair for that . . . Did you know that I have a tattoo as well?"

I didn't, though I have studied Blythe closely when permitted. I can definitively say she didn't have one in college and doesn't have one now anywhere that normally sees daylight. She pivots away from me on a heel, her backless dress framing a perfect expanse of white in the moonlight. Her hand brushes slowly down the smooth fabric to the juncture just north of decency. She pulls it down an exquisite inch to reveal two things.

The first is that she has a small Taijitu, the Taoist yin and yang symbol, right over her L5 vertebra. The second: that she has disdained the comfort of even a G-string tonight.

I find myself speechless. Blythe continues. "I know. A silly tramp stamp. How ridiculous, right? I often think of having it lasered away. But that little mark was very important to a confused college girl whose father had just died. And so I never get around to erasing it."

I clear my throat. "It's, ah, fascinating, but—"

She turns back to me, knowing her display had the desired effect. "So to me, Blake and I were more like the poles of a magnet. Bound together, irreducible, but at the same time opposite."

"Blythe, that's a lovely metaphor, but you're evading my question."

She holds up her hand, commanding patience. "I'm not. You want to know about my brothers' sad end, and I'm telling you the way I see it." She looks like she's about to say something cutting to me, but then she purses her lips and peers back out across the park. "Take Billy. Do you know why he chose Sade for his absurd production?" She waits for a response, but I just stare back at her, wanting to see where this is going.

She continues. "Sade was a philosopher of power and its dynamics." Her lips draw a sip of scotch, and her other hand traces a sinuous pattern on the stone in front of her. "To Billy, power was something to be struggled against rather than channeled."

I picture him lying next to his mother, her back a bleeding mess. "I wonder where he got that idea?"

"He was always that way. Unlike Billy, I see Sade as a novelty act. On the subject of power, I prefer Maxwell. His laws of electromagnetism. My little brother lived his life moving through his twin siblings' magnetic field. But he had this quality of *resistance*. If you remember your physics, what happens then?"

"Power is converted to heat."

"And what does heat do?"

"It dissipates."

Blythe nods sadly. "Sometimes, yes. But it can also burn. If the surge is too great, the resistor is destroyed."

"So it was all inevitable. Like clockwork."

"The laws of nature are immutable. Woe unto him that sets himself against them."

"And Blake?"

"Blake died from simple ballistics. Surely I don't have to explain that to *you*."

"He got what was . . . coming to him?"

Blythe shrugs. "I wasn't the one who dreamed of committing my younger brother in a jurisdiction where they still practice electroshock treatment. Remarkable how Billy's demise so closely fulfilled that fantasy. Just far more efficiently. And you certainly don't think such a vulgar display was my idea?"

"Blythe, I can't be in business with someone who has such fine aesthetic sensibilities."

She playfully feigns offense. "You want to abandon me? After all I've done for you?"

"I'm more worried about what you'll do *to* me. So here, I have something for you. A parting gift." I extract from my coat pocket a new bouquet of origami roses. But these I made with images rather than verse.

She seems charmed, but her eyes narrow as she unravels the first one.

A still I isolated from Billy's trove of necrotic family videos. The nasty conclusion of the force-feeding episode.

Continuing the theme, the next flower contains one of freelance photo-pharmacist Pete Novak's least-flattering shots of Blythe in distress.

Her fingers tear violently at the next one: a full nude she let me take of her in perhaps our most tender moment. That's when she really absorbs the pictures' message:

You *can't* trust me. I *will* hurt you.

But the next one puzzles her. A crime scene photo of Billy's disfigured corpse. An inset zooms in on an exposed fingerprint on the batteries' throw switch. Blythe raises an eyebrow at me.

"Amazing the police didn't run down an unidentified print at the crime scene. I guess someone else must have been there when he died . . . Can you account for *your* whereabouts?"

"Tampering with a closed case file? A rather fanciful use of your talents, James."

"Consider it a tribute. Using a technique I learned from you. You think it's *fanciful* because you weren't actually there. You didn't *do* anything, so you couldn't have left fingerprints, right? But you did *play a role,* and you *did* leave fingerprints."

I whip open the last flower for her. This one is not an image, but rather a transcript of my final NOD chat with Billy's avatar. The words are annotated with interstitial numbers denoting detailed timing metrics on each character as it was typed. Together, those measurements, called "keystroke dynamics," can be processed for any given person into a behavioral biometric signature. When I worked for Ravelin during college, they made telecommuting employees use an app that periodically verified your identity this way, and it had recorded Blythe's profile when she sent an email from my laptop. On matching her keyboard signature to Billy's av, at first I couldn't believe she'd risk hijacking it herself. But then Blythe probably didn't even trust McClaren with her most delicate business. Having known Billy from birth, she'd have been the best choice to channel him.

"That's clearly you, Blythe. Your w's and s's are real slow." I wiggle my left ring finger at her to contrast it with the crooked immobility of hers.

"Hardly proof of anything."

"No, just evidence. You think anyone might find it interesting that you were impersonating Billy online just after his death, but before you could have known about it?"

She doesn't make a sound, but her chest rises with a deep breath. She's mastering herself, suppressing rage. She couldn't even abide sharing power with her twin. Now my standing here with this scintilla of leverage must drive her insane. And beyond that, I suppose it will torture her that I found a crack in her masterwork. One that perhaps exposes a structural weakness and portends more cracks to come.

She says, "A very risky move, James."

"My point is, I'm through playing games. So are you."

"Oh, but there's a lot of fun for you and me still to come. You'll see." She casually tosses aside my flowers.

I'm surprised she's insisting on our new partnership. Has Blythe developed the same crush on the Dancers that everyone else did? I suppose to her they're a trophy of her conquest of Blake, or maybe worse: they're part of some dark stratagem I can't yet imagine.

"All I can see is your brothers' blood on your hands," I say, "and I don't want any more on mine."

I try my best at a penetrating stare. And maybe I do all right, because she meets it for a while as though she's deciding whether to argue. She pulls on her cigarette, down to its end, and flicks the butt to the street below.

Softly she says, "Maybe you don't see things as clearly as you think." Then she starts blowing the smoke directly into my eyes. I try to hold her gaze, thinking that this is some kind of test, but the smoke is too much, and I have to close them. Tears flood forth, and one escapes my left eye.

I'm amazed when I feel her lips catch it, as it trails down my cheek. Her hand at the back of my head, her body pressed close. A hint of her perfume induces a trill of vertigo. She makes a soft sound as she tastes it, like an alcoholic relishing her first sip after a decade of abstinence.

She whispers, "James, can't we just be friends again?"

Then she kisses me.

Part of me just wants to dissolve into her. But another, newer facet recoils.

She thinks I'm still so easy to seduce?

A year ago, I was deliriously happy to serve Blythe Randall in any way she might name. I delighted in making myself her creature. What she doesn't realize is that her deposed enemies Billy, Blake, and even Olya have given me a new banner under which to march. I have my own portfolio now, and I will pursue it with all the subtlety and ruthlessness at my disposal, regardless of her belief that she controls it. I am still formally a pawn, but I feel like one who's fought his way up the board to the seventh rank, on the precipice of promotion. Like her brother, she sees me as a knave, but I know that in the relentless shuffling play of the days ahead, I'll come out a king. And I want her to grasp that. To understand how things have changed.

Since that spring day in Cambridge on the steps to her apartment, I've often dreamed of once again kissing Blythe Randall. But I never imagined the touch of her lips would ignite a feeling of righteous rage.

I murmur against her teeth, "We were never friends."

Then my hand that was moving to caress her hair clenches and jerks her head back. My other hand moves to her throat, pressing on her larynx with my thumb. I thrust my tongue into her mouth.

I suppose I was hoping to shock her a little. Force her to take a cautious step back. To say to her:

We can do this, but it won't be like it was.

But Blythe just makes a low hum of appreciation. She steps into me, pressing her thigh hard between my legs. Then she bites down sharply on my tongue. My whole body convulses tightly with pain, bending her farther back. My teeth ram against her lips. I can feel her sucking, not content with my tears, now trying to taste my blood.

There we remain, locked in a farrago of pain and lust, neither willing to relent. And I know this position will define my life in the coming days.

It feels good.

ACKNOWLEDGMENTS

There are a number of people without whom this book would have remained at the far left of the idea/object continuum.

My family. Your boundless love and support have always amazed me.

Dustin Thomason inspired me to pick up my pen. He is an outstanding writer and a matchless friend.

Better writers than me have written encomiums to Jennifer Joel's many virtues as an agent, a word to which they tend to append modifiers like "super" and "über." As a person, she deserves the same prefixes, but to avoid some awkward constructions, I'll just say that she is simply wonderful.

Whatever meager pleasures this volume holds were coaxed to life by my editor, Sarah Knight. Rendering the dross from a manuscript is supposed to be a painful process, but I must admit I found it a rare pleasure to bask in the glow of her coruscating wit and perspicacity.

I'd also like to thank:

The good people at Simon & Schuster: Jessica Abell, Renata Di Biase, Jonathan Evans, Jonathan Karp, Molly Lindley, Aja Pollock, Richard Rhorer, Kelly Welsh, and Jason Heuer.

My early readers: Clay Ezell, Nick Snyder, Mike Fisher, Adam Hootnick, Sam Brown, John Crouch, and David Kanuth.

The faculty, staff, and students at the Interactive Telecommunications Program at NYU's Tisch School of the Arts.

ABOUT THE AUTHOR

Michael Olson, a Harvard graduate, worked in investment banking and software engineering before earning a master's degree from NYU's Interactive Telecommunications Program, where he designed a locomotion interface for virtual environments.